HIS PREGNANT ROYAL BRIDE

BY
AMY RUTTAN

BABY SURPRISE FOR THE DOCTOR PRINCE

BY
ROBIN GIANNA

MILLS & BOON

Royal Spring Babies

Unexpected royal heirs for two Italian princes!

Dante and Enzo Affini, Venice's hottest doctors,
have a secret…they're also Italian princes! Now, to
save their inheritance and the family name,
they'll need to marry and produce heirs—*stat*!

For Nurses Shay Labadie and Aubrey Henderson
a six-month stint in Italy teaching new nurses is the
escape they both need. But as romance blooms in the
spring sunshine they find themselves with new roles
entirely…as royal mums!

Read Dante's story in
His Pregnant Royal Bride
by Amy Ruttan

Read Enzo's story in
Baby Surprise for the Doctor Prince
by Robin Gianna

Available now!

HIS PREGNANT ROYAL BRIDE

BY
AMY RUTTAN

Published in Great Britain 2017
By Mills & Boon, an imprint of HarperCollins*Publishers*
1 London Bridge Street, London, SE1 9GF

© 2017 Amy Ruttan

ISBN: 978-0-263-92635-4

Printed and bound in Spain
by CPI, Barcelona

Dear Reader,

Thank you for picking up a copy of *His Pregnant Royal Bride*.

I was privileged to write this duet with one of my absolute favourite people, Robin Gianna. When our editor asked if I wanted to write a duet with her for my fourteenth book for Mills & Boon Medical Romance I answered with a resounding *yes!*

The best part of writing this duet was when Robin, me and our editor were all at the RWA Nationals conference in San Diego and we got to hash out the timeline and plot soaking in the sun by the pool. Those kinds of editorial meetings don't happen very often!

Nurse practitioner Shay Labadie has had a pretty rough hand in life, but it doesn't deter her from doing work all over the world, bringing medicine to those in need. She's quite admirable, and her first name is after a friend whom I also find admirable.

Dr Dante Affini has also been dealt several blows, but has led more of a charmed life being an Italian prince. Though *he* thinks it's far from charming—and after a one-night stand leaves Shay with a baby *she* thinks he's not her Prince Charming either.

I hope you enjoy Shay and Dante's story.

I love hearing from readers, so please drop by my website, amyruttan.com, or give me a shout on Twitter @ruttanamy.

With warmest wishes,

Amy Ruttan

This book is dedicated to Robin,
my partner in crime for this duet. You were awesome,
and I would work with you again in a heartbeat.
I'm so glad we got to meet face to face *finally*!

For my friend Shay,
who is just as giving and admirable as my heroine. You do so
much and ask for nothing. So glad we're friends.

And of course Laura, my editor extraordinaire, who concocted
this idea. Also for Tilda, who always helps out with my AFS
and keywords and for stepping in
while the rest of us were in California.

Born and raised just outside Toronto, Ontario, **Amy Ruttan** fled
the big city to settle down with the country boy of her dreams.
After the birth of her second child Amy was lucky enough to
realise her lifelong dream of becoming a romance author. When
she's not furiously typing away at her computer she's mum to
three wonderful children who use her as a personal taxi and
chef.

Books by Amy Ruttan

Mills & Boon Medical Romance

Hot Latin Docs

Alejandro's Sexy Secret

The Hollywood Hills Clinic

Perfect Rivals…

Sealed by a Valentine's Kiss

His Shock Valentine's Proposal
Craving Her Ex-Army Doc

Tempting Nashville's Celebrity Doc
Unwrapped by the Duke

Visit the Author Profile page at
millsandboon.co.uk for more titles.

PROLOGUE

"THAT HAS TO be the most monotonous lecturer that I've ever had the displeasure to listen to," Shay teased as she took a sip of her pineapple cocktail. She glanced over shyly at Dr. Dante Affini, who was attending the same conference on trauma simulation as her in Honolulu. She felt as if she was talking too loudly, which was something she always did in the presence of a man she found utterly attractive. And Dr. Dante Affini was all that and more. Just a few days with him and she was a lost woman. Add in the tropical setting and drinks…

It was a perfect paradise.

Shay had intended to throw herself completely into her work, as she always did, but on the first day of the conference she'd bumped into Italian surgeon Dr. Dante Affini looking perplexed. He hadn't known where to go and she'd helped him.

Since she'd let him know that she was attending the same presentations as him, they'd been inseparable. She didn't mind in the least. Dante was handsome, charming, intelligent and single.

She bit her lip, blood heating her cheeks. What was she doing? She didn't get involved with doctors, but with Dante it was hard not to.

He didn't look down his nose at her for being a nurse

practitioner. Usually at these kind of conferences the
nurses stuck together and the physicians stuck together.
Except Dante seemed to be the exception. He'd turned
down golfing, dinners and drinks with the other surgeons to accompany her. They'd attended the same lec-
tures and seemed to agree on the same approaches to
medicine.

Now the conference was winding up and it had been
Dante's idea to get drinks.

She knew she shouldn't have accepted his invitation. It was not something she was used to doing, but
this was sort of a work vacation and for once, Shay
thought, why not?

Dante was charming, sexy, and she'd been so busy
with her work for the last couple of years that maybe it
was the perfect time to kick back and have some fun.

"*Sì*, that was most terrible." He shuddered and took
a drink of his pineapple juice, then turned around, his
dark eyes flickering out over the water. "It is a beautiful night."

Shay nodded. "The breeze is nice. It was sweltering
in that room."

"Yes, it was most unpleasant." He waved his hand in
a sweeping arc. "This, however, is paradise."

And he wasn't wrong. The sun was setting, like mol-
ten gold against the turquoise water. Palm trees swayed
gently in the breeze and the sky was darkening. Soon
it would be full of stars as the hotel where the conference was being held was off the beaten track. It was on
the North Shore and there wasn't much else around it.
No city, no noise and no distractions. It was heavenly.

"I wish I had more time to explore," Shay said wist-
fully. "I never traveled much until I joined the United
World Wide Health Association, but that's for work and

I don't get a lot of downtime on assignments. It's all about the work."

Dante shook his head. "That is no way to live life."

"Maybe not, but I love what I do."

He smiled at her, that charming, sexy, crooked smile she was getting used to seeing every day. She was going to miss it when the conference was over.

"Of course, who am I to talk about living life, *cara*? My main focus is also my work."

"See, then why harass me?" she teased.

"Still, when you take an assignment somewhere, you must have time off."

Shay shrugged. "A little bit, but lately my assignments have been to mainly Third World countries after they've suffered a natural disaster and it really isn't safe to wander away from base camp to take in the sights."

Dante grinned. "Did I mention how incredibly brave you are, *cara*? I admire that about you."

Warmth flooded her cheeks. She could listen to Dante talk all night. He had such a dreamy Italian accent but spoke English so fluently.

"I just do my job," Shay said, brushing off the compliment, because she was proud of the work she did. It was a way to honor her mother, who should be alive still, if it weren't for Hurricane Katrina and the aftermath. The ill-effects of a poisoned house had prematurely taken the life of her mother, in the end.

It was at that moment that Shay knew what direction she had to take her life.

She'd worked hard to get where she was.

Now her job was to train other nurses and first responders by using simulation, so that they could go into the war zones, the disaster areas, and save lives, because that was all that mattered.

Saving lives.

"You do more than that, *cara*. I see it—you care about people and that's what makes you special." That smile disappeared and he fiddled with the straw in his drink. "Not everyone cares so much about others."

She was glad that the sun was setting, so that he couldn't see the blush he was causing.

Dante affected her in a way no man had in a long time. She was nervous around him. Giddy.

If she were anywhere else, she'd distance herself from him, but because she'd never see him again she figured it was okay to engage in harmless flirtation.

In a fantasy.

Not that anything would happen between the two of them.

Says who?

"Thank you," she finally said, trying to shake out the naughty thoughts suddenly traipsing across her mind.

"So let's do something about your lack of exploring," Dante said, setting down his empty glass on the bar. "Come."

"What?" she asked, confused.

"Look, it's our last night in paradise. Let's walk down to the beach and take a walk through the waves, follow the shore. It's a beautiful night."

"I don't know…"

What're you waiting for?

She glanced up at Dante, who stood in front of her, those dark eyes twinkling in the waning sunlight, the breeze making his short mop of ebony curls stir. His white cotton shirt billowed, so she could see the outline of his hard, muscular chest. His bronzed skin glowing in the waning light and, of course, that lopsided smile.

"What about the *luau*? Aren't we supposed to go

there and network? You've traveled so far to attend this, don't you want to mingle?"

He snorted. "I have done enough networking to last a lifetime. For once I've no desire to talk about medicine. Tonight is a beautiful night. Let's go."

Go.

"Okay," Shay said, not needing any more convincing. She finished her drink and set her empty glass down on the bar and took his hand. It was strong and she was surprised how easily her hand slipped into his. She hoped he didn't notice that her nails were much too short, that her palms were rough from the hard physical work. She envied well-manicured nails, perfectly coifed hair, women who had time for makeup and clothes that weren't torn, stained or scrubs.

Only Dante didn't seem to care.

She couldn't believe that he'd chosen to spend all his free time with her this week.

A surgeon and a nurse.

Don't worry about that now. Just enjoy it. Live the fantasy for one night.

They walked away from the bar, down a winding sandy path to the beach. It was tranquil and a bit deserted at the moment. It was perfect.

"Hold on," she said. She let go of Dante's hand.

"What're you doing?" he asked.

"Taking off my shoes. The sand is getting in and I hate that feeling of sand in your shoes."

He chuckled. "Good idea."

They kicked off their shoes and carried them as they headed down to the shore. The sun was almost gone, as if it were disappearing behind a curtain of water. It was picture-perfect. The water licked at their toes as they walked in silence along the shoreline.

It was the perfect end to the conference.

Tomorrow she'd be flying back to New Orleans for a short time and then off on her next assignment to the Middle East. Always moving, as she'd been doing her whole life. No stability. No roots. New Orleans was just a base for her, but it really wasn't home since her mother died and she didn't know why she kept returning to it.

"You seem sad all of a sudden, *cara*."

The way he called her *cara* made her tremble with anticipation.

"I was just thinking how wonderful this week has been." She bit her lip and sighed. "It's been amazing getting to know you, Dante."

He smiled and then ran his knuckles across her cheek. "I've enjoyed my time with you as well, *cara*."

Shay's pulse began to race and she closed her eyes, his touch making her heart skip a beat, and then, before she had a chance to say anything else, his lips claimed hers.

She dropped her shoes to the sand and sank into the kiss, wrapping her arms around him and pulling him close.

Dante's kiss deepened, his tongue pushing past her lips; it was a kiss that seared her soul.

"Shay," he whispered, his mouth still close to her, his hands cupping her face. "I'm sorry, I couldn't help myself. You're so beautiful, so wonderful…" He kissed her again.

"I don't want this to end," she whispered against his ear as he held her close, his hands drifting down her back.

"Me neither."

"Then let's not let tonight end." She took his hand. "Let's go to your room…"

"Are you sure, *cara*?" he asked.

"Positive. We can just have tonight. I'm not looking for anything long-term, Dante."

Just passion. Unforgettable passion.

That was what she craved right now.

He smiled. "I want tonight too."

Dante took her hand and they picked up their shoes and headed back to the hotel, to his room and something wonderful that she'd always remember...

Dante didn't know what he was thinking when he bent down to kiss Shay, other than that the need to connect with her was so totally overwhelming. With the tropical wind blowing wisps of her honey-blonde hair around her heart-shaped face, he couldn't resist her siren call.

He didn't know what possessed him, other than absolute desire and need, because he'd sworn when Olivia broke his heart he'd keep away from women. Love was a loss of control and he hated losing that loss of control.

Only from the moment he'd met Shay, when she'd reached out to help him, he couldn't help himself. He knew he should've stayed away, but couldn't. Her brown eyes were warm, friendly, and the more he got to know her, the more he felt completely at ease with her.

To the point where his carefully constructed walls came down.

"*Cara*, I want you so bad," he whispered against her neck.

"I want you too," she said, her breath hot against his skin. It drove him wild.

It's only for one night.

And he had to keep reminding himself of that. That it was only one night.

She only wants tonight. I can give her tonight.

His heart didn't have to get hurt.

You don't have one-night stands, a little voice reminded him, but he shook that thought away. His brother did and he fared just fine. Dante was not his father. He wasn't married, he wasn't hurting anyone, they were both consenting adults.

This was what his younger brother, Enzo, lived by; he could do that too, if only for one night.

Shay sighed as he ran his fingers through her silky hair as she wrapped her arms around him. Her long, delicate fingers tickling at the nape of his neck.

Mio Dio. It was only for tonight.

He could give himself over to one night. One night didn't mean forever.

It couldn't.

CHAPTER ONE

DANTE CLENCHED HIS fists as he jammed them into the pockets of his crisp white lab coat. Everything about him was controlled and ordered. Only today his schedule was off, and he was not in the mood for meeting the practitioner from America and running a simulation lab with him. And it wasn't just for one day; he'd then have him working under him as a surgical nurse in his operating room for twelve weeks.

Twelve weeks might not seem long in the grand scheme of things, but if Dante and this nurse practitioner didn't get along, then twelve weeks would feel like an eternity.

He remembered the last American from the United World Wide Health Association he'd worked with two years ago and that had been a nightmare. She'd been totally unorganized and needed constant guidance, which had driven him crazy.

Not all Americans are bad.

And his mood lightened as he thought of Shay and that stolen night in Oahu. She was the first woman he'd been with since Olivia had crushed his heart. Shay was one American he could get used to having around. Even now, months later, he could still feel her lips on his.

Only she was off who knew where on her latest

assignment and he had to make nice with a stranger. Someone he didn't trust, and it brought back why he was in a bad mood.

His father. Someone else he absolutely didn't trust.

At dinner last night with his younger brother, Enzo, Dante had learned that their father, Prince Marco Affini, had once again sold off more of the family land. And he was eyeing the land their late mother had left in trust for Dante and Enzo until they married and produced an heir. At least their father couldn't sell it off yet. Unless they married before they turned thirty-five and produced an heir within a year of that marriage. Last night Enzo had reminded Dante once again that soon Dante would be turning thirty-five in a matter of months, without a marriage in sight.

Dante was painfully aware that his villa on Lido di Venezia was in danger of being sold as well, because that had been his maternal grandfather's home.

The villa on the sandbar, a ten-minute ferry ride from Venice proper, was part of Dante's inheritance. It would be his as long as he married and produced an heir by the time he was thirty-five, according to the stipulations of the trust fund and the marriage contract between his parents, as his mother had been a commoner and his father of royal blood.

And his thirty-fifth birthday was approaching fast, without a wife or heir in sight.

And whose fault was that?

It was his. He knew it; he just didn't have any desire to get married after what had happened with his ex, Olivia, and he didn't want to have a child out of wedlock. Even if he did, that wouldn't help him recover his inheritance, such were the archaic terms of the trust.

If he didn't get married and have a child, he would

lose his home, everything that was meant for him by his late mother, including his beloved vineyard in Tuscany.

His grandfather had worked that vineyard. It was his pride and joy. Even though the family had money, his maternal grandfather always took pride in working his land. A work ethic that Dante had picked up on. He loved saving lives and he loved the life that bloomed in his vineyard in Tuscany.

Dante loved it there.

He loved working the land himself as well and the thought of someone else owning it was too much to bear.

It kept him awake most nights and he had the legal receipts to prove that he'd tried to get around the trust his mother signed on her wedding day, but it was ironclad. His father had the upper hand, until Dante and Enzo were married.

Dante downed the shot of espresso he'd grabbed before he headed to the lecture hall where he'd welcome the new United World Wide Health Association nurses and first responders who had come from all over Italy to join the organization. Here they'd learn what they needed to know, and then they would disperse over the world, providing health care.

Dante admired them and, even though he didn't want to be here and meet with his new associate from the United States, he knew he couldn't take his frustrations out on them.

He took a deep breath, ran his hand through his dark hair as he glanced in a mirror briefly, cursing inwardly for not having shaved the stubble from his face, and he hated the dark circles under his eyes, but he hadn't got much sleep last night.

Once, he'd had the chance to save all the land meant

for him, but that had cost him his heart and he swore he would never fall into that trap again. He just had to get used to the fact he was going to lose it all.

He was going to let down his brother and the memory of his mother.

His father would sell it all off and Dante would have to find a new place to live in a matter of a few months. He shook his head as he tried not to think about that now. He had to be charming and affable as the head of trauma at the Ospedale San Pietro.

Bracing himself now, Dante opened the door, ready to greet the American.

"*Ciao*, I'm Dr. Dante Affini, Head of..."

The nurse turned, just slightly, and Dante couldn't believe who he was looking at. His pulse raced and a rare smile tugged at the corner of his mouth. It was Shay!

She looked stunning. She was absolutely glowing, her cheeks rosy with a bloom she didn't have before.

Her honey-blonde hair wasn't as long as he remembered. She'd cut it, shorter in a bob, but it suited her delicate heart-shaped face. Those dark brown eyes of hers were warm and welcoming as she smiled at him, her pink lips soft and inviting. He could still feel them pressed against his. A blush rose in her round, creamy cheeks, deepening the healthy glow. Her lithe frame was fuller, but the curves suited her. "Hello, Dante."

"Shay?" Dante whispered, and then he smiled, realizing it was her who was here to work with him. "What are you doing here? I thought... I thought Daniel Lucey was going to be running this program."

"He was," Shay said. "But something came up for him, so I jumped at the chance to come to Italy and take an easier job for a while."

"An easier job? You're never one to back away from a challenge, *cara*."

A pink blush deepened on her cheeks and she tucked away an errant silky strand behind her ear. "I know, but I have no choice." She bit her lip. "Dante, I took this job because…because I'm pregnant."

Pregnant. Shay was having a baby?

It hit him and for a moment he wasn't sure he'd heard her correctly. Well, that explained the glow and the newly acquired curves. And then another realization struck him…

"Is it… Is it mine?"

"Yes." She bit her lip in a way that had driven him wild before but now filled him with a sense of trepidation.

A baby.

He had put up the walls to protect himself for a reason and he'd been a fool for letting her in back in Oahu.

It had been a moment of complete weakness on his part.

Dante scrubbed a hand over his face.

Why didn't she tell me? Was he really the father? Olivia had led him to believe that she carried his baby, only then he'd found out she'd tricked him. She'd already been pregnant when they'd slept together. Olivia had viewed Dante as perfect daddy material for another man's child…

He was angry. Angry at himself for thinking Shay might be different, but apparently not. He should've known better—a week and a one-night stand were no time to get to know someone. To trust someone.

A pink blush tinged her creamy cheeks. "I took this job so that I could tell you in person."

"Why didn't you tell me sooner?" he demanded. "Why didn't you contact me before you showed up here?

As soon as you found out? It's been months, Shay. You can understand my trepidation. My anger, surely?"

She winced. "I know. But I've only very recently found out myself, Dante. I'm sixteen weeks."

"Four months in and you expect me to believe that you just found out?" Dante scoffed.

"Yes. I was working in a war-torn area. My periods have always been irregular and I put their absence down to stress and travel. I wasn't keeping that close an eye on dates, but something told me that it had been too long. I took a test, which came out positive, but then there was no way to contact you. Communication was spotty."

Dante saw red. "You were pregnant in a war zone?"

Her eyes narrowed. "There are lots of pregnant women in war zones."

Dante cursed under his breath and scrubbed a hand over his face. "That's not what I meant."

"Sure sounded like it." She crossed her arms and he noticed her breasts were fuller and he recalled at that moment the way his hands fit so nicely around them.

Get control of yourself.

"Fine. So you couldn't get word to me."

"No, I thought it would be news better delivered in person."

"I want a paternity test," he demanded.

Shocked and hurt, Shay glared at him. "It's your baby, Dante. I haven't been with anyone else."

"You didn't even know you were pregnant right away, so you understand my hesitancy. We used protection," he said.

"A faulty condom. They're not infallible." Shay sighed. "And I don't sleep around. I don't sleep with strangers."

"Wasn't I a stranger, *cara*?"

She shot him daggers. "I didn't come here to make you a father, Dante. I actually took the job because it paid well, so that I could take a longer maternity leave when I return to the States."

"So you considered not telling me?"

"Of course not. You have the right to know about your child, Dante. What I'm saying is that I don't expect anything from you."

Everything was sinking in and he was having a hard time processing for a moment. He wanted to believe that she was telling him the truth, but he'd been burned before. And thanks to his father's indiscretions the entire world seemed to know that he was a prince, poised to inherit a vast estate of land and money. Wasn't that what had drawn Olivia to him?

Of course, if Shay was pregnant with his child, it solved all of his problems.

He had to be married and have an heir by the time he was thirty-five. There was nothing in the will that stated he had to stay married. And while Olivia had made him very wary of marriage, he had wanted to be a father for as long as he could remember. He wanted the happy family he'd never had growing up. Plus, he knew that Shay was passionate about her job. She wouldn't want to settle down in Italy with him—hadn't she told him that she feared staying in one place for too long? What if he could get full custody of the baby? Have the child he'd always wanted without risking his heart.

"Dante, say something. Anything," Shay said. "I know this must be a terrible shock."

Before he could say anything there was a knock on his door. His assistant poked her head round it. "Dr. Affini? The trainees are gathered in the lecture theatre and are waiting for you."

Dante acknowledged the woman before he turned back to Shay. "We'll talk later. We have a job to do."

Shay smiled, relieved. "Yes. We have a job to do."

He'd let her have relief for now, but this was far from over.

Shay had wanted to tell Dante that she was pregnant from the moment she'd found out. She was frustrated when she realized she'd put their child in danger, and then when he'd insinuated that, she'd felt even guiltier. She wasn't irresponsible. Once she'd known she was expecting, she'd been flown out, leaving her free to take over this assignment from her colleague Daniel, who'd sadly just been diagnosed with stage two colon cancer. She'd dreaded telling Dante here, at work, but she respected him and he deserved to know about their child. She also wanted him to know that she didn't expect anything.

She wasn't looking for a marriage or even for him to be part of the child's life if he didn't want to be.

She knew firsthand what it was like when a man was forced into staying.

Her own father had made that painfully clear to her until the day he'd left her and her mother.

So she knew what it was like to be rejected by her father and she didn't want that for her child. And that was why she'd been terrified of telling Dante. Terrified he'd reject her and the baby, which would make the next twelve weeks working with him miserable.

Glad to be able to focus for the moment on the job at hand, Shay took the time it took them to make their way to the lecture theatre to chat about the assignment with Dante.

"I think I'm pretty much up-to-date on what Daniel

was planning to do and how he was going to implement the simulation and training program," Shay said as she skimmed through the binder that she'd been given as she'd boarded the plane.

"So, what happened to Daniel?" Dante asked.

"Cancer," Shay said sadly.

"That's too bad. I wish him a speedy recovery, but I wish they had told me he wasn't coming." Dante rubbed his dimpled chin, and those butterflies that liked to dance around in the pit of her stomach months ago were starting up again. She'd forgotten how he affected her. He was still so handsome, the stubble on his chin suited him and she resisted the urge to tuck back the errant strand of his thick black hair.

"I thought you had been informed that Daniel was no longer coming," she said.

"Clearly not," he snapped.

"Dante, you're clearly not okay with this."

"I'm fine," he said, and he took the binder from her, not even looking at her.

She knew he wasn't. This was not the same man she'd spent a fairy-tale week with in Oahu. Then again, she hadn't really been herself either. Like when she'd decided to throw caution to the wind and have a one-night stand.

"Okay, you're fine, then. Shall we go and talk to the trainees? They are waiting."

"Of course." Dante didn't even look at Shay as he opened the door on the far side of the room. It was as if he was angry that she was here.

Can you blame him?

They walked out onto the stage of the small lecture theatre. The first two rows were filled with new United World Wide Health Association recruits, men and women who would be taking a crash course in first response and trauma.

Dante's job was to teach them trauma surgery and Shay was going to run them through a course of simulations. Based on situations she'd found herself in when she'd first started with the United World Wide Health Association.

She kind of envied all those hopeful faces, the thirty-odd new recruits. Her first days in the UWWHA working the field were some of her favorite times. Before she took this assignment she'd been going to take a field job in the Middle East to help vaccinate refugees.

Only that was before she'd found out she was pregnant. She couldn't go then and had been weighing up her options, and then this position had become available. The more romantically minded would probably call it fate.

This would be her last foreign assignment for a long time and she was going to make the most of it.

Her career and her unborn child mattered to her. She was going to make sure her son or daughter had a good life and this job in Venice would give her a strong foundation. Even if she had to give up on her dreams for now.

The recruits were from all over Italy and some from Switzerland and France. They could all speak English and French, which Shay understood, and she was glad when Dante started to speak French to them over Italian, which she was still trying to pick up.

If her news had shaken him before, Dante didn't show it now as he spoke highly of the United World Wide Health Association and the twelve-week training program they would be completing at the hospital under his and Shay's guidance.

A baby hadn't been in her plans either, but it had happened and she was going to be a good mother and continue with her career. Even if it was going in a slightly different direction than she'd thought. She wouldn't pine away after a man who didn't want her as her mother had done.

"Your dad'll come back, Shay. You'll see. I'm his wife. He went to Alaska to work for the crab season. He'll be back and he'll take us all up to Alaska."

Of course, he never did come back.

He was still alive, the last Shay heard, but didn't want anything to do with her.

He'd moved on and he certainly didn't care that their house had been destroyed by Katrina and that his wife had died soon after from mold poisoning.

"Shay Labadie will explain the simulation scenarios you'll be going through." Dante stepped away from the podium and Shay shook the thoughts of her father from her head.

She was here to do a job.

And she always did a good job. Always saw a position through to the end, no matter what life threw at her.

She got up and explained the simulations that she would be running them through and answered questions. When she was done, the director of the UWWHA took the podium and she went and stood beside Dante. There was tension pouring off him and he barely looked at her.

Not that she could blame him.

She had dropped the fact that he was going to be a father on his lap.

She would've been more surprised if he weren't shocked by the prospect.

Once the director finished talking, there was a mix

and mingle session, so that everyone could get to know one another. Shay walked toward the stairs at the end of the stage, but Dante grabbed her arm, holding her back.

"A moment *per favore*, Shay." He pinched the bridge of his nose and sighed. "First, I was serious when I said I would like a paternity test done."

"Okay." He'd been right when he'd reminded her that they were strangers who'd slept together, much as it smarted that her word wasn't enough to convince him that she didn't sleep around. "Anything else?"

"This is hard for me to say."

"Dante, you don't have to do anything. I already told you that I'm not asking for anything."

"I know you're not," he said quickly. "I am."

"What… I… You're what?" Shay didn't know how to take that response. Now she was shocked, so she asked cautiously, "What're you asking for?"

"Not much. Just that if the paternity test proves that I'm the father—"

"Which it will," she interrupted.

"*If* it does," he said through clenched teeth, "I want you to marry me."

Of all the things she'd thought he'd say, that wasn't one of them.

She hadn't been expecting that.

CHAPTER TWO

"YOU WANT…WHAT?" Shay was trying to process what Dante had said and she wasn't sure that she completely understood him. "Could you repeat that?"

"I said that if the paternity test proves I'm the father I want you to marry me." There was no smile on his face, no glint in his eye letting her know that he was joking, because he had to be joking, right? Men just didn't ask women they'd slept with once to marry them, did they?

"That's what I thought you said, but then I was thinking that there was no way you could be asking me that." She tried to move past him, because this was a bit crazy. This was not the Dante she remembered, the Dante she knew.

You don't know Dante, remember?

And she didn't. Usually she knew the men she slept with a bit better, but when she'd been in Oahu she'd thrown caution to the wind when she'd succumbed to Dante's kiss.

Even now, standing here in front of him, she had a hard time trying to forget the way his arms had felt around her. The way he'd whispered *cara* in her ear.

This reaction to him is why you're pregnant in the first place.

"Well, I'm not asking you," he said.

"You're crazy." She tried to leave.

He stepped in front of her to block her. "I'm not asking you, Shay. I'm telling you. If I'm the father, we will get married."

What?

"You're telling me?" She cleared her throat. "Seriously?"

Dante nodded. "Yes. You will marry me."

Shay tried not to laugh at the absurdity of it. This was not real life.

"And what about the paternity test you're so adamant I take?"

He glared at her. "I only want marriage if the test proves I'm the father."

"And if it doesn't?" Which was absurd. She hadn't been with anyone since him, and before him there'd been no one else for a long time.

"Won't it?"

She crossed her arms, glaring at him. Suddenly she was having a hard time finding him charming. Sexy, yes, but charming—heck, no. More annoying than anything.

"You're the father," she replied icily.

"Then you will marry me once we receive the results."

She snorted. "How romantic."

"Nothing about this is romantic, *cara*." The endearment he used on her, his voice still deep and rich. She could hear that whisper in her ears: *cara*.

"Do you love me?" she asked point-blank, shaking those thoughts from her head.

He cocked his eyebrows. "This has nothing to do with love."

"So the answer is no," she said.

"Were you expecting me to say yes? Other than one week together, we don't know each other."

"Exactly, so why would I marry you?"

He frowned. "To give our child legitimacy. A stable home. The guarantee that it will have two parents. This is a business arrangement for the sake of the child."

The premise of giving her child a good home life was very tempting, but she knew how this played out. She'd been that child after all and she wouldn't put her child through that. Through the resentment, bitterness and heartache. To the point that her father had walked away and didn't even want to see her again.

No, she didn't want that for her baby.

She didn't want her baby to feel that pain. Only he seemed to really want this baby and her father had never wanted her.

Another parent involved, especially a stationary one, means you can pursue assignments anywhere in the world.

"I'm not going to marry you," she said. "I'm here to work." She tried to leave the room, but he stepped in front of her, grabbing her by the arm, his dark eyes blazing.

"I don't think you know what you're talking about."

"I think I do," she snapped, shrugging her arm out of his grip.

"So I'm not to have access to my child?" he demanded.

"I never said that."

"You won't marry me. So that means I won't see this child. You're only in Italy for twelve weeks. Then what happens? You won't even be here when our child is born."

"Dante, I'm not denying you access to your child. I want you to be part of his or her life. We don't have to get married to raise this child. We don't even need to live in the same country."

He opened his mouth to say more when his pager buzzed. He looked down. "Incoming trauma, *dannazi-one*. This conversation isn't over." He stormed out of the room, his white lab coat billowing out behind him from his long strides. He was a force of nature to be reckoned with.

Shay breathed an inward sigh of relief, because for now she was able to get a breather, but she knew that this was probably far from over.

Dante stuck his head back into the room. "Are you coming, Shay? There is incoming trauma and you're to be my nurse for the next twelve weeks. I need you by my side."

By his side.

Only she wasn't sure she was going to survive the next twelve weeks. By the way things were going she was either going to kill him or fall in love with him.

And succumbing to the passion, the desire, she felt for him was not an option. Neither was falling in love.

She had to guard her heart.

Shay was not her mother and wouldn't be easily per-suaded by loving a man. This was *her* life and she was going to live by her own wit.

"Of course."

She shook her head; she had to get back in the game and focus on her work here. This was her job and, when she'd found out that she was pregnant after one night of forbidden passion, she'd sworn that she wasn't going to let the pregnancy interfere with her job performance.

She was a damn good nurse practitioner and simulation trainer. And that wasn't going to change.

Even though she was starting to blossom and her center of gravity was shifting, she was able to keep up with Dante's quick pace as they navigated the hallways through the hospital. He finally slowed down when they entered the trauma ward, where there was a flurry of activity. Shay could see water ambulances outside a set of automatic doors, where they were bringing in stretchers of patients.

"What happened?" Dante asked in Italian, that much she understood. The man spoke quickly and then pointed to where Dante was needed.

"Shay, this way," Dante called, waving his hand and directing her to follow him.

They entered a private treatment bay, where a man lay seriously wounded.

"He's American. Your presence might calm him," Dante whispered.

Shay nodded. "What happened?"

"A *vaporetto* was tossed when a large cruise ship came into the lagoon. The cruise ship sent a wave into St. Mark's Square and there were some injuries there as well."

"Vaporetto?" Shay asked as she pulled on a trauma gown and gloves.

"Water taxi," Dante said as he pulled on his own gloves. "This has been happening more and more. Especially during the summer months, when the tourists flock the city. Too much traffic." He shook his head with disgust.

Shay nodded and headed over to the patient, who was conscious and had a mask on. His brown eyes were wide with fear as he looked around the room.

"I can't understand a word," he mumbled through the oxygen mask.

"Me neither," Shay said gently. "I'm learning, though."

"You're American?" he asked, a hint of relief in his voice.

"I am. I'm a nurse practitioner with the United World Wide Health Association. Can you tell me what happened?"

"I don't know, I don't remember. One moment my wife and I were taking a water taxi from Lido di Venezia to St. Mark's, and then the next thing I know we're in the water. Oh, goodness, where is my wife?"

"What is her name?" Shay asked.

"Jennifer Sanders."

"I'll find her for you in a moment," Shay said gently. "It's important we make sure you're okay first."

"I can't move. I can't feel my legs," the man said, his voice rising in panic.

Dante shot her a concerned look. "What is your name, *signor*?"

The man looked at Dante. "Are you the doctor?"

"*Sì.* Can you tell me your name?"

"James, but my friends call me Jim."

Dante smiled at him. "I'm going to examine your abdomen. Tell me if anything hurts, and then we'll get an MRI of your spine."

The man nodded. Shay lifted his shirt and there was dark bruising; his belly was distended, which was a sign there was internal bleeding. The bleeding would have to be stopped before they could worry about his back. In this case internal bleeding trumped paralysis.

The man cried out when Dante did a palpation over his spleen.

"We need to get a CT scan of his abdomen, see how bad the bleeding is," Dante whispered to Shay.

"Where do I go to order that?" she asked.

"I will. You stay with him. Prep him for the procedures." Dante left the room.

Shay calmed their patient down and got an IV started, drawing the blood work needed before surgery. She had no doubt that with extensive bruising and pain Jim would need surgery and fast.

"What's your name?" Jim asked.

"Shay Labadie," she said as she took his vitals, writing them down.

"Baton Rouge?" he asked.

"No, close, though. New Orleans proper." She smiled.

"I thought it was a Louisiana accent. I'm from Mississippi. Picayune to be exact."

"Not far, then." She smiled at him warmly, trying to reassure him as his blood pressure was rising.

He grinned faintly as his eyes rolled back into his head and the monitors went into alarm.

"I need a crash cart!" she shouted, slamming her hand against the code blue button as the rest of the team in the room jumped into action. Some situations transcended the language barrier.

"Nurse Labadie, if you contact Dr. Prescarrie, he is the neurologist. He'll be able to determine the extent of the nerve damage in our patient." Dante wanted to keep Shay busy, keep her away from the OR table, but she didn't budge. She stood by his side, passing him the instruments he needed without him having to ask for them.

She knew exactly what he needed and when.

And she was so calm about it. That was what bothered him the most. As if nothing fazed her.

She was good at her job.

Though he shouldn't be surprised. He'd been impressed by her when they were in Oahu together at the conference. Only he hadn't got to see her actually work. Now he had that privilege, but he was also very aware of the fact that she was pregnant.

With his child.

Maybe your child.

He was still reeling over the realization Shay was here and pregnant with his child as he removed Mr. Sanders's badly damaged spleen.

"I will contact him, but does he speak English?" she asked.

"He speaks French and I know that you can speak that. I heard you speak that before."

"Okay, I'll have him paged once Mr. Sanders is stable." She handed him a cautery that he didn't ask for, but damn if he didn't need it right at that moment.

"Grazie," he said grudgingly.

"You seem tense, Dr. Affini," Shay remarked.

"Of course I'm tense. I have a man open on the table."

And you've just walked back into my life carrying my baby.

Her presence here totally threw his controlled world off balance. Thoughts of Shay were kept to the privacy of his memories. To the nights he was alone and lonely, wishing he could have more than he was allotted in life. That was when he thought of Shay and their time together.

He'd romanticized her. The one stolen moment he could treasure forever and now she was here and he wasn't sure how to handle it.

Her presence unnerved him completely.

"Is there anything I can do to ease your tension?" she asked. "I mean, if my job as a scrub nurse isn't up to scratch…"

"It's fine. There is nothing you can do. Well, there is one thing, but you refused." He quickly glanced over at her and he could see her brow furrow above that surgical mask.

"This is not the time to discuss it." There was a hint of warning in her voice.

Dante raised his eyebrows. He'd never heard Shay speak in that tone before. Even at the conference when there were idiots either hitting on her or talking over her, because she was *just a nurse*, she'd always smiled sweetly and taken them down a peg. This was something different.

A clear warning.

"Why not? I like chatting while I work." He didn't, but he liked getting under her skin the way she got under his.

She snorted. "You didn't seem very receptive to talking before."

"It depends what the subject is," he teased.

"Well, I can say in no uncertain terms the subject you want to discuss, Dr. Affini, is off-limits."

He chuckled but didn't say anything further to her as he completed the splenectomy and stabilized the patient. Once he was done, Shay walked away from him and he could see her on the operating theatre's phone, obviously paging Dr. Prescarrie about Mr. Sanders's spinal injuries.

Not only was he impressed by her skill in a surgical situation, but he admired her strength. Women in his circles usually would balk under interrogation.

Of course, women in his circles, women like Olivia, wouldn't even be in an operating theatre, getting their hands dirty.

"What you do is noble, Dante. It's just that I don't want to hear about it. Can't you just keep that to yourself?"

"And what am *I supposed to talk about, Olivia? Fashion, cars?"*

"The vineyards and, yes, it wouldn't hurt you to immerse yourself in the world of privilege you were born into."

Dante snorted as he pulled off his gloves and gown, disposing of them.

Olivia had hated that he was a trauma surgeon, working in a public hospital rather than in a private clinic. And his choice of surgery. Why couldn't he do something like plastic surgery?

In her mind, a prince who was a surgeon needed to do something glamorous that dealt with the glitterati, not just anybody who stumbled in through the doors.

Only that wasn't him. That was his father's world and he loathed it.

Dante might be a prince, poised to inherit a large vineyard in Tuscany and his villa on the Lido di Venezia, as well as a hefty sum of money, but Prince was just a title. It wasn't as if he were a member of the British royal family set to inherit the throne.

Being a prince was just a status in Italy. Nothing more.

His work as a surgeon meant so much more to him.

Working with his hands, doing something important whether it was tending the vines as his grandfather so lovingly had or saving a life.

That was what mattered to him.

Just like the baby that Shay was carrying inside her.

If it's yours.

Even though there was no long-term future for Shay and him, he was determined to be a good father if she would just let him.

"Dr. Prescarrie should be down soon," Shay remarked, coming into the scrub room. "He insisted on his own scrub nurse, though."

"As well he should," Dante said as he washed his hands. "You're on my service."

Shay rolled her neck and winced.

"Are you well?" he asked, concerned, seeing the discomfort etched on her face.

"Yes, just tired. I'm still getting used to the time change. A bit jet-lagged still."

"Why don't you go home and rest?"

She frowned. "I'm fine. I can still work and my shift isn't over yet."

"Shay, you need to take care of yourself. You're possibly carrying my baby."

There was a gasp behind them and they both spun around to see another nurse standing there, her brown eyes wide with shock as she looked between them.

"Sì?" Dante asked in exasperation and frustration. He had no doubt that the nurse had overheard.

"Siamo spiacenti, il Principe, non volevo interromperla." She was apologizing for interrupting them, but Mrs. Sanders was being treated for a broken wrist and was inquiring after her husband. The patient was worried. Dante told the nurse that he would be there shortly to speak to her.

The nurse nodded and left.

Shay was standing there just as stunned. "She just called you *il Principe*. Why did you refer to you as the Prince?"

Dante sighed. This was what he'd wanted to avoid. It was a title and a burden to him.

He was Dante and nothing more.

"Because I am," Dante said.

"You're a prince? A real prince?"

"Sì..." Dante sighed. "I am, so your child will also inherit my title if the child is mine. You may be carrying a royal baby."

"Shay!"

Shay just shook her head and kept walking. She was trying to process what Dante had said to her: that her child was going to have a royal title. Only *if* the baby was his and that annoyed her even more. He was so suspicious of her. She hadn't known that he was a prince, so he couldn't accuse her of fortune hunting.

But maybe that's why he's so suspicious of paternity?

This was all just too surreal.

Of course, it was only fitting that he drop a bombshell on her, just as she'd done to him.

"Shay!"

She stopped and sighed. She couldn't act like this. This was not professional and she'd promised herself that she would be above all professional when dealing with Dante. She was an adult and this was their child.

"I'm sorry, Dante," she said. "I guess it was a bit of a shock to find out who you are."

"It doesn't change who I am, though," he said gently.

"How would I know that? I barely know you." She shook her head. "We're strangers."

He sighed at that. "This is true. One week at a conference means nothing."

"I do realize we have to get to know each other if we're both going to be involved in this child's life."

"*Sì*, I agree. Which is why you will marry me if the test is positive."

Shay rolled her eyes. "Not this again. I'm not marrying you, Dante. I'm not going to marry someone I don't love."

"I'm not talking about a marriage of love," he said matter-of-factly. "I'm talking about a marriage of convenience. Just for a year. You live under my roof and we pretend to be man and wife in public."

"Dante, I'm only here for twelve weeks."

"So? You're going on maternity leave when you get back to the United States, *sì*?"

"Yes, but…I have to go back to the States. My work visa is only good for twelve weeks."

"If we marry, then you won't need a visa. You say it's my child, so why not have *our* child here, in my country?"

"I…I can't—I won't—give up my life, Dante."

"After a year is over, then you can walk away. With our child, as long as I have parental rights. I will continue to financially support the child."

"What do you gain from this?" she asked, confused. It all seemed too easy.

"An heir." He dragged his hand through his dark hair. "I will support the child either way, but while you're here in Italy, under my roof, I can protect you. Care for you."

She bit her lip, mulling it over, but she didn't want to marry. Ever.

Unless it was for love. Absolute, head-over-heels, can't-get-enough-of-each-other love. She let a hand drift over her belly.

"I can't, Dante," she said.

He frowned. "You're confused. Of course you are. I

can see it. You should know that the baby won't inherit any of my family land if he or she is not legitimized."

"Is that a bad thing?" Shay asked. "Perhaps it's better for our baby to be away from all of that."

His eyes narrowed. "I take my family history very seriously. Being an Affini heir is a thing of pride."

And then she felt bad because she was insulting him. His values.

Dante was not American. He came from a completely different world than she did.

How can you have family pride when you know nothing about the name you were born with?

Still, she couldn't agree to marry him. Not now. She needed time to think and she wanted to talk to her friend and colleague, Aubrey, about it. She was so confused.

"We should go and talk to Mrs. Sanders. I'm sure she's worried." She turned and kept walking toward the room where Mrs. Sanders had got her broken wrist taken care of. Dante thankfully took the hint as he fell into step beside her.

Mrs. Sanders was lying in a bed, her wrist in a cast, and Shay could see the pain and worry etched on her face. She opened her eyes when they walked into the room.

"Please tell me you have word on my husband," Mrs. Sanders said.

"I'm Dr. Affini and I did the surgery on your husband."

"Were you told why he went to surgery?" Shay asked gently.

"He had internal bleeding?" Mrs. Sanders said, a hint of uncertainty in her voice. "That's all I know."

"Your husband had major lacerations to his spleen," Dante said gently. "I had to remove it."

Shay rubbed the patient's shoulder as she began to cry.

"He came through the splenectomy well," Dante said. "Dr. Prescarrie is our neurologist. He is going to check out your husband's spine."

"Why?" Mrs. Sanders asked, her eyes tracking to Shay and then back to Dante.

"He was complaining of loss of sensation before we took him into surgery," Dante said. "Dr. Prescarrie will be able to determine if the paralysis is temporary and what damage was done to the spine. We take loss of function very seriously."

"Oh, no. This is our thirtieth anniversary. Our kids surprised us with this trip to Italy. We're on a tour, you see…"

"Were you with the tour company when it happened?" Shay asked.

Mrs. Sanders shook her head. "No, we were having some free time in Venice. We're leaving for Tuscany tomorrow."

"Give me the number of the tour operator and I'll explain what happened. She can contact your family."

"It's in my purse over there." She inclined her head. "Thankfully, I wasn't thrown into the water. Our passports are in there too if you need them."

Shay smiled and brought Mrs. Sanders her purse, holding it open so the patient could pull out the information. Shay took it.

"I'll call the tour operator and they'll take care of your belongings and everything," Shay said. "Don't you worry. Just rest."

Mrs. Sanders nodded and clutched her purse with her good arm.

"Dr. Prescarrie will update you on your husband as

soon as possible, Signora Sanders. For now you'll stay in this room. Try to rest." Dante patted the patient's leg and they walked out of her room. Dante stopped at the nurses' station to give instructions to the staff about Mrs. Sanders's stay, before he headed back toward Shay.

"That was very good of you to say you'll call the tour company."

"Well, they're so far from home." Shay glanced down at the information in her hand. "Is there a place I can call from in private?"

"*Sì*, follow me." Dante held out his arm and led her to another part of the hospital until they were standing in front of an office. "This is my office and you may use the telephone in there to contact the tour operator."

He opened the door for her and flicked on the lights.

"Thank you, Dante."

He shrugged. "Take your time, but before you go I want to finish our conversation."

"I thought we *were* finished with that particular conversation."

A small smile twitched his lips. "No, we're not finished. Far from it. Besides, you have a test to go through, *cara*."

Dante shut the door and walked away, leaving Shay alone in his office. She breathed a sigh of relief as she took a seat in his leather office chair and punched in the number. She was connected right away to the tour operator and she explained the situation to them. Everything was worked out. Their room in Venice would be held for them for as long as they needed and the tour company would contact the emergency contacts in their file.

The tour company would also contact the insurance and everything would be taken care of.

Satisfied, Shay disconnected the call and leaned back

in Dante's swivel chair. She closed her eyes and the baby fluttered around, feeling like a butterfly. Reminding her again that she was working a bit too hard.

The ob-gyn she'd seen in the United States had said she could do this work, but he had warned her to take it easy.

The only reason she had clearance to take this job was because it was less strenuous than the assignment she was originally on. Running a training and simulation program, as well as assisting a trauma surgeon in the operating theatre, should be a breeze.

The problem was, she hadn't taken a break.

Her blood sugar was dropping and she needed to eat something.

Something decent.

And she needed rest.

Dante might think their conversation wasn't over, but as far as she was concerned it was for the evening. She was going to head back to the villa she and her friend Danica were sharing, eat and get some sleep. Tomorrow was going to be a long day; she was going to run her first simulation.

She got up and found her way back to the small office she had been given on the other side of the hospital. She grabbed her purse and sweater. She headed toward the back door and from there it was a short walk to the house the United World Wide Health Association had rented for their staff.

If she had a moment, she'd talk to Dante again and tell him again that she wasn't going to marry him.

Convenience or not, she was a big girl and could take care of herself.

She didn't need his protection.

As she stepped outside she was blinded by flashing

lights and a rush of people crowded her, pressing her back against the wall. She shielded her face, but she couldn't understand what they were asking her.

She caught a few words, like *prince* and *baby*.

Then there was a roar and string of loud, harsh words and strong arms came around her, pulling her close, and she realized it was Dante, shielding her. She clung to him as he shouted at the group of reporters and ushered her back inside. Once they were back inside and the shouting from the mob of reporters was drowned out, she sighed in relief.

"What in the world…?"

"The press got word that you might be carrying my heir," Dante snapped.

"*That's* what they were asking me?"

"*Sì,*" he said, his dark eyes twinkling with a dangerous light, his hands on his hips, and he began to curse in Italian again.

"I thought that Italian princes were common?" Shay said, mimicking him. "I mean, not like the British royal family…"

"Yes, but with my family there is a bit more scandal. So my brother and I are often in the spotlight. We're favorites of the paparazzi."

"And I just gave them their latest scoop." She ran a hand over her belly. "Is this going to happen all the time?"

Dante scrubbed a hand over his face. "*Sì.*"

"So that's what you meant by protecting me?" she asked.

He nodded curtly. "Where are you staying?"

"At the United World Wide Health Association house. It's not far from here."

He shook his head. "Not tonight, you're not. You're coming to my place."

"I am not!" she said, getting annoyed with him.

"You're going to cause a bigger scandal if you don't agree to my marriage suggestion, especially if the child is mine," Dante snapped. "You could ruin my reputation at this hospital."

Shay bit her lip. She didn't want to ruin his career or his reputation. "You want a marriage of convenience?"

"*Sì*, that way I can protect you. I have a restraining order against the paparazzi and it will protect you also, if you marry me."

"So just on paper we'll be married."

"*Sì*, but to make it look real you will have to move into my home for a year." He rolled his neck and tugged at the collar of his shirt, as if it were suffocating him. It clearly bothered him just as much as it bothered her.

"Do you have enough room?" Shay asked.

He chuckled. "I have an entire villa to myself on the Lido di Venezia. I can give you your own wing if you desire. Just say yes. Let me protect you and our child."

Even though she should say no, she didn't want paparazzi stopping her and accosting her when she moved around Venice. Especially where there was a language barrier. Dante could keep them at bay. She ran her hand over her belly again.

This was his baby too. Even if he didn't believe it at the moment.

What choice did she have? It was just for a year. Only she couldn't do it. She couldn't agree to the marriage.

"You're coming with me," Dante said. "We'll get the paternity test done now, put this doubt to rest."

"I don't have a say in this?"

"No, you don't."

And she had a feeling this was one of many arguments she was going to have with him over the course of the next twelve weeks. He'd won this round, but she'd win the next.

CHAPTER THREE

"YOU DID WHAT?"

Dante glanced into his office, where Shay was curled up on his sofa, sleeping. She was resting after the paternity test. Now they were waiting for the results and Dr. Tucci promised to rush them. Before they left, Dante was going to make sure that they were at least on their way to being man and wife, even if Shay kept saying no. He was still having a hard time trusting her, but deep down he felt as if this child was his. So he was going to make sure she married him. Then he could protect the trust his mother left and have something for his child. His child wouldn't have to worry about the future the way his father made Enzo and him so worried. Dante wouldn't sell off his child's inheritance just because he or she wasn't married by the time they were thirty-five. He wouldn't have such a foolish restriction.

Once he brought Shay back to his villa, the press couldn't hound her. If she stayed by his side, she'd be safe as well.

There were still a few steps he had to take. Like convincing her to say yes and stay in Italy. *If* the child was his, he'd do the right thing to protect his child.

And if it's not?

He glanced at Shay sleeping so peacefully and he

didn't even want to think of her betraying him the way Olivia had. His memory of Shay had been so pure and untainted.

The memory of their night together was the only thing besides the vineyard and surgery that made him happy. If she betrayed his trust like Olivia, that memory would be shattered. He'd have nothing pure to cling to when the loneliness gnawed at him.

"Dante, are you even listening to me?" Enzo asked on the other end of the phone.

"*Scusate*, it's been a trying day." He rubbed his temple where a tension headache was forming.

"I would say so," Enzo commiserated on the other end.

"I'm getting married. I just have to obtain a Nulla Osta as quickly as possible."

"She's not Italian?" Enzo asked.

"She's American."

"Why do you want to marry an American?"

"She's carrying my child."

"Are you sure?"

"*Sì*, I believe it is mine."

"You don't sound sure."

"The paternity test results will be ready soon." Dante sighed.

There was silence on the other end. "Dante, I know I have been bugging you to get married, but…did she even agree?"

"Not yet."

"Not yet?" Enzo asked.

"You don't have to say anything else," Dante said, cutting his brother off. He knew exactly where Enzo was going with this and he didn't want to be reminded about Olivia and the baby that wasn't his right now.

Shay was not Olivia.

"I don't want you to get hurt again," Enzo said gently. "It killed me to see you so hurt last time."

"I appreciate that, Enzo. However, if this is my baby, I will marry her."

"What if she's after your money? Your title? Even if the baby is yours, she could be just after the same things that Olivia was."

"She's not," Dante said. "She's already refused to marry me, remember? Several times. It's almost getting embarrassing now."

Enzo laughed. "Still…"

"No, there is no still. Shay's not after my money or anything. There will be ground rules to this marriage. It's just a marriage of convenience. Nothing more. She can continue to do her work, our baby will be protected and I will keep my inheritance. The trust Mother signed over to Father before she knew any better."

"What do you need from me?" Enzo asked.

"She's staying at our place."

"What do you mean?"

"Our childhood home, the one that was sold off before mother died and is now being rented to the United World Wide Health Association. She's staying there."

"Ah, so you want me to go collect her stuff?"

"Or at least tell someone there to collect it for her and then bring it to my place. That's where she'll be staying from now on. She was mobbed on her way out of the hospital this evening. The whole world will soon know about the Affini heir."

"I can't believe you did it, Dante. I can't believe

you're going to get married and have an heir all within a year and so close to the cutoff date. You did it. You saved Grandfather's vineyard and Mamma's villa."

A smile crept across Dante's face as the reality sank in.

He had. He'd managed to keep a hold of all that was promised to him. All that money and land wouldn't pass back into their father's greedy hands. The land he loved so much, the vineyard, all of it would be saved. The relief that washed over him in that moment was almost palpable.

"Could you go and talk to her roommate as soon as possible?" Dante asked. "She's tired and I'm taking her back to my villa. She needs her rest."

"*Sì*, I'll go there as soon as I finish up at the clinic."

"*Grazie.*" Dante hung up the phone and then knelt beside Shay. She looked so peaceful sleeping, her face at ease, those long blond eyelashes brushing the tops of her round cheeks. He resisted the urge to reach out and run his thumb across those smooth, soft cheeks or to kiss her pink lips as he had back in Oahu.

The memory of which was still imprinted onto his soul. And pregnancy just made her all the more beautiful.

She glowed.

Don't. Don't get attached. The results aren't in. Don't set yourself up for hurt.

"Shay," he said gently. "Wake up."

She roused. "Is something wrong?"

"It's time to leave. The paparazzi are still waiting out back, but I have a water taxi waiting for us to take us to Lido di Venezia. They won't follow us there."

"And the results of the test?"

"They'll be ready tomorrow morning. Come, stay at my place tonight, where I can keep you safe."

She nodded drowsily. He stood and helped her to her feet.

He guided her out of his office, down a winding staircase to the canal that bordered the hospital. The water-taxi operator helped Shay down into his boat and Dante followed.

It was dark out, but the city helped light the way. The hospital wasn't too far from the lagoon, but behind him he could hear the singing of the gondoliers, tempting tourists to take a ride. Shay settled against the back of the seat.

"I'm sorry, I can barely keep my eyes open." Her head was nodding.

"Put your head on my shoulder." He rested his arm against the back of the boat and she leaned into him. He could smell her perfume. Soft, feminine. Lilacs.

It reminded him of summers spent in Tuscany. Of the flowers blooming in his grandmother's garden, warmed by the hot sun. He couldn't help but smile. It was so right. It all seemed so right. Everything he wanted.

Be careful.

As they left the canals and headed out into the lagoon, there were stars in the sky. The city light drowned them out, but tonight the sky was clear enough you could make out a few. Ahead the Lido di Venezia was lit up with lights from restaurants and homes that littered the sandy shoal. Even farther away there were a couple of cruise ships and you could hear the music wafting from the upper decks.

It left a bad taste in his mouth.

Venice was becoming too much of a tourist trap.

Which was why he preferred Tuscany.

Sure, there were tourists, but there was more space. And there were no tourists at his grandfather's vineyard.

My vineyard.

He glanced down at the small rounded swell that Shay was instinctively cradling in her sleep. That was his child. And even though he wasn't sure, he reached out to touch it.

"Where are we?" Shay asked, waking with a start. He pulled his hand back and moved his arm.

"We're almost to my home. It's a short walk from the pier to my villa."

"I'm sorry I fell asleep. I usually have more stamina."

"You're pregnant. It's fine."

And it was more than fine.

For his family's legacy it was a lifesaver. And for his heart, his longing for a child he'd thought he'd never have, it was a dream come true.

As long as it's yours.

And that little naysaying voice slammed him back to harsh reality. He was putting his heart at risk again.

Dante climbed out of the water taxi first at the docks and then held out his hand for Shay. Which was good; she wasn't that sure-footed on boats anymore, since her center of gravity had shifted.

In some of the places she worked, boats were a way to get around, a way of life, so she was annoyed when Dante had to help her out of a modern, luxurious water taxi. It wasn't as if it were a skiff in the middle of a fast-flowing river in the South American jungle.

However, she'd forgotten how well her hand fit in

his. How safe he made her feel, just like that night on the beach in Oahu. And she sighed; it slipped out unintentionally.

"What?" he asked as he helped her onto the pier.

"Nothing," she said, smiling up at him.

He smiled too and paid the water-taxi captain.

"Ciao," the captain said, waving at them as he puttered away out toward Venice. The moon was high in the sky, the dark water calm; only a few ripples from the water taxi disrupted the mirrorlike quality of the lagoon. It reminded her of nights in the French Quarter, by Jackson Square, and looking out over the Mississippi. Then there were the few scattered memories of her father taking her to Lake Pontchartrain to fish, before he left them. The moon would be so high over the large lake and New Orleans out on the delta would glow and come to life.

It was all so perfect, this moment. But that was the thing. It was just a moment. Even when the results confirmed what she was saying, she couldn't believe he'd change his tune. He was so untrusting, so guarded, and she couldn't help but wonder why. Moments didn't last. She should know. Her father had proved that, and once her father had left, those nights had no longer been so perfect.

And this situation with Dante was far from perfect.

"Come," Dante said, interrupting her thoughts. "It's only a short walk to my villa."

They walked up the ramp from the dock onto the street.

Shay was surprised to see a few cars and a bus stop.

As if sensing her shock Dante chuckled. "There are no large canals here. Solid land here."

"I'm surprised you don't live in Venice."

He frowned. "I used to. I grew up there."

"Do your parents still live there?"

"No," he said tersely. "Our family home is no longer in our family."

"You sound annoyed by that."

"It's a long story," Dante said. "Besides, I prefer living here on the Lido di Venezia. It's peaceful here. There are tourists on the beach side, but I live on the lagoon side. I enjoy having a garden and trees. And most of the beaches at this end are private and owned by the hotels. Though to the south there are public beaches. The Adriatic is warm and very popular for young children. I spent many summers swimming here."

They turned down a small side street off the main street, the Gran Viale Santa Maria Elisabetta, not far from the lagoon, where residents could catch the ferries and *vaporetti*.

Shay was expecting a small home and was shocked when he opened a gate to a large, square villa that seemed to take up the entire block off the main street. At the top of the villa there looked to be a patio that would have views over the lagoon and to Venice.

"I shouldn't be surprised," she mumbled. "You are a prince, after all."

He grinned and pushed open the creaky iron gate. "This was my maternal grandparents' summer home— they were wealthy but not royalty. Unfortunately, it fell into disrepair."

"And you're putting it back together?"

He nodded quickly. "There are many rooms."

Dante unlocked the front door and led her inside. When he flicked on the light, Shay gasped at the beauty of a place so old. The stucco on the wall was painted in terra-cotta. The foyer was round like a turret, which you couldn't tell from the outside, which was square.

There were many arches leading off to various empty rooms.

"I haven't had much time," Dante said apologetically. "Just the kitchen has been renovated on this ground floor and the master suite, terrace and a couple of bathrooms on the next level."

She followed him past numerous rooms. There was a large room that looked as if it had a dining table and suspended over it was a beautiful glass chandelier, unlit as it hovered above the ghostly occupants.

"This is the kitchen. It backs onto the garden. You can't see much, but I have a couple of kiwi trees and an olive tree out there as well as a small pool." Dante flicked on another light, which illuminated a white, large and modern kitchen. "Are you hungry?"

"Yes," Shay admitted.

He smiled. "I thought as much. You need to eat."

She took a seat at the large wooden kitchen table. The garden was in darkness, but she could make out the reflection of water as it bounced off the tile of the terrace.

"It's beautiful. How old is this villa?" she asked.

"This villa was built in the mid-eighteen-hundreds to replace a crumbling home that my family had owned since the fifteen-hundreds. This land actually housed many crusaders during the Fourth Crusade." He brought her a cold glass of mineral water. "Drink it—the limes are actually mine too."

Shay took a sip. "Crusaders? How do you know?"

"Everybody knows," he said offhandedly. "Did you not learn about the Crusades in school?"

"No, it really wasn't on our curriculum."

Dante *tsked* under his breath. "The Lido was home

to about ten thousand crusaders, spurred on by Pope Innocent III to sack Constantinople. They were block-aded here for a time because they could not afford to pay for the ships being built. In fact, some of my ancestors fought in the battle of Zara, but it wasn't until the fifteen-hundreds that my family gained notoriety and inherited the royal title. Of course, as this was my mother's fam-ily's home, my royal title has nothing to do with that at all. It's just a bit of interesting family history."

"I'm afraid I don't know much about my family at all."

Dante cocked an eyebrow. "Don't you?"

"No. Labadie is a French name. That much I know. My father's family came to New Orleans before it was purchased by the Americans. When it was still part of France, they, I believe, drifted down from the Maritimes in Canada during the Seven Years' War. Mostly Cajun."

"Seven Years' War?" Dante asked.

"Oh, didn't you learn about that in school?" Shay teased, and they both laughed at that.

"How does leftover risotto sound?" he asked. "Or perhaps some cheese?"

"Risotto sounds fine."

Dante went to heat the food and Shay glanced around the kitchen. She didn't do much cooking; she knew how to cook on cookstoves or an open fire. Basically any-thing that was propane-operated, because sometimes where she was working there might not always be elec-tricity or even clean water.

This kitchen was opulent to her.

Even her mother's kitchen hadn't been this nice.

And then after Katrina, when the house had been condemned and her mother was dying from the effects of the mold she'd picked up in her lungs after the dikes had burst and flooded their home, the small run-down kitchen had been absolutely destroyed. Shay had had to go back into the home and try to salvage anything she could.

Only there had been nothing left to salvage, really.

A few pictures and birth certificates that had been stored in a flood-proof and fireproof box. And whatever else her mother had managed to cram into her carryall when she'd climbed out through the attic to the roof, waiting for help as the floodwaters rose.

"You look sad, *cara*."

"Do I?" she asked.

"Sì." He set the plate of risotto in front of her and then sat down next to her with his own plate. "Is something wrong?"

"No, I'm just tired." She plastered a fake smile on her face and took a bite of the risotto. "Oh, my goodness, this is so good."

He grinned. "I like to cook."

"You're not a traditional prince, then."

His brow furrowed. "What do you mean, 'traditional'?"

"You're a surgeon, you like to work with your hands and you cook. You don't have any servants."

He laughed. "I do have a lady come and clean my house, but you're right, I do most of it on my own. My maternal grandfather was a winemaker. He had a large vineyard in Tuscany and, though he was extremely wealthy, he taught me the value of hard work. I enjoy it."

"Well, you're good at it. I'm afraid my cooking would not be up to par. The only thing I can make, if I have the ingredients and the patience, is *boudin*."

"What is *boudin*?"

"A sausage stuffed with rice and green peppers."

"I would like to try that sometime."

Shay chuckled. "I'm not sure I'm up to *boudin* making at the moment."

"I can get you all the ingredients here."

"I'm sure you can, but I have a simulation course and training to run. Not to mention I'm to assist you in surgery. I'm here for work, Dante. Nothing else."

He frowned. "I'm passionate about my job too, but you have to live life as well. Work is not life."

"It is for me."

"And what happens when you have the child?" he asked. "Our child. Are you going to ignore our child for work?"

"No," she snapped. "I will balance it. A woman can work and be a mother. I think seeing me work will be a good example for our child."

Dante sighed. "I'm not saying that at all. Of course it's a good example, but you said you don't do anything *but* work. What do you do for fun?"

And the question caught her off guard, because really she didn't do much.

When she was on assignment, she put her whole heart and soul into the job.

There was no time for much else.

"You know what, I'm really tired. Is there a place I can sleep?"

"Of course, follow me."

Shay followed Dante out of the kitchen and up the winding staircase to the second floor. There were many rooms and a large open area with a couch and a desk. A living room. He led her to the back of the house and flicked on a light.

"This is the only room with a bed in it at the moment. When you move in, I'll move out of here."

"This is your room?"

"*Sì*, it is also the only bedroom with a private bathroom. I can use the one downstairs. It is no trouble."

"Where will you sleep?"

"The couch. I have some work to do. I'm not tired yet. You rest."

"I can't kick you out of your bedroom."

"You can." He smiled. "Get some rest and we'll talk about our plans for marriage tomorrow, but only if the results are positive."

"Sure. Okay." She rolled her eyes. Dante was so stubborn, so untrusting.

He nodded and shut her in his bedroom. Shay sighed and sat down on the edge of his large bed, sinking down into the soft duvet.

Tomorrow she'd tell him that it wasn't a good idea.

They weren't going to get married.

It was a foolish idea.

She lay down on the bed and thought about how she was going to tell him her reasons, but before she could get too far into her plans she drifted off into a deep, sound sleep.

CHAPTER FOUR

THE INCESSANT RINGING woke Shay up. And it took her a moment to realize where she was. She scrubbed a hand over her face and dug her phone out of her purse. It was Aubrey.

"Hello?" she said, trying not to sound too groggy.

"Are you okay?" Aubrey asked excitedly on the other end.

"Fine, just…you woke me up."

"Where did you sleep? I called last night and Danica told me that you were staying with Dr. Affini at his home and she's to send your belongings there."

"No. I'm not staying here permanently. I'll call Danica and tell her. It was just for last night. It's a long story." Shay sighed.

"Well, I told you to tell Dante about the baby, not to move in with him," Aubrey teased.

Shay laughed. "It's the pregnancy hormones that made me do it."

"I'll say."

"Where are you today?" Shay asked, hoping Aubrey was nearby. She needed to talk to her face-to-face. Aubrey had taken an assignment outside Venice but did move around a bit in Italy.

"Actually, I'm in Venice today, believe it or not."

"I'll tell you all about it at lunch, then. When is your lunch break?" Shay asked.

"Two. Do you want to meet for lunch at Braddicio's near the hospital? I heard it was good. And I know where that is."

"Sounds good," Shay said, trying to stifle a yawn. "I'll explain everything there."

"Okay, be careful."

Shay disconnected the call and then headed to the bathroom, where she quickly showered before re-dressing in yesterday's clothes.

The bathroom was white and modern like the kitchen, except for the deep, large claw tub with a shower hose placed on a rack in the middle of the room. There were long windows and the blinds were closed. There was a bit of sunlight peeking through the sides of the roman shades.

She pulled on the string and drew open the blinds, gasping when she noticed French doors that led out to a rooftop terrace. She unlatched the French doors and headed outside. From the terrace, the master suite faced the Adriatic. She could see the blue water and the sandy beaches that made the Lido di Venezia a favorite spot for tourists.

She closed her eyes and drank in the scent of fruit trees flowering in the spring, mixed with sand and surf. When she looked down, she could see the high stone walls that bordered Dante's garden. The fruit trees, the olive tree and the small pool that Dante was currently swimming laps in.

Naked.

Shay meant to look away, but couldn't. She couldn't help but watch him. His bronze form cutting through the turquoise water like a blade. It was mesmerizing.

And she recalled very vividly what it was like to run her hands over that muscular body, to feel him pressed against her, his strong arms around her, holding her. His lips on her skin. Her blood heated. Drawn to him, she was so weak.

Don't look. Go downstairs and catch a ferry back to Venice. Back to the place you're staying, so you won't be tempted.

And she was so tempted by Dante.

She tore her gaze away and collected her purse and made her way downstairs.

When she got to the stairs, she could smell coffee. It was inviting and she desperately wanted a cup, but coffee was off-limits. She made her way to the kitchen, just as Dante came walking in through the open terrace doors. He had a towel wrapped around his waist, but she got an eyeful of his broad, muscular chest.

"You're awake," he said, his deep voice making her quake with a sudden need for him.

"Yes." She tried to avert her eyes from him, because she remembered all too well that body. The touch of it, the taste of it, the way he felt in her arms, his kisses burning a path of fire across her skin. "I hope your pool is heated."

"*Sì*, it is. How did you sleep?"

"Very well. Your bed is very comfortable and I feel bad for taking it. I have a perfectly good bed where I'm staying."

"You're going to be my wife and you're carrying my child. *This* is now your place," he said matter-of-factly.

"Dante, I'm not going to be—"

"You need to eat," he said, cutting her off, which made her grind her teeth a bit. Was he this annoying in Oahu or were her hormones amplifying his annoying, arrogant habits?

"I'm trying to talk to you, Dante."

He was looking in the fridge. "How does some fresh fruit and yogurt sound?"

Great.

And her stomach growled in response.

Traitor.

"Dante, this is serious. More serious than fruit and yogurt."

He turned around then, one of those dark brows cocked. "Oh?"

"I'm not going to marry you, Dante. We can't get married."

"*Cara*, the only way I can protect you and the baby is by marrying you."

"What about the paternity test?"

"Dr. Tucci called," Dante said offhandedly. "The results came in. The child is mine."

Shay tried not to roll her eyes. "I know that, but that doesn't change the fact that I can't marry you."

"It's not permanent—the marriage, I mean. There will be rules. You will have your own room, your own space."

"You're going to give up your bed for a year?"

"I'll get another bed and I'll finish the other bedroom up on the second floor. It's not a problem. And then I'll start on the nursery."

"Dante, it's not as easy as this." She ran her hand through her hair to stop her from pulling it out.

"Why can't it be? This is a business arrangement to protect our child, and my child will have my name. A good name," he said as he scooped fresh berries into a bowl. "Now eat your breakfast and I'll shower and change before we head back to the hospital."

Dante was shutting down any further discussion to the matter and that was highly frustrating for Shay. She couldn't remember him being this stubborn before. He didn't even want to discuss the matter. Didn't he know what he was doing? He was going to blame her in a year for ruining his life.

Just as her father had done all the times when he'd been unhappy. Which had been a lot.

Sure, there had been moments when her father had been happy, but they had been few and far between. Now she couldn't even remember them.

She couldn't even remember her father's face.

All the pictures of him had been lost during Katrina, except for one that her mother had clutched to her chest when she'd taken her last breaths. And Shay had been so angry that her father had left them that way, left them in poverty, that she'd buried that picture with her mother in St. Louis Cemetery on Canal Street in New Orleans.

At least Dante wanted to give their child his name. Dante was offering their child roots, history. Permanence.

Something she couldn't give their child. Not really. He had land that was centuries old. Other than the house that Katrina had destroyed, there was no childhood home. Her mother and her always moving.

It still haunted her, the looks, the heartache of her mother, and she couldn't put her child through that. Even if it meant that she would be protected from the paparazzi. She didn't need that protection. She could take care of herself. She'd been in worse situations before and had managed.

You weren't pregnant before.

She shook that niggling thought from her head. She also couldn't help but wonder what Dante had to gain by marrying her, by supporting her. She had a hard time believing it was just for the sake of the child.

Just marry him. Take the protection. Do your work and give your child access to his or her father.

The only thing that would be different in her situation was that she would never pine over a man who didn't want her. She wouldn't waste away as her mother had. She couldn't stay in Italy and rely on a man to help her raise her child, even if that man was her baby's father.

She was stronger than that.

He'd watched her sleep. He hadn't meant to go back into the room, but when he'd been on the couch last night she'd been all he could think about.

Shay had been plaguing his thoughts since their stolen night together in Oahu and now she was under his roof. Carrying his child.

And this morning, Dr. Tucci had confirmed what he'd known, deep down. He was just too afraid to hope, too afraid of being hurt to let himself believe it.

Shay had always been beautiful, but now, pregnant with his child, she was even more so and he couldn't help but think of the night of passion they'd had together. The night that had brought about this baby and their reunion.

The first woman he'd been with since Olivia and he'd had no qualms about taking her to his bed that night months ago. He'd dated since Olivia, but never had he made love to another woman until Shay. Usually he would talk himself out of it, but with Shay the desire had been too great.

He'd wanted her.

He *still* wanted her. That had never changed. He still desired her. The urge to take her in his arms and kiss her again was too much to bear.

She was in his villa. In his bed.

He'd sneaked into his bedroom, now her bedroom, to check on how she was doing. He hadn't been able to help himself.

Shay had been sleeping, but she'd been huddled in a ball in the middle of the bed, shivering. He had forgotten that he'd left a window open. Even though it was spring and temperatures were rising, the nights were still chilly. Especially the breeze coming off the Adriatic and the lagoon.

So he'd covered her with a blanket, made sure she was comfortable.

As in the taxi, he'd wanted to touch the rounded swell of her belly, but he wasn't sure.

Dante hadn't wanted her to wake, so he'd backed away and gone back to the living room, where he'd spent the night tossing and turning on the couch.

He wasn't sure what he was doing by asking her to marry him. He'd never intended to get married after what happened with Olivia, even if that meant he was going to lose everything. The vineyards, the villa and the inheritance.

The money didn't matter to him so much, but losing his grandfather's vineyard and this villa was what was crushing him. Now Shay was pregnant with his child and all his problems were solved.

Were they?

Why did he feel so guilty about this situation? And he couldn't help but think of his own parents' loveless marriage. Well, loveless on his father's part, because even though his father insisted that he'd loved their mother, a man who loved a woman wouldn't cheat on her repeatedly as their father had.

Perhaps the guilt stemmed from the fact that it seemed too easy that his problems were solved.

Shay had made it clear that she didn't want to marry him. She didn't love him.

He didn't want to ruin her life by forcing her to marry him, but it was the best thing for the baby.

He could protect them. He was going to be a father.

Why did it have to be her to come to Venice and not Daniel? Only, if she hadn't, would he ever have known about his child? He sometimes wondered if fate had a twisted sense of humor. Nonetheless, she was here and pregnant with his child and he was going to do right by them.

Both of them.

He was going to protect them from the paparazzi and anyone else who wanted a piece of the Affini name. He quickly had a shower in the main suite's bathroom, to wash the chlorine from his skin. He noticed that the French doors leading to the terrace were open and he wondered if Shay had ended up out there and seen him in the pool.

When he went for his morning swim, he didn't even think about putting on a bathing suit. He wasn't used to it, but if Shay was going to move in with him he'd have to remind himself of common decency.

Dante got dressed and ready to go back to the hospital for his shift in the emergency room. He had to complete rounds with students, check on his patients, including Mr. Sanders from yesterday.

When he came back downstairs, Shay was pacing, having finished her yogurt and berries. She shot him a look of frustration, but he didn't care. There was going to be no more talk about it. They were going to get married. He was going to take care of them.

By marrying her he could gain control over the vineyard and the villa, and then he could properly take care of them. His father wouldn't have any hand in it. His child's inheritance would be safe. He wouldn't sell off the estate, the land, piece by piece as his father was doing. His child would never look on him with disdain, the way he looked upon his father.

He would never hurt his child. He would be a better man than his father was.

And this was definitely his child, unlike what had happened with Olivia, when the child he'd thought was his hadn't been.

"You told me it was mine! I believed you."

She shrugged. "I wanted to marry you."

"Why? If the child wasn't mine..."

"The title. The name. Affini is respected."

"You were going to let me believe that your baby was mine, but really it's another man's? A man you were having an affair with before we even got together. Why?"

"Oh, come on, Dante. I don't love you. You don't love me. Not really. You were just excited about the prospect of family, of settling down and raising a child. I don't want that. I thought you were different. I thought we'd go to parties and hire a nanny."

"I never wanted that. That was how I was raised. I don't want that for my child."

She glared at him with those dark, hardened eyes. "Well, it's a good thing this child isn't yours."

"Are you ready to go?" he asked, shaking away that painful memory.

"I've been more than ready. I finished my breakfast

a while ago. I would've left sooner, but I didn't know my way back to catch the water taxi. I'm a bit turned around here."

"We'll take the ferry to Venice—it's running right now—or a *vaporetto* if we miss the ferry. Although the water buses are smaller than the ferry, I prefer the ferry, but they do the job."

He led her out the front door and locked up. It was a beautiful sunny day and everybody was out on the street. He put his arm through her arm.

"What're you doing?" she asked.

"Just leading you. Making sure you don't step out into the street."

"I've been all over the world in worse situations than this, in worse conditions than this. I'm not going to just step out into the street," she teased, the smile replacing the frown of worry that had been there moments ago.

"Nonetheless it is my pleasure to do so."

And it was. He liked walking with her. And he couldn't remember the last time he'd had company to work. It was nice.

They walked in silence down the Gran Viale Santa Maria Elisabetta toward the ferry landing. The ferry was there; they paid their fare and got on board just before it departed. He walked her up to the top deck to enjoy the sun and the breeze off the lagoon.

She was still slightly frustrated with him as she leaned over the railing to look out over the water. He could tell by the way her brow was furrowed and her lips were pursed together.

"How was your breakfast? Was it adequate?" he asked.

"It was good," she said seriously. He chuckled, and then she smiled again. "It was good. Thank you."

"I'm glad to hear it. You have to remember to eat small meals all day long. It's the best for you and the baby."

"I know," she said.

"Do you have a doctor here in Venice yet?"

"No, I have to find one."

"I could send you to the clinic to talk to my brother. He's a family physician."

"Don't you think it would be odd that your brother would be my doctor in this situation?" she asked.

"Hmm, perhaps you're right. You need to go see Dr. Tucci, then. He's the ob-gyn that did the paternity test. He works in the hospital. He's quite good and he speaks English as well, as you know. He's one of the best."

"Dr. Tucci—that's good to know. I wasn't sure who to go see. I wasn't sure that he worked in the hospital. I liked him."

"I would like to go to the appointment," Dante said.

"You want to go to my appointments?" Her finely arched eyebrows rose in surprise.

"Of course. It's my baby. I'm concerned about its health too."

"Yes, of course you would be." She sighed. "When we get to the hospital, I will make an appointment on my next break, but this morning I'm swamped. I have to plan the first simulation. The trainees are with another physician this morning, so that gives me time to plan an exercise they would face in the field."

Intrigued, he asked, "What were you thinking of?"

"I was thinking of a natural disaster, like a flood or forest fire."

He nodded. "That sounds good. You should do a flood. There're lots of floods here, especially when the big cruise ships come into the lagoon and they flood

San Marco's *piazza* quite often. I mean, look what happened to Mr. Sanders in the *vaporetto* that was capsized because of one of those cruise ships and the big bow waves."

"I understand that. Flooding would be a big deal here, especially since this city is basically sitting on wooden planks. I'm sure that you face that issue all the time, but this is a city. These trainees will be going out into Third World countries where the flooding is different. Where the conditions are not so sanitary."

"Have you ever been in a flood where the conditions are not so sanitary?" he asked.

Shay frowned, her gaze drifting out over the water. "Yes, yes, I have."

"Where?"

"New Orleans," she said in a faraway voice. "Katrina."

She turned and looked away from him. It looked as if there were tears in her eyes as she said it.

"I'm sorry, *cara*," he apologized. "I didn't mean to bring up something that would be hard for you. I forgot… you're from New Orleans, aren't you?"

"Yes, it was terrible. The conditions were so bad."

"It wasn't just the hurricane, though?"

"No, it was after that. I was in school, training at the hospital and helping people escape. Taking care of those who couldn't flee. First we got out the infants, and then moved down the priority list. It was pretty scary. I was one of the last people to leave as the hospital flooded."

"I bet that was scary," he said, placing his hand over hers and giving it a reassuring squeeze. There wasn't much more he could say. He'd read about the devastation.

"That was the first and worst flood I've ever been in. I've been in other floods, but Katrina was definitely the worst," she said quietly, looking off into the distance. "I don't really want to talk about it, if you don't mind."

He nodded. "I'm sorry for bringing it up, *cara*. I didn't mean to cause you pain."

"It's okay. You didn't hurt me. You're right, they could have to deal with flooding in a city like this, a city like New Orleans, during a natural disaster. They could be posted anywhere. The conditions weren't sanitary in New Orleans. There was no power, no clean water. So yeah, maybe I'll do the first simulation in a setting like this. A setting where everything you thought you had, because you're not in a Third World country and are used to having, is no longer available. You have to learn to boil water in unsanitary conditions, where your supplies can run out. Thanks for that, Dante. I think that's what I'll do today."

"I'm always here to help. I'm part of this program too. I wish I could help you more, but I have rounds in the emergency room today. And I would like to check on Mr. Sanders."

"Did you hear anything about his condition after Dr. Prescarrie saw him?" she asked.

Dante sighed. "Yes, there was some damage to his spinal cord—it's bruised and there's swelling. We're hoping his paralysis isn't permanent. He's in the ICU. The internal bleeding has stopped. That's the main thing."

"That's good," she said. "I hope his paralysis isn't permanent. That's the last thing he needs on a trip of a lifetime, all because a cruise ship taking it too fast caused a *vaporetto* to capsize."

He nodded. "Yes, it's these things that annoy us Venetians about the tourist industry. So many tourists."

"You don't like tourists?"

"We like them. I mean, it's a way of life, but then there're things like the cruise ships coming in too fast and flooding San Marco's *piazza*, and there are issues with overcrowding. It's not the same as it was when I was young."

"I bet it's not," she said. "New Orleans gets tourists, especially during Mardi Gras. It's insane around the French Quarter. You can't walk around anywhere. It's just packed full of people."

"So you understand what I'm talking about."

"I do get it," she said. "They bleach Bourbon Street every night."

"Bleach the street?"

"Oh, yes." She grinned. "Bourbon Street is a very popular party street. There are a lot of bars and people drink a lot and sometimes they can't always find a bathroom."

He wrinkled his nose. "That's terrible."

"It is," she said. "Every night after last call and into the early morning the street cleaners go out and bleach the street with lemon and bleach. It's very citrusy if you walk down Bourbon Street just after they've sprayed it, but if you walk ahead of the cleaners, like I did one night trying to get to work, you learn to appreciate the bleach."

They laughed together at that as the ferry pulled into the docks.

It was a short walk from the ferry to the hospital. And there wasn't any press around. Dante made sure she got to her office and was settled, before he headed to his.

"Shay, if you need anything, please have me paged. I'm here for you, *cara*."

She nodded. "Thank you, but I've arranged to meet

my friend today for lunch and talk to her about a few things, because I'm honestly not sure about this, Dante. I mean, a marriage of convenience… I can't agree to that."

He held up his hand, cutting her off. "It's for the best. Trust me."

"How can I trust you? We barely know each other."

He understood that. He understood about not trusting someone. His trust had been shattered when Olivia broke his heart.

"You just have to," he said, and he walked away.

Not even sure that he could trust her either.

Dante made his rounds pretty quickly, which always gave him a bad feeling because when the emergency room was quiet it would inevitably become busy in the near future. Which meant trauma.

After he did his rounds and checked on the stability of Mr. Sanders, who was doing well in the intensive care unit, he headed back to his office. He resisted the urge to go and find Shay to see how she was coming along with the simulation planning because he wanted to give her some space. He had a feeling that he was overwhelming her and he didn't blame her one bit. He was feeling a bit overwhelmed himself.

When he walked into his office, he saw Enzo standing in front of his desk, his back to him. The expensive suits his brother always wore gave him away.

"Enzo, aren't you supposed to be at the clinic?"

Enzo turned around and flashed him that impish smile he'd had since he was a young boy. "Is that any way to talk to your brother? Not even a *ciao* and asking how I am doing, just straight to the point of why I'm here?"

"Yes, usually it is. You're a pain in my side." Dante laughed.

Enzo just shook his head. "I have some good news—"

"Did you do what I asked?" Dante said, interrupting him.

"Yes, I left a message with someone from the United World Wide Health Association who was at the house. I told her where Shay was and where she was going to be moving to. She said she would try to find time to pack Shay's personal belongings, but I don't know."

"Well, they haven't yet," Dante said.

Enzo shrugged. "I can't help that. I did what you asked me to. I wasn't about to go into some woman's room and rummage through her things. Especially if she's rooming with another woman. I really don't feel like being beaten up by a bunch of United World Wide Health Association workers. I have a practice to run and I'm going to be getting one of those United World Wide Health Association nurses in my clinic soon to deal with the tourists."

"You don't sound very happy about that," Dante said.

Enzo shrugged again. "Am I ever happy about stuff like that? It is what it is. Maybe she'll have a lighter hand with the tourists. Sometimes I don't have enough patience with them."

"So intolerant," Dante teased.

"Look, I have some news. Do you want to hear it or not?"

"*Sì*, I want to hear it."

"I have a friend who works for the civil court. I explained your situation and they are very aware of our situation with respect to our inheritance and the trust fund."

"Oh, yes?" Dante was now very interested.

"And instead of the four-day waiting period to get your Nulla Osta they were able to give it to me today. All you have to do is get Shay to sign it stating that there is no impediment for you two to marry, and you can marry today, provided you have two witnesses."

"I hope you'll be one of the witnesses."

"I'll try. Truly," Enzo said. "I want to make sure this is seen through. I'm still worried, Dante. I still have my misgivings about this."

"I know you do, but, trust me, Shay is pregnant with my child. The paternity result said so. I met her at that conference in Hawaii months ago. We had one night of passion. We did use protection, but you know that doesn't always work. And now she's expecting my child."

Enzo nodded. "Don't you think it's funny, though, that she came here? I mean, people know about us. The paparazzi follow us around even though we have restraining orders. Everyone knows our father is a womanizer and has sold off pieces of Affini land, just so he could pay for all his mistresses, and that he'll eventually sell off our mother's land too if he gets the chance. Affini men are cheaters, both in matters of money and women. It was the same with his father too. Affini men are a bunch of womanizers. What if she hears about that?"

"What if she does?" Dante asked, getting impatient. He knew all this. Why was Enzo so worried?

"Isn't that why Olivia went after you? She could claim that you were not being faithful to her, even though she was ultimately not faithful to you. Women like that are just looking for a handout."

"I am aware of the situation, Enzo. Because it's happened to me. It won't happen this time. This is my child. With Olivia it was different. She was pregnant before we met—that's how I knew the child wasn't mine. It was better I found out. It hurt a lot at the time, that's true, but Shay *is* pregnant with my child. I'm going to take care of them even if I have to give them a handout. I'm going to support her. I'm going to make sure my child is taken care of. That's the kind of person that I am."

Enzo shook his head. "This is why I don't want to get involved with any woman. Just give me casual relationships."

"Casual can lead to a baby too," Dante said. "Look what happened here. Shay and I were only ever going to be a onetime thing and now she's pregnant with my child. If it wasn't for the fact that I was approaching my thirty-fifth birthday, I wouldn't be pushing this marriage so hard. I would support the child, don't get me wrong," Dante said quickly. "Because, unlike you, I want to be a father."

There had been so many times when he was in that villa that he'd felt lonely. He wouldn't admit it, but it was true. It hurt thinking about what could've been with Olivia if she hadn't betrayed his trust, if that child had been his. He wanted a family. Despite the fact that his father was a womanizer who had broken his mother's heart. He wanted what he'd never had as a child. A happy family.

Love from both parents.

What his mother had mourned, because she'd had that as a child and hadn't been able to give it to her sons.

Dante had loved his mother. She was a good mother. He loved Enzo and having a brother. He'd loved spending time with his maternal grandparents in Tuscany. Every summer they would spend their time there when they weren't in school. Then there were the times his mother would take them to the dilapidated villa that was now his home. They would spend time running on the sandy beaches at the Lido, eating olives and picking fresh fruit.

It was a happy time.

On the Lido they had been away from the hustle and bustle. From the lonely nights when their parents had gone to parties and entertained. From the fights and arguments their parents had had. From the heartbreaking cries of their mother as her heart had broken more every time their father had cheated.

He wasn't going to do that. Enzo was more afraid of becoming a womanizer than Dante was, but Olivia had crushed every little piece of trust he'd had and he wasn't sure he ever wanted to take the risk of having what he'd always wanted.

Family.

Shay showing up in Venice pregnant was scary. He was terrified, but he was going to do the right thing. Even if the marriage was for show and nothing was going to come of things between the two of them, he was going to have a child. An heir. He was going to be a part of that child's life forever. He didn't take his duty lightly.

He was going to make sure his child was happy. His child wasn't going to suffer the way he and Enzo had suffered. He wasn't going to hurt Shay, or his child.

"Come on, let's go get Shay to sign this." Dante took

the forms from Enzo. "Then you can meet her and see for yourself that she's nothing like Olivia."

"I look forward to meeting her. Another time, though. I have work to take care of."

"You can come meet her here before you go."

They walked through the halls of the hospital to the other side where the simulation training was going to take place, but they found that Shay's office was locked. Dante knocked, but there was no answer.

A nurse walked by.

"She went out for lunch," the nurse said.

"Do you know where?" Dante asked.

"*Sì*, Braddicio's, which isn't far."

"Do you know when she'll be back?" Dante asked.

"I don't know," the nurse said. "The simulation is ready, but the trainees are still working with Dr. Carlo, so it's been postponed until they are done working with Dr. Carlo."

Dante cursed under his breath. *"Grazie."*

"Well, now what?" Enzo asked. "I don't have much longer before I have to get back to the clinic."

"How about we go to the restaurant? I need to talk to her privately away from here anyway. You can distract the girlfriend she's having lunch with while I talk to Shay."

"No good," said Enzo. "I'm truly sorry, but you're on your own."

Dante cursed under his breath. "You're a thorn in my side, Enzo."

And all Enzo did was grin.

CHAPTER FIVE

SHAY WALKED INTO BRADDICIO'S, which was tucked down a small canal, off the main canal near the hospital. She'd been here before. It was a nice Italian bistro, dark and romantic, and the food was good. Shay loved it here. When she went inside, Aubrey was already sitting there, waiting. She looked worried as she watched the door.

Shay headed to the booth in the corner where Aubrey was waiting for her. When Aubrey's gaze landed on her, she could see the relief wash over her face.

"Oh, thank goodness," Aubrey said. "I've been so worried about you. You didn't go into too many details on the phone this morning and I figured you couldn't speak freely. I hopped a train for you, I'll have you know."

"I was fine, Aubrey. I was with Dante—the father of my child *and* a highly respected surgeon," she teased. "I was in very good hands."

"I know, I know. I was just concerned when you weren't at the house when I called last night. I know I pushed you to take this job here and to tell Dante about his child, but I didn't expect you to run off with him."

"I didn't."

"Clearly. Still, I was picturing all these horrible things happening to you." Aubrey grinned. "I'm relieved."

"What kind of horrible things? The worst he could do is lock me up in his villa…"

"He owns a villa?" Aubrey asked with surprise. "Where?"

"The Lido di Venezia."

"He has a villa on the Lido?" Aubrey asked, impressed. "Wow, Venice is expensive."

"He's a prince."

Aubrey's mouth dropped open, her eyes wide, and she shook her head. "A what?"

"A prince. The father of my baby is a prince. Yesterday when I tried to leave the hospital after my shift ended I was accosted by the paparazzi because my baby is the Affini heir." She'd lowered her voice, not that there were many people in the restaurant while they were having their lunch break, but, still, she didn't want someone to hear.

"So that's why he wants to marry you? Because he's a prince?"

"Something like that," Shay said. "He said he could protect me. He has a restraining order against the press. Once he had me in his arms, they didn't come back again. They didn't follow us to the Lido to bother us either."

Aubrey frowned. "He wants to marry you to *protect* you? That sounds a little old-fashioned. What did you say?"

"I told him no, of course, but he's so insistent. Which is why I wanted to talk to you."

"Do you *want* to marry him? I thought you didn't want to get married."

"I don't, but he wants to give his child his name. And it would be more of a business arrangement. Dante said it need only last a year."

"You don't need to be married for him to give your child his name, you know," Aubrey said.

"I know, right? I mean, it's just that he's royalty and their name is well-known—it's a legitimizing thing apparently. And…with my work…well, I could continue to do my work if he was involved."

"You don't have to be married for him to be involved in your child's life. Or for you to be able to continue with your career, Shay."

"I know. I'm so confused. When I woke up in his bed this morning in his villa, it felt right being with him, but… I don't know."

Aubrey's eyes widened. "You spent the night in his bed, in his villa?"

"Yes." Shay winced as Aubrey groaned. "But he was the perfect gentleman and slept downstairs on the sofa all night," she added quickly.

"Oh, Shay, are you still attracted to him?"

"Yes."

Aubrey looked even more concerned then. "And he only wants to be married for a year? That seems weird."

"I know." Shay sighed. "It sounds a little too good to be true, but there you have it. I don't know what to do."

"Well, at least he wants to be involved with his child's life."

"Yes, that much he does," Shay agreed.

"That's a good thing." Aubrey had issues with her own father, just as Shay did. Which was probably why they'd bonded so quickly when they'd met in their first years during the UWWHA. Aubrey was the one who had been so insistent that Shay find Dante and tell him about the baby. Aubrey was also the one who'd found out about this job and suggested that Shay take it when Daniel dropped out.

Shay didn't know what to do, which was why she was glad Aubrey was visiting today. She needed to talk it out. That was how she rationalized things.

"I wonder what's in it for him," Aubrey mused.

"That's exactly what I was thinking. I don't understand. Couldn't someone just offer to get the mother of their child on their restraining order without them having to marry?"

"Yeah," Aubrey said. "I'm not familiar with how that works here. I'm not too familiar with Italian laws."

"I don't know what to do," Shay said. "He promises that the marriage won't interfere with my work and that it's on paper only. Once the year is up, I'm free to go. He'll grant me a painless divorce. No fighting over custody, which we'll share. We're going to have contracts drawn up and everything."

"It just sounds *off*, Shay." Aubrey didn't look convinced. "Please promise me that you'll get a lawyer to look over everything. Especially when dealing with Italian laws as a foreigner."

"I know. I will. I just want my child to have their father in their life."

Aubrey nodded sadly. "I understand that. I get that, but you have to protect yourself too."

"There is nothing to protect myself from. I don't own any assets. It's Dante who should be worried, even though I have no interest in his money. Or his land. Or his title."

Or him? a little voice in her head asked. She shook that thought away. She did have an interest in him. A big interest, which was what had got her into this situation in the first place. Only she would never hang on to past relationships. Once it was over, it was over. With Dante, it wasn't. There was something different about him.

You're carrying his baby, that's why.

She hadn't known she was pregnant for weeks after conception, yet she'd thought of Dante every day since they'd parted. So what was it about him? Why was Dante different from her other few fleeting relationships?

You've never been this attracted to someone before.

And she *was* attracted to Dante. She still desired him. Just being around him made her pulse quicken, her blood heat, and the urge to kiss him again was strong.

"I'm not just talking legal stuff."

"Oh?"

"You're attracted to him and yet you're agreeing to this cold and loveless marriage."

Blood rushed to Shay's cheeks and she groaned. "Yes."

"Tread carefully. I don't want you to get hurt."

"Why don't we order something? I'm starving," Shay said, keen to shake away thoughts of Dante and kissing him. "I haven't had anything to eat since this morning when he made me fresh fruit and yogurt."

Aubrey chuckled. "He made you fresh fruit and yogurt?"

"He's a good cook. I tasted the risotto he made the night before. It was delicious. He says he likes to do it."

"Well, that's at least something, because you are a terrible cook."

They both laughed at that as the waiter came over to take their order. Shay ordered a glass of Italian soda, while Aubrey got to have wine.

They continued talking about their work and how

Aubrey's work was going farther south in the country, and Shay talked about the simulations she was going to run the new trainees through. It was nice to chat like normal again. To not talk about babies or marriage.

"Oh, my," Aubrey said, perking up.

"What?"

Aubrey nodded at the door. "I think your husband-to-be just walked in."

Shay turned and saw Dante standing in the doorway of the restaurant.

"What is he doing here?"

Dante caught her gaze and then headed over to their table. By the firm set of his jaw and his tight gait he was on a mission.

"*Scusami*, I'm so sorry for intruding on your lunch." Dante smiled briefly, but charmingly, at Aubrey.

"What're you doing here, Dante?" Shay asked.

"I need to speak with you alone, Shay." Then he turned to Aubrey. "If you'll excuse us? This is important."

Aubrey was going to say something, because she didn't look too thrilled at having their lunch interrupted, but Dante turned his back on her. Shay sighed—this arrogant side was not what she was used to from Dante—and slid out of the booth. Dante led her away and Aubrey looked none too happy about being left alone. Her lips were thinned and her arms tightly folded across her chest.

Not a good sign. Dante didn't know what kind of trouble he was in.

"What, can't it wait until I go back to the hospital?" she asked.

"This." He held out a paper. "This is a Nulla Osta. If you sign it, we can get married this afternoon."

"Dante! This afternoon? We have to finish our shift

and I haven't even agreed to marry you yet!" She rubbed her temple. "You're very persistent."

He grinned. "I know."

"Maybe I should get a lawyer."

"Shay, I promise you, you don't need a lawyer. This is just a form that states that there's nothing to stop us from getting married. You sign it and we head to the courthouse to get married now. I will provide you a contract outlining the details of our marriage within five days to a lawyer of your choosing."

"So, I have to stay married to you for a year?"

"*Sì.*"

"This is not a real marriage, though?" And warmth flooded in her cheeks as she asked that question. It was a polite way of saying that there would be no sex between them.

"Correct. You will have your own space at my villa."

"What happens after the year is up? You said I wouldn't have to fight for custody."

"*Sì*, we will have joint custody. I will take our child when you need to work. Our child will have my name and will be taken care of. You, as our child's mother, will be as well. Finally, our child will have dual citizenship."

"I don't know…" Then she thought of the schooling her child could receive with Dante's money and connections. The opportunities she'd never had as a bright child growing up in the lower ninth ward of New Orleans, moving around constantly. No roots. No family ties. No father.

She bit her lip.

Do it for your child.

"Where do I sign?" Shay asked.

Dante pulled out a pen, but before she could sign on

the dotted line his pager went off. He pulled it out. "Incoming trauma. I knew it was too quiet this morning."

"We should go, then," Shay said.

"Sì."

Shay turned and saw that Aubrey was frowning, her eyes narrowed as she glared at Dante.

"I have to go, Aubrey. There's incoming trauma," Shay said.

Aubrey nodded. "Don't worry. Go. I'll settle up and we'll talk later. I have a train to catch." It was as if Aubrey knew that Shay would agree to the marriage of convenience in the end.

Shay smiled and mouthed, "Thank you," as she left the restaurant with Dante. Her mind was still reeling with the fact she'd decided to marry him.

Even though she was terrified at the prospect.

Dante hated fires.

He hated when people were burned. He never did like it when people were injured, but burn victims always hit a little too close to home. His best friend had been caught in a fire and had received burns to seventy percent of his body. He'd lived for a few short days in complete agony.

And this situation was no different.

The young man was in pain and Shay was moving quickly in the chaos of a busy trauma room. He appreciated it. She knew what to do. He didn't have to tell her what to do. She just did it. She set up the IV with antibiotics and painkillers while Dante examined the extent of the burns.

"Was it a house fire?" Dante asked the paramedic who brought the patient in.

"Sì, it was."

Once Dante learned that, he changed his tactic. He knew that when some of the old houses caught fire, they were very enclosed and it wasn't just the burns that could kill.

It was the carbon monoxide poisoning in the blood. The patient's lungs could be scorched.

He could suffocate.

Dante immediately listened to the patient's chest. His breath was hoarse, labored. He tilted the patient's head back and examined his throat, to see black.

"We need to intubate him," Dante said to Shay. "Get me an intubation kit."

She nodded and went over to the cabinets in the bay, pulling out an intubation kit. Dante tilted the patient's head back once more and quickly intubated him. Shay bagged him once the tube was in, pumping air into the man's lungs until they could get him up into the ICU.

There wasn't much he could do for the third-degree burns in the trauma bay.

The man's blood pressure was high and he was now intubated. They had to get him stable, and then they could take him into surgery where they would clean his burns and help prevent infection.

"I want a CBC drawn. I need to see how much carboxyhemoglobin is in his blood."

Shay nodded. "I'll do that."

"When he's stable and we have his labs back, we'll get him into the operating room."

Dante watched as Shay hooked the man up to the ventilator. The man was now in an induced coma, but it was good. This way he wasn't in pain.

Once they had the patient as stable as they could, porters came to take the patient up to the ICU. Dante and Shay removed their gloves and moved to the next bay, making their rounds through the influx of patients that had come through, but there was no one that needed immediate attention, as the burn victim had needed.

"I'd better get to my simulation training," Shay said. "I just got a page that they're ready for me now that Dr. Carlo is done with them."

"Do you need any help with that?" Dante asked.

"No, but maybe you could walk me out of the emergency room to my office? I still haven't got the lay of the land yet."

He chuckled. "Of course."

Dante led the way out of the emergency room.

"How long will the training last?" Dante asked.

"Why?"

"The courthouse closes at five."

"Oh. Right. Do we have to do it today? I signed the form. Can't we wait? I promised I would marry you. I won't run. I can't."

She was nervous and Dante found it endearing.

"*Sì*, we have to do it today because you signed the form and dated it."

"Okay, I'll make sure I'm done in time. How long will it take and who will be our witnesses?"

"It should only take a few minutes and I've asked Enzo, but he might be busy. Do you think your friend Aubrey will step in?"

"No, she's headed back to Rome, where she's working at the moment. And my roommate is packing my belongings, since I'm apparently moving in with you tonight."

"That makes me very happy." Dante grinned that charming lopsided, dimpled smile that made her weak at the knees.

And it was true. Once she was under his roof, then he

would be more at ease about this whole situation. There he could take care of her and take care of their baby.

"Does it make you happy?" she asked.

"It does. This will benefit us both, Shay."

"That's what I can't figure out. How does this benefit you?"

"By having the baby in my life, that's how it benefits me. Being a father is an honor and something I have always wanted. My name, and passing it down, is important to me." He didn't know why he couldn't tell her the real reason, why he didn't tell her about the trust fund, other than the fact that the last time he'd told someone about it, she had used him. Shay knew he was a prince, knew that he owned the villa, but she really didn't understand the scope of what was at stake.

And he just didn't trust her enough yet to tell her.

He couldn't tell her.

"So, when should I come back?" Dante asked as they stood in front of the training room.

"Two hours should suffice. The simulation is ready to go and they have to complete it in a certain time or else they don't pass."

"You're tough," Dante teased.

She grinned. "Working with the United World Wide Health Association isn't an easy ticket. It's hard work. I was put through my paces and I plan to do the same for them."

"I don't doubt it. I'll come back in two hours, then, and we'll make it official. That way you can move freely throughout Venice. The restraining order will protect you and our baby."

Shay nodded and headed into the training room.

Dante turned and walked back to the emergency room, but first he pulled out his phone and tried to call Enzo. There was no answer and it went straight to voice mail.

"Can you meet Shay and I at the city hall at half past four? She signed the papers and we're going to make it official." He disconnected the call.

His stomach twisted at the thought of Shay becoming his wife.

Having a wife was the last thing he'd wanted, but also something he'd secretly always longed for.

He was so close to having it all, but then a sense of dread sank in his stomach and he couldn't help but wonder when it would all end.

When he would lose it all.

He'd learned very young that he couldn't take life for granted. That happiness was fleeting. So when would all of this be snatched away from him?

He hated the fact he was such a pessimist. He was a surgeon. He was supposed to be an optimist.

Only he didn't feel so optimistic at the moment.

He was only feeling dread over what the future held.

CHAPTER SIX

SHAY COULDN'T FOLLOW most of the civil ceremony, but she understood when the judge pronounced them man and wife.

"You may kiss your bride," the officiant said in English.

Shay's pulse raced. She hadn't anticipated that a kiss would be part of this marriage.

Since she'd agreed to the marriage she kept trying to think of it as a business arrangement for the benefit of their child, but now as she held Dante's hand, staring up into his dark brown eyes as his wife, the prospect of kissing him made her insides quiver. Her body responded with the familiar ache, because it knew what his kisses were like.

How they enflamed her.

Dante bent down and pressed his lips against hers briefly, but in that moment a jolt of electricity raced through her, her body recalling every kiss he'd shared with her. It lit a fire in her that had never been extinguished. This marriage of convenience was going to be hard.

Dante stepped away quickly, pulling at his collar again as the officiant led them to where they were to sign the certificate.

The court had standby witnesses, who signed their names after Shay and Dante had finished signing theirs.

She accepted congratulations graciously, but there was a little voice in the back of her head reminding her that this marriage was a sham.

That she shouldn't be here.

This wasn't real.

And it really wasn't.

She'd just entered into a marriage of convenience with the father of her baby.

This is for the baby. Dante won't leave the baby. He wants to be a father. He's not like your father.

As they stepped outside she took a deep breath to calm her erratic pulse.

"Shall we celebrate?" Dante asked as they left the courthouse.

"I'd rather have a nap," Shay teased. "I do need to collect my things if I'm moving in with you. And your lawyer will need to start looking into extending my visa."

"*Sì*, he will, and as for collecting your things—we can do that." Dante walked to the edge of the Grand Canal and flagged down a gondola.

"What're you doing?" Shay asked, bewildered.

"Flagging down a gondola. That's how we'll get to your residence. Or rather your former residence."

"A water taxi will do."

"I like this way better." He winked at her, those dark eyes of his twinkling, sending her pulse skittering.

Damn him.

"How do you know how to get to the United World Wide Health Association house?"

"Because it was my childhood home," Dante said quickly as a gondola pulled up. "Come on."

His childhood home?

He took her hand and helped her down the steps into the gondola.

"You know, we could've walked too. I don't think I've ever used the canal entrance before."

Dante smiled. "I know, but this is a celebration. We're married and the world is watching. We have to pretend that we're a happy couple out in public. You have just snagged one of Italy's most eligible bachelors."

Shay smiled ruefully as he took a seat beside her on the cushioned bench.

The gondolier used his long pole to push away from the canal ledge out into the Grand Canal. She hadn't done this before. Mostly she just walked where she needed to go. The United World Wide Health Association residence wasn't far from the hospital and Shay liked to walk, but as they slowly glided down the main canal she found herself relaxing into the ride. She could see smaller canals leading off the Grand Canal, overshadowed by old buildings and smaller bridges that connected one side to the other.

On the Grand Canal there were larger bridges, with tourists passing over them as the gondola glided underneath. She understood now why so many people loved this. Why it was popular with tourists. It was beautiful. It was calming and she was suddenly very aware that she was alone on a romantic gondola ride with Dante.

And he was so close, she could smell his masculine aftershave, feel his strong arm around her. His hand on her shoulder, his fingers making circles through the fabric of her scrubs, making her body yearn for something more.

You can't have any more. And Aubrey's warning about treading carefully went through her mind.

"So, the United World Wide Health Association residence was your childhood home?" she asked, trying to defuse the tension she was feeling and chasing the thoughts of kissing Dante away to something a little more tedious.

"*Sì*, my father sold it off a few years ago. He and my mother moved elsewhere." There was a hint of bitterness in Dante's voice.

"You sound sad about it."

"Annoyed," Dante said, and he ran his hand through his hair as he always seemed to do when he was distracted. "I didn't have as much of an attachment to that home as my younger brother did. I prefer the villa where I live and the vineyard in Tuscany."

"I would love to see the vineyard."

"You told me once that you never sightsee when you're on assignment. There is so much more to Italy than just Venice."

"Isn't that blasphemy?" she teased. "You're Venetian."

He smiled. "Perhaps, but I am Italian first."

The gondolier pulled up in front of the United World Wide Health Association house, tying up his gondola as Dante asked him to wait. Dante climbed out and helped her out of the gondola.

"Why are you asking the gondolier to wait?" Shay asked. "I didn't think they crossed the lagoon."

"No, they don't, but I thought it would be nice to take the gondola down the Grand Canal back to the hospital before we make our way to the ferry docks."

Shay didn't respond as they walked into the rental house that had once been Dante's childhood home. The moment they stepped over the threshold his demeanor changed. She could tell by the way his body stiffened. He jammed his hands in his pockets and kept looking straight ahead.

Even though he'd said that he wasn't attached to this home, it clearly brought up some painful memories for him. She knew the look, because that was the way she'd felt the day she'd walked back into her mother's house after the floodwaters had receded. After FEMA had told her it was marked condemned and that she was allowed one last look inside before it was demolished.

Yet it still stood. They hadn't demolished it yet.

It was boarded up and covered with graffiti, sitting among the wrecks and ruin of the lower ninth ward homes. People toured the area now, which ticked Shay off no end.

It was macabre.

Don't think about it now.

"I'll just go collect my suitcase. I won't be too long."

He nodded and stood by the door. She went upstairs to her room.

She collected her few belongings and left. She was sad that she wasn't going to be living here. She'd always lived on-site wherever the United World Wide Health Association housed her.

This was a first, living off-site.

It was nerve-racking.

This is for your baby. It's only temporary. Just a year. You were going to take a year maternity leave anyways after this twelve-week assignment.

Still, a pang of homesickness washed over her.

She couldn't remember the last time she'd ever felt homesick and she wasn't sure if she ever did feel homesick.

This isn't your home.

Shay didn't have a home. And she never had, really. She and her mother were always moving and this was no different. Only it was. Dante was offering her permanence for a year and permanence for a lifetime for their child.

With a sigh she walked back downstairs. Dante met her halfway up the steps and took her suitcase from her.

"Is this it?" he asked.

She nodded. "Yes. Everything I own fits into that suitcase and my purse."

He gave her a strange look. "Strange."

"It's not strange. I travel a lot."

"Don't you have a home in New Orleans?"

"I have a place to stay, but it's not much." It was just a bed, a couple pieces of furniture. That was all. It was just a place to stay while she waited for assignments.

"Good thing you're moving in with me, then," Dante said as they went outside and he handed her suitcase to the gondolier.

"Why is that?" she asked.

"Because every child needs a place to call home."

Shay's stomach twisted in a knot and she resisted the urge to say something further. About how not every child was that lucky, but it wasn't about that. He was absolutely right. Every child deserved a home and by agreeing to marry Dante, even if on paper only, she was giving her child something she'd never had.

A home.

Which was why she'd agreed to this marriage of convenience in the first place.

And that was the most important thing.

Dante stood at the nurses' station in the emergency department filling out a newly discharged patient's chart. Soon Dr. Salzar would come and relieve him for the night shift. Dante wanted to make sure that everything was in order for the sign-off.

He glanced up to see Shay leading a group of United World Wide Health Association trainees through the emergency room. He smiled watching her. She'd been so busy since they'd got married, he rarely saw her.

It had been well over two weeks of just moving past each other like ships in the night. No more than a greeting and the odd quick meal. And then the last five mornings when he'd finished his swim she had already left, taking the first ferry across the lagoon. At night when he got home from his shift she was always fast asleep. She wasn't totally at fault. He'd been busy preparing the contract for their marriage, and when the baby was born Dante's inheritance left by his mother in trust would be his at last. At least now with the marriage his father couldn't get his hands on it.

Almost three weeks now without really talking to Shay made him realize that he missed her.

What did you expect it to be like? It's not a real marriage. You're basically roommates.

Still, he wanted to get to know the mother of his child. This marriage might be keeping her here for the sake of their baby, but he found that he liked spending time with her when he saw her. And on the occasions when they worked together with the trainees he enjoyed his time with her and he found himself wanting more.

You can't have more. She's made it clear she doesn't want more.

Besides, the press were noticing the distance between them. He'd seen the headlines. He would have to talk to Shay later about putting on a better show of marriage. At least for the year. The last thing he needed was some kind of ridiculous headline to the effect that he was buying a baby or something.

"Dr. Affini?"

Dante turned around and his intern was standing behind him.

"How can I help you, Dr. Martone?"

"I have a patient in a trauma bay. I think you need to check his EKG."

Dante took the electronic chart from Dr. Martone and frowned when he saw the chart. The patient was a sixty-five-year-old man who'd presented with dizziness, nausea, shortness of breath and severe heartburn. The ST segment of the EKG was elevated.

"What do you think?" Dante asked as he flipped through the tests. Dante had his suspicions, but he was teaching Dr. Martone, who was fresh out of medical school and a quick learner.

"STEMI."

"Which stands for?"

"Segment elevation myocardial infarction," Dr. Martone answered.

"Let's go see the patient."

Dante followed his intern into the larger trauma bay. When he walked into the room, he saw the patient already had oxygen and that an IV was started. Shay walked into the bay on the other end of the open room.

"Do you need a hand, Dr. Affini?" she asked as she came up beside him.

"I do." He handed her the chart and went up to the patient. "*Buongiorno*, I'm Dr. Affini and I'll be taking care of you."

"It's a pleasure to meet you," the patient said, his breathing labored. "I'm Giovanni Scalzo."

"Can you tell me what brought you in here tonight, Mr. Scalzo?" Dante asked as he listened to the patient's chest.

"Indigestion," Giovanni said. 'I don't know what the fuss is all about. I was hoping for a prescription antacid."

Shay handed Giovanni an aspirin. "Mr. Scalzo, can you take this, please?"

Giovanni grinned up at Shay and Dante couldn't blame him.

"Anything for you, *cara*." Giovanni grinned again and took the aspirin.

Dante chuckled. "Do you have a cardiologist, Mr. Scalzo?"

Giovanni looked confused. "No."

Shay and he exchanged looks.

"Mr. Scalzo, I'm going to page our cardiologist on duty, Dr. Fucci, to come and take a look at your labs."

"Is something wrong with my heart?" Giovanni's monitors beeped as his blood pressure rose from panic.

Shay stepped forward and placed a hand on the patient's shoulder, instantly calming the patient down with the simple reassurance of touch.

"Don't worry, Mr. Scalzo, you're in good hands here. Your EKG was a little elevated and I'd like to run it by a specialist if that's okay with you?" Dante's question also calmed down Giovanni.

"*Sì*, that's good." Mr. Scalzo lay back against the bed. Dante watched his breathing become more labored.

"Are you in pain, Mr. Scalzo?" Shay asked.

"*Sì*, the heartburn burns my throat and my arms feel heavy."

"Give him some morphine," Dante said. Then he turned to his intern. "Page Dr. Fucci and prep the cath lab for a percutaneous coronary intervention."

"*Sì*, Dr. Affini," Dr. Martone said, taking back the chart.

Dante left the trauma bay. The next ninety minutes would be crucial for Giovanni. His heart muscle was dying, as was evident from the labs drawn by Dr. Martone.

Shay fell into step beside him.

"That's quite a way to end your shift, with a STEMI."

Dante nodded. "Dr. Martone is an excellent intern and Dr. Fucci will have the block taken care of in no time. When is your shift over?"

"Now. I'm done as well."

Dante cocked an eyebrow. "I don't think we've been off at the same time since we got married three weeks ago."

"You've been working late," Shay said, and then she winced, holding her belly, instantly alarming him.

"Are you okay? Is the baby okay?"

"Yes, I'm just tired." Shay smiled. "I'm fine. I think it's just a Braxton Hicks."

"So early?"

"I'm nineteen weeks pregnant now. Almost halfway there. Braxton Hicks can start in the second trimester."

Dante was going to make her sit down, when a code blue was called from the trauma bay where Mr. Scalzo was. They turned around and walked quickly back to his room.

Mr. Scalzo was unconscious, ashen and in full-blown cardiac arrest. His heart was tachycardia, pumping too fast, and no blood was getting through. There was no blood flow to his brain or other organs. He would be dead soon. Dr. Martone was pumping on the patient's chest hard, trying to get it back into a rhythm, but only the electrical shock would reset the cells of the heart to fall back into rhythm.

"What do we do, Dr. Martone?" Dante shouted over the din as he pulled on gloves.

"Shock the heart back into rhythm and intubate."

Dante nodded and turned to Shay. "Get me an intubation kit."

A defibrillator was primed and wheeled over to the patient. The electrode path was placed on Mr. Scalzo's chest.

"Clear!" Dr. Martone shouted.

They shocked the patient's heart, his muscles twitching as the electricity moved through his body. Now all Dante could do was watch the monitors and wait for the heart, which was now flatlining, to jump back into rhythm.

Come on.

The monitor beeped as a rhythm started.

Shay handed the intubation kit to Dr. Martone while Dante took the man's pulse to confirm that the heart was back in rhythm. Then Dante guided Dr. Martone as he successfully intubated the patient. Once the ventilator was breathing for their patient, Dr. Martone wheeled the patient out of the trauma pod to go up to the cath lab, where Dr. Fucci was waiting. The room cleared and Dante finished his notes, breathing a sigh of relief that the patient wasn't lost.

"Dante…" Shay said, her voice trembling.

"Sì?" He glanced up just in time to see Shay's knees buckle as she crumpled to the floor.

He raced to catch her, his heart hammering. *"Cara,"* he whispered, but she didn't respond. So he scooped her up in his arms and got her to the table.

"Dr. Affini?" a nurse asked as he hit the call button.

"Get Dr. Tucci here now!" he shouted.

Oh, God.

He took her pulse. It was low. And he couldn't help her. He'd lost control over this moment and he hated this loss of control. Hated that he was helpless, that she brought this side out in him in this moment.

He was in danger when he was out of control. And he didn't like this one bit, but all he could do right now was cradle her.

Protect her.

Protect his child.

Later he could bury the emotions. Right now he couldn't keep them back even if he wanted to. He was only glad that Shay couldn't see him like this.

CHAPTER SEVEN

SHAY STARED UP at the ceiling tile in Dr. Tucci's office, her hands folded around her belly as she took deep calming breaths. She was still feeling a bit shaky, but she felt fine; it was the baby she was worried about now. Dante was sitting next to her, which was a relief, because a moment ago he was pacing.

"You know, Dr. Tucci wasn't even on duty. He was at home," Shay said. "This is very good of him to see me like this. We seem to keep paging him at odd hours. First the paternity test and now this."

Dante just grunted and then got up and paced again. "I thought you were going to make an appointment."

"I did," she countered. "It was for next week. I'm only nineteen weeks, Dante. It's not until I'm in my third trimester that I see an ob-gyn every week. You're a doctor, you should know this."

It was a tease, but Dante didn't take the bait. He shot her a look of frustration. He dragged a hand through his hair and glanced at the watch on his wrist. It was at that moment that Dr. Tucci walked in.

"*Scuse*, I'm sorry that I took so long," Dr. Tucci said. He saw Dante. "Dr. Affini, I'm surprised to see you here. I thought you were on duty." Dante sat down muttering under his breath.

"I'm the father. Nurse Labadie is now my wife, so I just went off duty."

Dr. Tucci's brows arched at all the answers Dante was giving him, and then he grinned. "Congratulations. I guess I should call you Principessa now."

"You don't need to," Shay said quickly. "In fact, I'd rather not be referred to as that."

Dr. Tucci chuckled and Dante rolled his eyes.

"So what happened, Shay?" Dr. Tucci asked.

"She fainted," Dante said. "Her blood pressure was low. I took it in the emergency department."

Dr. Tucci nodded. "How far along are you?"

"Nineteen weeks," Shay said. "I think I felt a Braxton Hicks."

"I think it's too early," Dante said firmly.

"No, not too early. She's nineteen weeks. They can be felt as early as sixteen weeks. Especially if the mother is tired or under stress." Dr. Tucci shot Dante a knowing look.

Shay couldn't help but laugh. "So it was Braxton Hicks?"

"Well, let's have a listen to the baby's heart." He pulled down the Doppler monitor and lifted Shay's shirt. "The gel will be cold, I'm sorry."

"It's okay. I'm used to it."

Dr. Tucci squirted the gel onto her abdomen and turned on the Doppler. He pressed into her belly and Shay held her breath, waiting to hear that familiar rapid beat of the baby's heart. Dante was frowning and she could see worry etched into his face.

He hadn't heard the baby's heartbeat yet. He hadn't even so much as touched her belly.

Then the familiar thump of the baby's heart sounded

on the monitor and Dr. Tucci grinned at her. "Sounds strong, Shay."

She smiled and then glanced over at Dante. The frown of worry was gone and now wonder was spread across his face as he listened to the heartbeat from where he was standing.

"Have you had any bleeding?" Dr. Tucci asked, wiping the gel off her belly with a towel.

"No," Shay answered. "I had some mild cramping."

Dr. Tucci frowned. "The baby's heartbeat is fine, there's no bleeding, so I just think you're overdoing it. Let's check, though."

"How?" Dante asked.

"Ultrasound," Dr. Tucci said. "Just to make sure the baby is doing well and there's no internal bleeding from the placenta. I want to make sure it's intact."

Dante leaned forward, staring intensely at the screen, and Shay couldn't help but smile. He usually was so detached, but this was different. This was nice. He was so concerned about their child in this moment.

Dr. Tucci squirted more gel onto her belly and placed the wand on her belly. The screen lit up and her breath caught in her throat at the grainy image of her child.

Their child.

Dante was beaming as he watched their child and tears stung her eyes at his reaction. Usually he was so guarded, but there was no sign of that now. Perhaps he wasn't as cold as she'd first thought. Maybe she had nothing to really fear and he'd be there for their child.

"No bleeding," Dr. Tucci said.

Dante reached out and gripped her hand, grinning at her as he squeezed it and whispering, "Good."

Dr. Tucci took some measurements and then shut off the machine, wiping her belly again. "You're a nurse with the United World Wide Health Association program, *si*?"

"Yes," Dante grunted, his smile instantly fading. "She's running the simulation training as well as assisting me in the emergency room for the next nine weeks."

Dr. Tucci raised his eyebrows. "You're overdoing it, then."

"I eat small meals. I rest—"

Dr. Tucci shook his head, interrupting her. "You need a couple days to rest. I'm ordering it."

"Good," Dante said. "I'll take her home and make sure she rests."

"I'm on bed rest?" Shay asked, confused.

"No," Dr. Tucci said. "I want you to take three days off, and then you will go on light duty. Only half days. And that's an order."

"Grazie," Dante said. "And thank you for coming in on such short notice."

Dr. Tucci nodded. "I will see you next week and then for the scheduled ultrasound at twenty-six weeks. We'll make sure everything is still going well and take some more measurements."

"Okay," Shay said, but she wasn't exactly thrilled with the idea of going down to half days. That wasn't in her nature. Work was the only constant thing in her life, except now that it wasn't. What was she going to do with herself?

Dante shook Dr. Tucci's hand and then turned back to her when they were alone. "I'm glad the baby is well and that you're well. That it wasn't serious."

"Me too," she said. She sat up slowly. "Told you it was Braxton Hicks."

"It scared me when you fainted like that."

"I'm glad you were there to catch me." Then she blushed. "I'm okay."

He nodded and took her hand. "You will be. I'm going to take the next three days off as well and I'm going to make sure that you get rest. Proper rest. I'll cook for you and take care of you both."

Warmth spread through her chest. No one had ever taken care of her before. The idea of Dante being there for her was nice.

You can't rely on him always taking care of you. Remember this is just for a short time.

"You don't have to do that."

"I want to do that." He grinned. "Besides, I have some business to attend to in Tuscany and we can spend a couple days at my vineyard. It's quiet there and I think you'll get more rest there than you will here in Venice."

The idea of spending a couple days in Tuscany sounded heavenly, and if she couldn't work, then she was going to do what she always wanted to do, but never found time for, and that was explore.

"That sounds great." Her stomach grumbled and Dante chuckled.

"Let's get back home and get you something to eat. It's still early. We can hit a local bistro on the Lido if you'd like. I think we've both had a long, trying day."

"Now, that's something I can really get on board with." She took his hand as he helped her to her feet.

They grabbed their coats and she had her purse. She informed the other United World Wide Health Association nurses that she was ordered by Dr. Tucci to have three days of rest. She left her simulation training in the capable hands of Danica, who could take over for her because Shay had made up copious notes and prepared the next several simulations.

She and Dante then walked to the ferry pier and caught a ferry to the Lido.

After a short ride, they disembarked.

"The bistro isn't far from here. It's right across the Gran Viale Santa Maria Elisabetta."

"Good, I'm starving."

Dante grinned and took her hand. Just as he'd done in Oahu when they were walking along the beach at sunset. It felt so good, her hand in his large strong one.

"What're you doing?" she asked, shocked that he was holding her hand. She liked it, but she was surprised by it. He'd slung his arm through hers before, but holding her hand was more intimate. And she had to admit she liked it. It made her feel safe.

"For any press lurking around. You are my wife after all," he said, explaining it, and though it made perfect sense she was a bit disappointed in the answer.

What did you expect?

She didn't know and she didn't know why it bothered her so much.

The little bistro faced the Adriatic side and the warm breeze coming off the water was heavenly. The bistro was filled with tourists from the nearby hotels, but the maître d' found them a table out on the patio underneath lemon trees that were strewn with twinkle lights.

It was perfect and the angel-hair pasta with sun-dried tomatoes was heavenly.

It was delicious.

"You know, you make funny noises when you eat," Dante teased.

"What?"

He grinned, his eyes twinkling as he mimicked the noises she was making, noises that sounded decidedly naughty.

"Making those noises is a compliment."

"*Sì*, I know." He winked at her, grinning.

Her pulse began to race and she thought about the last time he'd looked at her like that and where it had led to.

"Have you been to this bistro a lot?" It was a foolish topic change, but she didn't want to start thinking about the last time they had shared a meal or a drink together so close to a beach.

"*Sì*, I have been here a few times, but never with a woman before if that's what you're getting at."

"No, I'm not." She looked away, knowing that she was blushing.

He winked and took a drink of his red wine, which looked so good, but she couldn't have a drop.

"Oh, I have this for you." Dante reached into his jacket pocket and slid a paper toward her. "It's in English. It's our marriage contract. It outlines our fifty-fifty custody, stipend for living and money for our child. As well as schooling."

Shay nodded as she read it over. The contract benefited her and their child. There was nothing hidden in the contract. It was straightforward.

"Also your visa, *cara*, is taken care of. My attorney arranged for it to be extended indefinitely."

"Indefinitely? I thought our marriage was only for a year."

"We're putting on a show, *cara*."

"Right. Good." She tensed. It all seemed too easy. Why was she uneasy about it?

Because you're having a hard time trusting him.

She didn't know how to trust.

Dante is not your father. He won't abandon our baby.

Shay signed the contract, although her stomach was doing flip-flops.

"Here you go," she said, sliding it back toward him. His fingers brushed hers and sent a jolt of electricity through her.

"Grazie, cara." He took the contract and placed it in his jacket. "Are you okay? Is it Braxton Hicks again?"

"No, I'm just tired." She rubbed her belly and the baby kicked. Hard, for the first time. She smiled, the kick reminding her why she was doing this.

"Is everything okay?" Dante asked again.

"Yes. I think everything is going to be okay."

Dante smiled and then paid the bill. He stood, holding out his hand. "Come, let's go."

Shay took his hand and he led her down to the beach. Her pulse began to race, thundering in her ears. She desired him. She still wanted him, even though she couldn't have him.

Dante affected her so.

They walked along the boardwalk instead of the sandy beach. It was a beautiful night. They didn't say much, but she wasn't worried about the silence between them. It was nice not talking and just enjoying the evening.

"It's a gorgeous night," Dante said.

"It is." She squeezed his hand. "Thanks for being there for me today."

"It's my job. That's our baby you're carrying, *cara*." And the way his dark eyes glowed she forgot for a moment who she was with and how this was only temporary.

She nodded. "Still, I appreciate it. I'm not used to having help."

"I understand." He stopped and tilted her chin so she

was staring deep into his dark eyes. "I will be there. I'm here to help you. You can rely on me, *cara*."

And though she wanted to believe him, she was having a hard time letting her heart do just that.

They sped along the winding road that was lined with tall cypress trees. Shay enjoyed the drive in Dante's luxury car. She hadn't even known that he owned a car, until they'd got to the mainland from the ferry and he'd walked her to a car park where the red two-seater was waiting. And she had to say it was a beautiful sports car.

Dante didn't say much on the drive, but she could tell that he was visibly relaxing. He wasn't as tense as he was when he was in Venice. He was smiling to himself the closer they got to Arezzo. Dante's villa was on the outskirts of the city, lying in a valley below the city, but far enough away to enjoy the peace and quiet of the countryside.

"You know," she said, "this is a very nice sports car."

"Grazie." He grinned at her briefly.

"Not very practical, though," she teased.

"What does practicality have to do with it?" he asked.

"There's no backseat—where are we going to put the baby?"

"We?" he asked.

"You." She cursed under her breath for making that assumption. This wasn't a real marriage. There would be no we at all in the near future. Just you or I.

"I can get another car for when I have the baby." He tensed, his knuckles whitening on the steering wheel.

Shay wanted to change the subject. Obviously a touchy matter for him and it annoyed her that she got so upset about it. She knew what she was getting into, but she was so sensitive lately. One moment she could be fine and then next in tears.

"Why don't you tell me a bit about the vineyard?"

"It's been in my mother's family since the seventeen-hundreds."

"Everything in your family is so ancient."

He grinned. "*Sì*, you should've met my Zia Sophia. She was very ancient."

Shay laughed. "I don't think any woman appreciates being referred to as ancient."

"She deserved the title. Enzo and I would make bets on how old she actually was when we were young, because every year she seemed to get younger. I swear her last birthday she was claiming she was younger than me and I was twenty when she passed."

"So how old *was* she?" Shay asked.

"No one knows. There were no birth certificates, but the doctors suspected that she was over a hundred."

"I take it you didn't like her?"

"I adored her. Even if she hid her age. She was young at heart."

"Was she royalty too?"

He shook his head. "No, she was part of my mother's family. I think she was my grandfather's aunt, as he referred to her as Zia Sophia too. What about you? Any elders in your family."

"No."

"No?" he asked, confused.

"Well, there probably was. I wouldn't know. My parents were quite young when they got married and… let's just say their families were extremely religious and didn't approve of a child conceived out of wedlock. My mother was disowned and my father…" She couldn't finish that sentence.

"*Sì?* Your father…?"

Abandoned me.

"My father didn't talk about his family. All I know is the name is Acadian and most of my, I guess, blood relations are in New Orleans, but they didn't want anything to do with us."

Dante frowned. "That's terrible."

She shrugged. "I'm used to it."

"Still, not to know where you come from…"

"I know where I come from. I'm from New Orleans, Louisiana. That's where I'm from." She sighed. She didn't really want to talk about the fact she knew exactly who her family was; she'd seen them. Her mother's parents and siblings. They were a family of wealth and worth in the Garden District.

And they'd let Shay's mother suffer. They'd let her live in poverty.

And when her mother had died, none of them had come to the funeral. None of them had acknowledged Shay's existence. Frankly, she was better off without them. She'd made do without the traditional family for a long time.

Her baby wouldn't have a traditional family either, but at least he or she would have two parents who cared about them. Two parents who would give him or her all they needed.

Does Dante care?

She wasn't sure. He'd seemed concerned when she'd fainted, fascinated when he'd seen the baby on-screen and relieved when the baby had been deemed well, but she didn't know if it was because of a sense of duty or because he genuinely cared about the baby. He said he wanted to be a father. She still didn't know what was in it for him. He didn't touch her belly, didn't plan for the baby or talk about her pregnancy, other than insisting she marry him.

Yet he was always concerned about her getting her rest, feeding her, making sure she took care of herself. He was taking care of her now in a way no one had before.

That meant he cared, right?

"Ah, we're almost there," Dante announced as they turned off the main road, down a small dirt road that went through a small village. "It won't be long now."

"Oh, good," Shay said. And she enjoyed the sights of the small village as Dante slowly drove through, the dirt road giving way to a cobbled stone street. They went over a narrow stone bridge suspended over a gorge, a river tripping over rocks as it wound its way down the hill the village was on.

As they rounded a small square featuring a tall bell tower on the church, the dirt road dipped again into a valley. And when they turned the corner Shay gasped at the sight of acres of vineyards, stretching as far as the eye could see.

"*Bellissimo*, isn't it?" Dante asked, the pride evident in his voice.

"*Sì*," Shay said happily.

He turned up a long dusty drive. The name over the gate they drove under read Bellezza Addolorata.

"What does that name mean?" Shay asked.

"It's the name of the wine this vineyard produces. Sorrowful Beauty."

She cocked her eyebrows. "Ooh. Sounds wonderful."

"*Sì*, when you have the baby, we'll celebrate with a wine I've been saving for a special occasion. One my grandfather laid down."

"I look forward to that."

Dante parked in front of the house. When he opened the door to climb out, an older couple came out, smiling. Shay almost wondered if they were his grandparents, but by the looks of them they were too young. She got out of the car as Dante was embracing the couple.

He then turned, grinning, and gestured to her. "*Mia moglie*—Shay."

The woman shouted with happiness and then rushed her. Taking her in her arms and kissing her, while who Shay could only assume was her husband grinned, his hands thrust deep into his pockets.

Shay was bowled over by the woman clinging to her, saying things Shay could not understand but could only interpret as happiness.

"Who is this?" she asked, smiling back at the woman, who had finally let her go.

"This is Zia Serena and Zio Guillermo. Not relatives, but they have worked with my grandfather their entire lives. They're caretakers of the vineyard. Zia Serena took care of my grandmother after my grandfather died. They treat me a bit like a son, since they don't have children of their own."

Zia Serena nodded and then motioned to Guillermo as they marched back into the house.

"Well, the villa is big enough for them to live here."

"They don't live here. They own a house on the other side of the property. I called them and let them know we were coming. Zia Serena made sure the house was stocked. She's made lunch." Dante grinned. "We'll get you fed, and then you can rest in our room while I go inspect the vineyards with Zio."

Shay's stomach did a flip-flop. "Our room?"

He turned around. "Of course. We're married and Zia won't understand that ours is just a marriage of convenience. She's only prepped one room. There's a couch in the room. I can sleep there."

Her pulse pounded in her ears at the thought of sharing a room with him.

Even if he was sleeping on the couch.

She was apprehensive, but honestly she had no one else to blame but herself. She'd decided to sleep with him that night five months ago and she'd agreed to the marriage of convenience.

Dante had forgotten how much he loved sitting around his late grandmother's rough-hewn wooden table in her kitchen. Even though his grandmother had died a few years ago, he could still feel her presence in the brick walls and could still see her rattling the copper pots that swung on the ceiling in the gentle breeze wafting in through the open back door to the garden.

Zia Serena had prepared a light lunch, with a *Caprese* salad and fresh-baked bread. There was *espresso* and *biscotti*. Zia Serena didn't speak a lot of English, but she knew enough to tell Shay to eat and a few stories about Dante when he was young.

Much to Dante's chagrin and Shay's delight.

Once they were done with their food, Zia Serena insisted on cleaning up. Dante made sure that Shay was settled into bed with strict instructions to nap, before he followed Zio Guillermo out the back door and down into the vineyards.

"You've been gone too long," Guillermo remarked.

"I'm a surgeon. I've been busy."

Guillermo just *harrumphed* and then stopped to examine a leaf. "It's good you got married. Your grandfather would be proud."

Dante's stomach knotted when Guillermo mentioned his grandfather.

Would his grandfather be proud of the fact he'd got married only to legitimize the child and keep the land? Essentially his marriage was a sham.

He didn't think his grandfather would be so proud about that. However, the fact Dante was thinking of his child, willing to do whatever to properly raise his child, would make his grandfather proud.

His grandparents had loved each other. When he'd spent summers here, he could see the love between the two of them. Something his parents had never had. Although Dante was sure that his mother had loved his father at some point.

"You know, there were some men here last month with your father," Guillermo said with disdain. Dante knew Serena and Guillermo didn't think much of the man who'd broken his mother's heart. The royal title and status did not impress Serena or Guillermo one bit.

"Oh, yes?" Dante inquired. "What were they here for?"

But deep down he knew.

They were eyeing up the land to sell when Dante's thirty-fifth birthday came at the end of spring and the trust slipped into his father's hands. Thankfully, the marriage put a stop to that, and once the baby was born, then it would all transfer to Dante. And Dante knew that his father was not at all pleased about the prospect.

"Your father was going to sell this vineyard, *si*?"

Dante nodded. "They came to the Lido villa too, Zio. I sent them away."

And he had. He'd chased them off.

His father had no right to send out Realtors to his

property, even if time was running out for Dante to wed and have a child.

Guillermo chuckled and then clapped Dante on the shoulder. "I would've liked to have seen you chase them away. I would've liked to have seen your father's expression."

"He wasn't with them."

His father knew better than to come near Dante.

Dante had made it clear in no uncertain terms that he wanted nothing to do with him.

His father had done enough damage over the years, lying to them, breaking promises.

Guillermo spat on the ground. "He's a coward."

"*Sì*. I couldn't agree with you more." He dragged his hand through his hair. "Show me the rest of the vines you were worried about so we can figure out what's going on."

Guillermo nodded and kept walking on.

Dante trailed behind him, taking it all in, trying to remember everything his grandfather had taught him about the delicate art of winemaking. He glanced back up at the house and saw Shay standing on the terrace in a white summer dress. His heart skipped a beat. She wasn't looking at him; her eyes were closed and her face was tilted up toward the late-afternoon sun. There was a smile on her face and the wind blew back her short blonde locks.

He could see the swell in her belly, the perfect roundness, and his heart swelled with pride. When he'd seen his baby for the first time on the ultrasound, he'd realized that this was more complicated than a simple marriage of convenience.

He liked things simple. Cut and dried, but this was more. Shay was carrying his child.

His child.

She was more than a wife on paper. Inside her was a piece of him.

It wasn't just him alone anymore.

That was his baby inside. The fact that Shay was carrying his flesh and blood made him desire her all the more.

His. Yet he was afraid to think possessively over the baby. To reach out and feel the kicks.

Olivia had made him so wary. He'd been so hurt when he'd found out the baby he'd been hoping for back then wasn't his. She'd shattered all his hopes of a family. Shay promised him an inkling of something more, but he was so afraid to reach out and take it.

She turned back toward the open doors and headed back into the bedroom.

Dante sighed and turned back to the vines.

It was better he kept his distance from Shay. She'd made it clear that she was only doing this for the child's sake. She didn't want him. It was apparent when she was horrified about the idea of staying in the same room as him tonight.

Perhaps I should sleep in the barn?

Only he didn't really ever enjoying sleeping on a bed of hay. Not that there were any animals left in the dilapidated old barn besides field mice and the occasional owl. And he couldn't sleep in the living room. Zia Serena had promised that she would be back up at the house early to cook them breakfast. She'd insisted on cooking all their meals while they were here so Dante could focus on the vines and Shay could rest.

It was dark when Dante returned from the fields with Guillermo. He washed outside with Zio and they both wandered inside, where Dante could smell something he hadn't had the pleasure of tasting in a long time.

"Braciole!" he exclaimed.

Serena grinned and nodded. "Guillermo and I will be out of your hair soon, Dante."

"You can stay for dinner, Zia."

"No, you and your bride must have alone time."

"What's going on?" Shay asked.

"I was trying to convince Zia and Zio to stay, but they refuse."

"Oh, but they must! She cooked this food for us." Shay turned to Serena. "Please stay."

Serena patted her hand but shook her head. "We'll take our dinner back to our home. Sit, Dante."

Dante took a seat next to Shay while Serena dished up the tender steak stuffed with cheese, bread crumbs and raisins that had been marinated in tomato sauce. *Braciole* was served for special occasions in his house and it was accompanied by pasta and bread so you could soak up the sauce.

"I'll be back tomorrow morning." Serena kissed the top of Dante's head and took a small covered pan with their dinner out of the house. Guillermo waved as he followed the food and his wife.

Now it was just the two of them. And an uneasy tension fell between them. Last night at the bistro and then when they had been walking along the boardwalk, all he could think about was taking her in his arms and kissing her. He could remember the taste of her sweet lips, how she'd trembled in his arms when he'd made love to her.

He had been so close to her and he wanted that closeness again.

Only she'd made it clear she didn't want that. She had been so upset when he'd said he'd extended her visa to longer than one year. As if he were trapping her or something.

"What is *braciole*?" Shay asked. "Don't get me wrong, it looks so good—and smells good too."

"It is delicious. It's steak, pounded thin and stuffed. Then it's cooked in tomato sauce."

Shay cut a piece and took a bite. "Oh, my goodness, that's so good."

"See, I told you." He took a bite and it melted on his tongue. Not as good as his grandmother's, but almost there.

"How were the vines?" Shay asked.

"Healthy. There was a bit of a problem area, but I'll get it fixed. How was your rest?"

"Peaceful." She sighed and then smiled. "I really had a good sleep. I can't remember the last time I slept so well."

"You look beautiful tonight," he said, and it was the truth. He only ever saw her in scrubs. She was still wearing that white dress, but now she was wearing a stylish wrap over her bare shoulders, because it was a bit cool in the evening. It was still spring.

A pink tinge rose in her cheeks. "Thank you."

He wanted to say that she looked as if she belonged here in Tuscany, but he didn't.

"I brought a book to read tomorrow on that terrace." Serena chuckled. "Your Zia Serena was insistent I rest. She wants to bring me my meals when you're in the fields."

Dante chuckled. "Don't try to fight her. She'll win."

"I don't have any intention of doing that." Shay sat back. "That was an amazing supper. And I thought you were a good cook. Serena is just absolutely amazing."

"I'll tell her that," Dante said. "It will make her day."

She smiled. "Well, I think I'm going to head back to bed to rest. I'm not used to eating this heavy this late."

"Farmers have to tend the land until the last drop of light is gone." He stretched. "I'll clean up. Go rest like Dr. Tucci told you to."

"I'll leave a light on." There was a nervous tinge to her voice as she left the table to head upstairs.

"Grazie," he whispered as he watched her head up the back stairs to the bedroom above him. His pulse thundered in his ears. He glanced at the couch in his grandmother's sitting room. It was old, but it was a heck of a lot more inviting than taking a chance with his self-control upstairs.

CHAPTER EIGHT

WHEN SHAY WOKE up in the middle of the night, she expected Dante to be next to her. She'd actually fallen asleep in a curled position so that he'd have lots of room and they wouldn't accidentally touch.

She made her way down the stairs quietly and found that he was sleeping on the very short couch in the sitting room. He looked very uncomfortable and his legs were propped up over the end of the couch.

Her foot creaked on the last stair and he craned his head to look at her. "Shay, what're you doing awake? You're supposed to be resting."

"I woke up and you weren't there," she said. "I thought after the big fuss you made about sharing a room in order to keep up appearances that you'd come up."

Dante sighed. "I thought better of it."

She came down the last step into the living room. She sat down on an armchair across from the couch. "You don't look very comfortable."

"I'm not," Dante groused. "I remember it being a lot more comfortable when I was younger."

She chuckled softly. "You were probably shorter."

"*Sì*, I was." He laughed and then groaned as he tried to stretch his six-foot frame out.

"I shouldn't have made such a big deal. We're grown-ups. Come upstairs. We can share a king-sized bed." Her heart skipped a bit as the words slipped past her lips.

"Are you sure?" he asked.

"Yes." And she hoped her voice didn't quiver. She stood and held out her hand, hoping it didn't shake. "Come on. If you spend another couple hours on this thing, you won't be able to move in the morning."

He took her hand, making her skin prickle at his touch, and she led him upstairs. "Yes, and if I was limping too much, Zia Serena would insist on using her homemade liniment on my back."

"Is it any good?"

"Yes, but it stings so much and smells so bad."

"I can only imagine."

"I'm not sure you can," Dante teased. "It would curl your hair."

Shay laughed, but she was unfortunately familiar with scents that could curl your toes. She'd been in enough situations where breathing through your mouth was a better solution.

"Come on," she said, changing the subject. "You can stretch out, and then you won't get attacked by Zia Serena tomorrow."

They walked into the bedroom and she crawled back into bed, adjusting the pillows so she could lie on her side, which was the only comfortable way to do it.

Dante opened up the terrace doors to let in fresh air. The moon was high in the sky and bright, casting moonlight against the white bedcover. He padded over to the bed and lay down carefully on his back, with his hands folded behind his head.

"Does the breeze bother you?"

"No," she said. "It's nice. And the moon is so bright."

"*Sì.*"

"I guess that gives credence to that old Dean Martin song."

He grinned at her—she could see his dark eyes twinkling in the moonlight. "Don't sing it."

"Why?"

"I've heard you sing."

She gasped. "When?"

"You sing when you're busy and you've tuned the world out. I've heard you singing in your office and when you're chopping fruit. You sing, but I hate to tell you that you have a terrible singing voice."

Shay hit him with a pillow. "That's not nice!"

"I am only telling the truth, *cara*."

"Oh, and you sing *so* much better?"

Dante rolled over and leaned on one elbow. He began to sing in Italian. A rich, deep baritone that made goose bumps break across her skin. As if he was wooing her in song and it was working. At the end of the song he cocked his eyebrows, as if to say *see, I told you so*, so she hit him again with her pillow.

"And what was that for?" he asked, snatching the pillow from her.

"For upstaging me."

He chuckled. "I'm sorry."

"So how long have you run this vineyard?"

"This is my first year," he said.

"I'm confused. I thought your grandfather died a while ago and left you this vineyard."

"*Sì*, but it was in the family trust until I reached a certain age." He cleared his throat and looked uncomfortable. "Now I am of age. It is mine."

"Is that why your childhood home was sold?" Shay asked.

"Sì," he said bitterly. He was on his back again, frowning up at the ceiling.

"Was that part of your inheritance?"

"No, that home should belong to Enzo, but father sold it off before our mother died. He's determined to get it back. All I was left was this vineyard and the villa on the Lido di Venezia. That is all I wanted and that makes me happy."

"Are you going to give up surgery for winemaking, then?"

"No, I love being a surgeon. Even more than winemaking. Zio Guillermo is perfectly capable of running the estate while I'm gone."

"Just like a prince," she teased.

"How so?"

"Vassals and serfs to attend to your every whim."

He snorted. "I'm telling you, it's just a title. Prince means nothing in my country."

"It means something to some people."

"People who live too much in the past," he said hotly. "You know, Zia Serena starts breakfast very early. I think we should try to get some sleep. I know that you need your rest."

And with that quick change in demeanor she knew that the conversation was over. There was no use trying to dig further. She'd get nowhere. He was stubborn.

That much she'd come to learn in the short time she'd been with him.

It could be a good quality some of the time, other times it was downright annoying. Just like this time.

Of course, she was no better.

She was just as stubborn too.

That was what her mother always said, but Shay's stubbornness had helped her survive. It had helped her endure her childhood, where she'd often had to parent herself. It'd helped her survive Katrina, natural disasters when working with the United World Wide Health Association and her mother's death.

She was a survivor, and if that meant being stubborn, then so be it.

She was stubborn.

The scent of pancetta frying roused Dante, but it was the thumps to his hand that caused him alarm. As he pried open one eye he saw that his hand was placed on Shay's belly and the thumping was from the resident occupant taking up space in her womb.

It was his baby.

His baby was kicking him. It wasn't very strong, but he could feel it. Like a poke of a finger under a blanket against his palm.

A smile tugged on the corners of his lips.

He wasn't sure how his hand ended up there or why he was spooning Shay, who was still sound asleep, but in that moment he didn't care either.

And he couldn't figure out why he'd been so afraid of this moment, because it was nothing to be scared of. In fact, it made him feel more connected to it all. Perhaps that was why he was always so reluctant to reach out and touch the child growing under Shay's heart: because he was too afraid.

Afraid to feel that deep connection with a child who might be taken away from him.

He snatched his hand away and rolled over.

Shay stirred. "What time is it?"

"It's seven in the morning. Don't get up," he said, sitting up and putting his feet down on the cold tile floor.

"Too late. I have to get up." She got up and padded off toward the bathroom down the hall.

He chuckled and then got ready while she was out of the room so that he was gone before she came back. If she wanted to continue to sleep, he wasn't going to stop her. She needed her rest.

Dr. Tucci had made that clear.

Dante didn't want anything bad to happen to Shay or the baby.

After freshening up in the downstairs bathroom he headed into the kitchen, where Zia Serena was laying out a large breakfast. She didn't even look at him when he entered the room.

"Guillermo is waiting in the fields for you," Serena said. "Eat and then go out and see him."

"Is something wrong, Zia?" Dante asked as she set the plate in front of him. Usually she was all smiles, especially when she was feeding people, but this morning the smile was gone and replaced with a frown of concern.

"Guillermo wasn't feeling too well this morning but still insisted on going to the fields."

"He should stay home," Dante said.

Serena threw her hands up in the air in exasperation. "That's what I told him, but he won't listen to me. Perhaps if you talk to him."

Dante nodded and took a bite of his egg. "How has his angina been?"

"He takes the medication you prescribed for him, but he doesn't always listen to the local doctor's orders."

"That smells so good," Shay said as she came into the kitchen and took a seat.

Serena lit up when she saw her and she made a plate up for Shay.

"What're you going to do today?" Dante asked Shay.

"I don't know. I thought about going for a walk."

"Do you think that's wise?" he asked, frowning.

"Dr. Tucci said to rest, he didn't say anything about complete bed rest, so why can't I go for a walk?"

Serena nodded in agreement with Shay, though she was probably only picking up the odd word. She set the plate down in front of her and went back to the stove.

"This looks so good," Shay said, eagerly eyeing the scrambled egg, pancetta and mounds of fresh fruit.

"Well, if you want to go for a walk, why don't you come down to the fields with me? I need your second opinion on something."

"I don't know much about winemaking," Shay said. "I'll gladly go for the walk, though."

Dante waited until Zia Serena had left the room and then whispered, "Guillermo has angina."

"Okay," Shay said.

"He's been experiencing some pain and I suspect he's not going to the doctor. He won't let me near him, but maybe if I had a second set of eyes…"

She nodded. "Gotcha. It's something I would often do for the doctors when we were in remote villages. Patients may not trust the doctor but could always trust me and they'd open up to me."

He grinned. "That's what I'm hoping for. Guillermo is a stubborn man."

"Are you sure he's not blood related?" There was a twinkle in her eyes and he couldn't help but laugh a bit as he finished up his breakfast and put the dirty plate in the dishwasher.

Shay finished up and he took the plate from her.

They both donned a pair of wellies because the fields were a bit muddy after a fresh round of fertilization a day before they arrived.

Guillermo wasn't too far from the main house, which was good because from a few feet away Dante could tell that Guillermo wasn't doing so well.

"He's ashen," Shay whispered. "That's not a good sign."

"I know. Serena said he was complaining of heartburn and was feeling off, but he still insisted on doing his job."

And Dante was fearful that Guillermo, standing right in front of them now, was having a heart attack. And the nearest hospital was Arezzo, which was forty kilometers away.

"*Buongiorno*, how are you feeling this morning, Zio?"

Guillermo waved his hand but didn't answer. Also not a good sign.

Shay moved closer and Guillermo beamed at her, taking her hand. She just smiled at him and walked beside him.

"He's sweating profusely and it's not that hot out yet," Shay said over her shoulder.

"*Cosa ha detto?*" Guillermo asked. What did she say?

"Zio, did you take your angina medications this morning?"

"*Sì*, I did. I always take them, but this morning I'm having a lot of indigestion. My jaw hurts too."

Dante shot Shay a look and she nodded ever so slightly, as if in tune with his thoughts. Guillermo was having a heart attack.

"Guillermo, we need to go to Arezzo." Dante took his arm and Shay the other.

"Why?" he asked, his voice panicked.

"I want to get you looked at. I think it's more than indigestion. The hospital in Arezzo can take care of you."

Guillermo didn't try to fight, and when they got back to the main house Shay got Guillermo to sit down. Dante explained quickly to Serena what he thought was happening. And she took it in her stride, knowing that if she became overwrought it wouldn't keep Guillermo calm.

It wasn't long until an ambulance pulled up the long drive.

Dante explained what was going on with Guillermo. They got Guillermo loaded into the back of the ambulance and Serena climbed in with him to ride to Arezzo.

As the ambulance flicked on its sirens and headed away, Dante sighed. "I'm sorry."

"What for?" Shay asked.

"You were supposed to come here for rest."

"You shouldn't apologize for Zio Guillermo having a heart attack. That's not something you can control."

Dante cursed under his breath. "I should be able to control it. I like control."

"And you're a trauma surgeon?" she asked quizzically. "There's no control in that choice of profession."

He rolled his eyes and she just laughed at him.

"Well, now we have the house to ourselves." He ran his hand through his hair, because he was nervous at the prospect. At least when they were alone in Venice or at the villa on the Lido there were neighbors around. At the vineyard, they were truly alone.

And that terrified him.

* * *

Shay walked through the rows of vines, carrying an ice-cold glass of sweet tea for Dante. Dante had retreated to the vineyards after the ambulance left and she hadn't seen hide or hair of him all day. So she'd decided to make a pitcher of sweetened iced tea. Which was no easy feat.

She'd had to scour the kitchen until she'd found a few bags of black tea in the back of a cupboard.

She'd brewed it, strained it and poured it into a pitcher. Adding sugar until it was the right taste that reminded her of summer days when her mother would make sweetened tea for her. Then she'd taken one of the fresh lemons in the big bowl of fruit on the counter and sliced it thinly.

It was the best refreshing drink on a hot day and she could only imagine that Dante was out there sweltering. So she'd poured him a glass and put on her wellies under her long summer dress and headed out into the vineyard. He wasn't far from the house; he was working on the stretch Guillermo had been working on before they'd called the ambulance.

He was crouched down with pruners in his hand, staring at the leaves. His shirt had been abandoned and the late-afternoon sun made his bronzed skin glow like that of an ancient Roman god. The usually tame dark curls were haphazard and beads of sweat ran down his face and his large, muscular biceps.

She hadn't realized how muscular he was, until she saw him out here, working on the vines.

It was as if he were someone totally different, but the same.

Her heart skipped a beat and she couldn't help but admire him.

He was absolutely beautiful.

As if sensing her admiration, he glanced up. "Shay, are you okay?"

She shook her head. "Fine, I thought you might be thirsty."

"Sì." He stood and stretched and she tried not to stare at his half-naked body, because then that would remind her of that stolen night together. The way her hands felt running over his muscles as she clung to him. She handed it to him and he took a drink and then looked confused.

"What is this?" He was frowning.

"Iced tea, or, as we call it, sweet tea. True iced tea is—"

"Just cold tea." He made another face. "I don't like it. I don't like tea."

"What? Why?"

"It was kind of you, but I can't drink this." He handed the glass back to Shay.

"What's wrong with it? Is it too sweet?" She frowned at the cup in her hand, the condensation on the glass making her palm wet.

"I don't like tea."

"Why?"

"It reminds me of being sick."

She arched her brows. "Sick?"

"Sì, my mother would always make it for me when I was sick. I don't like tea."

Shay chuckled. "Is that why there was only a small amount in the cupboard?"

He grimaced. "Medicinal use only."

"Well, I tried. I might not be able to cook much, but I pride myself on my sweet tea."

Dante grinned. "Well, if I didn't associate tea with sickness, I'm sure I would enjoy it."

"Ha-ha."

He picked up a towel and wiped off his hands quickly. "Are you hungry, *cara*? Would you like some dinner? We can go into the village."

"That sounds nice."

"Let me just have a quick shower and we can head into the village."

They walked back in silence to the house. Dante had a quick shower and changed into jeans and a white crisp shirt that was unbuttoned at his neck and rolled up on those strong forearms. His curls were tamed once again, but he didn't shave his five-o'clock shadow off. And the bit of stubble suited him. Shay kicked off the cumbersome wellies and put on her sandals.

It was a short drive to the small sleepy village, which was built into the side of a hill and made of cobblestone. Dante found one of the few parking spaces, and then they walked together to the *piazza*, which was in the heart of the village.

A tall clock tower loomed over them and in the center of the *piazza* was a large fountain. The gentle breeze blew mist from the fountain onto them, but it felt good. It was a surprisingly warm day. Humid. Almost as warm as it was in New Orleans in the summer. Which was brutal for humidity.

Shay closed her eyes and she could almost swear she was home, except for everyone around her speaking Italian.

"This way," Dante said, and his hand touched the small of her back as he led them to a small bistro with an outdoor patio with red checkered tablecloths, which was tucked at the corner of the *piazza*.

"Ah, Principe! It's a pleasure to see you again." The maître d' turned to her and grinned. "Is this the Principessa?"

Shay plastered on a fake smile, but her stomach began to twist and turn as she thought about people knowing that she was married to him. She didn't like being in the limelight.

"Sì," Dante said graciously, but she could tell that he was annoyed by the attention too. Which just endeared him to her more.

Don't get attached. This isn't permanent.

"This way," the maître d' said, and he led them to a corner table out on the patio, so they could enjoy the twilight *al fresco* style. He left them with a menu, but Dante ordered for them.

"What did you just order?"

He grinned and winked at her. "You'll see."

"Hmm, well, I suppose I should trust your judgment. You haven't let me down yet."

"Of course, I could be getting you back for that sweet-iced-tea concoction you tried to force down me earlier today."

"I didn't force it down you." She laughed with him. She liked laughing with him.

It was like the way it used to be. Before she got pregnant. When they didn't have to link their lives together. They'd had fun in Oahu.

Too much fun, remember?

"So tell me about your mother," Dante said softly. "You speak of her and yet you don't."

"She died as a result of Katrina. It's why I joined the United World Wide Health Association. To help those who can't afford health care."

"I'm so sorry, Shay. How did your mother die?" he asked gently.

"The place she stayed at after the floodwaters receded was full of toxic mold, but she couldn't afford to stay anywhere else and she had to stay somewhere while she waited for FEMA to provide housing. She got really sick from the mold, and in the end the toxins overwhelmed her body."

"I'm really sorry." He reached out and placed his large hand over hers. It felt so good.

Be careful.

She cleared her throat. "Now, you tell me about your mother. You don't speak much about her either, but we're staying at her childhood home, yes?"

Dante nodded slowly. "She died a few years back. Cancer."

"I'm so sorry, Dante. That must have been hard to bear."

"Yes. She was a wonderful mother, but…" He trailed off and moved his hand off hers. "My father was difficult. She thought he was her prince and he was far from that."

I hear you.

"My father left my mother," she said. "He said he was going off to Alaska to crab fish and earn the money to bring us all up there. We never heard from him again."

"Did he die in an accident?" Dante asked.

"No, I know he's alive. I know for a fact he is. He just left us."

Dante snorted. "My father didn't leave my mother, not physically at least. That's not what marriage should be about. It shouldn't be a lie."

"I know," she said softly, but he didn't hear her or what she was implying about their own sham marriage.

The waiter brought their food.

"Panzanella," Dante announced. "I figured you wouldn't want to eat anything too heavy in this heat."

"Grazie," Shay said. The salad was filled with pieces of the traditional Tuscan bread, *fettunta*, and mixed with fresh crisp greens, tomatoes, cucumbers and onions. It was melded with olive oil and vinegar. There were also tuna and capers in this version.

It was delicious and, by the kicks she was getting, the baby approved too.

Once they were finished, Shay couldn't have dessert. She was too full. So Dante paid and they walked across the *piazza* in the dwindling light.

"I've enjoyed my time in Tuscany. It's sad that we're leaving tomorrow," she said.

"Sì, it's always hard to leave here, but I'm a surgeon and I love that just as passionately too." They stopped by the fountain to watch the water.

"It'll be good to get back to work," Shay said.

"You'll remember to take it easy," Dante warned.

She was going to respond, when she heard a screech and a crash. They both spun around in time to see two cars collide at high speed, flipping one car over and over.

When the cars finally came to a stop, Shay was running behind Dante as they rushed toward the scene.

CHAPTER NINE

SHAY SET UP a triage, as she'd done countless times in the field.

Thankfully, since the paramedics had arrived, she had more access to modern equipment. And these paramedics knew English as well. Which was heaven-sent, so she didn't have to keep getting Dante to translate for her. Though from being in Italy for almost a month now she was picking it up to the point she could be useful in emergency situations.

They had the patients laid out. Shay tagged them by priority, using the colored sticky notes that she always carried around in her purse.

The fire crew that was also on the scene was busy extracting one of the worst victims with the Jaws of Life. The crash scene was a jumble of twisted metal and fumes from the petrol.

Dante was assessing his patient through the wreckage, instructing the fire crew on how to extract him. He was up on the wreckage, aiding the occupant of the car through the broken windshield. And she couldn't help but admire him.

He was passionate about medicine. His passion and compassion just made her want him more. If she weren't pregnant, she would be doing the same thing. She'd done the same thing in the past.

Dante and she were so similar.

Only she couldn't help Dante and the driver of that vehicle right now. Instead Shay tended to the young couple who were in the other car, while paramedics helped an elderly man who had been in a third car that was involved in the wreck.

The young man who was being extracted had been going too fast and had lost control when he'd reached down to answer his phone. That was when he'd ploughed into the young couple.

Shay knelt beside them. The young man had a few lacerations, but the paramedics had strapped the young woman down, because she couldn't feel her legs.

"I'm so sorry this happened to you," she murmured as she took her pulse rate.

"You're American?" the young woman gasped. "Oh, thank goodness."

The young man looked at her. "We're here on our honeymoon. Beatrice and Tim O'Toole."

"I'm Nurse Labadie. Shay."

Beatrice sighed with relief. "I'm so glad. I wasn't sure how I could tell these paramedics that I'm…I'm pregnant."

Shay's stomach knotted and she placed a protective hand on her belly. "How far along?"

"Just eight weeks," Tim said. "We really need to know if the baby is okay."

Shay didn't want to say anything to them. The baby was so small, it could still be alive, but if there was damage to Beatrice's spine, then the chances were slim. She didn't want to give them false hope. The only way they would know for sure was by ultrasound.

Tim turned back to the paramedic who was dressing his bandage and getting him to climb onto a gurney to be taken to Arezzo.

"Tim?" Beatrice called out frantically because she couldn't turn her head all the way to see what was happening behind her.

"He's just being put into the ambulance. He's okay."

Beatrice let out a shaky sigh. "We were just married a week ago, but we've been together for a long time."

"How long?" Shay asked as she tended to some minor scratches.

"Since we were sixteen. He's my high-school sweetheart. We've been saving a long time for this trip."

Shay smiled warmly at her. "I'm sorry that this has happened."

"As long as we're both alive and the baby is fine, we can survive anything." There was a tremble on her lips as she talked about the baby and Shay couldn't help but wonder if she was thinking the same thing that Shay was: that the baby was lost. Her hand instinctively cradled her belly. As she did that Beatrice's gaze tracked down.

"You're pregnant?" she said, grinning at her.

"I am. I'm just halfway there."

"A boy or a girl?"

"I don't know. I thought it would be nice to have a surprise!"

"Your husband must be thrilled." Beatrice smiled and then winced.

Yes. Husband.

Thrilled she had right, because Dante seemed to really want this child, but Shay still wasn't used to calling him husband because the marriage wasn't real.

Only she didn't say anything as the paramedics came

and got Beatrice, loading her into the ambulance. The moment that she was loaded, Tim leaned over, bandaged up and bleeding, to take her hand. The way Beatrice looked up at him and the way he looked at her made Shay realize that she had never looked at Dante like that and he'd never looked that way at her.

Her mother had looked at her father like that, but he'd never reciprocated.

This was what true love was.

And they might lose their baby.

Shay touched her belly again as the ambulance doors closed and was reminded how life was so unfair. Dante came up behind her. He touched her shoulder. She turned around and saw his shirt was stained with oil and grease, as was his face. He was sweaty and looked tired. Almost beaten down.

"Are you okay?" he asked gently as he brushed her cheek with the backs of his knuckles. It was nice, but she didn't want the comfort. She was okay.

"I'm fine. My patient was pregnant, but only eight weeks along. I hope the baby is okay."

"Me too," Dante said gently.

She turned to see a blanket draped over the wrecked car and a sheet over a body on a gurney and her heart sank. Then she understood the weariness in his eyes.

He'd lost the battle.

"Oh, I'm sorry. You were working so hard." And then she felt bad for rejecting his comfort.

Dante sighed. "There was nothing more I could do. His body was too broken. Once he was extracted, the pressure on his internal bleeding released and he bled to death in seconds. I'm not even sure surgery would've saved him had I been able to open him up right here and now. So much damage."

"Mi scusi, Dottore..."

Shay turned and saw policemen there and she knew that they wanted a statement from him.

"I'll be back as soon as I can, then we'll get you back to the villa so you can have a peaceful sleep before we drive back to Venice tomorrow."

She nodded and he went to speak to the police about the accident. Shay wandered back over to the fountain. There were still a few curious onlookers to the accident and a few people were praying.

She sat down on the ledge of the fountain, watching Dante speak to the police officer and trying to keep her eyes off the young man whose life had been cut short due to a careless mistake, but, mistake or not, a life had been cut short. Possibly two. And if Beatrice was paralyzed, her life would be changed forever.

A twinge of pain raced across her belly. She sucked in a deep breath as it passed, assuming it must be Braxton Hicks as she had overdone it this evening. She'd spent the last couple of days relaxing and on her last night at Dante's vineyard she'd thrown herself into the fray of her work.

So she was making herself stressed again. She deep-breathed through the pain.

And soon it was gone.

She was mad at herself for not listening to Dr. Tucci and running a small triage in the middle of a *piazza*.

Because that is your true love. Work.

And what else was she supposed to do?

She couldn't leave that young couple there. Broken and in a foreign country. Pregnancy or not, she'd signed up to be a nurse. To help others.

She would continue to take it easy because that was

how she could help her baby, but she had to help others too.

Her work was her love. Her reason for living.

And it was the only thing that remained true in her life.

They'd been back in Venice for a few weeks and Dante had been trying to catch up on all the work that had piled up. He knew that Shay had been as well, though most of the paperwork she did from the villa. Ever since they'd left the vineyard she'd been unusually quiet. He knew the easy workload was getting to her and now she was over halfway through her pregnancy.

He thought maybe it had to do with the accident and he thought it would cheer her up to learn that Beatrice's baby had survived and that she wouldn't be paralyzed. There was temporary paralysis, but it would abate and Beatrice would be able to walk again.

All she had said was "That's good."

Then he thought perhaps she was worried about Guillermo. She'd taken such a shine to him. When he gave her a status update on Zia and Zio, how Zio had had a mild heart attack but would recover quickly, she gave the same answer and returned to her paperwork.

He shook his head and flicked through the stack of mail his maid had left on the kitchen counter of the villa. Mail he had been ignoring because he'd been so busy.

A heavy cream envelope stood out from the rest and he opened it, groaning as soon as he saw the word *masquerade*. It was an invitation to the hospital's annual charity masquerade ball, which would raise money for funding. It was always a huge success. Everyone dressed up in their finest and hid behind Venetian masks.

It was a fancy dress gala along the lines of Venice's

most infamous carnival, which was usually held in the winter months. He hated going to these affairs. Anybody who was anybody attended this event. Even heads of state, and as he was technically a head of state he had to attend. Plus he was Head of Trauma and collaborating with the United World Wide Health Association.

It was pretty much mandatory that he be there.

"What's that?" Shay asked as she came into the kitchen carrying an empty bowl.

"An invitation to a gala fund-raiser for the hospital."

"Ooh," Shay said, sounding intrigued and showing more interest than she had in the last weeks, which made him happy. "It sounds fun."

"It's not, but it's for a good cause." He stared at the envelope.

"Well, aren't you going to open it?"

"Should I?" he teased.

"Yes."

He broke open the seal and read it over. "Hmm…"

"Well, when is it?" she asked.

"It's tonight."

"Too late to RSVP?" She sounded disappointed.

"Do you want to go?"

"Not really, but you should."

"I don't want to go." He leaned across the counter. "Why, do you want me out of the house?"

"I don't…" She sighed. "I feel like I'm holding you back. You've been hovering over me like a ticking time bomb since Tuscany. I'm fine and I want you to have fun."

"Trust me, this gala isn't fun."

"Well, if you have to RSVP, then you don't have to go. You could just ignore it."

"No, it's more of a reminder. I go every year." Dante

cursed under his breath. "I was hoping to catch up on some paperwork for the simulation program this evening."

"I can do that, you go." She turned her back to him, washing her dish in the sink.

"You're going to do my paperwork?"

"Sure," she said brightly. "Then you can get out instead of watching a pregnant woman sleep."

"You think you're getting off that easy?" he said as he grinned from ear to ear. "You're coming with me."

The bowl clattered in the sink and she spun around. "I'm what?"

"You're my wife." He grinned, enjoying the look of distress on her face. "And you're coming with me."

"Uh, no, I'm not."

"Of course you are. You are a princess. It's your duty." He grinned.

"Duty?" she asked, her voice rising an octave.

"*Sì*, you're coming with me." He pinned the invitation to the corkboard in the kitchen. "You seemed so excited before."

"That's when I thought you were going. I can't go." She ripped the invitation down from the corkboard and handed it back to him.

"Why not?"

"Dante, I don't have anything to wear, for starters." Then she pointed to her belly. "I don't think they make ball gowns for pregnant women."

"Of course they do. There have been pregnant women who have gone to balls before. You're coming." He slapped down the invite and walked out of the kitchen, grinning to himself because he knew full well that she was following him out of the room.

"Dante, I don't go to fancy galas." Her voice was panicked. "I've never been to one."

"Now's your chance." He was really enjoying this.

"You're teasing me."

"Well, I am a bit, but I would like you to accompany me."

"I don't want to go. I should be resting." She jutted out her chin, her pink lips pursed together in defiance.

He laughed out loud. "That's the first time you've used that as an excuse here."

"Well, a gala is… It sounds terrible. I'm not one for crowds. Can't you go by yourself?"

"You are my wife."

She crossed her arms. "I don't even know where to get a dress from. I would call Aubrey, but she's working today. How am I going to find a dress?"

"The Lido has many shops around here. You can go and find a ball gown in one of them. I'm certain."

Her mouth opened and closed a few times, as if she was going to say something, but instead she left the room, calling over her shoulder, "I'll wear what I have, but I'm not going shopping."

"The gala starts at eight. I'll be home at five to get ready, so hopefully you're ready then."

Dante picked up his keys and his briefcase. He was going to have his assistant pick out a dress for Shay and make sure it was delivered in time. She was his wife and he wanted her to feel good. She was beautiful, sexy, and he wanted the world to know it.

When he walked into the Palazzo Flangini tonight with Shay on his arm, he was confirming to the world, and to his father, that he was married. That he had it all.

That he was going to have an heir and his father's chances for getting a hold of his vineyard and the villa were gone. Dante had no doubt that his father would be there tonight with one of his mistresses and he hoped his father heeded his advice from his mother's funeral about not approaching him.

Dante had no interest in mending broken fences with that man. A father in name only. Dante would be a better father than his ever was. A better husband too, for as long as Shay would have him.

Tonight he wasn't just wearing a Venetian mask, he was wearing a different mask. One of a loving husband and father. He had to show the world that Dante Affini was happily married. And maybe then people would leave him alone.

His marriage had put an end to all that talk about the trust fund and his father's cheating. It was bad enough his mother had suffered through all those stories in the paper about his father stepping out with different women.

All Dante wanted, all he'd ever wanted, was a quiet life.

Was that too much to ask for?

The box containing the most beautiful black lace ball gown arrived at lunchtime with a note from Dante that asked her to take the ferry into Venice and then catch a *vaporetto* to the Palazzo Flangini on the Grand Canal. He also sent a Venetian mask on a handle; white, painted with black and silver filigrees.

It reminded her of Mardi Gras in New Orleans.

The only difference was that usually involved beads and bright colors such as purple and green.

This was more elegant, more sophisticated, and she was terrified. She doubted anyone would be flashing their boobs for beads tonight. She'd never done that, just as she'd never been to a gala before. She hadn't even gone to her own high-school prom. She was so worried about making a bad impression and embarrassing Dante. So she really wished that she weren't going. She was clumsy and awkward, even more so being pregnant.

However, the dress was stunning. As were the matching shoes, which were thankfully small kitten heels, and jewelry. He'd thought of everything. Except that he wouldn't be escorting her. She had to make her own way to the gala.

Dante had apologized in the note, explaining that he had to work late on a trauma case that had come in, but he promised to meet her there.

"How will I even know who he is if everyone is wearing masks?" she mumbled, looking up from the note while sitting cross-legged on his bed, and Dante's cleaning lady overheard her.

"He'll be wearing a matching mask. That's how it's done. His will be more masculine, though." Maria, the cleaning lady, patted her shoulder.

"Thanks, Maria."

Maria nodded and continued her cleaning of the en suite bathroom.

Shay stared at the gown again.

She really didn't want to go, but she didn't want to let Dante down either. And it could be good to mix and mingle with those who might donate to the United World Wide Health Association. Dante wanted this marriage of convenience. He was giving up a lot to be part of his child's life. So the least she could do was play the part.

Ever since they'd got back from Tuscany she had been a little standoffish with him because she'd thought it was for the best, but she'd been so lonely. Especially since she was on modified duties and everyone else she knew was busy with their own jobs.

She hated this feeling of helplessness she'd been experiencing lately.

She missed her work. She hated being on light duty.

She missed being in the emergency room, triaging, teaching. She missed being a nurse.

Pretending to be a wife tonight was something not very high on her list of priorities, but maybe tonight she could make connections. Tell more people about the good work that the United World Wide Health Association did.

At least that way she was doing something. She glanced at the clock. She had three hours to get ready and head over to the Palazzo Flangini.

Once Maria was done with the bathroom, Shay took over and had a shower. Her hair was a short stacked bob, so she added some curls with her curling iron, pulled on the beautiful lace dress and did her makeup. By the time she was ready, it was time to catch the ferry from the pier to Venice.

Maria walked out with her, locking up, so Shay wouldn't have to worry about wrecking her dress trying to latch an ancient iron gate.

As she walked down the main road on the Lido to the pier there were a few curious onlookers. Especially since she was carrying a Venetian mask, but she tuned them out as she boarded the ferry, just before it left. Once she disembarked at the Venice pier, she found the water taxi that could take her down the Grand Canal to the famous Palazzo Flangini, where they held the Venice Carnivale every February.

It was getting dark and the canal was lit up. There

were many water taxis vying for the water entrance to the palace. Once she was at the entrance, she was helped up out of the water taxi and showed the doorman Dante's invitation. She followed the crowds inside, holding the mask up to her face as they walked into the main room, where the gala was being held. Except it wasn't one big room, but different rooms. The walls were covered with Renaissance artwork, the ceilings were gilt and there were lots of marble columns.

People in the party filtered around from room to room, chatting, and Shay didn't know how she was going to find Dante in this mess of people.

She kept to the outside of the flow of people wandering around the *palazzo*. Until a tall man in a designer tuxedo, holding a more masculine mask with the same markings, approached her. He moved through the crowd easily. They parted for him as the Red Sea parted for Moses. His presence seemed to command it so.

"Ciao, cara."

Her heart skipped a beat. She recognized his voice and he moved the mask off his face to bring her hand to his lips, kissing her knuckles, which made her stomach flutter.

This is just a show. It's all just a show.

Only it was fooling her, this show she kept reiterating she was acting through. Her heart fluttered and the baby kicked in response to her accelerated pulse rate.

She moved aside the mask. "You look very handsome."

He grinned. "You are absolutely stunning."

Warmth flooded her cheeks and she covered her face again. The mask was coming in handy for that.

"You're too kind."

"I'm not being kind. It's the truth." He leaned over and whispered in her ear. "You're glowing, *cara*, and I find it absolutely sexy."

A shiver of anticipation ran down her spine as he took her arm and led her away from the safety of the wall out into the mix.

"Thank you for the dress," she said. "It's wonderful. I don't feel like a beached whale in this."

"Since when have you looked like a beached whale?" he asked.

"Since this bump is getting bigger," she teased.

He chuckled. "You're beautiful. Radiant."

She blushed again. They moved through the social circles. Shay shook hands with a lot of people whom she couldn't speak to, but she knew that Dante was talking up their simulation program and that was all that mattered. They finally moved to a room that was full of art being auctioned off as part of the fund-raiser. The room was also thankfully mostly devoid of the crush of people, which was good because she was getting hot.

And she was exhausted by socializing with a language barrier.

"My father is supposed to be here," Dante groused. "I haven't seen him."

"And that's…?"

"Good." Dante squeezed her hand. "He likes these events. I don't. I didn't want to see him tonight, but then with you here and our baby…well, I was hoping to run into him."

"I take it my presence won't make him happy?"

"No."

"Why?" she asked, confused.

"Because he never wants me to be happy."

Her heart skipped a beat. "And you're...happy?"

"*Sì*, right now, I am."

She gasped and her pulse raced. She wanted to tell him she was happy around him too, but couldn't.

"I'm tired, Dante."

"We'll go soon, *cara*. I know you're tired."

"Thank you." She held the mask at her side and didn't look at the contemporary art that was on sale, but the Renaissance craftsmanship that was carved into the post and lintels of the *palazzo*. She ran her hand over it and she got a secret thrill of delight touching something that was so old.

"It's beautiful, isn't it?" Dante asked.

"Yes, it is. You know, Venice in some ways reminds me a bit of New Orleans."

Dante arched a brow. "How so?"

"It's close to the water. We also have canals, though not as many as you."

"Go on," he urged, smiling at her, those dark eyes twinkling. Her knees went a bit weak because the suit he was wearing fit him like a glove. It was all she could do to tear her eyes from him.

"We have Mardi Gras and you have Carnivale," she said.

"I think that's the Catholic influence," he teased.

"Perhaps, but I doubt Venice has voodoo roots."

"I don't think so."

She grinned. "So one difference."

"What else is the same?"

"I've seen plantations, on the inside, with similar architecture."

"Wasn't that the Neoclassical movement?"

"Could be," Shay said. "I wouldn't know. I didn't take history, remember?"

He shook his head. "I shall have to school you on history."

"No, thanks." And they laughed together. Her pulse was racing, they were so close, and she was fighting the urge to reach up and kiss him. "Should we make that last round?"

He sighed.

Was that disappointment?

"*Sì*, let's…" He trailed off as he stared over her shoulder. Shay turned to see what had caught his attention. It was a tall, beautiful Italian woman all dressed in red.

She was absolutely stunning.

"Do you know her?" Shay asked.

"*Sì,*" he said, through gritted teeth. If he'd been a dog, Shay would have sworn his hackles would be raised as he glared at the woman.

The woman, as if sensing she was being glared at, turned and looked at them standing at the other end of the corridor.

"Dante?" the woman asked as she glided over to them. "I thought that was you, *mi amore*."

Mi amore? My love?

Dread knotted her stomach and for the first time in her life a flare of jealousy rose in her as the stunning woman called Dante her love and touched his arm as a lover would. She was relieved to see that Dante was none too thrilled to be in the woman's company and did not return the endearment.

"Olivia," Dante acknowledged gruffly. "I thought hospital functions were beneath you?"

"Usually, but a carnival-inspired one sounded too chic to pass up. Besides, Max wanted to come. His hotel chain is donating a vast quantity of money to the United World Wide Health Association." Olivia's cold olive-colored eyes landed on Shay. Her gaze raked her up and down, judging her and looking at her as if she were a piece of dirt. "I see you're not alone either, *mi amore*. Who is this?"

"Shay," she said awkwardly. "I'm a nurse with the organization that you donated money to."

Olivia snickered. "*I* didn't donate. My Max did."

"Well, then, remind me to thank Max," Shay snapped, instantly detesting this woman.

"Bringing a nurse to a society function, *mi amore*. How classless."

"Why? She has every right to be here, and Shay also happens to be my wife—Principessa Affini." Dante smiled down at her, with pride on his face, the way Tim had beamed down at Beatrice when they were in the back of the ambulance. Shay's heart swelled and she held on to Dante's arm.

"Your...your wife?" Olivia asked, stunned.

Dante grinned at her, but it was cold. Calculating. It made Shay shudder, and then he reached down and touched her belly, the first time he'd ever done that.

"We're having a baby." Dante took her hand and kissed it. "We're so happy. Aren't we, *cara*?"

"Yes," Shay said breathlessly. Her heart skipped a beat. Maybe he did want more. Maybe this wasn't like her parents' marriage. Maybe it was real and she was just too blind to see it. Why *couldn't* they be happy?

Olivia smiled, but it was forced. "Well, I see you got what you always wanted. A little nobody who will bear your fruit and drudge beside you in that sham of a hospital."

"Don't you dare speak about my wife like that. You

have no right!" Dante growled, and a few people nearby stopped their chatter and looked. The last thing Dante would want was the press to hear about this and report on it. Shay knew how much he detested any publicity.

"Dante, it's okay." Shay tugged on his arm. "She's not worth it."

"You're right, *cara*. She's not. Good evening, Olivia." He grabbed Shay's hand and led her in the opposite direction, out of the corridor. She could barely keep up with his pace as he weaved through the crowds. Once they were at the exit, Dante waved down a water taxi. His face was like thunder as he helped her down into the boat and gave the captain strict instructions to the Lido as he climbed on board and sat next to her.

"Is everything okay?" Shay asked.

"Fine." Dante scrubbed his hand over his face. "I'm sorry Olivia said those things to you. She's mean and spiteful."

"It's okay, but I have to agree with you there."

"No, it's not okay. You're my wife. It's most definitely not okay."

"Who was she?"

"A former acquaintance." He turned to her. "She means nothing to me. You mean so much more to me, *cara*."

Tears stung her eyes and he slipped his arm around her and held her close.

Shay wanted to believe him, because he meant so much to her too.

CHAPTER TEN

THE LAST THING Dante wanted Shay to know about was his past with Olivia, but when he saw Olivia at the gala he'd become so angry. The way Olivia had looked down on Shay had angered him. No, it'd infuriated him.

His fight-or-flight instinct had kicked in and he'd wanted to fight.

And now he was angry at himself for engaging with Olivia. For not walking away and for her showing up and spoiling a magical night.

And it *was* a magical night. Shay looked so stunning in that dress. The moment he'd seen her standing off to the side, pregnant with his child, his first thought had been *She's mine*.

When he'd seen her there, he'd no longer wanted to be at that gala. He'd wanted to take her home and take that dress off her. He'd wanted to hold her in his arms and kiss her. She'd never looked so beautiful before.

He'd wanted her so badly, but he'd known they had a duty to do and he wasn't sure if she wanted him the same way that he wanted her. So he'd tamped down his ardor, but it had been so hard, and then Olivia had shown up, angering him. Directing pointed barbs at Shay, who was a thousand times a better woman than Olivia ever was, and he couldn't help but wonder what he'd seen in

Olivia in the first place. They were polar opposites in personality. Shay was caring, kind and Olivia was self-centered and selfish.

The ride home in the water taxi was silent.

Shay didn't press him with any more questions.

Which was a relief. If she pressed him, he'd lose control and it wouldn't take much. His grasp on the reins of his emotions were wearing thin.

He didn't want to get into it. He didn't want Shay to know about his secret shame. The way he'd been duped by Olivia.

Once they were back at the villa, though, she made him a cup of espresso and sat down at the table with him.

"Tell me about Olivia," she said gently.

He shrugged. "There is not much to tell. She's a former acquaintance. We had a falling-out years ago."

"Obviously there's something. It was like you'd seen a ghost. You two were lovers?"

"We were. Long ago. It's not important." Dante loosened his bow tie and unbuttoned his collar.

"How long ago?"

"Long." He cursed under his breath. She deserved to know the truth, but he didn't want to talk about Olivia. "I don't want to discuss it, *cara*. It's a painful memory best left in the past."

"Okay. I'm sorry."

"You have nothing to be sorry about, *cara*. It's my fault."

"How?"

"For getting involved with a woman like her. She's a user," he said bitterly. "She wanted to be with me because I was a prince. She just wanted to be a princess."

"Ah, so that's why she seemed so ticked when you referred to me as your Princess."

"*Sì*, it was a dig." He sighed. "You see, not many people knew I was a prince until my father started selling off Affini land and real estate. Then it was outed that there were two Affini men who were bachelors, set to inherit a vast fortune. She wanted in, so she took advantage. That's why I get so angry seeing her."

Shay's eyebrows rose when he said vast and he braced himself for the fact that she would ask how much was vast, but she didn't ask him that. It was as if she didn't care about his money, but he found that hard to believe. Most women he met in his circles cared only about money and status.

Whereas Shay seemed to care most about helping those who couldn't help themselves. Even though Shay had admitted she came from the poorest of the poor in New Orleans, money wasn't what attracted her. Doing good and being passionate about saving people's lives was what mattered to Shay.

And he couldn't help but admire that; but he still wasn't sure that he could trust her.

He wasn't sure that he could ever open his heart up again.

And he hated himself for that. For being so hard-hearted.

"I'm sorry she hurt you so bad."

Dante cursed under his breath. "*Sì*, I was hurt, but I'm angry that she showed up tonight. And that she treated you so badly."

"I'm okay. She can't get to me. I've heard worse. Although it killed me that she's so beautiful and tall. Elegant."

Dante brushed his hand across her cheek. "You are more beautiful, *cara*."

She deserved so much better than him.

Shay placed her hand on his shoulder, rubbing it and trying to console him in that sweet, simple way she did.

She was an angel.

He'd forgotten.

He smiled down at her. And then he touched the swell, where their baby was, and her eyes filled with tears. "I'm happy. What I told her was true. I'm happy about the baby."

"You've never… You've never touched the baby before," she whispered as she placed her hand over his. "I liked when you did earlier at the gala and I like it now."

"I have felt the baby, but you were asleep when I did." The baby pushed back. A strong kick against his palm. Last time it was a tiny poke.

"This baby takes after its daddy, that's for sure—he kicks me enough to annoy me," she said, trying to make light, and he chuckled.

"I know," he said, and he tilted her chin to make her look up at him. Those beautiful dark eyes of hers, those soft pink lips—he'd forgotten how truly beautiful she was. He leaned in and kissed her. It was as if he were tasting ambrosia. He wanted more and he knew that if he pursued this further one kiss would never be enough.

"Dante," she whispered against his lips. "What're we doing?"

He didn't respond; instead he scooped her up in his arms and kissed her again. "I believe I'm taking you upstairs, *cara*."

Shay didn't say no, instead she kissed him back, those long slender fingers of hers brushing the hair at the nape of his neck as he carried her up the stairs to his bedroom. He'd never made love to a pregnant woman before and he wanted to be careful with her.

He didn't want to hurt her.

And most of all, he wanted to take his time.

He set her down on the floor and cupped her face to kiss her again. He couldn't get enough of her kisses. He undid the zipper in the back and helped her out of the black lace dress while she kicked off her shoes. The dress pooled at her feet as he kissed her neck, knowing how that spot had made her moan with pleasure before.

She let out a sigh, her arms wrapped around him as he trailed his hands down her bare back, undoing her strapless bra. Her hands undid the buttons to his shirt and slipped inside.

He loved the feel of her hands on his chest. Those soft, delicate hands.

Shay finished undoing the buttons of his dress shirt. Then he shrugged himself out of his jacket and let her peel off his shirt.

"I've missed you," she whispered as he held her close.

"*Sì, cara.* I've missed you too."

She led him to the bed and sat down on the edge as she guided him down with her. They sat on the bed, kissing and touching. Just as they had that night in Hawaii. Only this time it wasn't the sounds of the Pacific Ocean and palm trees swaying outside the bedroom, but the sounds of the Lido at night. Of a cruise ship blaring a horn as it came close to the lagoon.

It was the night sounds of Venice, but he drowned them all out, because all he wanted to hear tonight was Shay, moaning in pleasure and calling out his name.

Shay hadn't expected the kiss, but she didn't stop it because she wanted more than anything to be with him. She wanted that kiss. For just one brief moment she wanted to be happy.

To remember a time when she had thrown caution to the wind and experienced real passion. To that one perfect night.

Even if that one perfect night had led to an unplanned pregnancy and them being in this situation now. She'd always sworn to herself that she didn't want to have a sham marriage and she should push Dante away. Only she couldn't.

Right now, she wanted to feel.

To taste passion one more time.

His mouth opened against hers as she kissed him, his kiss deepening. His hands were hot on her bare back, holding her tight against him. And then he pushed her down on the mattress, lying beside her.

She'd never wanted someone as badly as she did Dante.

Even though they'd been apart for months, that hadn't changed. And she'd known that the moment she'd laid eyes on him that day in the hospital.

She desired Dante above all other men.

She *craved* him and that thought scared her because she knew he didn't feel the same about her. She was treading a dangerous path.

The kiss ended and she could barely catch her breath, her body quivering with desire. He trailed his hands over her body.

"Shay," he whispered. "I've missed you."

He wanted her, just as much as she wanted him. A tingle of anticipation ran through her. She remembered his touch, the way he felt inside her, the way he made her feel when she came around him.

No words were needed, because she knew they both wanted the same thing.

"So beautiful," he murmured, pressing a kiss on her shoulder. His hands skimmed over her again.

When he kissed her again, it was urgent against her lips as he drew her body tight against his. Their bodies pressed together and warmth spread through her veins, then his lips moved from her mouth down her body to her breasts.

She gasped in surprise at the sensation of his tongue on her nipple. Her body arched against his mouth and the pleasure it brought her, her body even more sensitive to his touch thanks to the pregnancy hormones.

"I want you, so much," she said, and she was surprised that she'd said the words out loud, but it was the truth.

Dante kissed her and she was lost, melting into him. "I'll be gentle, *cara*. Please tell me if I hurt you or the baby. I don't want that."

"You won't hurt me. I just want to be with you again, Dante."

He stroked her cheek and kissed her again, his hand trailing down over her abdomen and then lower. Touching her intimately. Her body thrummed with desire. She arched her body against his fingers, craving more. Wanting him.

Their gazes locked as he entered her. He was murmuring words in Italian, just as he'd done before, and that made a tear slip from her eye.

"I'm sorry," he whispered. "Did I hurt you?"

"No, I'm just remembering. Good things." She kissed him. "Don't stop. Please don't stop."

"I won't." He nipped at her neck and began to move gently. Slowly. He was taking his time. She wrapped her arms around him to hold him close as he made love to her. He kissed her again and then trailed his kisses down her neck to her collarbone. It made her body arch and she wanted more of him. She wanted him deeper and she wrapped her legs around his waist, begging him to stay close, but she couldn't get him as close as her body craved, because of her belly.

"*Cara*, let me help you," he whispered as he rolled her onto her side. He helped lift her leg and entered her from behind, her leg draped over his. His hand on her breast as he made love to her.

Her body felt alive. She had never thought a feeling like this would be possible. She had never thought that she would ever get to experience it again with him.

Even though her relationship with Dante was not real and had an expiration date, she couldn't help but care about him. Deeply.

Maybe love?

She shook that thought away. There was no room in her life for love. Just her work, just her baby.

Their baby.

And this moment.

She wanted to savor it. He quickened his pace and she came, crying out as the heady pleasure flooded through her veins. Dante soon followed and then gently eased her leg down. She rolled onto her other side to look at him.

Dante was on his back, his eyes closed. She slid close to him and laid her head against his chest. He slung his arm around her, his fingers making little circles on the bare skin of her back.

"*Cara*, that was…"

"I know," she said.

He kissed the top of her head and held her close. She didn't want to leave this bed. She didn't want to leave his side. And that thought terrified her.

She was just like her mother.

Shay was falling in love with a man who didn't love her back. A man who'd married her because there was a baby on the way.

Only she couldn't let that happen.

She wouldn't spend her life pining for a man who didn't want her.

She had to put a stop to this. To bury her emotions in her work.

Only she was so comfortable in his arms that soon she forgot about all her worries and fell into a deep, blissful slumber.

CHAPTER ELEVEN

SHAY WOKE UP in Dante's arms. As she had every day for the last week. And every day she kept telling herself this couldn't happen again.

She was weak, and he only had to whisper *cara* and she melted into his arms.

Not that it was strange to wake up beside him. She was getting used to it. During their couple of nights in Tuscany she had slept beside him and that hadn't fazed her one bit. And now, for the past seven days she'd enjoyed waking up in his arms. His breath on her neck as he slept.

It was almost natural, as if she were meant to wake up beside him.

And with that came the truth that she could no longer deny: that she was deeply in love with Dante.

Maybe always had been, and she was mad at herself for falling in love with him. She'd promised herself that she wouldn't fall in love with someone unless they reciprocated it. Sure, Dante lusted after her, but did he love her?

She didn't think so. Yet the way he'd been so protective of her last week at that gala, the way he'd told her that he was happy, the way he'd made love to her every night gave her hope. And that was scary.

She couldn't trust hope.

She slid out of bed and quietly got ready for the day. Just as she had when she'd first moved in with Dante and headed to the hospital to run a triage simulation set in the mountains.

Today was a day that she could be at the hospital and it was the perfect place to hide. Which was why she was here setting up a triage situation.

Tarps? *Check.*

Rope? *Check.*

She went over her list on her computer pad as she laid out all the equipment. She had ten different patients in the form of mannequins who were all suffering from various ailments, but as she stared at the checklist on her computer pad she couldn't think about the various trauma that she could be facing during a volcanic eruption.

All she could think about was her own personal volcanic eruption that had happened last night. Thoughts of Dante and his lovemaking were taking over her every waking moment.

This was exactly what she didn't want to happen.

He was starting to invade every part of her. And on cue their baby kicked as if to remind her that was true.

She glanced up at the projector screen where she'd posted the levels of triage as it pertained to assessing people in the field for care. Especially when there were mass casualties involved. And a natural disaster such as a volcanic eruption or a flood, among other things, could bring in a lot of casualties.

She'd seen a volcanic eruption when she'd been working in the southern part of Mexico. A volcano had erupted and the lahar not only killed hundreds of

people, but injured hundreds more. They'd had everything from broken bones, to impalement, infections
from the lahar's mud getting into open wounds and
dry drowning.

In cases where many were hurt, she'd learned a useful tip from the US Army about dividing casualties into
Immediate, Delayed, Minimal and Expectant.

Each of the mannequins fell into those categories,
and if the trainees had been listening, they should be
able to figure out what dummy fit into what category.

"Shay?"

She turned around to see Dante, dressed in his scrubs
and white lab coat, standing in the door of the room
where she was running the triage simulation.

"Yes, how can I help you?"

"You left very early this morning," he said as he shut
the door behind him.

"Well, I was anxious to get this simulation set up."
She didn't look at him; if she looked at him too long,
she'd succumb to his charms again. She'd throw herself
into his arms and beg to stay with him.

And that wasn't what she wanted.

Her career path was with the United World Wide
Health Association. When her time was up here, she'd
travel on to somewhere new, once her baby was old
enough to travel with her. Of course, she would be doing
training and teaching jobs in cities as opposed to dangerous fieldwork. There wasn't really any permanence
to her job, a place to make roots, whereas Dante was
settled here.

He had land here. He had roots.

He would never ever leave Italy. She knew that.

How could they ever even conceive of being together?

"Shay, about last night…"

"No, we don't need to talk about last night. It was wonderful, but I get it. It was one time. Of course, every time we sleep together we remind ourselves it's only one time and then fall back into bed together. We have to stop. We've breached the terms of our marriage contract. It has to stop."

It was harsh, but she had to put an end to it to protect herself. She had to put an end to it before she got too carried away.

A strange look passed on his face briefly. "Yes. One time."

"Is that all?" she asked, trying to ignore the fact that he'd moved up behind her. Last night when he'd come up behind her, he'd been buried inside her. And her blood heated as she thought of that intimate embrace. His hand cupping her breast, his kisses on her neck as he whispered sweet nothings in her ear.

"I guess," he said. He sounded disappointed. "Do you need help with setting up the triage?"

"No, I'm good." What she needed to do was get him out of this room before the trainees came in and saw her lip-locked with Dr. Affini.

"I can help. You're supposed to take it easy."

"I'm good," she said. Then she smiled at him. She had such a hard time resisting him, but she had to. She couldn't let this go any further. It was a marriage of convenience, not a real marriage.

It wasn't permanent. Just like everything else in her life.

He liked control and she thrived on flux and change.

How could a marriage work with two individuals so different?

No, it was better this way.

"What time is your appointment with Dr. Tucci?" Dante asked and she could hear the frustration in his tone.

"Four o'clock. It's the ultrasound. Do you still want to be there?"

He nodded. "*Sì*, I will be there. I will escort you up there myself if you don't show up in time."

Shay rolled her eyes. "Well, if you would let me get to this simulation, then the sooner it can be done and the faster I can get up to Dr. Tucci's appointment."

"Fine. I will see you here at three fifty-five."

"Unless a trauma comes in?" she asked.

"Correct."

Shay breathed a sigh of relief that he was gone and didn't seem to be bothered by the fact that she was brushing him off. Which just firmed her belief that these feelings she had for him were one-sided.

And that nothing would come of this marriage, other than that her baby would have his surname and have his or her father in their life.

When he'd reached out for her this morning, she hadn't been there. For the past few mornings she'd been in bed beside him, but this time she wasn't, and he'd panicked.

Dante didn't know what to think about that. Only that he'd expected she would be there.

Part of him was relieved that she wasn't, but the other part of him was hurt that she'd left. *What did you expect?*

He didn't know.

Yes. You know.

Only he didn't want to admit to it, because he didn't believe in it. Sure, there were people who could find happiness, but he wasn't sure that he was one of them.

He turned back to look in the room where she was teaching the nursing trainees about mass casualty triage.

A smile tugged on the corners of his lips.

They'd come from such different backgrounds. Shay was so strong. She never gave up and he admired her fortitude. It was what he was attracted to when they'd met at that conference. She didn't give a damn about what others thought of her; he wished he had an ounce of that.

Only it bothered him seeing his name and his family's name splashed over the front pages because of his father's exploits. How the world knew everything about his family and how he couldn't even go for a cup of coffee without the paparazzi lurking around the corner.

He hated it.

And that was why he tried to keep a low profile wherever he went. Why he didn't want to make a fuss, but Shay was so strong. She just jumped into the fray.

She'd been thrust into poverty as a child and he hadn't wanted for anything.

Except love.

He shook that thought away.

Love was not for him. Affini men were notoriously a bunch of womanizers.

You're not. Your mother's father wasn't.

"Dr. Affini, there's someone in a trauma pod who is insisting you attend to his stitches," Dr. Carlo, one of the interns, said as he ran up to him.

"You know how to deal with unruly patients, Dr. Carlo. I don't need to see him."

Dr. Carlo frowned. "I tried all the tactics you've been teaching us to deal with difficult patients, but this man is insistent and he's bleeding profusely."

Dante groaned. "Take me to him."

Dr. Carlo nodded and they walked to the emergency room. There was a small trauma bay that was used for lacerations that was far off from the larger trauma bays that were for patients who were in distress. Patients that needed a large team surrounding them to save a life.

Dr. Carlo handed him the electronic chart and the name that popped up caused Dante to take a pause. Marco Affini.

No.

He hadn't seen his father in years, save for pictures splashed across the headlines.

Dante had had his solicitor tell his father that he was married and a baby was on the way, because Dante couldn't stand the thought of talking to the man again.

Even when he turned in his marriage certificate to stop the process of his father having his inheritance, his father would have wanted to speak to him about the mistake he was making and Dante wouldn't have anything to do with him.

Now he was here. In Dante's emergency room. His father had his back to him, but Dante could see the arm laid out on a tray; a nurse was still cleaning the deep wound on his forearm. There were bloody towels in the trash bins. He'd had a significant blood loss.

"You can leave, Nurse. I can take care of this patient." Dante clenched his fist.

His father turned then. "Ah, look who has finally decided to come pay his respects."

The nurse peeled off her gloves and slipped out of the trauma bay, as did Dr. Carlo. Dante shut the door.

"You were giving my interns a hard time, I hear," Dante said, setting the chart down and peeling off his white lab coat, before slipping on a trauma gown and gloves.

"Is all that gear necessary?" his father asked in a snarky tone.

"Yes, this is standard protocol."

"I'm your father. The same blood runs through our veins."

Dante snorted. "That's debatable."

His father glared at him. "What is your problem?"

"My problem is that you wouldn't let my intern do his job. How else is he going to learn?" Dante snapped as he sat on the rolling stool in front of his father and began to finish cleaning the wound the nurse had started on.

"I don't want some student stitching me up. I'd rather have you," his father groused.

Dante rolled his eyes and continued to clean the laceration. He was trying to tune his father out.

"I didn't get to congratulate you personally on your marriage." His father's voice was laced with sarcasm.

Dante snorted. "As if you actually *wanted* to congratulate me. You were just angry that you couldn't get a hold of Nonno's vineyard or the Lido villa. Or my money."

"You still have to produce an heir," his father said.

"Shay's already pregnant. Congratulations, Nonno," Dante said scathingly.

His father's face paled, his mouth opening and closing like a fish out of water. "Pregnant?"

"Sì."

"Are you sure it's your child this time? Does she know about Olivia and that child that you believed was yours but wasn't?" His father was clearly relishing digging at Dante's old wounds.

Dante glared at him and then injected freezing into the cut, causing his father to curse. It took every ounce of strength not to jam the needle in hard, but he was a doctor and he would never jeopardize his career because his father was making him angry.

He got up and discarded the needle in the hazardous material receptacle. "So how did this happen? Did the current girlfriend discover you in bed with another woman?"

Marco sneered. "No, I was in a minor altercation."

Dante shook his head. "You're unbelievable. You know that? Why are you here? You didn't need to have me stitch up your wound. Are you here to torment me because I took away your opportunity to sell Nonno's vineyard off to the highest bidder?"

"What're you talking about?"

Dante leaned over him. "I know. I know that you've had investors out there poking around. I know that big company wanted Nonno's wine under their wing. I know that you've been waiting like a caged animal, waiting to sell it. And now you can't."

"You think you know me so well? You don't."

"So you've come here to make amends?" Dante asked sarcastically.

"No," Marco said. "I came here to meet your bride."

"To find out whether there was an heir on the way."

His father turned and wouldn't look at him.

Dante just shook his head and opened a stitch kit. He began to close his father's wound. Angry that he'd had to deal with his father today. Angry that his father was so unchanged.

So ignorant, so greedy.

He would never be like him. He could never be like him.

"You'll need to stay here until the effects of the painkillers wear off. Sit back and relax and I'll send an intern to discharge you." Dante peeled off his gloves.

"You shouldn't have got married," his father said. "You're an Affini. We're not faithful."

Dante glared at him. "I may be an Affini, but I'm not like you at all."

With that, he left the room.

His father would never change. He would never accept the blame for what he did to Dante and Enzo's mother. For what he did to them.

And for that Dante would never forgive him.

And he would never forget.

Shay was lying on the bed waiting for the ultrasound.

More important, she was waiting for Dante to show up, but he was forty minutes late to her appointment. She'd had him paged, but he wasn't answering.

Which was unlike him. Even if he were tied up with a trauma, surely he'd have found a way to get a message to her?

"Are we still waiting?" Dr. Tucci asked, coming into the room.

"No, he's probably stuck with a trauma."

Dr. Tucci nodded. "Yes, it's always hard for an emergency room doctor to make appointments."

"I'm sure it's the same for an obstetrician," she teased.

Dr. Tucci grinned and tapped the side of his nose as he rolled the ultrasound machine over. "I could've tried to wait another ten minutes, but I do have a consult in about twenty minutes that will now be pushed back."

"I'm sorry about that," Shay apologized. "Usually he would get some message to me about why he was late."

Would he? Do you know him that well?

She shook that thought from her head.

"It's okay, Principessa." He grinned and lifted her

shirt, tucking a paper towel just under her breasts, and Shay tucked a towel into the waist of her scrub pants, which she had pulled down. "This will be cold."

The gel squeezed out of the bottle with a little spurt of air and he turned on the monitor. She turned her head toward the screen. She closed her eyes and took a deep breath as Dr. Tucci placed pressure against her abdomen.

"Ah, there is Baby."

Shay looked at the monitor and she could see the outline of her baby, moving, the flicker of a heartbeat and the string of pearls that represented the spine.

Her heart stopped for a moment and her eyes filled with tears as she stared at her baby.

Little hands and a tiny nose and she couldn't wait to see him or her in person and hold them.

I'll take care of you.

"Do you want to know the sex?" Dr. Tucci asked as he moved the ultrasound wand over her belly.

"You know?"

"Well, I have a pretty good idea. It's not one hundred percent factual, but this baby is in pretty good position to show me." Dr. Tucci grinned. "Or shall we wait for Dr. Affini?"

"No, I'll tell him later." If he couldn't be here, then she'd tell him herself. "I'll only tell Dante if he wants to know."

Dr. Tucci nodded. "It's a girl."

A tear slipped out of her eye and rolled down her cheek; she wiped it away with the back of her hand. "A girl?"

"Sì," Dr. Tucci said happily as he continued to tap the keyboard, taking measurements.

Shay's heart overflowed with love. It was the first

time since the stick had turned blue that she'd felt a real motherly connection. Probably because she was so focused on her work. So focused on keeping everything in her life the same, but nothing was the same anymore.

Nothing could be the same.

This little girl was her whole world.

"There, all done." Dr. Tucci wiped the ultrasound gel from her belly. "I'll email you the pictures of the baby. All looks good for twenty-six weeks."

"Thank you."

Dr. Tucci nodded and left the exam room.

Shay cleaned herself up. It was sad that Dante hadn't been here to see it, to share this moment, but his demeanor had changed when she'd reminded him that their marriage was a business arrangement.

I need to find him.

She left the exam room and headed down to the emergency department. She checked the updated chart and saw that Dr. Affini was in the far trauma bay. She headed down the hall and entered the room.

Only Dante wasn't there. Just an older gentleman, clad in expensive designer clothes, who had obviously been treated for a laceration to his forearm, because it was bandaged and there were blood-soaked towels in the trash.

"I'm sorry," she said. "I didn't mean to walk in on you."

He smiled and there was something familiar about the way he smiled, but his eyes were cold. He was a handsome older man, but there was no warmth about him, which gave her a bad feeling.

"You're not interrupting at all." His gaze raked her body up and down, eyeing the belly and frowning in disappointment. "Have you come to discharge me?"

"No, who is your doctor? I can check to see if they have the orders up."

"Dr. Dante Affini," the man said in a weird tone. "He's my son and I know he's anxious to get rid of me."

So that was why she'd seen the Affini name on the chart.

"You're Dante's father?"

He narrowed his eyes. "Yes. I'm Marco and you must be the blushing bride."

"Yes. I'm Shay."

"And that's my grandchild, is it?" He snorted. "Or is it someone else's?"

"The child is Dante's," Shay said, instantly detesting him. "What're you implying?"

"He didn't tell you?" There was a pleased glint to the man's eyes. "Olivia."

"What about her?"

"He was engaged to her and she was pregnant, with what he thought was his child, but of course it wasn't. What a huge blow to his ego."

"I'm not Olivia," Shay snapped. "I would never do such a thing."

"Even for wealth?"

"Money is not important to me."

"I find that hard to believe." He leaned forward. "Money is power."

"Money is not everything." She didn't like Dante's father at all and now she understood why he didn't like his father much either.

"Then why did you marry him?"

"To give my child a father."

Marco snorted. "Do you know why he married you?"

"For our child."

He shook his head. "For money."

"I don't have any money. I work for the United World Wide Health Association. I'm not in it for the money. Your son helps people as well and he doesn't get paid astronomical amounts."

Marco grinned deviously. "He didn't tell you?"

"Tell me what?" Her stomach twisted in a knot. She didn't like the way this conversation was going; she should just leave, but she couldn't move.

"He only married you to keep his trust fund. Dante and his brother have to marry by the time they're thirty-five and produce an heir from that marriage in order to keep their inheritance. If they don't, then they lose it all. It goes back to me. All their mother's dowry, which she left in trust to those boys, becomes mine again."

Her heart was crushed. She knew there was a reason why he'd been so insistent that they marry, but she didn't want to believe it.

She wanted to believe better about him.

"Shay, your father will come back. I believe in him. He's a better man than you give him credit for."

It was the douse of cold water she needed.

She fled Marco's room, tears threatening to spill.

She had to find Dante.

She had to find out if it was true, or whether his father was just being cruel.

Only deep down a little voice told her what she already knew.

And she was angry at herself for letting her guard down.

CHAPTER TWELVE

"I've been trying to get a hold of you for days. Where have you been?" Dante asked as Enzo answered his phone.

"Working," Enzo said quickly, and Dante sensed there was something more going on, but he didn't have time to pry at the moment. "What do you need, Dante?"

"Father came into the emergency room with a laceration to his right forearm."

There was silence on the other end. Then Enzo cleared his throat. "Are you okay?"

"I'm fine."

"Are you sure?"

"I said the last things I needed to say to him." Dante snorted. "He's not changed one bit, has he?"

"I don't think that he'll ever change, to be honest." Enzo sighed. "How did he get the laceration?"

"I never did find out. All he said was that it was a minor altercation," Dante said. "I just stitched him up. He told me my marriage is doomed and I left. I'll have to go back and discharge him soon. Especially before Shay runs into him."

Enzo was quiet on the other end. "He said your marriage was doomed?"

"He's not wrong," Dante said. "He said all Affini men were doomed."

"Damned might be more appropriate," Enzo groused.

Dante grunted in response. "I have to find Shay. I have to tell her about the trust fund and Olivia."

"I already know," she said.

Dante spun around to see Shay standing in the doorway, her eyes moist with unshed tears and her arms crossed. "I have to go, Enzo." And he disconnected the call.

"It's true?" she asked, coming into the room and shutting the door behind her.

"What were you told?"

"Your father told me that you married me only to keep your trust fund from reverting to your father. You married me because the baby guaranteed that the money, the land would be yours. And he filled me in on your exact acquaintance with Olivia, but that doesn't bother me. I'm not like her and I'm sorry if you think that I was when I first showed up. I understand your distrust."

"You met my father?" He scrubbed a hand over his face. "I'm sorry you had to meet him."

"He wasn't exactly pleasant," Shay said. "And didn't seem too thrilled about the prospect of the baby. Of course, now I know why. You're taking money out of his pocket."

"Is that what he told you?" Dante asked.

"Are you denying it?"

"No, but we need to talk about this calmly. For the baby."

"Calmly?" she asked, tears in her eyes. It hurt his heart knowing that this was hurting her. He didn't want her to get worked up. She was too fragile.

"Shay…" He tried to hold her, but she moved away from him.

"Tell me," she said.

It's for the best. Tell her the truth.

"*Sì*. That is why I married you. It's my thirty-fifth birthday soon and our marriage put a stop to my father taking away the vineyard and the Lido villa until an heir, our baby, was born."

She shook her head. "Why did you hide this from me? Why didn't you tell me about this before?"

"Would you have married me?"

"No. Probably not." She sighed. "My parents were forced to get married and my mother loved my father. Dearly, but he didn't return those feelings. It broke her heart. She just pined for him until the day she died. I don't want that. I never want that."

"Well, why did you marry me, then?" he asked. "Did you think that this could possibly lead to something more? You reminded me yourself just this morning that this is a business arrangement."

Shay winced as if she'd been slapped and he regretted the choice of words.

"I want my baby to know their father," she said, her voice shaking. "I thought you…"

"Thought what?" Dante asked, trying to stay calm to keep her calm.

"I don't know," she said quietly.

"Then why are you angry for my reasons?"

"Because you don't want this child. Not for the reasons I thought you did."

"And for what reasons did you think I wanted this child?" he snapped. "You show up here pregnant, my one-night stand. What am I supposed to think? I've been used before, people after my money. People after my title."

"I don't want any of those things," she said. "I never have. I'm not Olivia."

"I find that hard to believe. You grew up with nothing. You've probably been dreaming of a knight in shining armor to take you away. To save you. Well, I'm not him."

Shay glared at him. "I know you're not him. I'm painfully aware of that fact."

"So now you know the truth," he said in exasperation. "The reason I wanted you to enter into a marriage of convenience with me for a year. I thought you understood the parameters to our marriage. Everything was laid out in the contract. I thought you understood that it couldn't go further than this. I thought you didn't want more, but I was wrong. You want more than I can give you."

"I wish you would have told me the reason why you wanted the marriage." Shay couldn't even look him in the eye. "This is why…marriage just doesn't work. Unless both people love each other. It just… It can't work."

"I can't give you anything more," he repeated.

"I don't want more." A tear slid down her cheek, but she held her head up high.

"Are you going to ask for an annulment?"

She shook her head. "No, I won't let you lose your property. Especially to that man. I signed a contract. I'll stay your wife. You'll give my baby a name, but when my twelve weeks' contract is up I'm leaving."

"You can't leave," he said, but he felt terrible.

"Then give me a reason to stay," she said.

Only he couldn't, because he was too afraid.

He was a horrible human being.

Why did he have to hurt her?

Because it's for the best?

Only he wasn't so sure about that.

"I'd better go," she said. "I'm going to pack and move back to the United World Wide Health Association quarters."

"What?" He stepped in front of her. "You don't have to do that."

"What's the point of staying at the Lido?"

"We have to keep up at least the pretense of being married. If you move back into the United World Wide Health Association quarters, then people will know that our marriage is a sham or on the rocks and my father will put things in motion to take back the land."

"What does it matter?" she snapped. "I'm not going to divorce you and the baby will be born. Who cares what the press thinks? Who cares what people think?"

"I do! I care. It's my family name, but you wouldn't understand about family, would you, since your own father didn't want you?"

The sting of her hand slapping him burned, but he deserved it.

She pushed past him out into the hall and he stood there, holding his face. The feel of her palm still burned into his flesh and in that moment he realized his father had been right. He was exactly like him.

It had been two weeks since their fallout and it still tormented her. He never came back to the villa. She lived there alone and, even though she was used to being alone, without him it was lonely. She missed his arms around her at night, and then she was angry at herself for shedding tears over Dante. For missing him, when he clearly didn't want her.

What did you expect? Love?

She'd thought he was different. She'd hoped he was different, but he wasn't. He was exactly the same.

The same as his father, the same as her father. So she made up her mind. Her twelve weeks were done. She was going to leave and head back to New Orleans. The place she always returned to. The only home she knew, even if it wasn't much of one.

Shay leaned against the wall, fighting the tears that were threatening to fall, and she cursed herself inwardly for letting herself fall in love with a man like her father. Something she'd always sworn she wouldn't do, but she'd done it. And she realized that she was just like her mother.

The only difference was that she wasn't going to pine away.

She was going to keep working.

She was going to make damn sure that she forgot about Dante Affini.

How can you forget about him when you carry a piece of him inside you?

Now she had to get up the courage to find him and tell him she was leaving. Contract or not, she was going back to New Orleans. Her baby wouldn't be used as a pawn for a trust fund. A sharp pain stabbed her just under her navel and she cried out. She was getting too worked up. She was supposed to be taking it easy.

Part of her wished that she'd just headed to the Lido instead of trying to find Dante. If she'd headed back to the Lido after the run-in with his father, then she wouldn't have heard from Dante's own lips the real reasons why he'd married her. Wouldn't have had it confirmed that he thought so little about her and the baby. That he'd just wanted the baby because the baby would ensure his inheritance.

Nothing more.

He didn't love the baby and she realized that she would be giving her baby the same kind of father she grew up with. It truly was all about business.

The pain hit again and she doubled over; her heart began to race. She was dizzy and she felt as if she was going to be sick.

It's stress. Just stress. You have a flight tomorrow you have to catch.

Only the pain hit once again, with a lightening of her belly, and she knew it was something more than just Braxton Hicks. She slid down the wall, crying as the pain overtook her body. She was down a hallway that wasn't busy in the evening. A hall that was filled with offices that were closed. She was alone.

Oh, God. Don't let my baby die.

"Shay? Oh, God, *cara*…"

She rolled her head to look down the hall. She could see Dante running toward her and, even though her heart had been broken by him, she'd never been so happy to see him.

He was kneeling beside her. "What's wrong?"

"Pain" was the only word she could pant through the pain racking her body. The world was spinning and she brought her hand up from where she had been clutching her lower belly. There was bright red fresh blood on her palm.

"Oh, no," she whispered. Red fresh blood was never a good sign in a pregnant woman.

She was only twenty-eight weeks along. It was too early to have her baby.

"Oh, God, *cara*, you're bleeding." She was scooped up into his arms. He was holding her close. "We'll get you help, Shay. Please stay with me."

"It's too soon, Dante. Please help our baby. Please."

She gripped the lapel of his white jacket, holding tight to him as her body attacked her. Shay knew what was going on: she was in premature labor. She'd seen it so many times in Third World countries. And if she was bleeding, that didn't bode well for her or the baby.

Her labor was progressing so fast. Why was it happening to her? Was it punishment for entering into this sham of a marriage?

She had just seen Dr. Tucci two weeks ago.

All she wanted was for her baby to live. She couldn't care less about herself. Her baby had to survive. Her baby needed a chance at life.

Dante carried her into the trauma bay. The largest trauma bay and she buried her head in his neck while the pain coursed through her body. She was scared that he'd brought her here. The largest room was saved for the direst situations. How did she go from being normal and healthy to critical?

"Help. Me."

"I know, *cara*. I know." Dante set her down on the examination table. "Someone page Dr. Tucci to Trauma, *stat*!"

He held her hand as the trauma nurses and residents began to fill the room.

As she stared up at him she found herself slipping away from him. In more than one way.

"Shay, please stay with me."

She turned her head away as the nurses slipped on the oxygen mask. She couldn't look at him. He was concerned only because the death of the baby meant that he would lose everything. All his land, his money.

He didn't deserve to be in this room with her, but she couldn't tell him to leave either, because he was the only familiar thing in this room. She didn't like being on the other side of a trauma as she took deep breaths and tried to fight the urge to slip off.

Dr. Tucci came bursting into the room.

"I'll be back," Dante whispered in her ear. He went to speak to Dr. Tucci.

Shay tried to focus on what they were saying, but she couldn't. Instead she closed her eyes and listened to the heart-rate monitor that they had on her belly. The baby's heart rate was speeding up, but it was still there.

Her baby was still alive for the moment.

"We have to get her into an operating theatre now," Dr. Tucci shouted above the din. "Dr. Affini, you have to leave. She's your wife. You can't be in there with her."

"Husbands go into the operating theatre all the time when their wives have C-sections."

"I don't want… I don't want him in there," she managed to say from beneath the mask.

Dr. Tucci nodded at her. "Dr. Affini, please leave the bay."

Dante looked back at her, but she looked away.

If he only wanted their baby for monetary reasons, then he had no right to be here with her while she was losing it. He had no right to share in the pain she was feeling.

"Shay, we're going to put you under general anesthesia. It's safer for you both. We have to move fast," Dr. Tucci said. "Do I have your consent?"

Shay nodded. "Yes. Please save us."

And that was the last thing she could remember before the world went black.

CHAPTER THIRTEEN

ALL DANTE COULD do was watch the clock on the wall. That was all his mind would let him do, because he couldn't let his mind wander to where it wanted to go. He couldn't let it wander to down the hall where Dr. Tucci was trying to save Shay's and his baby's lives. It crushed his heart that he had pushed her away.

That he'd hurt her. Those two weeks apart had made him regret his harsh words.

All he could think about was earning her love back again and not knowing how, but he was going to try. Without her...his world spun out of control. It was colorless. There was no light. No sun.

And the way he'd hurt her to protect his heart sickened him.

That he was like his father.

You're not your father.

He hid his face in his hands and tried to shake all the thoughts away. All those dark thoughts that were niggling away in the dark recesses of his mind.

The one that stuck out the most was that he'd failed Shay and the baby.

He'd absolutely failed them.

Don't let them die.

It was a silent plea, but one that he was hoping wouldn't fall on deaf ears.

Not today.

Lives were saved every day and he wanted to be there when Shay's life was saved, because that was all he had to cling to at this moment.

Dr. Tucci came out of the surgical hall. Still in his scrubs. The grim expression on his face made Dante want to scream; his heart sank into the soles of his feet. Further. Into the depths of absolute despair as Dr. Tucci approached him.

"Please," Dante whispered. "Please don't tell me… Don't tell me she's gone. Please."

Dr. Tucci sighed. "She survived, and so did the baby, but it's not good. Shay lost a lot of blood. A lot. We hung a lot of packed cells."

"What happened?" Dante asked.

"Placental abruption." Dr. Tucci ran a hand over his bald head. "We never know when they're going to happen. It can happen so fast. Just be thankful that it happened here in the hospital and we were able to get the baby out. Usually, by the time the women get here the baby has suffocated and the mother has bled to death."

Dante felt dizzy and he sat back down. His head in his hands, his eyes stinging from unshed tears that would not come.

Dr. Tucci sat beside him and patted his back. "The baby will be fine. She's strong."

Dante glanced up at him. "She?"

"Yes, I forgot you missed the last ultrasound. You have a little girl. She's very small, but already she's a fighter. Ideally we'd have started on steroids in utero to help mature her lungs, but obviously in this case there wasn't time. We have her hooked up to oxygen and various drips to support her while she continues to grow. Of course, you know that she'll have to stay in the NICU until she gains to what should have been close to her birth weight. We also don't let premature babies go home until they're close to their original due date."

Dante nodded. "I know. Thank you, Dr. Tucci."

"We're not out of the woods either, yet, with respect to the Principessa. The damage to her uterus was extensive. The placental abruption ripped through the wall of her uterus. It was a full uterine abruption. I had to perform an emergency hysterectomy. Shay will not carry any more children."

Dante nodded again.

Dr. Tucci left.

This is all my fault.

He was the one who'd got her pregnant and then broken her heart.

He was no better than his father. All because he was afraid of letting someone else in.

Dante left the waiting room and wandered up to the NICU. The nurse on duty pointed him in the direction of the incubator where a tiny baby weighing no more than a couple of pounds was hooked up to a bunch of machines that were helping her live.

He was scared to approach the incubator. He was afraid of what he was going to see. And he wasn't sure that he was ready for this. That he was ready for a daughter.

This is what you wanted, remember? Before Olivia crushed your hopes and dreams.

All he'd ever wanted when he was young was a family. Not that he didn't love Enzo or his mother, but he wanted some sense of normalcy. He'd wanted that family with a mother, father and child. A loving family who would celebrate holidays together.

Just as his mother had with his *nonno* and *nonna*.

They had loved each other.

All of them.

And that was what he'd always craved when he was younger.

He took a step toward the incubator and looked in to see his daughter. His beautiful daughter. She was so small and fragile. A tear slid down his face as he looked at her.

And he knew in that moment what he was.

He was a father.

This was his child.

"Can I touch her?" he asked the nurse.

"Of course," she said.

Dante put on hand sanitizer and the nurse opened one of the little portal doors to the incubator. He slid his hand in and rested it on her back. There was downy fine hair on her skin. The lanugo she'd never shed because she was born premature.

She was warm, but under the palm of his hand where she fit so well he could feel her chest going up and down. And the small flutter of her heart.

His baby.

His child.

His future.

Dante slipped his hand out of the incubator and left the NICU. He went up to the ICU, where he gowned and masked to go see Shay, who was still receiving a blood transfusion and still not awake. She was still under anesthesia, in an induced coma while they monitored her.

When he walked into the ICU room, he cried out at

the sight of her. She was so pale against the crisp white hospital sheets. She was ashen.

Oh, God.

He'd been responsible for this.

The woman he loved had almost died. The realization hit him hard and it wasn't the realization that he loved her, it was the fact that he'd allowed himself to say that to himself for the first time without hesitation. Without conjecture.

He was in love with her. It was more than a marriage of convenience. It was real. She was his everything.

And it didn't matter to him about his inheritance or the trust fund. If he couldn't have her or the baby in his life, if they didn't get their chance to be a family, then life was not worth living for him. He would give up everything, his pride, his family name, everything that he'd thought he wanted, to have a chance with Shay.

To do things right. To be a real family.

"I'm sorry, *cara.* I will make things right. I promise."

Dante left the ICU room and knew exactly what he had to do. He couldn't be selfish anymore. As he left the intensive care unit floor and passed through the waiting room he saw that his father was here. Two visits in two weeks was more than he'd seen Marco Affini in the last five years and it was two too many.

Dante couldn't figure out why his father was back, but he was unwelcome.

His father turned as if sensing him there.

"What're you doing here? Why did you come back?" Dante asked.

"To see if the child survived. There was a lot of press. Word got out that Principessa Affini almost died. That she was hanging on by a thread."

"It's not any of your business and you know the press always gets things wrong."

"Were they wrong?"

"No, but it still doesn't concern you."

"I think it does," Marco said. "Well, did they live?"

"Do you care?"

Marco shrugged. "It would be a shame, but no, not really. Not for the reasons you think I should care."

"*Sì*, they both survived. So you can go now."

"I think I'll wait."

Dante clenched his fist. "Waiting around to pick at the bones?"

Marco snorted. "Hardly. I actually wanted to wish you a happy birthday. Today is your birthday, is it not?"

"I'm surprised you remembered."

"You're my son," Marco said.

"You've never remembered before now. Or was it because today happens to be my thirty-fifth birthday? Today's the day you could've had it all." It was a dig and Dante didn't care. He deserved it. "And now none of it's for you. You lost it."

"It could still be mine. I hear the baby is sick and that your wife is unable to bear any more children. If your baby dies, then that's it. Unless you leave *this* wife and find another you can breed with."

Dante resisted the urge to pummel his father in the waiting room. "I would gladly lose it all for Shay. If our baby doesn't survive, I will stay with Shay. I love her. I won't abandon her like you abandoned my mother."

"I loved your mother, Dante. It's just that Affini men aren't faithful. My father wasn't, nor his father before him…"

"I *am* faithful. I have always been faithful and I will continue to be faithful. I am an Affini and I am faithful.

I am more of a man than you ever were or will be. Now, if you have nothing further to say to me, then I think this is where we part company."

Dante's pulse was thundering between his ears. He was reaching out to give his father a chance.

His father sighed and then nodded. "Good luck."

Dante shook his head as he watched his father leave.

He watched the last of a long line of Affini cheaters walk out of his life forever, because his father was going to be the last of the Affini men to be unfaithful. He wasn't going to follow in his footsteps and Enzo had no plans to settle down. Ever.

He briefly mourned the loss of his father. For the father he could've been, but Marco Affini was weak. Dante refused to be weak.

He was going to fight for what he wanted.

He was going to be strong like the person he loved and admired the most.

He was going to be strong like Shay.

His wife.

CHAPTER FOURTEEN

I'M THIRSTY.

That was Shay's first thought as she started to come out of the anesthetic. The groggy fog that compelled her to keep sleeping, but the more she struggled to stay asleep in that warm, hazy, pain-free cocoon, the more she became aware of her surroundings.

And most important, the fact that she was no longer pregnant.

She let out a small cry.

I've lost her. My baby.

And she began to weep. She wanted her mother there to console her. To ease the pain. Her whole childhood she'd been the balm to ease her mother's pain when she was sobbing over her father. Now she needed her mother's arms to wrap around her and hold her close.

To ease the heart-wrenching pain that was tearing away at her very soul.

The baby she would never get to see.

A nurse rushed in, speaking Italian to her, trying to get Shay to calm down, but she couldn't stop the sobs from racking her body, because nothing could bring back her baby.

"I'll take care of her," a deep, gentle voice said.

Shay turned her head to see Dante standing beside

her bedside. He was in his scrubs, but they were wrinkled and she noticed the cot in the corner.

He'd been sleeping here?

She glanced back over at Dante, who was issuing instructions to the nurse, who was nodding and then left the room. It was just Dante and her.

There was no baby.

There was nothing for them.

"What…?" She trailed off because she couldn't even finish the sentence. It was too painful.

"She's alive," Dante said. Then smiled. "Our daughter's alive, beautiful and in the NICU."

Tears streaked down her face. "I thought I'd lost her."

"No, *cara*. You didn't lose her. It was I who almost lost you…" He took her hand and kissed it, tears pouring down his face. "I almost lost you."

"What do you mean?"

"Your placenta abrupted, and it was so forceful it caused your uterus to do the same. It was a full uterine rupture. You almost died."

"Oh, God," she whispered.

"They had to remove your uterus to save your life. You needed several units of packed cells. You almost died. I'm so sorry, Shay. I'm devastated that you won't be able to carry another child. I'm so truly sorry, *cara*."

Tears streamed down her face.

"I'm so sorry," she whispered.

"No, never apologize," Dante said. "Never. You're alive and our daughter is alive. There is nothing to apologize for."

"What does it matter to you? You don't love me." Shay tried to take her hand away. "You have your heir. You don't need me anymore."

"You're wrong. I need you, *cara*." He kissed her hand

again. "I love you more than anything. Our two weeks apart were torture. You are my world. I am nothing without you, *cara*."

"How can you love me? You only married me for the baby..." She started to weep but shrugged him away when he touched her. "You only wanted me for the baby, so you can keep your inheritance. You have that. Don't you want someone else who can give you more children? You wanted a family, to be a father."

"You're sounding like my father," he said sternly. "Besides, I am a father.

"You're being cruel."

"You're talking nonsense." He reached for her hand. "I love you, Shay. I was terrified, yes, and my heart was broken and I couldn't trust that emotion. Love was dead inside me until you came along. I don't care if I lose everything by being with you. I love you. I love you, *mi amore*. You're all that I need. You're all that I want."

"You love me?"

"*Sì*, I would give it all up for you. Only you, and if our child hadn't made it, I would still want you. Almost losing you was too much to bear. You are my heart. My soul. My everything."

"You weren't the only fool, Dante. I was a fool too." Shay sighed. "I was so afraid of falling in love and having to give up everything I knew. Giving up my career for a man. I didn't want to be my mother. I was trying so hard not to be her, when I was turning into her."

Dante chuckled. "I understand. I was trying so hard not to be my father I was doing the same. I was turning into him. The only difference in our situations is that you loved your mother. You miss your mother. My father and I, there is no love lost. All we share is a genetic link. We are not the same."

"I am very glad for that."

Dante smiled and then leaned over and kissed her. "I'm afraid I tore up that contract."

"Our marriage contract?"

He nodded. "I want you for more than just a year. I want you for a lifetime."

Shay began to cry again and he kissed her.

"Are you ready to see your daughter now?"

"Yes."

Dante called the nurse, who brought in a wheelchair. He helped Shay into the wheelchair and made sure she was comfortable. He wheeled her down to the NICU, and when they entered that room full of incubators her heart skipped a beat. Dante wheeled her over to the incubator across the room. He lifted the pink blanket and inside was a tiny baby on a ventilator.

Her little girl was so small and fragile. She was hooked up and there were many lines and leads on her tiny pink body, but Shay knew instinctively this was her baby.

"She's so small." She began to weep, not being able to hold in the emotions any longer. She'd thought she'd lost everything when she woke up. She'd thought she was waking up into some kind of nightmare, but instead she was waking up to a dream that she never wanted to end.

A dream she didn't even know she wanted until she thought it was all lost.

That it was all gone.

Dante opened the incubator and with the help of the NICU nurse they lifted the tiny baby girl from the incubator to place her on her mother's chest. Shay's heart overflowed with a love she hadn't even known was possible. A blanket was wrapped around her little girl and

Shay placed her hand over the tiny round back, holding her close.

"It's okay," she whispered. "I'm here and so are you. I haven't left you."

Dante placed a hand over hers. "We're both here now, *mi amore*. And we're not leaving."

The familiar little heartbeat thrumming against her calmed Shay and the baby's vitals kicked up a notch in response to being held.

"That's a strong heartbeat," Dante said. "She's a real fighter."

"Yes. She is." Shay ran her fingers over the tiny feet that had kicked her.

Her baby was alive.

"I thought I'd lost this," Shay whispered. "I hope I never feel that way again."

"Me too," Dante said. "It was the worst feeling ever. If I lost either of you…I couldn't go on living. You are both my heart. My loves."

"I feel the same," she whispered.

"*Cara*, our little girl needs a name. I wanted you to name her."

"Me?"

"*Sì.*"

"Sophia," Shay said without hesitation. "My mother's name and your long-lived *zia*. I hope you don't mind."

"I don't. That is a good first name and how about Maria for the second? That was my mother's name."

Shay nodded. "I like that."

"Sophia Maria Affini. Or rather Principessa Sophia. It has a nice ring to it."

"It does." Shay sighed. "I guess I should tender my

resignation with the United World Wide Health Association."

"Why?" Dante asked.

"It seems I'll be staying in Italy for a while."

"You don't have to resign from the United World Wide Health Association."

"Why not?"

"Because I've tendered my resignation at the hospital. I have to give them six months' notice and finish up the work that you started."

"What?" she asked, surprised. "You resigned?"

"*Sì*, I joined the United World Wide Health Association as a trainer. I won't be doing any kind of missions that you used to do, because we have a child, but I will finish your work while you recover, and then in six months we'll head to America, where I will spend three months training trauma surgeons to head out to disaster zones. Then, who knows where we'll go? I was told that training can happen all over the world in various cities. The point is, we'll go together. The three of us. I requested that you will work alongside me. I can't work without you."

"But…but you love Italy."

"*Sì*, I do, but I love you more and your work is important to you. It's your passion and it's all you have, besides us. Anyways, Venice is our home base. We'll come back for summers on the Lido and Christmases in Tuscany. I have enough money to pick and choose when I want to work and where. Besides, time in Tuscany while you're healing will be nice. Serena and Guillermo can't wait to spoil this little girl. Italy is just a place we hang our hats. The three of us is what makes a home."

Shay smiled. Yes. Italy was a great place to live, as New Orleans had been. Just a place she'd passed through since her mother died, but her husband and her daughter were her life. Wherever they were together they were home. And for the first time in her life she had a home. Love and roots that were all her own.

* * * * *

Look out for the next great story in the
ROYAL SPRING BABIES *duet*

BABY SURPRISE FOR THE DOCTOR PRINCE
by Robin Gianna

And if you enjoyed this story,
check out these other great reads
from Amy Ruttan

ALEJANDRO'S SEXY SECRET
UNWRAPPED BY THE DUKE
TEMPTING NASHVILLE'S CELEBRITY DOC
PERFECT RIVALS...

All available now!

BABY SURPRISE FOR THE DOCTOR PRINCE

BY

ROBIN GIANNA

Published in Great Britain 2017
By Mills & Boon, an imprint of HarperCollins*Publishers*
1 London Bridge Street, London, SE1 9GF

© 2017 Robin Gianakopoulos

ISBN: 978-0-263-92635-4

Our policy is to use papers that are natural, renewable and recyclable
products and made from wood grown in sustainable forests. The logging
and manufacturing processes conform to the legal environmental
regulations of the country of origin.

Printed and bound in Spain
by CPI, Barcelona

Dear Reader,

Deciding to set this book in Venice, Italy, was easy—
such a magical place! Then my editor Laura asked
if I'd like to have the book be part of a duet with the
wonderful Amy Ruttan. Brainstorming the story with
Amy was a lot of fun—as was figuring out the last
details with Amy and Laura poolside in San Diego at
the RWA conference. A writer's life is rough! ;-)

In the story Aubrey thinks she's going to Italy to nurse
there, and to support her pregnant friend Shay… Until
Aubrey meets a gorgeous Italian man, Enzo Affini,
and can't resist a hot one-night fling. Except when she
returns to Venice two months later she learns he's the
doctor she has to work for!

Enzo is suspicious of Shay showing up in his brother's
life, and when Aubrey comes to work for him he
wonders about her, too! Until a shocking event forces
him to rethink his life and what's most important to
him.

This story is about trust and betrayal and learning that
the things we may believe about ourselves aren't always
true. I hope you enjoy it!

Robin xoxo

I'd like to thank my duet partner, Amy Ruttan, for being so great to work with. Let's do it again, sometime, Amy!

Also, another huge shout-out to my wonderful friend Meta Carroll for helping me with the medical scenes in the story—thanks and smooches!

After completing a degree in journalism, then working in advertising and mothering her kids, **Robin Gianna** had what she calls her 'awakening'. She decided she wanted to write the romance novels she'd loved since her teens, and now enjoys pushing her characters towards their own happily-ever-afters. When she's not writing, Robin's life is filled with a happily messy kitchen, a needy garden, a wonderful husband, three great kids, a drooling bulldog and one grouchy Siamese cat.

Books by Robin Gianna

Mills & Boon Medical Romance

The Hollywood Hills Clinic

The Prince and the Midwife

Midwives On-Call at Christmas

Her Christmas Baby Bump

Flirting with Dr Off-Limits
It Happened in Paris…
Her Greek Doctor's Proposal
Reunited with His Runaway Bride

Visit the Author Profile page at millsandboon.co.uk for more titles.

CHAPTER ONE

AUBREY HENDERSON LIFTED her face to the lagoon breeze and smiled, soaking in the incredible history, vivid colors, and sheer amazement that was Venice, Italy. How lucky was she to have snagged a temporary job here? She might have spent only two days in Venice before leaving for her two-month nursing job in Rome, but every detail of those hours felt etched in her brain.

Which included every detail of her illicit, probably ill-advised, and beyond wonderful fling with Enzo Affini. That one night felt burned into her mind—and body, as well—and just the thought of him made her silly heart both skip a beat and burn with annoyance.

Maybe they'd left it a little vague, but hadn't he implied he'd be in touch? What exactly they'd said to one another when they'd parted in the wee hours of the morning didn't seem too clear anymore, but still. She'd expected he'd at least call her while she was in Rome, since he knew she was coming back to Venice around now.

Knowing she might run into him in the flesh had her feeling nervous and excited and ticked off all over again for making her wonder if she'd ever hear from him. Then ticked off at herself for wondering at all.

Then annoyed even more when she realized that

when the phrase *in the flesh* had come to mind, an instant all-too-sexy vision of the man's glorious body made her feel a little breathless.

Ridiculous. Time to concentrate on why she'd come to Venice, which had nothing to do with a handsome Italian prince who was obviously the love-'em-and-leave-'em type. Which was okay. She didn't care if she saw him or not. In fact, she had no desire at all to see the guy, since he clearly didn't want to see her.

No, she'd come here before to support her friend Shay, who'd recently married Enzo's brother, Dante. Now she was here to work in the clinic, enjoy that adventure, and meet with the art and architecture preservation society she'd donated more money to in her mother's memory.

Her mom had always been fascinated with Venice and its incredible history, and it had only been her fear of travel and crowds that had kept her from coming to explore it. Seeing the fresco she and her mom had "adopted," paying for its restoration before her mother had died, would be sad but wonderful, too. Her mother's legacy as a preservationist in New England had now been expanded across the ocean, and that thought brought her smile back and her thoughts completely away from Enzo Affini.

Really. She wasn't going to think about him again. Period.

A renewed pep in her step took her down narrow stone passageways in front of colorful homes, over numerous charming footbridges, then across the *piazza* toward the well-marked clinic she'd be working in for the next four months. When she opened the wide glass door, a bell chimed. Inside, a friendly-looking, middle-aged woman sat at a rather spartan desk. Aubrey had been told most of the people here could speak English, but wouldn't they appreciate it if she tried a few of the Italian phrases she'd learned?

"Buongiorno. Mio nome e Aubrey Henderson. Um... sono qui...per lavorare."

She struggled to remember more, then abandoned the effort when she saw the quizzical and amused expression on the poor woman's face. Doubtless she was completely butchering the pronunciation.

"I'm a nurse with the UWWHA, assigned to the clinic here starting today."

"Welcome. We've been expecting you. And let's speak English, shall we?" said the woman, her smile widening.

"That sounds good." Aubrey smiled back. "I'm working on the language, but I'm not too good at it yet, obviously! I'm hoping by the end of the time I'm here, I'll be practically fluent."

"Learning a language takes time, but working with patients will teach you much. I am Nora, and you can ask me for anything as you need it, *si*? Come with me." She stood and gestured to the door behind her. "I'll show you where you can put your things. We have a small staff here—you may already know we have just one doctor and nurse working each day, which sometimes gets very hectic. The doctor who is director of the clinic is here today, and he will be the one to show you around. A patient is here right now, though, so the doctor may not be available for me to introduce you at the moment. When you see him, can you introduce yourself? I must greet patients as they arrive, you see."

"Of course. And I confess I don't really know much about how the clinic runs," Aubrey said as she followed Nora down a brightly lit hallway. "I saw the opening in Venice and jumped at the chance to work and explore here." Had jumped at the chance to explore a certain unbelievably sexy prince, too. Except she wasn't thinking about him ever again.

The place was very modern and scrupulously clean. Aubrey glanced into a few rooms to see each had a blue and white examination table, along with the usual medical necessities that you'd see in the United States. Not exactly plush and comfy-looking, but they'd do the job.

Nora opened a tall cupboard door made of the same white material as the rest of the built-in furniture in the space. "Here is a locker for your things, with your uniform inside. I don't see the doctor, so make yourself comfortable and he will be with you soon. Okay?"

"Okay." Nora left her alone and Aubrey was about to put her purse inside the locker until she wondered if maybe she was supposed to change into her uniform right then. Probably yes, since she assumed she would be working with patients right away? Why hadn't she asked Nora those things while she was still here?

Aubrey nearly went back out to the reception area but decided that was silly. If she got into uniform and it turned out to be just an introductory day, it was no big deal. At least she'd be ready, right?

Finding a bathroom, she changed into the crisp white dress, smiling at how it was oddly old-fashioned compared with what nurses wore in the US today, and yet the whole place felt ultramodern. She dropped her clothes and purse into the locker, then hovered around, not sure what to do next. The various drawers and cupboards tempted her to open them up and poke around on her own, but she figured it would be more polite to wait until she was invited to do that.

She stood there for a good ten minutes, and each minute that dragged on felt more awkward. And didn't it make sense to acquaint herself with where things were, in case she needed to take care of a patient sooner rather than later? But luck being the way it was, just as she opened one of the cupboards above the long countertop a deep voice spoke from behind her.

"*Buongiorno.* You must be the new nurse from the US."

Jumping guiltily, she nearly slammed the cupboard shut and turned with a bright smile. Then her heart completely stopped when she saw who stood there.

Enzo Affini. The man who'd unfortunately kept coming to mind since she'd returned to Venice. The man whose hands and mouth had been all over her two months ago. The man who hadn't bothered to call her again after that very intimate night together.

Aubrey felt a little as if she might just fall over, as though she'd been physically struck at the surprise of seeing him right there in front of her. She barely noticed the elderly man standing next to him as Enzo's dark eyes met hers for several breathless heartbeats. He recovered from the shock more quickly than she did, moving next to her to get something from the cupboard she'd just been snooping in, then turning to the elderly man with instructions. Aubrey didn't hear a word he said, feeling utterly frozen as she watched Enzo and the patient move down the hallway, with Enzo opening the door to the reception area for him, then following behind.

Aubrey sagged against the countertop, her hand to her chest, trying to breathe. Did she have any chance of slipping out the back door before he came back? Though if she did, what would that accomplish? She'd come to Venice to work. Was it her fault that he, incredibly, worked at this clinic, too? Gulping down the jittery nerves making her feel numb from head to toe, she forced herself to stand as tall as possible and stared at the door, willing herself to look calm and confident.

Proud that she managed to be standing there in a normal way when the door opened again…assuming he couldn't see her knees shaking…she met his gaze. The look on his face was completely different than the last time she'd seen him, which was the night they'd parted in the wee hours of the morning. Then, his eyes had been filled with warmth, his sensuous lips smiling and soft.

These lips could have belonged to someone else. Hard and firmly pressed together. His silky eyebrows formed a deep V over his nose as he stared at her.

"Aubrey. To say this is a surprise is an understatement. How did you know I work here?" His voice was a little hard, too. Ultra-chilly. She'd have to be dense as one of the posts sunk into the silt of the lagoon if she couldn't read loud and clear that he was not pleased to see her *at all*.

Something painful stabbed in the region of her heart, but the nervousness and, yes, hurt filling her gut slowly made way for a growing anger at the strange suspicion in his eyes. As if she'd come here on purpose to stalk him or something. "I didn't. I didn't even know you were a doctor. Something you conveniently forgot to mention."

"You knew Dante is a doctor."

"So that meant you had to be one, too? From the way you talked about the restoration of the old homes here, I thought you were an architect or in the construction business or something. You at least knew I was a nurse traveling with Shay." She wasn't about to add that her attraction to him and excitement about deciding to let herself enjoy a little carnal pleasure on the trip had been foremost in her mind, not the thought of what he did for a living, since right now *he* clearly had other things on his mind. Like being ticked off that she was there.

Well, he wasn't the only one feeling beyond annoyed right then. It was painfully obvious that he'd never planned to contact her when she was back in Venice, and she wasn't sure if she was angrier at him for that, or at herself for wishing he'd wanted to.

"I assumed you were working at the hospital with Shay."

"Well, you assumed wrong, the same way I did." She tipped her chin and stared him down, her chest pinching tightly at the way he was looking at her. As if she were some black rat that had scurried out of the sewer into his clinic.

A long slow breath left his lips as he stuck his hands in the dress pants that fitted him as impeccably as the ones he'd taken off as fast as possible the last time she'd seen him. His white lab coat was swept back against his hips, and even through his dress shirt his strong physique was obvious. The body she'd gotten to see in all its glorious detail.

The jerk.

"Our time together before was...nice, Aubrey. But this is a problem."

Nice? The most incredible sexual experience of her life had been *nice* for him? "Why?" she challenged, beyond embarrassed and steaming now. "You're obviously a man who enjoys women. I enjoyed our night together, too. But that's long behind us. Now we move into a professional relationship, which won't be a problem for me at all."

Liar, liar, pants on fire, her inner self mocked.

Though maybe it was true. Right now, if he tried to kiss her, she just might punch him in the nose.

"Listen." He shoved his hand through his hair. "I think it's better if we look at other options."

Other options? The rise of panic in her chest shoved aside her anger with him. Nora had said he was director of the clinic. Did that mean he could toss her out if he wanted? She knew there weren't any positions available at the hospital. What if there wasn't a single other place to work in all of Venice?

"Enzo, there's no reason we can't work through this. I—"

"Dr. Affini." Nora rushed into the hallway with a boy who looked to be about seven trailing behind. Blood stained his torn pants and dripped onto the floor with every step he took. "Benedetto Rossi is here. He fell off his bike. I tried to call his father and his *nonna* but haven't reached either of them. I'll keep trying."

"All right." Instantly, the frown on Enzo's face disappeared, replaced by a calm, warm smile directed at the boy. "Were you taking the corners too fast again?" he asked in English.

The boy responded in quick Italian, gesturing wildly and looking panicked. Enzo placed his hand on the boy's shoulder and led him to an examination room as the boy talked, his head tipped toward the child as he listened. Aubrey hurried to follow. Enzo might not want her here, but maybe she could prove he needed her anyway.

The boy stopped talking to take a breath, and Enzo took advantage of the brief break in his recitation. "Sit up here." He swung the child up onto the exam table. "And speak English, please. I know your *papà* likes you to practice, and the nice nurse here is American. I'm going to take a look, okay?"

Benedetto nodded and sucked in a breath as Enzo leaned over to carefully roll back the boy's ripped pants. The skin beneath sported a wide, bleeding abrasion. It was a nasty one, to be sure, but at first glance it didn't look to be deep enough to require stitches. Not that his leg couldn't still be fractured in some way.

Time to show how competent and vital to this clinic she could be, right? Before Enzo booted her out the door for having *nice* sex with him?

Aubrey shoved down the anger and worry and stab of hurt still burning in her chest and opened a few drawers. Pulled out the supplies she'd need to stop the bleeding, washed her hands, and snapped on gloves. "That's an impressive scrape you've got there," she said to the child, smiling to relax him. And herself, if she was honest. She was glad Enzo had asked the boy to speak English, because she hadn't been able to understand a single word he'd said. "You're obviously a very tough guy. Is your bike okay?"

"No." The panicked look came back. "The wheel is bent, and the tire is flat. *Papà* is going to be angry."

"Oh, surely he won't be angry when he sees you were hurt," Aubrey said.

"Yes, he will." He licked his lips and turned his wide-eyed attention back to Enzo. "Nonna will be, too. I was supposed to be getting bread and *seppioline*, but I went to play with Lucio first. And then I fell off my bike near his house."

"Let's worry about that later." Enzo straightened to send the boy another wide smile he should patent to relax a patient. Or kindle some other reaction, depending on the circumstances and who he was sending it to. "First, we're going to stop the bleeding. Then we'll take an X-ray to look inside your leg. Luckily your *papà* signed papers allowing me to treat you the last time you were here."

"X-ray?" Tears sprang into the boy's eyes. "You think my leg might be broken?"

"I don't think so, no. But we'll check just to be sure." Enzo patted the child's shoulder and glanced at Aubrey as she cleaned the wound. "Looks like you have that under control. I'm going to get the portable X-ray."

"Yes, Doctor," she said, oh, so coolly and professionally, staring at the boy's leg because she didn't want to look at Enzo's wickedly handsome face. Be distracted by all his undeniable beauty, and get mad at him all over again.

He returned just minutes later, rolling the cart to the table. "Between the blood and rips, I'm afraid these pants are ruined, Benedetto. I'm going to cut them off so we don't have to slide them down over your leg."

"What? How will I get home without pants?"

"We keep spare clothes here for things just like this. No worries, okay? Nurse Aubrey here will find you something. Now, this won't hurt at all, and you'll get to see a picture of your bones afterward, which I think you'll like."

Enzo was so incredibly gentle as he lifted the child's leg to place the X-ray plate under his calf, her vexation with the man softened slightly. The steady stream of calm, amusing conversation he kept up with the boy actually had the child laughing, which was a dramatic difference from the scared tears of earlier. She had to grudgingly admit that the man had a wonderful bedside manner. In more ways than one, darn it.

Enzo straightened, and his dark eyes lifted to hers. "This will take just a short time to develop."

"I'll wait to dress the wound until you've taken a look. Then find those pants you talked about. Unless you want to wear the ones I brought, Benedetto? They have little flowers on them—quite pretty."

"Eww, no!" He obviously knew she was kidding, because he laughed, and the impish smile she'd so enjoyed on Enzo's face the first moment she'd met him returned as he winked at her.

"Benedetto wearing flowered pants to the fish market just might make the fishermen's day, don't you think, Aubrey?"

"I don't want to wear them, but I want to see you in them, Nurse Aubrey! I like flowers on girls' clothes."

A laugh left Enzo's annoyingly sexy lips, and the eyes that met hers held a hint of the amused look she remembered too well. "You're smart for being so young. Very, very smart. I'll be right back."

Hopefully this proved they could take care of patients and interact just fine, and the weight in Aubrey's chest lifted a little. She absolutely did not want to have to leave Venice before she'd learned more about how her mother's foundation could help restoration projects there. Before she'd barely had a chance to explore this unique city. Enzo Affini might be superficially charming and very irksome, but she was confident she could look past all that and think about him in a strictly professional way while she worked here.

She could and she would.

Aubrey chatted with the child until Enzo returned, and she quickly looked away from him, because every time she let her gaze run over his dress shirt and doctor coat she remembered the strong body, smooth, tanned skin, and soft dark hair on the muscular chest beneath it all. Which made her feel a little warm, and while she wanted to think it was her anger bubbling up again, she knew the ridiculous truth.

Mad at him and hurt by him and needing to keep her distance from him didn't seem to affect being *attracted* to him one bit. What in the world was wrong with her?

"Good news, Benedetto. No fracture." Enzo's voice warmed the whole sparse room. "So Nurse Aubrey is going to get you bandaged up while I go take a look at your bike. See if I can fix it so it's good as new. Is it outside?"

"Sì." The boy's eyes lit in surprised excitement. "Can you do that?"

"I'm going to give it a try. Aubrey, when you're done, please get a tube of topical antibiotic from the drawer for his *papà* to pick up later when he comes back for us to change the dressing. And will you look in the cupboard next to yours to see if there are any pants that would work for him?"

"Of course." She watched his tall frame leave the room, completely failing in her determination to not admire that beautiful dark hair and his broad shoulders and the elegant way he moved.

Ugh. She quickly turned back to Benedetto. Being sweet to this child and fixing his bike didn't erase the reality that the man had virtually accused her of hunting him down just moments ago. A Jekyll and Hyde type, to be sure.

When she had the boy's leg securely bandaged, she stood and smiled. "I'm going to look for those pants. Be right back."

The first cupboard had a neatly stacked pile of all kinds of clothes, but after fishing through them she couldn't find a single pair of pants. The one next to it had what looked like running shorts and a few T-shirts, and a lone pair of gray sweatpants. More searching proved there was nothing else around, so she took the sweatpants back to the exam room, dug into her purse for her sewing kit, and showed the child the pants. "This is the best I can do, I'm afraid. They're way too big for you, but I'm going to make them fit as best I can. Okay?"

"Okay." He eyed them doubtfully. "How can you make them fit? They are huge."

"Ah, I have many talents, young man. You just wait. Can you stand up without it hurting too much?"

She helped him from the table and held the pants up to his waist. They draped a good foot and a half onto the floor, and she made a pencil mark. Then she took scissors from the drawer, cut off the bottom half of the legs, then cut into the elastic waistband. Removing a big chunk of fabric, she then stitched it back together as the boy patiently watched.

"Eccoli!" she said, feeling pretty satisfied with her work and her ability to come up with a good Italian word to boot. "Step into them and see if they'll stay on you now."

Once he'd pulled them on, he stared down at the pants, then up at her with a big smile. "They are okay! I didn't think you could. Thank you very much."

"You're welcome. Here's that tube of antibiotic Dr. Affini wants put at the front desk for your dad or your *nonna* to pick up. Now, let's go see how he's doing with your bike."

She tried hard to ratchet back the way her heart squished as they stepped out to the *piazza*, trying to shore up her negative feelings about the man currently crouched on the stone pavement. His head was bent over the bicycle wheel as he used some kind of wrench on it. He'd taken off his lab coat, and his necktie was askew and tucked inside the buttons of his shirt. Midmorning sunshine gleamed in his hair, and his eyes were narrowed as he concentrated on his task.

"Can you fix it, Dr. Affini?" Benedetto sounded both worried and hopeful.

"Good…as…new. You're going to ride like the wind." One last turn of the wrench, then he stood to pump a little more air into the tire. Obviously pleased, he brushed his hands together, beaming a smile at the boy. "How's your leg feel?"

"Okay. Thank you so much. I'm going to get the things my *nonna* wanted, then go straight home."

"Here are the instructions for your *nonna* and *papà* on when to come back, and later, for changing the bandage again and using the antibiotic ointment." He pulled a folded paper from his pocket, and his eyes met Aubrey's. "You did put the ointment at the desk?"

"I gave it to Nora after we set him up with new pants."

"*Bene.* They—" He stopped short as he looked at the child's pants, then, after a long pause, laughed out loud.

"What?" she asked, bristling that he obviously thought her sewing job was amusing. Or bad. Or something. "There wasn't anything that would fit, so I made a bigger pair fit at least a little."

"I see that. They look very good on you, Benedetto. Very good." He reached to give the child a quick hug. "Now you go run your errands. Come back tomorrow to let us take another look and change the dressing, and ask your *nonna* or *papà* to call me before that if they have questions."

"Okay. I don't think Papà will be as mad now that my bike is fixed. Thank you again!"

Aubrey watched the boy mount the bike and ride it slowly and carefully away, and she smiled. "He's being very cautious now, I see."

"Not for long, I'm sure." Enzo's amused gaze met hers. "Good thing you made the pants fit so the legs wouldn't get caught in the chain and make him fall again."

"Yes, good thing. So why were you laughing at my sewing job?"

"I wasn't laughing at your sewing job. I was laughing because those are—were—my pants."

Her mouth fell open. "What? They were in the cupboard you told me to look in! With some shorts and T-shirts and…and…" The vision of the neatly folded shorts and manly T-shirts in that cupboard made her voice fade away. Why hadn't she realized those items were all the same size, when the ones in the other cupboard had been a total mishmash? Heat washed into her face. So much for showing she was indispensable around here. "I'm so sorry. Really sorry. I thought—"

"Aubrey." He pressed his fingertip to her lips. "It's fine. Sometimes I run when the clinic's slow, and I keep clothes here for that. Obviously, they served Benedetto well. Between you and me, his father is very old-school and can be hard on him when he makes mistakes. Not having to show up in bloody, torn pants with a broken bike is a good thing."

"What about his mother?"

"She died a few years ago."

Her heart squeezed for the little boy who had lost his mother far too soon. Having her own mother for twenty-seven years hadn't been nearly long enough. She looked into Enzo's eyes and could see they'd shadowed with sadness for the boy, too. Probably for the child's whole family, since he obviously knew them fairly well, and seeing how much he cared melted her heart. Just a little, though. "Poor little thing," she said softly. "It's good that you fixed his bike for him, then."

"And I thank you for making the pants work. We Venetians take care of our own."

Not being a Venetian, she knew he wasn't talking about her, but somehow it felt absurdly nice to be included in the thought. Which reminded her how much she wanted to stay here for the next few months, and how Enzo Affini had implied just a bit ago that he didn't want to work with her in the clinic at all.

"So." She squared her shoulders and looked him in the eye. "We were having an important conversation about my job and future here, and you need to know I'm not leaving."

"No?" His lips quirked at the same time that suspicious frown dipped between his eyes again. "And if the director of the clinic, who would be me, says you have to? That he'll find you employment somewhere else in Italy?"

"I've already worked two months in Rome. And I've come to Venice now because this is where I want to be. Didn't taking care of Benedetto prove we can work together just fine?"

"Aubrey, I cannot promise that I wouldn't allow myself to be seduced by you again."

Her mouth fell open. "I didn't seduce you! I believe it was you who seduced me. And I *can* promise that it won't happen again. I don't even find you attractive anymore." Which was kind of true. For good reason.

And yes, her nose was growing a little, but she'd stick with that half-truth if it killed her.

A slight smile softened the hard lines on his face. "That I know is a lie. Shall we agree that the seduction was on both sides? And that's the problem, because I can't have an affair with someone who works at the clinic."

"Listen. I know we only got together at first that night because you wanted to ask me questions about Shay." Knowing that hadn't kept her from jumping into bed with him, though, had it? "It was just a one-night thing. I have zero desire to…to co-seduce you again."

"And if I can't say the same thing?"

She wondered if he knew he spoke the words in the same low, sexy rumble he'd used when they'd kissed and made love, and she sucked in a breath as memories of all that shimmered between them. "Then that's your problem, not mine. Though you clearly didn't want to anyway, since you never called me in Rome."

Oh, hell. Did those words really fall out of her mouth? Implying she'd wanted him to, and wondered if he would, and hadn't liked that he hadn't? Lord, that was the last thing she'd wanted to admit.

"Aubrey. It wasn't—"

"Skip it." She held up her hand, desperate to stop him from giving her some lame excuse he didn't really mean. "We'll just have to figure out how to work together. I have no doubt we can act like mere acquaintances and pretend that night never happened."

"That would be extremely difficult. For me, at least."

"Uh-huh. And since we're going to have a professional relationship, please stop with that tone of voice and…and those kinds of comments."

"I thought you no longer find me attractive, so why is that a problem?"

The way her heart fluttered and her breath caught at his physical beauty and sexiness and utter male appeal, she knew it would be tough going to learn to be immune to it.

"It's not. Now, I'd appreciate it if you'd give me a tour of the facility, so I'll know where everything is when a patient arrives, Dr. Affini." She moved past him to the clinic door and paused there. "Shall we?"

CHAPTER TWO

ENZO STUDIED THE woman standing there by the door, looking expectantly at him. Coolly, her pretty chin tipped up as her eyes challenged him. Those eyes had seduced him the second he'd met her two months ago, at the same time he'd wondered what her story was, and her friend Shay's, too, who'd shown up in his brother's life pregnant.

He still had no idea if the two women had an agenda that included snagging two doctors who also happened to be princes, and whose problems with their inheritance had been well-documented in the press. He'd planned to just talk with Aubrey the night they'd spent together, but talking and laughing had led to kissing, then touching, which had led to other, more than pleasurable and memorable things he hadn't been able to stop thinking about ever since.

But getting involved with a woman—a woman he wasn't sure he could trust—at the same time he was trying to save his heritage had seemed like a bad idea.

And now here she was, in his clinic, in all her beautiful glory. *Stunned* would be the only word that could describe how he'd felt when he'd seen her standing there, looking sexier than anyone should be able to look in a nurse's uniform. How coincidental was it that she'd just happened to be signed up for employment there?

Too coincidental, as far as he was concerned.

"You working somewhere else makes more sense. I'll make a few phone calls to the hospital and the other clinic. I can't promise to find you a position there but can also look at Verona or Padua for temporary nursing opportunities."

"This is ridiculous." She folded her arms across her chest and stared him down with such laser intensity, a lesser man might have caved right then and there. "You need a nurse here, obviously, or I wouldn't have been hired. I want the job, I'm qualified for the job, and I'm here now ready to work. Did I do well helping with Benedetto?"

"Yes. But that's irrelevant to the problem."

"Are you saying that you're so chauvinistic and weak around women that you wouldn't be able to behave professionally around me?"

"What? Of course not." He couldn't decide whether to laugh, or be irritated, or both. And admit that their night together had happened because he'd been unable to resist being with her then, so yeah, maybe he was weak. "You're pretty sassy for a woman who wants her boss to keep her around."

"And you're pretty insulting, implying I hunted you down in coming to work here." She stepped closer and poked her finger into his chest, her eyes flashing blue-gray fire. "I can show you the letter from the UWWHA confirming my employment here, which is dated long before we met. And I'm not going to let a mistake from two months ago keep me from having this job now. So you're stuck with me, and I'm stuck with you."

He grasped her hand in his, planning to move her

finger from his sternum, but found himself curling it against his chest instead. "A mistake, was it? You didn't seem to think so that night."

"That night, I didn't know what I know now." She yanked her hand from his. "And neither did you. So we act like adults and work together like adults. Professional relationship, pure and simple. Now, let's get on with you showing me around here, before more patients show up."

He felt his lips curve, despite knowing that if he agreed to keep her here, it might well be a disaster waiting to happen. He'd been attracted to her smarts and beauty and sense of humor before. Add to that her spunk and tough attitude?

Irresistible.

Dio. He sighed and stepped around her to open the door. "I have a bad feeling the next few months are going to challenge me at a time I have too many challenges already," he said. "Lead on, Aubrey Henderson. I'll show you the ropes if you promise not to hang me with them."

"I never make promises I'm not sure I can keep," she said in the sweetest of tones, smiling up at him, her eyes filled with victory, flashes of exasperation, and a touch of the teasing look he'd fallen for before. "But I'll do my best, Dr. Affini. That I can promise."

Several days working at the clinic hadn't dimmed Aubrey's enthusiasm for the job, it had made her even more excited about it. Seeing the clinic sign up ahead had her stepping up her pace the same way it had the first day she was there. She was so glad she'd embarked on this adventure, in spite of Enzo Affini's insulting attitude and the uncomfortable tension between them.

Why in the world had she decided to sleep with him that first night she'd met him? What a mistake that had turned out to be! It was so obvious now that she never should have gotten involved with him, especially since she'd known all along that the main reason he'd offered to show her around Venice was because he'd wanted to pick her brain about Shay.

Except she just hadn't been able to resist, fool that she was.

Now, though, she was going to concentrate on work and only work. Thank goodness Enzo hadn't made her go somewhere else, since taking care of mostly tourists was so interesting. In some ways completely different than what she'd done back at home, and in other ways it was exactly the same. And the locals she'd seen so far in the clinic had been a fascinating mix of characters, from charming and sweet to gruff to downright cranky. Though she supposed that would describe all the people in the world—when it came down to it, everyone was much more alike than they were different, weren't they?

She changed into her crisp white dress and glanced in the locker-room mirror. Caught herself thinking about how surprisingly well it fit and how flattering it was and how Enzo just might think so, too, and why did even her simple uniform make her think about the man? Pathetic. What was wrong with her that she still caught herself feeling doe-eyed over a guy who'd wondered if she was trying to trap him or something?

Cool, professional relationship only. No fighting or kissing allowed. They'd done pretty well with that the past couple days. Surely after a few more it would feel as if their time together before had never happened?

Yeah, right. Whenever they were alone in a room,

the low sizzle humming between them was very hard to ignore.

Nora poked her head into the locker room. "I have a British couple here to see the doctor. A Mr. and Mrs. Conway. You want to get started with them first?"

"Of course." She ushered the middle-aged couple to one of the exam rooms. "Hello, I'm Aubrey Henderson, the nurse on staff today. Can you tell me what you're here for?"

"I've been pecked by a bird," the woman exclaimed. "By an awful dirty bird, and it hurts!"

"All right. Let's have a look." Aubrey was about to shut the door for privacy when Enzo appeared, filling the doorway with his big, irritating, masculine presence.

"Mind if I stay?" he asked. His face was impassive, but she could see a glint of amusement in the depths of his dark eyes at the woman's dramatic statement. "I need to evaluate how our American nurse is doing."

"Of course," Aubrey said before the patient could answer. And was that what he really wanted, or was he there to just rattle her again, knowing this was probably not a serious situation? "This is Dr. Affini."

"I'd like to see what the doctor thinks about this!" the woman exclaimed. "I've probably got some disgusting disease."

"Mrs. Conway, why don't you sit on the table here and show me where it hurts? Sir, you can sit in one of these chairs."

"Right on the top of my head, that's where it hurts! Bleeding, too." She held up a tissue with some specks of blood on it, waving it first at Aubrey, then Enzo. "What if I've been exposed to some terrible bird infection?"

Aubrey donned gloves and gently pushed the woman's hair aside to find a small, reddened indentation. "I can see this probably hurts. But I don't think it's too serious. Let me get some antiseptic to clean it with."

"Not too serious? You'll change your mind when I tell you the story." The woman sat straighter and waved her hands. "I'm minding my own business on a park bench in that big main square where the basilica is. Pigeons were walking around, and I pulled a little treat from my purse to give to one. Then this great, giant black bird dive-bombs me from the sky and grabs the treat from the pigeon!"

Aubrey pulled the cotton and antiseptic from the cupboard, and, when she turned, saw Enzo's eyes dancing and his lips obviously working to not smile at the dramatic recitation. Feeling her own mouth dangerously quiver, she quickly turned back to her patient to keep from looking at him. "And then? How did your head get pecked?"

"So I pull another treat from my purse, and the nasty black bird takes it, drops it, then scares me to death when he suddenly flies up, flapping his great wings in my face as he does. Lands there, right on my head! I shrieked, of course, and jumped up, and it pecked me. Hard! Why, I'm lucky it wasn't my eye he put out."

Aubrey glanced at Enzo. Fatal mistake, as his expression clearly showed he wanted to laugh, and a chuckle bubbled in her own chest when she saw how he was struggling.

Turn away. Do. Not. Look. At. Him.

She quickly turned to the woman's husband, who appeared more weary than worried. "Did you see what kind of bird it was?"

"Some black bird. Don't know what kind, I'm not a birdman. Especially Italian birds. Medium sized. Yellow beak, I think." He turned to his wife. "You brought it on yourself, you know. Who gives a pigeon mints to eat? The bird that pecked you was probably so shocked and ticked off, it felt it had a right to attack."

"Well, I never!" The woman looked beyond insulted as she flung her hand toward her husband. "And this is the kind of support I get after giving him thirty years of my life!"

Oh, Lord. Aubrey held her breath. Dang it, she would have been fine if not for Enzo's unholy grin. She would.

"I…I think I've cleaned it well, Mrs. Conway," she said.

"What do you think, Doctor? Don't you think I may get some nasty infection or disease? A filthy bird in a filthy square full of filthy people is bound to have given me something awful. Don't I need an antibiotic or something?"

Aubrey was impressed at how carefully he looked at the tiny wound, since he knew as well as she did that it was nothing. "Nurse Henderson has done a good job of cleaning it, Mrs. Conway. I'm sure you'll be fine, but if you have any problems with it, be sure to stop back and we'll take another look."

"We're leaving tomorrow anyway. Thank heavens for that. And what a waste of time to come here for help." Looking miffed and completely unsatisfied, she slid off the table, and Aubrey led her back out to the lobby, making sure to not look at Enzo as they passed. The woman's parting words before she walked out the door had Aubrey holding her breath hard again when she went back to the room to be sure it was clean for the next patient.

Enzo appeared again in the doorway. "Ah, she's the kind of patient that makes this job worthwhile. A pick-me-up from the more serious stuff we deal with, don't you think?"

Aubrey couldn't hold it in another second, and she pressed her hands against her mouth to subdue the laugh that spilled out. "That's for sure. You know what she said when she left?"

He folded his arms across his chest. "What?"

"She said, 'What does that doctor know about birds? He's obviously a quack.'"

His sexy laughter joined hers, and she quickly pulled him into the room and shut the door behind them. "Shh! They might have come back for something! What if they hear us?"

"Hear us what?"

She looked up into his eyes, still filled with mirth, but something else, too. That dangerous glint that made her heart flutter and her skin tingle.

She drew in a deep breath. "What is it with you? One minute you're unpleasant, and the next you're throwing out sexual innuendos. Didn't we agree we had to be professional with one another? I think I'm holding up my end here."

"I also said I didn't think we should work together because I knew I'd have problems with that."

Oh, my gosh. Why did he keep saying things he shouldn't in that deep, rumbly voice that sent a warm flush across her skin, reminding her of their first day and night together?

"Enzo." After his name, words seemed to dry up on her tongue and she just stared at him.

"Yes?" He took a step closer. He smelled wonderful, and his body heat seemed to envelop her. He obviously knew what unwelcome thoughts had suddenly crowded her brain, because his gaze settled on her lips.

Which parted involuntarily, and her own small movement toward him that brought her nearly against his chest was completely involuntary, too, and when his arms wrapped around her and his head lowered toward hers all protest and common sense left her mind as her eyes drifted closed in breathless anticipation.

"Dr. Affini? Aubrey?"

Her eyes snapped open to see his, dark and dangerous and full of heat, staring right back at her. Time seemed to halt for several heartbeats until they both managed to gather their wits at the same time. She stepped back as he let her go, his chest lifting in a deep breath.

"Saved by Nora." He stared at her for one more second before turning to open the door.

She watched him disappear into the hallway, and the air she'd been holding in her lungs whooshed out. She was in so much trouble here. No matter how many times she remembered his suspicions, no matter how often she reminded herself they had to keep a professional distance, she just kept forgetting.

And it clearly wasn't her imagination that he kept forgetting, too.

CHAPTER THREE

ENZO WAS MORE than glad the Restore Venice Association meeting was about to start. That people were finally wandering off to find seats instead of asking him endless questions about the house that was no longer his, talking about how it was going to be ruined if he didn't get it back, and grilling him on what he was going to do to save it.

He sat toward the back of the room, resisting the urge to slouch in his seat to become semi-invisible. And yes, that probably made him a coward. But since he had no real answers yet, having endless conversations about the house that represented the past seven hundred years of his mother's family history, and his own, and how he had to keep it from going under the wrecking ball, made his gut churn.

He pulled the program from the pocket of his jacket and just as he was about to look at the meeting schedule, a flash of something bright blue or green in the aisle near him caught his eye. He looked up to see that the flash of color was a dress on what looked to be a very attractive body, at least from the back. The fabric skimmed the curves of a sexy feminine derriere that swayed slightly as she walked.

Who was she? He knew most of the people who attended these meetings and definitely would have re-membered that body. The woman turned her head to smile at the person standing to let her sit next to him, and Enzo's lungs froze in his chest.

Aubrey.

What the hell was she doing here?

Her silky golden-brown hair skimmed her cheek as she sat, and a slender hand shoved it behind one ear as she dug into her purse for something, coming up with the same program he held in his hand.

He and Aubrey had managed to work together with-out fighting, or, worse, kissing, if he didn't count that one near miss yesterday. But now the suspicions about her that had stayed on a low simmer—along with the sexual attraction between them—came bubbling into full boil. First she showed up at his clinic to work, and now she'd decided to come to an art and architecture meeting attended only by Venetians and academics from universities in other countries?

Tourists never came. Neither did many Italians from other areas, because they had their own preservation concerns. And yet here she was, and how was he to be-lieve it was about anything other than her ingratiating herself into his life even more? Doubtless knowing all about his family's problems and the house he loved that she happened to be currently living in.

Did she know he'd owned it before and had rented it out to the UWWHA as he'd planned its renovation? Know that his father had sold it out from under him, and it was about to be resold at a profit? Was renting it from the UWWHA part of her plan somehow?

Enzo's blood ran cold. If Aubrey was trying to charmingly, spunkily wiggle her way into his life, did that mean Shay had done the same thing with his brother? Was there any way this could be another big coincidence?

Seemed incredibly unlikely, but suspicion without proof just festered, and Enzo had enough to worry about right then. So the only solution was to be brutally frank with Aubrey. To ask her some hard questions, and hopefully be able to figure out if she was being honest with him or not. Which might be very difficult, considering he'd had to consciously fight being attracted to her seeming sweetness and smarts and beauty every hour they'd worked together the past few days, but he had to give it a try.

Barely paying attention to the speakers and conversation, Enzo sat through the first half of the meeting trying to decide if he should tackle Aubrey during the break, or wait until it was over. Feeling on edge, he was still pondering that question during the break when the decision was made for him.

A flash of color had him turning from the coffee stand in the front hallway to see her marching right up to him, a militant expression on her beautiful face.

"Just so you know, I had no idea you'd be here today."

"No?" The woman must be a mind reader. "Then why are you here?"

"Because I'm interested in Venice's future. In the restoration of its buildings and artwork."

"So you know nothing about my current situation." He said it mockingly, and she frowned at his tone.

"What situation? Unless you're referring to having to work with me, which you've made more than clear is something you'd rather not do."

"I've seen you're a woman who says what she thinks. So I'm just going to come right out and tell you what I'm thinking. Which is that it's really bizarre that Shay shows up announcing she's pregnant with Dante's baby, and within days she's married to my brother. Then you and I get together, and two months later you magically show up at my clinic to work." He set his coffee down and folded his arms across his chest. "And now you claim to have an interest in the restoration of Venice's buildings, which…shockingly…is my passion, too."

She stared at him, an even deeper frown creasing her brow. "I'm not following."

"Then let me be clearer." He stepped closer, hoping to intimidate her and make her come clean. "What I'm saying is that I can't help but wonder if you and Shay researched Dante and me, and decided two doctor princes would be a nice catch, then figured out how to weasel your way into our lives."

"What?" Her mouth fell open in a gasp. "You have an ego the size of Mount Vesuvius, you know that? I'm not even going to dignify that accusation with an answer. You can believe what you want to believe. But if you think insulting me is going to get me to leave the clinic, you've got another think coming. I'm staying until my contract is over, so just deal with it. And you're going to feel pretty ridiculous when you realize your fantasies of me wanting to trap you into something were all in your own small mind."

She spun away and stalked off, and he stood there long seconds just watching that sexy behind of hers until she went through the doorway to the meeting room again.

He let out a long breath. Maybe his strategy had backfired this time. But if she and Shay weren't what they seemed, he had to believe that, sooner or later, one of them would tip their hand and the truth would come out.

The president of the association spoke in English as he opened the second half of the meeting. The back of Enzo's brain absently noted that there must be university guests from other countries for this portion of the presentation and discussion. Then his focus snapped big-time to the speaker when the next words out of the man's mouth were a name.

Aubrey Henderson.

What the...? He sat up straighter to watch her stand and make her way to the lectern, noticing that plenty of the men in the room seemed to be admiring her swaying walk as much as he had been earlier. Until he'd been shocked to see whose enticing body was wearing that dress.

"Two years ago, Ms. Henderson graciously adopted the renovation of the large fresco depicting angels and warriors in one of the churches at San Sebastiano. The twenty-five thousand dollars she donated have brought this art treasure back to life, and we encourage all of you to visit and admire it. In recognition of this gift, we present this plaque to show our appreciation."

Applause greeted Aubrey as she accepted the plaque, then stood with the president as photos were snapped. If he'd been surprised before, this time Enzo could barely wrap his brain around what he was witnessing.

Aubrey had donated money to a restoration project in Venice? Two years ago? And not just a little money, but a very nice chunk—enough to completely pay for that project, which was one of so many beautiful old masterpieces in Venice that needed repairs.

Her smile seemed to light the whole room as she leaned toward the microphone, holding the plaque to her breasts. "Thank you. I appreciate this recognition, but it was our privilege to be able to adopt the fresco project. My late mother, Lydia Henderson, lived her life working to save old buildings from being demolished instead of renovated. She led numerous architectural review boards in Massachusetts and elsewhere in New England. During her illness, we decided to donate to this project because she was fascinated with the history of Venice and had always been drawn to images of angels and warriors. She often said that all of us had a chance to be both in our lives. I'm proud to say that she truly was an angel and a warrior, and I hope to live my life at least a little bit like she did."

Even from the back of the room, Enzo could see her blinking back tears as she said one more thank you, then headed back to her seat. It seemed she'd taken only a few steps before her gaze lifted to his. Her eyes narrowed and her graceful gait seemed to falter for a moment before she turned her attention to finding her seat again.

Dio. What was he supposed to think now?

He stared at the back of her silky head and had no idea of the answer to that question. But one thing he did know?

He owed her an apology.

Obviously, she had good reason to be at the meeting that had nothing to do with him, and, yeah, she'd been right. He did feel ridiculous that he'd assumed otherwise.

He huffed out a breath, not wanting to have to give her that *mea culpa*, but knew he had no choice. The meeting seemed to drag on forever, his eyes on the back of her head instead of the speaker for most of it. Finally, the crowd stood and he jostled his way through the throng until he was able to catch her just as she was walking out the door.

"Aubrey. Wait. I need to talk to you."

She stared straight ahead across the *piazza*, walking faster. "You've already said plenty, Dr. Affini."

"I want to apologize."

"For what?" She finally turned to look at him, and if the daggers she was sending from her furious gaze had been real, he'd be lying dead on the pavement. "Accusing me of showing up at your clinic to trap you? Of stalking you at the architecture meeting? Of faking an interest in restoration? You overestimate yourself."

"I know. And I'm sorry. I am. Truly."

"Hmmph." The sound she made wasn't exactly an acceptance of his apology, but at least she slowed down a little, instead of surging through the crowd as if she were in a sprint race.

He reached for her arm to slow her even more and was glad but a little surprised that she didn't yank it loose. "Aubrey. Things are…difficult right now. Which maybe is making me think and act in a way I shouldn't."

"Now, isn't that an understatement."

"So can we put this behind us?" He tugged on her arm to force her to look at him. He wanted to see her soften and forgive him, and why that felt so important, he had no idea, since he still wasn't sure what to think about her.

"I'll do my best." She finally turned to him, and the blaze in her eyes had thankfully cooled. "But only because I love being here and enjoy working at the clinic. And I'm not going to let you ruin either one of those things for me."

This time, she did pull her arm loose, and without another word she took off at a fast pace again. He slowed and decided to let her go. Time to think up a new strategy on how to handle beautiful and mysterious Aubrey Henderson.

* * *

"Stop being negative. We still have time," Enzo said to his accountant and fellow preservationist, Leonardo. Not sure if he was trying to convince Leonardo or himself, he paced the upper floor of the one home he had left in his possession in Venice, staring unseeingly at the finely woven antique carpet covering the *terrazzo* floor. "I'm working on raising more money for the purchase and have also liquidated some assets, which you'll see transferred to the account in a few days. Almost all our vineyards had a good harvest, with more grapes sold this year to other wineries than last, and our own vintages are selling well. Dante gave me the numbers a few days ago. It's coming together."

At least, he hoped it was. His gut tightened at how much money he still needed to buy back the childhood home he loved, but he was determined to make it happen.

"But the new owner told me he expected the sale to the hotel chain to go through within the next three weeks," Leonardo said.

"Which gives us two and a half to beat them to it."

"I was looking through all the photos of the house you gave me. Whether the sale goes through or not, I'll need more of the exterior, the internal courtyard, and the bedrooms to provide to the commission proactively, so they'll agree to a six-month delay of the interior demolition the hotel is planning. Buy us some time to convince the commission to refuse to allow it. If the sale ends up going through to the hotel, maybe they'd end up selling it back to you if they can't remodel it the way they want to. So can you get those for me?"

"Yes." Or at least, he hoped he could. He might not be the one who owned and rented the property to the UWWHA anymore, but he did know a certain beautiful, questionable tenant living there. If she wasn't so angry she refused to talk to him anymore, let alone allow him in the house. "I'll get them to you as soon as possible. *Arrivederci*."

Familiar burning anger swelled in Enzo's chest as he hung up, but he fought it down. Holding close the bitterness and fury he felt was a distraction he couldn't afford. Despising his father and his selfish actions didn't change a damn thing.

No, Enzo just had to work harder and outbid the hotel chain. That was all there was to it.

Thinking of the house had his thoughts turning to Aubrey again. He could picture her sleeping in one of the run-down but still beautiful bedrooms, her shining hair spread across the pillow. Curled up reading a book in a chair in front of one of the massive stone fireplaces. Wandering the halls admiring the amazing rooms and artwork and antiquities.

He dropped into a chair to stare out over the Grand Canal. *Confused* was probably the best word to describe how he felt about her. Along with suspicious and extremely attracted.

Were she and Dante's lover—no, wife, now—two women with an agenda? So many things pointed to *yes, maybe*. Then again, there was something so appealing, so seemingly genuine about Aubrey, something that drew him to her in a way that he couldn't quite remember happening with another woman. He'd seen it when she'd cared for Benedetto, then fixed up Enzo's pants for the child, which made him chuckle all over again. And a number of other times as they'd taken care of patients together.

Yet there were all those coincidences that made it hard to believe she was for real.

So where did that leave him?

The same place he'd always been. Still planning to save his inheritance here and in Arezzo a different way. Through hard work. Still planning to never marry, regardless of what that meant to the future of the properties that should be his.

Except Aubrey didn't know that.

Feeling oddly unsettled, he decided to give Dante a call. Between his brother's new wife and his always busy job as a trauma surgeon, Enzo hadn't seen the man in weeks. He hoped that meant everything was reasonably fine, but he wanted to hear that for himself. With any luck he'd be available to talk, and not in the middle of surgery, and Enzo was glad Dante picked up after only two rings.

"To what do I owe the honor of hearing from my brother, since you haven't called me for weeks?" Dante said in his ear.

"The phone works both ways, you know. I figured you were busy with Shay and didn't want to bother you."

"You've been bothering me your whole life, so why change things now?"

"Point taken." The smile in his brother's voice made Enzo smile, too. "How's work?"

"Busy. So busy that we haven't been able to get back to Arezzo for a while, but we plan to soon. How about you?"

Hearing his brother say "we" when it came to his life and travels sounded so strange, but, with a baby on the way, he'd be saying that for the rest of his life, wouldn't he? Something everyone would have to get used to. "Busy, too. Always is during the heavy tourist season, as you know. How's Shay? Feeling all right?"

"She's well. Getting more round, but feeling good."

Why the conversation felt so awkward to him, Enzo wasn't sure, but he sensed that his brother wasn't feeling awkward at all. He sounded happy, maybe? Excited? Enzo hoped so, and also hoped his brother's heart wasn't going to get mashed up over all of it. "Glad to hear it. Well, I just wanted—"

"What's the situation with the house?" his brother interrupted. "Last time we talked you were having trouble raising enough funds."

"Still working on it." No point in adding to his brother's concerns, since they'd already collaborated to borrow as much as possible against their wineries.

"I heard that Aubrey Henderson is back in Venice with the UWWHA and living at your house now."

"It's not my house anymore, remember?"

"It will always be your house." Dante's voice was fierce. "I'm still exploring a few other possibilities for raising money, and I know you're going to find some way to buy it back. No one is as determined as you when you set a goal for yourself."

"Thanks. And I am determined." Somehow, his brother's vote of confidence eased the tightness in his chest a little, even if they were just words and not money in the bank.

"So how's it going with Aubrey working at the clinic, or shouldn't I ask?"

"How did you hear about that?"

"You know how women like to talk," his brother said drily. "I heard it from Shay. But she didn't have to tell me you went out with Aubrey. I had a gut feeling you'd end up in bed with her when you told me you were going to introduce yourself to ask questions about Shay. Despite my telling you I knew the child was mine."

His brother's voice was chiding, but he didn't sound

annoyed with him anymore. But who wouldn't have wanted to find out more about the woman his brother wanted to marry? "Maybe your gut feeling was just indigestion."

"Or not. Aubrey's a beautiful, smart woman and I knew you wouldn't be able to resist. And neither would she. If there's one thing the Affini men are good at, it's charming women, right?"

"I hope we have more going for us than that, since it's one of the many things about our father that we both despise."

"Yeah." Dante's joking tone disappeared. "Listen, I just got a surgery consult. Thanks for calling, and I'll talk to you soon."

Enzo stood to shove his phone in his pocket, sling his camera around his neck, and grab the keys to his boat. He jogged down the curved stone staircase of one of the several homes that had been in the Affini royal family for centuries.

It struck him that the way to find answers to his questions about Aubrey seemed obvious. What was that old saying? Keep your friends close and your enemies closer? He had no idea if Aubrey was friend or foe, but keeping his distance from her wasn't the answer, since he couldn't feel good about making her leave the clinic and find a job somewhere else, especially now that her wanting to be in Venice might be partly because of her late mother. He understood that kind of loss, and if staying here helped Aubrey heal a little, she should have that chance.

And hopefully, spending time with her both at work and socially would eventually tell him the truth.

If he could keep his damned libido out of the picture, that was. Keeping the enemy close was one thing.

Sleeping with the enemy? That was something he was sure never ended well.

It was handy that he was the one who drew up the clinic work calendar. That allowed him to be sure to have her time off scheduled for when he wanted it to be, and the thought made him smile for reasons he shouldn't be smiling. Before he started the motor to his boat, he pulled out his phone again. The sound of her answering with a cheerful hello on the other end of the line made him smile even more, and he shook his head at himself. Hadn't he just reminded himself moments ago that he had to keep an emotional distance from her?

If just the sound of her voice made him smile, that wasn't going to be easy. Though he had a feeling that smile would go away quickly when she learned it was him calling.

"Aubrey, it's Enzo. I was wondering if by chance you were at the house you're renting. I need to get inside to take a few photos."

CHAPTER FOUR

"TAKE A FEW PHOTOS?" Aubrey's voice in his ear sounded beyond surprised. "What do you mean?"

"I'll explain when I see you. If you're available?"

"Why should I be? Oh, wait, it's because I'm trying to snag a prince doctor for another notch on my bedpost."

"That's not exactly what I said."

"That's right. It actually was that I'm trying to *weasel* my way into your life. Because I'm cunning and deceitful and…and squirmy."

"But you're a beautiful squirmy weasel." He couldn't help it, something about her outrage made him want to tease her even more, though he could hardly blame her for being angry about all he'd said. "If I apologize again, will you let me take the photos?"

"I'll consider it, if it's a good apology and you tell me why you need the photos."

"I apologize for being suspicious of you and your motives." He wouldn't share that he still was. "And I'll tell you when I get there."

"Well, I'm not there right now. I just finished lunch and am outside the restaurant."

"Where?"

"I don't know, exactly. I'm a little lost, to be honest."

He could picture her face scrunched up in thought the way it did at the clinic sometimes. "What's the name of the restaurant?"

"It's called…um…Trattoria da Agnolo. It's off some *piazza*, a little way from a small canal."

He had to chuckle at her description. "Everything is just a little way from a small canal in Venice, or off some *piazza*, but I know where you are. Walk back to the canal. I'll pick you up and drive you back to the house."

"Drive? What do you mean?"

"Drive in Venice means by boat. I thought you said you'd done your homework?"

"If you want me to let you in the house, you'd better be extra, super nice, Dr. Affini, to make up for being so nasty to me."

"I'm not going to be nasty anymore. But I don't have to be super nice, either, because your employment at the clinic is in my hands, remember?"

"And you might remember that the UWWHA has very strict rules about the conduct of the health centers that employ their nurses. They don't like doctors who insult us and try to lord it over us."

Her words pulled a chuckle from his chest that he couldn't hold back. The woman was such an attractive mix of smart and spunky, and he wondered if she knew it. If all that was designed to sucker unsuspecting men into falling for her before she snagged them in her net, or if she really was as wonderful as she seemed. "I'll be there in five minutes to pick you up."

"No, that's all right. I can find my way back to the house. I'm pretty sure it's not too far. I'll just meet you there."

"I'm happy to—"

"No," she interrupted, and her voice sounded nearly panicky. Surely she didn't think he'd fire her if they spent time together that wasn't strictly professional? Then again, he'd said some pretty unpleasant things, so he couldn't exactly blame her for wanting to keep her distance.

He maneuvered his boat through the canal, and as he approached the house he looked for her. Even with a number of people walking on both sides of the canal in front of his house—correction, *formerly* his house—he spotted Aubrey instantly. The golden highlights in her shiny brown hair caught the early-afternoon sunshine, and her gorgeous body wore a sundress that stopped a few inches above her knees, showing off her shapely legs. The sound of his motor must have caught her attention, because she turned, then instantly sent him a half scowl. The boat skimmed to a stop in front of her, and he stood to grab a wooden post to steady the boat and tie it.

"Ciao. Thanks for letting me come by," he said as he climbed onto the walkway to stand next to her.

"I'm still mad at you. But I confess I'm curious why you want to take photos here. Do you have some connection to this house?"

He looked down at her, wondering how much he should share. How much she might already know. Since the sad and infuriating truth was public knowledge at this point, he didn't see a reason to try to keep it a secret.

"I do. I'll tell you about it as I take the photos."

Aubrey concentrated on carefully putting the old, intricately forged key into the lock and turning it this way and that, her tongue cutely poking out of the side of her mouth as she did. It had been tricky to manage for as long as Enzo could remember, and he couldn't help but tease her about it.

"For a woman so good at creating a small pair of pants from a large one, you seem to be having some mechanical difficulties."

"It's hard to open. I swear I've stood out here five minutes every time—why doesn't whoever rents this house to the UWWHA put on a new knob and lock?"

"It's important to keep the original hardware and historic charm when possible. I thought you said you were a preservationist."

"I am. And you're right." She huffed out a frustrated breath. "I need to have the kind of relaxed attitude the ancient Venetians had, instead of my twentieth-century hurry-up impatience, don't I?"

"Yes." He reached around her, his arm skimming against her warm skin, to take the key from her hand. He inserted it again, and, with a quick turn to the left, the lock clicked and the door swung open.

She stared up at him. "How did you do that?"

"Magic fingers." He wiggled them at her, and she frowned.

"Huh. I don't want to think about the various times you use that line. And what you might be referring to."

"What do you think I might be referring to?" They stepped inside the large entryway, wide sunbeams striping the *terrazzo* floor from every west-facing window. He knew exactly what her words made him think of, and he found himself leaning close to her. A little test to see if she'd take it as an opportunity to start flirting with him again. "Are you remembering our night together?"

"No." Pink tinged her skin. "I just figured a guy like you enjoys making sexual innuendoes to either make women feel uncomfortable, or to think bad thoughts."

"And which are you experiencing at the moment?"

With her hands on her hips, she took a quick step left and frowned up at him. "Listen. You can't be all nasty and accuse me of stalking you, then the next day come on to me. We agreed that if we're going to work together, we need to keep our distance. Treat one another professionally. So tell me why you want to take photos of this place, and how you're connected to it."

He didn't want to talk about the dire situation he faced, but he might be able to tell if she already knew. "Do you know that this place is close to being sold to a large hotel chain? Afterward to be gutted of everything historic except its exterior and turned into a modern hotel?"

"What? That's terrible!" The surprised dismay on her face seemed real. "How can that be allowed?"

"We live in a democracy, and, while we have architectural rules in place, the economics of Venice are a worrying reality. More and more tourists, fewer residents. Many of us are trying to reverse that to some degree, but it's a complicated and difficult task. A lot of houses are now empty, some even slated for demolition. The cost is great to restore them, and when you do you must have someone who can afford to live there."

"I saw in the meeting that there's an architectural review board that a hotel chain or whoever has to go through for permission to tear up a house like this one. It's so incredibly beautiful, I can't imagine it."

His heart warmed at her words, even as he wondered again if she already knew all the truth about it. "It's in great disrepair, as I'm sure you've seen. At times, even some of the tenants working with the UWWHA have complained about the bathrooms, the broken flooring, the peeling frescoes."

"Then they're just stupid," Aubrey said hotly. "If they can't see beyond superficial things like that to love and adore the amazing handwork of the tiling and *terrazzo* and artwork, the incredible design, the awe-inspiring history of a place like this, they should go work somewhere like the US, where a house just eighty years old is considered historic. Every time I walk in this house, I love it more."

"A woman after my own heart," he heard himself murmur. Then mentally stepped back. Distance, remember? *She may not be who she seems.*

The eyes looking up at him were wide and worried. "So, you said you have a connection to this house? Do you think you'll be able to stop the hotel from gutting it?"

"I'm doing everything I can to prevent them from buying it. Getting it into the hands of someone who will renovate and preserve it the way it deserves to be. Who will live in it and love it for the rest of their life."

"Do you have someone in mind? Someone who wants to buy it?"

"Yes. I do." He looked down at her seemingly earnest face. "That someone is me."

Aubrey blinked up at Enzo in shock. "You're trying to buy this house? But what about the house you live in now? Are you hoping to renovate it, then resell it?"

"No." She watched him move around the spectacular room, absently picking up a vase here and a decorative plate there, which Aubrey had been surprised to see lying around. Surely a few of the tenants might have had sticky fingers, unable to resist taking home an antique "souvenir."

"Then what?"

He turned to look at her, his expression deeply serious. Even pained. "This home has been in my late mother's family since the portal was built in the fourteenth century. The second and third floors were added in the fifteenth century, and the top floor, always my favorite as a child, was built in 1756."

Surprise left her staring for a long moment. "So you visited family here as a child?"

"I lived here as a child. Grew up in this house from nearly the day I was born. Of all the properties my family has owned, this one means the most to me. My father kept mistresses in a few of the homes belonging to his side of the family. Always claimed it was his right to do with his own properties as he pleased. And he continues to prove he believes that today, selling away what rightfully should belong to Dante and to me, having been held in trust for us. Except my father has control of that trust."

The bitterness in his tone was unmistakable. "This was one of the houses he sold out from under you and your brother." She didn't say it as a question, because the truth of that was obvious, and her chest filled with a mix of emotions. She wasn't sure what they all were, but she knew for certain the main one was anger. A different anger than she'd felt toward Enzo when he'd been so accusatory at the architectural meeting.

This anger was on behalf of a man who had lost the home he obviously loved. Fury that the buyers didn't care at all about it, ready to pass it on to a hotel chain that couldn't care less about destroying its history, wanting only to transform it into a modern, money-making hotel. Disgust and pain swept through her. Sympathy for both men that their father was as selfish, coldhearted, and uncaring about his sons as her own had proven to feel toward her.

"Yes." Intense dark eyes met hers again.

"But if it was your mother's, how did your father have control of it?"

"When they married, she signed over her property to him. I never asked her why, if it was just expected, or if he insisted. I didn't realize what could happen until she was gone, and it was too late. Now I'm doing all I can to get it back."

"I'm glad, then, that I decided to look past your meanness yesterday." She said it to lighten the weight in her chest, at the same time reminding him she hadn't forgotten about it. And that she expected him to be nicer from now on. "What do you need pictures of?"

"I need better ones of the outside, but will do that last, because any changes to the exterior are regulated much more than the interiors are. And, Aubrey?" His serious dark eyes met hers. "I am sorry about yesterday. I should have kept my mouth shut and not let my worries push me to say things I shouldn't. But I need to look after my brother, you know? We've both had our share of women pretending to be attracted to us just because of our titles and profession. Forgive me?"

She found it hard to believe any woman would have to pretend to be attracted to either of them, but she wasn't about to say so. "Yes. So long as it doesn't happen again."

"Thank you." A real smile touched his eyes. "Okay with you if I go to the bedrooms and baths? Then I want to take pictures of the top floor."

"This way." She started to walk, then stopped to shake her head at herself. "Wait. You know this house a lot better than I do. Lead on, Dr. Affini."

She followed him up the stairs and watched as he snapped photos of some of the incredible things that had amazed her from the second she'd first walked in the place. "I couldn't believe it when I saw the first fresco in the entry. Then about fell over at the sight of all the gilded stucco on the next level. And the art on the ceiling!" She knew she sounded like a little kid in a candy shop, but that was exactly how she felt. "Just like something out of one of the museums I went to in Rome. I never dreamed I'd ever get to live in a place like this. When I heard the UWWHA had a house to rent, I figured it would be some plain, utilitarian thing."

"I'm glad you're enjoying it." His smile was back in all its attractive glory, and the power of that alone made her feel stupidly weak in the knees. "Wanting to share it for a while was part of the reason I first offered it out to rent as I made plans for its renovation, until my father sold it. The house I'm living in now was already in the process of being restored, and being there as much as possible to supervise it all had seemed like the best plan."

"Well, getting to live here for a while is like a dream come true." She realized that was insensitive, since it had been yanked out from under him. "I'm sorry. Here I am going on about getting to live here, and you can't anymore. Which really makes me mad, just so you know."

"Thank you. Makes me really mad, too." His impish smile widened to show his straight white teeth. "And I have to tell you that your American accent and the way you say things is very cute."

"I don't have an accent. Except maybe when I'm trying to badly speak in Italian."

"Oh, you definitely do."

His warm expression made her lungs feel a little squishy and she frowned to hide it. She refused to think about his words and the low, sexy tone he'd spoken them in as they moved up the intricately carved stone staircase. A complete reversal from the hard words he'd flung at her yesterday.

"One of my favorite rooms here is the library," she said, both to distract herself and because it was true. "So huge! And the ceiling is stunning. The bookcases are in remarkably good shape, too. But the windows are quite leaky and let in an awful lot of light that is doubtless damaging the paintings in the ceiling, not to mention being hard on the books. What are your options for replacing those while still making them look original?"

He stopped dead as they reached the next level, staring at her. "I guess you really do have an interest in historic renovation."

"So you truly thought I went to yesterday's meeting just to stalk you?" She folded her arms across her chest. "Like I said, you're unbelievably egotistical. For your information, my mother's passion for restoration is a part of me. And while doctor princes aren't one of my interests, I have lots of other ones. To me, people who don't are boring as heck."

"Which you most definitely are not, Ms. Henderson." Their gazes seemed fused together for long seconds before he moved toward the bedroom she was currently using. Which made her suddenly, horrifyingly, remember that she'd left clothes strewn around, including some personal items she'd rather not have this hunk of a man see, and never mind that he'd seen a whole lot more of her than just her underwear.

She pushed past him and rushed into the room, grabbing clothes up off the floor and from her bed. And why did it have to be this day of all days that she hadn't taken time to make it?

"Um…let me get this stuff out of your photos."

"It looks like you have more clothes out of the drawers and armoire than I have inside mine. But I think you should leave them." The amused eyes meeting hers danced as he reached out with the curve of his finger to hook the pink underwear lying on the bedspread. "I'll be presenting these photos to the Preserve Venice Committee. I suspect they'll be even more interested if I show how people actually live here, don't you?"

"No, I don't." Heat rushed into her face as she snatched her underwear from his grasp. "I don't normally leave my stuff lying around, so I'm really sorry about that."

"Are you kidding? You're apologizing for leaving your underwear and nightwear out?" He picked up her flimsy black gown by the spaghetti straps and held it up to her. His smile faded a little, his eyes darkened, and his voice went even lower than before. "This bedroom was mine as a child. As a teen, I had many sexual fantasies in this room, and, believe me, seeing what you sleep in has made my day almost as much as it would have back then. Problem is, I'll probably be imagining you in it when we're working together tomorrow."

Oh, Lord. There it was, shimmering between them like a hot, bright light. The connection that had drawn her to him from the moment she'd met him. The chemistry that had sent her headlong into his arms and his bed before she'd thought too hard about it.

No doubt he could see exactly what she was thinking and feeling, despite desperately trying to shore up her past anger with him. Because he leaned closer to brush his mouth against her cheek. Slipped it across her mouth, his breath mingling with hers before he pulled away. The sizzling thoughts swirling in her brain were clear on his face, too. Just as she took a step back and started inwardly scolding herself for letting herself think about the annoying man that way, she could see him mentally and physically retreat, too.

"Got to get these pictures taken. Thanks for letting me in to get this done." He slipped the camera off his neck and seemed to concentrate awfully hard on adjusting the lens. "The hotel's supposed to close on the house in three weeks, so you'll be around for the news."

"Good luck. Let me know if there's anything I can do to help." Probably shouldn't be offering, considering everything, but wouldn't anyone feel bad about his situation?

His gaze moved from the camera back to her. If he was trying to put cool and collected between them instead of hot and alive, he failed miserably. Because it looked for all the world as if he was mentally undressing her, and she just couldn't help the quiver her body responded with.

"I think you know that's an offer I can barely resist, Aubrey Henderson." His chest lifted in a long breath, then, as he turned to walk to the next room, she heard him murmur, "Just barely."

CHAPTER FIVE

How was Aubrey supposed to actually get any sleep in the bedroom she'd unfortunately learned had been Enzo's as a child?

A bedroom he'd apparently slept in from childhood until recently. *Recently* being when he'd decided to rent it for a short time while he renovated his other house, a move his father had apparently taken as a green light to sell the home Enzo loved. Not that it sounded as if the man who was both Enzo's and Dante's father needed any real excuse to steal from his sons.

That awful reality still burned in her gut for both of them. She couldn't even imagine how that must have felt—how upsetting it would have been for Enzo in particular, selling off this house that held centuries of his mother's history, and his own.

Thinking she couldn't imagine how that felt wasn't exactly true, though, was it? She sure knew from painful personal experience how deceitful and self-centered some fathers could be.

Aubrey glanced at her watch, trying to process all the emotions swirling around inside her. Sympathy for Enzo and what he was going through. Annoyance with his weird suspicions and insults. Confusion about why he seemed to run hot and cold with her, which made her determination to keep things professional and stay angry with him none too easy.

Since she had twenty minutes before she needed to be at the clinic, the burning need to talk to Shay about it all conflicted with her worries that she shouldn't bother her friend at this strange time in Shay's life. And was "strange" an understatement, or what? Aubrey could only hope she was doing okay, and wanting to know that, too, prompted her to give in. To stop walking and sit on a warm wooden bench in the *piazza* near the clinic and pull out her cell phone. All kinds of tourists walked by, from young and old couples, to big tour groups, to families, as she soaked in the amazing beauty and sense of community that was Venice. Children laughed and played, pampered dogs on leashes nosed their way around, and pigeons pecked at invisible delicacies from the old stone at her feet as she dialed Shay's number.

"Hello?" Shay's voice came through, strong and vibrant. "Aubrey?"

"Hey, you! I was wondering how you're feeling. How it's going. You okay?"

"Life has certainly taken a new twist for me, but I'm doing all right. You probably remember the past couple months I was feeling really tired, but now I feel great."

"I hope you're taking good care of yourself. Making sure you get plenty of rest and keeping a little easier pace than usual."

"That's what Dante said."

Was Aubrey imagining a smile in her friend's voice? She hoped and prayed that, however things turned out long-term, it would prove to be good for everyone involved, including the little baby Shay carried.

"I'm glad he's taking care of you, and I hope you listen to that resting thing." Now that she felt good about her friend's health and state of mind, she licked her lips to move on to the other subject on her mind. "What's Enzo been like to you? Has he been a jerk?"

"A jerk?" Shay sounded surprised. "No. I've only seen him a couple times, and he was a little cool but not a jerk. Why, has he been nasty to you?"

The way he spoke to her at the meeting had definitely qualified as *nasty*, but his apology for that had seemed sincere. Hopefully. She had to work with the man, after all, and he'd been pleasant yesterday—and the brief brush of his lips on hers had been more than pleasant.

She shook her head in annoyance that she'd let herself enjoy it. "Never mind. We're managing to work together. And by the way, I wanted to ask, did you know that Enzo used to own the house we rented from the UWWHA? That he and Dante grew up there?"

"I did know. Enzo took me there to get my clothes when I moved in with Dante, and told me then. Though he acted kind of stiff and odd about it. I'm not sure how much of that was because of me and the baby and Dante, and how much was about their dad selling off the property."

"I can't believe their father is so selfish and awful." Though she shouldn't have any trouble believing it, considering she'd experienced the same thing for a short time, too.

"I can't, either. And it's such a beautiful house, standing so tall with those small canals on both sides of it. Almost like an island itself, isn't it? I can't imagine how Enzo feels about losing it. And this house that's Dante's? It's amazing, too. Incredible, really."

"Who would have thought you'd meet a prince and marry him?"

"Not me, that's for sure," Shay said. "I don't need

anyone to take care of me. At least, I didn't think so until I got involved with someone famous. Who I didn't even know was a prince or famous, and that has sure complicated things. But it's just temporary, you know. We're only staying married for a year. Until the crazy stalker camera people out there forget about me, and when the excitement of an Affini heir is old news. So the baby and I can stay safe."

"It's been that bad?"

"Unbelievable. They practically knocked me over a few times getting pictures." Shay sounded angry, and who could blame her? "I have to admit it was scary, which is the only reason I went along with his marriage suggestion."

Aubrey still found all of it hard to believe, especially their sudden marriage. But since she'd never been in such an odd and difficult situation, she definitely couldn't and wouldn't judge her friend. She moved on to more basic conversation, asking Shay how her work at the hospital had been, and sharing a few of her experiences at the clinic. Yakking with her the way they had in the past had her smiling so much, she nearly forgot to check the time. "Oh, my gosh, it's late! I've got to get to work now. Don't be a stranger! Call me with any news, promise?"

"I promise. You keep me posted, too, okay?"

"I will. Talk to you soon." Aubrey hung up and stood, feeling so much better now that she'd talked to Shay. Thankfully, she'd sounded pretty good, so Dante must be treating her well. Not that she was surprised, since, despite Enzo's weirdness with her, she'd seen that, for the most part, he was basically a good guy.

Which was such a bland, understated way to describe the dynamic, sometimes-charming, caring doctor Prince, it didn't even come close.

"Aubrey." Enzo moved into the doorway of the clinic room she was tidying, and she looked up. Her eyes locked on his broad chest, then moved up to that absurdly handsome face, and she quickly busied herself with finishing her cleaning before he could catch her absurdly and inappropriately eyeing him.

"Yes?"

"I'm going on a house call. Hotel call, actually, not too far from here. I may need you. If we get a patient here that needs immediate attention, one of us can come back."

"Okay." Being around a patient and having work to do would be the distraction she needed to get her head on straight. Or at least she sure hoped it would.

"We're going to see an elderly tourist, female, who's been walking a lot the past couple of days, apparently more than she's supposed to. My friend who manages the hotel told me she isn't feeling very well, but doesn't seem in enough distress to warrant a hospital visit. She has a history of congestive heart failure, but of course we'd need to confirm that's what the problem is. The granddaughter doesn't want her walking here, though, so we're going to go to her."

"What do I need to bring? Nitropaste? Lasix?"

"And a little morphine, in case it is congestive heart failure. Blood-pressure unit and cuff, phlebotomy items and an IV line."

She nodded. "I'll have it all ready shortly."

"Thanks. I'll be in my office."

Proud that she'd resisted the urge to watch him leave, Aubrey gathered up the items, put them in a plastic

Ziploc bag she found in the cupboard, then found herself glancing in the mirror. Her ponytail was looking a little loose and she pulled the band out, brushing it to tidy it again. She tried to convince herself it was so she'd look professional for the patient, but she shook her head at the stupid reality that it was partly so she'd look good, period.

Even walking briskly along the wide promenade to the hotel, Enzo proved to be a good tour guide, pointing out historic buildings, homes, and hotels and giving a brief history of each. The hotel manager greeted Enzo warmly, was cordial to Aubrey, then ushered them up elegant floral-carpeted stairs to a small but beautifully appointed room.

"Thank you so much for coming," said an obviously American woman about Aubrey's age as she opened the door wide. "I feel bad that my grandma and I may have overdone it walking and seeing the sights. Should have kept a closer eye on her and not pushed it, but Venice is so tremendous that we got carried away." She frowned and glanced at the older woman sitting across the room in a plush, wingback chair. "I didn't want to put her through the ordeal of going to a hospital if we don't have to, but I felt we needed to know if we should be worried or not."

"That's why we're here," Enzo said, introducing himself and Aubrey, and the woman in turn introduced her grandmother. Aubrey could see by the way the younger woman stared at Enzo that she was as dazzled by his easy smile and good looks as Aubrey had been from the second she met him. As every woman on the planet would be, no doubt, if they didn't know what a split personality he had.

He crouched in front of the white-haired woman,

who leaned against the back of the chair holding both hands pressed to her chest. "Tell me how you're feeling."

"Short of breath. But it's barely anything. Really. My granddaughter just likes to worry about me."

Aubrey could immediately see that the woman's breathing was a little labored, but Enzo just smiled as though they were having a regular conversation. "Because that's what granddaughters are supposed to do when it comes to their beloved *nonnas*."

"We've had such a wonderful time." The woman's eyes shone, and her wrinkled face smiled broadly. "The basilica—why, it was more incredible than I ever would have dreamed. And going up the tower to see the islands, and the terra-cotta rooftops of the city! And taking that boat thing down the canal to see the houses along the water—the history! Unbelievable. Seeing Venice in pictures isn't anything close to actually being here, is it?"

"No, it most definitely is not." His smile widened and the way he glanced up at Aubrey made her heart do that annoying, squishy thing again. "You are a woman after my own heart, Mrs. Knorr."

"You're so handsome I'm sure there are lots of women after your heart, young man. I'd heard Italian men were beautiful, and have seen for myself it's true. And here you're proving it again."

"Thank you. Sometimes it is true that women show up in my life, but they are not necessarily after my heart." Another glance up at Aubrey, this one odd and questioning, and her throat tightened that he obviously wasn't completely over wondering about her. "Does your chest hurt?"

Yes, Aubrey wanted to say, *because of you and your*

attitude. But of course she knew he was asking the patient and not her.

"Just a few twinges," Mrs. Knorr said. "Really, I don't want to be a bother. I'm sure I'm fine, and I'm having a wonderful time. Just a little tired."

"Let me take a listen anyway." Enzo pressed his stethoscope against various parts of her chest, his face inscrutable. "May I look at your ankles?"

She stuck out her foot, and he gently tugged her socks down to press his fingers against the obviously swollen flesh. He drew the socks back up before reaching for her hands and the nail beds were clearly purple. Aubrey hadn't listened to their patient's lungs, but it was pretty apparent that heart failure was likely the problem.

Enzo pulled up a chair and sat in front of the woman, looking at her. "Your heart is a little out of rhythm. Does that happen sometimes?"

She nodded as the granddaughter answered. "She's had fibrillation on and off for some time. Takes a heart medicine to control it. And a little water pill in the mornings."

"They work. They do, Doctor." The eyes that had looked so excited before now reflected the worry on her granddaughter's face. "I don't want to ruin our trip and don't want anyone fussing over me. I'll be fine."

"Only the right amount of fussing, I promise." He patted the woman's hand, and the sweetness of the gesture and the warm expression on his face made her own darn heart about go out of rhythm, too. How could the man be beautiful and smart, so incredibly caring, and the best kisser in the Northern Hemisphere at the same time he was so skeptical and wary with her?

"You are having a little congestive heart failure. But I don't think you need to go to the hospital. So here's what we're going to do," he said. "We're going to have you take the water pill three times a day for three days, and see if that helps with the fluid in your lungs. Increase your beta-blocker, too. Don't worry—" more patting and sweet smiling "—I'll write all this down for you. Aubrey is going to take your blood pressure, and we'll see if we need to tweak the medicine for that, as well. Then draw your blood, just to check a few things, like your potassium and sodium, and to make sure you're not anemic. Okay?"

"Okay. That all sounds good." She gave him an obviously relieved smile.

He stood, and Aubrey worked to do as he'd asked while he spoke to the granddaughter. "When are you leaving Venice?"

"We were supposed to leave tomorrow, to go on to Florence, then the Tuscan countryside. But maybe we shouldn't. Maybe we should arrange to go home."

"Can you stay in Venice three more days, so we can look at her again? If she's feeling better, I don't see any reason why you can't continue your vacation with maybe a couple fewer stops."

"That's what I want to do," Mrs. Knorr chimed in. Aubrey smiled at the stubbornness that suddenly was loud and clear in her voice. She reminded her a lot of Aubrey's nanny, the retired nurse who'd been obstinate and awesome and was the reason she'd decided on that profession. "I love it here. Three more days sounds perfect, and we can just cut a few days off the rest of our trip somewhere else."

"I love it here, too," Aubrey said, hoping to distract her as she drew the woman's blood. "I get to be here for four months, and I know even that isn't going to feel like long enough."

As she capped off the vials Enzo's gaze caught hers. Held. The man was becoming more and more of a mystery, because she had no idea if he was thinking good things or bad things about her, and decided she couldn't worry about it.

As if that were possible. She focused on being efficient as she worked to gather everything up while Enzo wrote down his instructions, going over them with both women again before they left to go back to the clinic.

"You were so good with her, Dr. Affini," she said as they walked. That was matter of fact, right? Just honestly expressing her admiration with his bedside manner. *Oops. No thinking about his bedside manner.* "Are all elderly patients smitten with you?"

"Definitely not." He grinned at her. "I had one lady throw every pillow on her settee at me the second I walked in her house. And older Italian men tend to be the worst patients in the world, believe me. I'm sure you'll experience one or two while you're here."

"Older men in general are the worst patients, if you'll pardon me saying so. Sexist though that might be. You think you'll be cranky in your old age? I mean, crankier than you already are?"

He laughed. "Most definitely. In fact, it's in my genes. Along with other unfortunate traits."

He didn't look as if he was kidding, but she didn't ask what other traits he could be talking about. Keeping it professional. She could do it.

The rest of the day went by in a blur. Aubrey felt downright exhausted after the influx of patients they'd taken care of all day. Everything from tourists who got overheated to cuts that needed to be stitched to a broken arm and gashed head after a poor guy intently admiring the city fell down a long set of stone steps. They ended up keeping the doors open until seven o'clock when finally the last patients had been treated and were on their way.

With a last swipe of antibacterial wipes along the countertops, she stepped back, satisfied that the exam rooms were ready for the following day. Time to maybe do some evening walking around the city she still had barely toured, then have another wonderful dinner somewhere. Her breath suddenly hitched in her chest as she stood at the sink washing her hands, and she didn't have to turn to know the figure that came to stand close behind her was Enzo. And how did her heart and lungs know work was over and she could think about *him* again, darn it? Being able to concentrate on their patient load all day had convinced her she was over it.

Trying hard to pretend she wasn't ridiculously aware of him, she nonchalantly dried her hands on a towel. Which was tugged from her fingers before a large warm hand grasped hers, the other sliding a cool glass of sparkling water into her palm.

"You've had a long day, and you're probably thirsty. Thanks for hanging in there so long."

"You did, too." She let her eyes meet his over the glass as she took a drink, thinking how very thoughtful he was to have brought it to her. She hadn't even realized she was thirsty—how had he? "And no thanks are needed. That's why I'm here."

"Still, you did a great job. Even not speaking Italian, it amazes me how well you're able to communicate with the locals anyway."

"Hey, I'm learning to speak Italian! A little, anyway. A few words and phrases."

"Yes, you are. Even Venetian Italian." He smiled. "Pretty soon you'll be talking like a native."

"Wouldn't that be wonderful? Sadly, that's probably not a reality, in just a few months." And she'd probably forget all of it after she went back home. Still, the idea of being able to pretend for at least a little while that she was part of this amazing city filled her heart with some emotion she couldn't quite place.

"You never know. I'm impressed with your progress."

"Um…thanks." The admiration in his gaze made her feel warm, or maybe it was his closeness, and she took another big swig of water to cool it before setting the glass on the sink. "I better get going."

"To where?"

She moved to her cupboard to grab her things, hyperaware that he followed. Since she didn't yet have any idea where, and didn't want to think too hard about what *he* might be up to that night, she tried for a joke. A joke she couldn't deny she hoped would needle him a little. "Maybe I have a date."

Even from the corner of her eye, she could see him stop dead. "A date?"

"You know, where you eat somewhere with someone, and explore a bit? A date."

"With who?"

She turned to him and folded her arms across her chest, absurdly pleased that she'd gotten the surprised and disconcerted expression from him she'd wanted. "What's with the questions? You got out of me all I know about Shay, and, since you accomplished that on *our* date, what I do outside the clinic isn't really your business, is it? Maybe me going on a date would finally prove to you that I'm not here because I was pursuing you or something."

"First, you knew when we met that I wanted to learn

more about the woman my brother was to marry. Second, I've apologized for the things I said. I realize how stupid it was of me, now that I've gotten to know you better and see the kind of person you are. I'm truly sorry it even crossed my mind to accuse you of that. But there probably is one thing you don't know that you should." The small hallway felt even smaller as he moved close. "Which is that being with you that night was the best thing that's happened to me in a long time."

For once, the eyes meeting hers weren't laughing, or suspicious. His brows weren't dipped into a frown. His lips weren't curved into a teasing smile. Instead, his expression was serious and sincere and her heart started beating in double time. She tried to shore up her defenses because the last thing she needed was the complication of a man who hadn't tried to get in touch with her after their oh-so-memorable night together, who'd been suspicious of her when she'd first come back to Venice, and who was her boss to boot.

And never mind that it was a beyond tempting complication that seemed more tempting with every second that passed.

"I've got to go." She turned and hurriedly grabbed her stuff, shut the cupboard door, and started to move past him, but his hand reached for her arm to stop her. Slid slowly down her skin to twine his warm fingers with hers.

"A long day deserves a nice night," he said quietly. "For both of us. Would you join me for dinner? Then a little more touring of Venice to see things we didn't see last time? Unless you must honor your date, of course."

"I…I think it can be rescheduled." She couldn't help that her response sounded a little breathy, because the way he was looking at her and touching her seemed to steal every molecule of oxygen from her lungs. Making her feel the same way she'd felt two months ago that first night they'd met.

"*Bene.* You have a change of clothes here? I think you'll like what I have in mind."

CHAPTER SIX

"I'M PRETTY SURE that was the best dinner I've ever had. Though I fear I may gain ten pounds by the time I leave here." Aubrey sat back in her chair and watched Enzo pay the bill, his head tipped downward as he did. The night lights by the canal touched the silky black hair that he wore slightly long, and she couldn't help but admire the adorable little waves curling against his neck that were usually a bit hidden by his lab coat. When he looked back up at her with the smile that had dazzled her two months ago and again tonight, her silly heart skipped a beat.

The evening with him had been wonderful, as she'd known it would be. Magical, just like the first night she'd met him. Getting to roam romantic and incredible Venice, not just once, but twice with a man as amusing, intelligent, and physically beautiful as Enzo Affini was something she'd never forget.

Hadn't forgotten even a little in her two months away from Venice.

No wonder she'd fallen into bed with him last time. Not that she had any intention of repeating that all too memorable experience, especially knowing now that he wasn't really perfect in every way.

"Between seeing patients and touring the city, we've

walked a lot today. You needed the sustenance." Enzo stood, and why did just his smile keep making her feel a little weak in the knees? His hand wrapped around hers as it had on and off all evening, and it felt perfect and electric and she wasn't sure how much of that was the magic of Venice, and how much was the magic of Enzo Affini. A very lethal combination. "Let's take the *vaporetto* to my boat, hmm? Then I will take you to your house."

Boat? Her tummy tightened at the suggestion—as much as she adored Venice, being on the water made her nervous—and she drew a deep breath to calm it. "You mean your house."

"It's not my house again yet. Unless you mean you want to go back to the house I'm living in, instead?"

His eyebrows were raised, and his dark eyes shone with both amusement and the banked-down heat she'd seen in them on and off all day.

"No way. I could be a stalker, remember? Not smart of you to take a chance. And we work together now. But I appreciate your asking for clarification," she said in a prim voice that got a chuckle out of him.

They headed toward the water taxi, and the closer they got, the more her breath quickened until she felt she might hyperventilate.

Stop being stupid. Being around water all the time while you're here is going to help you get over this, right?

Still, staring at the dark sky surrounded by even darker water as they stepped onto the taxi, she found herself gritting her teeth and hanging tightly on to his arm. She was glad it was far less crowded than earlier that night, which had just added to her anxiety somehow. Despite having plenty of room, he slid his arms around her waist and pulled her back against him just as he had when there had been a few dozen people pressing shoulder to shoulder. The way he held her made her feel safer, ridiculously, and even as she reminded herself again how silly her fears were she found herself clutching the forearms looped across her stomach.

"You don't have to hold me this close anymore, you know." She'd said it to force herself to be brave, but she was more than glad when the arms around her didn't loosen. Her words had come out a little breathy, but she couldn't help that. Between his closeness and her worry, she was surprised she could breathe at all. "I can stand up on a moving boat quite well when people aren't jostling me."

"I know. Which should tell you that's not why I'm holding you close." His voice was soft, his lips right next to her ear in a feather touch against the shell before moving slowly down to rest below the lobe.

For a split second she was surprised. Until the feel of his mouth on her skin had her relaxing, melting back against him at the deliciousness of it and making her forget that they were on dark water that might swallow her up. That he was her boss and all the other reasons she shouldn't let him kiss her again.

Her head tipped back against his collarbone as her hands caressed the large, warm ones pressing against her belly. It wasn't a conscious invitation for him to explore further, but he obviously read it that way, since she could feel his lips smile against her skin before his mouth moved down her throat, the tip of his tongue touching the base.

"It's a good thing the stop near my boat is close by," he said. "Otherwise I might have to kiss you right here in front of everyone. Not that Venetians would mind, but tourists, maybe yes."

"I thought kissing wasn't allowed between clinic employees."

"It's not. But for just this moment, I want to pretend we don't work together."

"But we do work together." And why had she said that, when only negative things could come of it? Those things being that he'd make her stop working at the clinic after all, or he'd decide not to kiss her. And she definitely wanted both of those things a whole lot whether she should or not.

"Sorry, I can't hear you. The wind's in my ears." With his warm, slightly rough cheek touching her temple, they rode across the water without another word passing between them as the breeze caressed her. It felt wonderful, but not nearly as wonderful as the feel of his skin against hers and the exquisite sensory overload that completely overpowered the fear that had squeezed her chest just moments ago.

The *vaporetto* finally docked, and Enzo released her for just a second before grasping her hand to help her off. That familiar fear skittered down her spine again, and she was beyond glad to be off the darn boat. Also glad Enzo had found a very nice way to distract her, and sure hoped she didn't freak out riding on his small boat.

"My skiff is just over there." The pace he kept was so fast, she might have tripped if she hadn't been in the comfy, crepe-soled sandals that were her favorite for long tourist walks.

"Do you have a curfew or something?" she asked breathlessly, feeling nearly dragged behind him as he held her hand tight. "Do you turn into a pumpkin at midnight? Oh, wait, that was Cinderella's coach, not the Prince."

He turned his head to flash a grin at her that somehow managed to look impish and sexily seductive at the same time. "Guess you'll have to stay with me until midnight to find out, hmm?"

Then just as he'd practically started sprinting the second they got off the boat, he came to such an abrupt stop in the shadows beyond a streetlamp, she collided into him as he turned toward her.

"Gee, give a girl a warning, would you?" She pressed her free hand to his chest to separate them and found hard muscle there, and heat, and…and…what had she been about to say?

"Sorry. Here's your warning. I'm going to kiss you now."

And with that promise rumbling deeply from his throat, he pulled her flush against that warm, firm chest, lowered his head to hers, and did exactly that.

The kiss started out gentle, sweet, his mouth moving on hers in an unhurried exploration that stole her breath and sent her heart into slow, rhythmic thuds against her ribs. He tasted a little of the Chianti they'd shared, and of fantasies come to life again, and of him.

Especially him.

The hands she had pressed flat against his pectorals slipped upward of their own will to wrap around the back of his neck, and she could feel his palms splay wide on her back as his arms tightened around her. The kiss deepened, their tongues danced, and Aubrey hung on for dear life as her knees weakened under the sweet assault that felt so beyond a mere kiss there wasn't a name for it.

His lips separated from hers, just enough to let her

drag in a much-needed breath at the same time his chest heaved against hers. "You taste amazing, *mia bellezza*. Just like you did the last time we were together."

"You…you do, too." And wow, was that ever true. She stared up into his eyes, and even through the darkness she could see the blaze in their deep brown depths. That taste filled her with a hunger she'd felt only one time before, which had been the last time they'd kissed. A hunger for the life adventures she'd promised herself, for moving on from betrayal, for…for Enzo Affini, smart or not.

"I have to tell you something," he said.

The blaze in his eyes was suddenly joined by an odd seriousness. Maybe even troubled, and her chest felt as if it caved in a little. "Oh. You're…you're involved with someone else?"

"No."

"Okay, that's good." More than good, but then that left lots of other possibilities of something even worse. "You still think I'm a stalker? You murder unsuspecting tourist employees and throw them to the sharks?"

"No. Didn't I already tell you I knew I'd been stupid?" His lips curved slightly. "And I don't believe I've ever seen a shark in the lagoon, or one of the canals. But the truth is almost as bad. The Affini men are a bad bet. I hope Shay knows that. And I want you to know it, too."

"Why?" She searched his face, wondering why he'd gone from kissing her breathless to pulling back like this. And should she really be worried about her friend? "In what way are you a bad bet?"

"Just take my word for it." His expression was downright grim now, even as his eyes still looked at her as if kissing her again was as high on his list of desires as it was on hers, and his hands held her waist so tightly she expected to be pulled back against that hard chest at any moment.

"Shay's a big girl. She's planning on her relationship with your brother to be temporary, and what's best for the baby," she said. "As for me, I'm a big girl, too. I'm not betting on you. I'm just enjoying kissing you. A lot. And I don't think kissing and…and stuff has anything to do with betting. Does it? You're completely confusing me here."

"Aubrey." He said her name in a low voice that held a smile and something else that made every inch of her insides vibrate, and she found herself moving against him instead of waiting for him to draw her closer. "I know you can't be confused about how much I enjoy kissing you. Even though I shouldn't. And if you are, I'll have to make it clearer."

And with that, he lowered his mouth to hers. Kissed her until all thoughts and questions disappeared, replaced by heat and want and a desire so intense, she felt woozy from it. After long, breathless minutes, he raised his head, lifting one warm hand to cup her cheek, running his thumb across her moist lower lip.

"Are you sure you don't want to quit working at the clinic and just have a hot affair with me instead?"

"Not fair to ask me that question right after you've kissed me like that." And was that ever true. The way her insides were quivering told her to hand in her notice that very second. Who needed work when she could have Enzo Affini for a few months? "But, no, much as I'm tempted, working at the clinic is important to me."

"I know." He smiled and slowly pressed his lips to first one cheek, then the other before lightly kissing her mouth. "I was kidding. Sort of."

He released her and stepped back, and she instantly

missed his warmth. "I should get home now. To your home. I mean, your home that's temporarily my home." Lord, kissing the man had clearly shaken her brain as much as the rest of her.

"Thanks for making that clear." Enzo's impish smile was back in full force, and he reached for her hand. "Tomorrow when we see one another at work, we'll pretend tonight didn't happen. If we can."

"Yes. I'm sure I can manage that." Which was a total lie. Her still-tingling lips and wobbly knees told her that, for her at least, pretending that would be impossible.

For the first time all day, there was a lull in the action at the clinic, and Aubrey took the opportunity to get a cold drink and catch her breath, glad the office was about to close. Crazy busy days there had left her with little time to think about the evening she'd spent exploring the city with Enzo. To think about how it had felt when he'd held her and kissed her, which was a very good thing.

During clinic hours, there hadn't been more than a few quick moments to reflect on their odd and confusing relationship. Learning they worked well together, and were able to set aside their attraction to one another while taking care of patients, was a relief. But the other times? When there were gaps between patients? The heat they kept on a back burner would suddenly flare into a warm simmer in an instant.

A teasing grin, or a gentle finger flick to her cheek, or a long look from his dark eyes, would tell her he was remembering their kisses, or maybe even thinking about that first night they'd met over two months ago. Then she'd recall exactly how all that had felt, which would leave her a little short of breath.

So, what were they going to do about it? Was Enzo going to stick to the "keep their distance" thing? Did she want to? And really, hadn't they already violated that rule at least a little?

She had no idea what the answers were, but maybe trying to make a few friends in Venice would keep her from thinking about him so much when they weren't working together. Meet some of the UWWHA nurses who worked at the hospital, or get involved with the various restoration and preservation groups and learn more about the city and its history and challenges.

Yes. That would be a good plan. Learn something, maybe contribute as well, and have more things on her mind than Enzo Affini.

Aubrey was just about to pull out her tablet to see about any meetings the organizations might have scheduled, and look at the UWWHA social loop to see if any of the nurses might be planning a get-together that night, when Nora came into the back hallway.

"We have a Russian couple here. Wife is twenty-five weeks pregnant and is feeling uncomfortable. I'm going to bring her to exam room two."

"All right." Aubrey washed her hands, then greeted the couple with a smile. "Hello. Tell me why you're here."

"My wife is pregnant. Not feeling okay." The man's expression was strained, and his English was hard to understand. Aubrey knew difficulty communicating usually made patients feel even more anxious, and she smiled wider to try to reassure him.

"Tell me how you're not feeling okay," she said to the dark-haired woman, who looked to be in her thirties and reminded Aubrey a little of their Russian housekeeper, Yana, who'd ruled the roost for years when she'd been growing up. "Are you in pain?" Aubrey repeated the word in Russian, hoping to gain her confidence. She didn't speak much of the language, but could manage the basics.

"No." The woman looked at her with surprise, then a smile as she cupped her hands around her round belly, speaking rapidly in Russian until Aubrey had to stop her.

"I'm sorry, I don't understand. I only know a few words, from an old friend."

The woman stopped speaking, but still smiled. "Okay. Just, um, balling. Here."

"Cramping?"

"Yes." She nodded and seemed a little relieved that Aubrey understood what she was trying to say. "Cramping."

"All right. Let's put a gown on you, then get your feet up, and I'll take a listen to baby." She helped the woman undress, then had her lie down on the exam table. After putting a few pillows beneath her legs, she pressed a stethoscope to the woman's belly, relieved to hear a steady heartbeat there. "Baby's heartbeat is normal, so that's good. I'm going to talk to the doctor, okay? Be right back." She patted the woman's shoulder, adjusted the pillows, then went to look for Enzo.

His office door was open, and she was glad to find him there filling out paperwork. "We have a patient who's twenty-five weeks pregnant and experiencing cramping. Baby's heartbeat is steady. Do you want me to do an ultrasound? Or do you want to do an internal exam first?"

He looked up and her heart gave an unfortunate little kick when his dark eyes met hers. Hadn't she just been feeling proud that the simmer between them was mostly absent when they were working? "I'll come do the exam, then we'll decide."

Enzo gave the couple his usual, calm smile, asked questions about how she was feeling, explained what he was going to do, then snapped on gloves as Aubrey helped adjust the patient's position. "You'll feel me touching you, and some pressure, okay? This will just take a moment."

Aubrey watched Enzo's face as he examined the woman's cervix, and though his expression didn't change she could tell instantly that he didn't like what he'd found.

He took off his gloves as Aubrey moved their patient into a more modest position, keeping her legs elevated on the pillows. "I'm afraid there is some dilation of the cervix. Not much, but more than should be there at twenty-five weeks. I want you to go to the hospital for treatment that we can't give you here."

"Hospital? No." The woman suddenly looked a little mulish. "We are on vacation. No hospital."

Enzo glanced at Aubrey, and his look told her loud and clear that he might need backup about this. "If you go into preterm labor, your baby could be born way too soon. It's important that you have the baby monitored for a bit. If they determine that baby is trying to come too early, there are medications that can be given to you through an IV that will stop the process and let baby grow inside you longer. Depending on what they find, they may even want to give you steroid injections to be sure baby's lungs will develop before it's born."

"We go home soon. I will see the doctor there."

The husband hadn't said a word, and it seemed clear that he'd go along with whatever his wife wanted.

"Please let me call the hospital. An extra day or two here is worth your baby being born healthy, isn't it?"

"No. Thank you."

The woman swung her legs over the table and picked up her clothes, clearly intent on leaving. Enzo opened his mouth to say something more, but Aubrey put her hand on his arm to stop him. Her Russian might not be very good, but she understood this woman a little and wanted to give it a try.

A halting conversation with the patient finally had her yielding, and her expression went from stubborn to resigned. Enzo's eyebrows were raised, but he didn't say another word except to tell Aubrey he'd call for the ambulance boat to take the woman to the hospital, probably worried that he'd jinx the process and she'd change her mind.

By the time the ambulance came the office was closed for the day, and it was all Aubrey could do not to drop into a chair and stay there awhile. Enzo returned through the back door after talking with the EMTs, raising his eyebrows at her.

"When were you going to tell me you had special skills with difficult patients? That was amazing."

"I just got lucky." She had to admit she felt good the situation had gone well. Glad the woman and her baby were going to get the help they needed. "Our Russian housekeeper, Yana, was the most stubborn woman I've ever known. She was very suspicious of doctors and hospitals, and refused to see anyone but a Russian doctor whose practice was almost a hundred miles from our town. I channeled my memories of why she felt the way she did when I was talking to our patient. I guess it worked."

"I guess it did." He reached for her hand and brought

it to his lips, his eyes smiling at her above it. Heating, too, as that *thing* that was always simmering there between them started to boil a little higher. "You are a constant surprise, Aubrey Henderson."

"I try to keep you guessing and on your toes, Dr. Affini," she said lightly, hoping he couldn't tell that just the touch of his lips on her hand and the way he was looking at her had her heart doing a little tap dance.

"You successfully do that every day. In more ways than one."

The dark eyes meeting hers were full of admiration, maybe a little confusion, and a whole lot of desire. She recognized it, because she could feel it melting her bones.

"Aubrey."

His deep voice vibrated through her, and her answer back was breathless. "Yes?"

"Would you join me for a cruise on the water to see some of the islands in the northern lagoon? They're very different from the glamorous Venice you've seen, and one has interesting buildings and church ruins I believe you'd enjoy. I'll pick up some things for a picnic dinner. What do you say?"

He was watching her with the small smile touching his lips that was always so appealing, but the question in his eyes seemed to say that what he was asking was important to him. And how could she say no to an excursion to a part of the lagoon she might not get to see her entire time here, if not for him? The thought of cruising on that dark water made her stomach squeeze, but she knew if there was one person who could make her face her fear of that, it was this caring and empathetic man.

"I'd love to. But I'm happy to get the food together."

"Let me. I have favorite delis I know that will pack

us a picnic you won't forget. I'll pick you up at the house at six, *sì*?"

"Sì." Her chest bubbled with pleasure just at the thought of spending another evening with Enzo Affini, even as she promised herself it absolutely would not end anything like the first delicious one they'd shared.

CHAPTER SEVEN

WITH BAGS OF food and a few bottles of wine from one of the family wineries at his feet, Enzo sent his boat through the canal toward his old home. He hadn't looked forward to an evening with a woman this much in a long time. Not since the recent night they'd spent touring and eating and kissing. Not since the incredible night he'd spent with Aubrey two months ago, and he didn't have to think too hard about what all that meant.

Maybe this was a bad idea. Maybe it wasn't. Maybe it didn't matter either way, because he'd given up on keeping their relationship strictly business, not just because he'd failed miserably at it. Because he'd come to believe that, unbelievably coincidental as it had seemed that Aubrey had shown up in his life, there'd been a reason for it. And not the reason he'd originally wondered.

It was meant to be that he and Aubrey would have four amazing months to spend time together. For her to have a native Venetian show her the most amazing city in the world. For him to have something in his life to enjoy while he dealt with the very stressful and unenjoyable battle to get his mother's house back from the brink of destruction, and into the family fold again.

The more he was around Aubrey, the more he wanted

her. Warm and smart and a little sassy, and how was he to resist that lethal combination?

Clearly, the answer was that he couldn't. And he'd given up trying.

His heart gave a strange little kick in his chest when he saw Aubrey waiting for him next to the dock. She smiled and waved, and he nearly ran the boat into one of the wooden posts, he was so intent on looking at her beautiful face and body, her silky hair lifting a little in the breeze.

He managed to safely secure the boat right next to her. A gust of wind blew her dress up a little, and was it his fault that he was below her and had to look?

"Hey!" Both her hands pressed down her skirt and she frowned at him. "No peeking up my dress."

"Need I point out that I've already had the pleasure of seeing way more of you than that?"

She gasped, but it almost sounded like a shocked laugh, so he was pretty sure her offense was mock. Though why he'd let such a thing fall out of his mouth, he wasn't sure. Or maybe he was, because he couldn't help that the vision of her beautiful, naked body often filled his mind.

"That kind of remark definitely doesn't qualify for us having that professional, friendly relationship we're trying to have."

"That was friendly, wasn't it?"

"Maybe in Italy. At home it's called sexual harassment."

"Is it? To me, sexual harassment is more like—"

"Stop now, before I call the UWWHA on you. And refuse to come on this excursion after all."

He'd already told himself to shut up already and laughed at how outraged she somehow managed to look, even when her beautiful eyes were twinkling. "Sorry. I'll behave. Come on. Your chariot awaits."

"Does Prince Affini say that to all the girls he picks up?"

"Only the ones he wants to picnic with." He reached for her hand. "Watch your step."

She hesitated for a moment before finally extending her hand. He folded her soft palm in his, surprised at the strength of her grip as she stepped carefully into the boat. So carefully, in fact, he looked up at her instead of at her sexily sandaled feet, suddenly realizing she looked surprisingly scared. "Does getting into the boat worry you?"

"Of course not. Um…okay, yes. I'd hoped I'd be so brave you wouldn't notice."

Her teeth sank into that delectably full lower lip of hers, and he let go of the post to grasp her elbow, keeping her steady on the gently bobbing boat as he lowered her onto the seat. "What should I have noticed?" But he had a feeling he already knew.

Wide blue-gray eyes met his, filled with embarrassment and worry. "I'm…I'm afraid of water. Like, dark lake water or ocean water. It's silly, I know. Ridiculous. I can even swim fine and have no problem in a clear swimming pool. But when I was really little, I fell off the dock of the big pond on our property and thought I was going to drown for sure until one of our groundskeepers jumped in and fished me out. I've been weirded out by it ever since."

He hadn't asked about her background, but if they had housekeepers and groundskeepers, that usually meant wealth. But, of course, he'd figured she must be well-to-do when he'd first learned about her donation to restore that fresco.

He remembered the way she'd clung to him on the *vaporetto*, realizing now that perhaps it had been as much about her fear as about wanting to be close to him. Had he not noticed because all he'd been able to think about that night was how much he wanted to kiss and touch her? The alarm in her eyes was more than real, and he thrashed himself for not seeing it before.

"I'm sorry I didn't realize you were scared. I wish you'd told me before now." He sat close enough to wrap his arm around her, this time to comfort instead of maneuvering into a good position to kiss her, though he couldn't help but think about that, too. "Perhaps driving around on the canals and riding more often in the *vaporetto* will help you manage it better, hmm? Though I have to say I'm surprised at your insistence on staying in Venice instead of going to the mainland. A woman with a fear of water clearly likes to torture herself if she wants to live in a city built on water."

He smiled at her, relieved to see her smile back, even if it was a weak effort. "Actually, I did it on purpose. Not to torture myself, but to deal with it. Get past it. My mother had a terrible fear of being in public places around a lot of people, and it was paralyzing for her. I promised myself I wouldn't live my life like that, that I'd figure out a way to get over it. Four months here should do the trick, don't you think?"

"When did your mother pass?" he asked quietly, understanding well that pain and loss.

"Just over a year ago." She looked away across the water, and the pain on her face was so intense, he squeezed her shoulder in support. When she turned back to him, her smile was wider, but still forced. A clear message that they were closing the subject. "I'm starving and very excited about this picnic idea. Where are we going again?"

"To an island in the northern lagoon that's mostly deserted, but beautiful in its own way. The marshes and mud flats around it are totally different from here, and much of the island itself is marshy with rough fields. It's quiet, unlike the busyness of Venice. I think you'll like it. And, Aubrey?"

"What?"

"I promise I won't let you fall overboard."

She smiled, but it didn't banish the worry in her eyes, and his mouth lowered to hers for a soft kiss to reassure her before he'd even realized he'd done it. And that simple touch of his lips to hers made him want so much more.

When his lips parted from hers, he was glad he'd kissed her, because the eyes wide on his were filled with something very different from worry now, and it was all he could do not to go back for another, deeper kiss.

He drew in a breath and forced himself to stand again, his arm around her waist as he moved them to the rear seat.

"Sit in the back with me. It'll make the bow sit a little high in the water, but you'll be close to me." Normally he would have had her stay in the center of the boat for better weight distribution, but he wanted to keep his arm around her. Make her feel secure. And it had nothing to do with wanting to touch her soft skin and hold her close. And he was getting really good at kidding himself when it came to Aubrey Henderson.

They passed boats like his, larger tour boats, and the ferry that stopped at a few of the islands. Her excited exclamations at the various sights made him smile, glad he'd had the idea to bring her here. He watched her point at old buildings and churches as they went by, and each time she did she'd turn to look at him with a bright smile. He stared into her eyes as she talked, wondering how she described their color. Sometimes they were the gray of the water, tinted with a blue reflection of the sky. Other times they seemed more blue than gray, with interesting flecks of green and gold. Holding a smile inside that she was able to enjoy the ride in spite of her fear, he felt as buoyant as the boat skimming across the water.

"So, where exactly does Dante live? And, I guess Shay now, too."

Her odd tone of voice had him stealing another look at her. She wore a slight frown, and her lips were cutely twisted as though she was wondering about that marriage as he was, which lightened Enzo's heart even more. If she wasn't too sure about the two of them marrying, that would mean there was no agenda on Shay's part, just a situation where a night of lovemaking had led to unexpected consequences.

"Dante's home is on the Lido di Venezia. The very long island you can see past Guidecca, which is across from San Marco's."

"Is it as old as yours? I mean, the house I'm living in now?"

"No. His is practically new. Built in the fifteen-hundreds. Needs a bit of work, though."

She laughed. "Only in Italy is something built in the fifteen-hundreds practically new."

"Much of the rest of Europe would object to that statement. Though I believe our history is the most interesting, which isn't bias, of course."

"It is. It's incredible. Imagine knowing who your ancestors were so long ago, and that they lived and loved in the very house you grew up in. You have to get that house back, no matter what."

The fierceness on her face reflected just how his heart and gut felt on the matter, and it amazed him that she seemed to understand that. "I agree, *bellezza*. Believe me. And I will, no matter what it takes."

He didn't want to think about all that now, and the tough odds against him. He wanted to enjoy a special evening with this very special woman.

They sat in silence as they approached the island, and he didn't try to analyze the sense of peace he felt being with her at the same time he felt utterly wired. "I'm going to dock here. We'll walk along the canal, but, unlike the ones you've seen before, this one will be practically deserted. Then I'll show you the old churches, and then we'll have our picnic on a favorite green space Dante and I used to bring girls."

"I can imagine what you both had planned when you did that."

"And sometimes those plans would backfire if the mosquitoes came out. Smelly repellent isn't quite as appealing as cologne."

"Except rubbing it on the girls would have been a good excuse to touch them."

"There was that, yes."

Her soft laughter slid inside him, and he reached to tuck the silky strands of hair that had escaped her ponytail behind her ear. Let his fingers travel down her jaw before sliding his hand down her arm to hold hers as they exited the boat.

Her exclamations and excitement as they walked along the deserted canal made him feel as if he were seeing everything with new eyes himself, despite having been there dozens of times. They trudged over the grasslands and saw the ancient churches and abandoned homes, and she seemed so pleased, he was glad he'd brought her out here, despite her fear of the water.

"You're right—this place is very different from Venice." Aubrey spread the blanket over the flat, over-grown grass next to the lagoon. "Feels almost wild, you know?"

"Yeah." He wanted to tell her that watching her tempting rear move around as she bent over to straighten the blanket was making him feel a little wild, too. Be-cause hauling her into his arms, lying down on that blanket, and kissing her until neither of them could breathe seemed like a much better idea than a picnic. He inhaled a deep breath of the salty air and concen-trated on pulling out the food. "After we eat, we'll take the boat to meander through the channels a little more, where we'll probably see wildlife, then we'll head back."

The picnic food seemed to taste even better than usual, and he was glad he'd brought one of their winer-ies' best vintages to share with her. "Did Shay tell you about the Affini estates in Tuscany? We have extensive vineyards, and several wineries. Dante and I are pretty happy with this batch of Chianti. I hope you like it."

"It's really good." Her eyes closed briefly as she took a sip, apparently letting it linger in her mouth. The ex-pression on her face reminded him of the night they'd made love, and he turned his attention to the horizon to subdue the way his body reacted to the memories. "And believe it or not, Shay and I really haven't had a chance to talk about more than the, um, situation. I don't really know much about the Affini family other than what you've shared with me."

"And that's probably just as well." Talking about his family situation was one sure way to kill his libido, and he managed to get them settled onto the blanket without laying her down on it and kissing her breathless.

As they ate they shared stories of patients that had both of them laughing, along with a few that brought tears to Aubrey's eyes, turning them into another fascinating shade of gray-blue tinted with green.

"What color are your eyes?"

She paused from eating a chunk of bread and looked up in surprise. "My eyes?"

"Yes. I'm slightly color blind, and every time I look at them, I wonder."

"That must be so strange! Do you have to spend your life figuring out what color things are, or are you just used to not being sure?"

"Neither. Most of the time I don't particularly care." He leaned closer, lifted his hands to cup the softness of her cheeks as he turned her face, watching her pretty eyes catch the lowering sunlight. "But knowing the color of your eyes feels important."

"They're…they're just a mix of colors. Change with what I'm wearing, and the light, and how I'm feeling, I guess. I always wished I could say they were blue or green or gray, but never knew how to answer that on my driver's license questionnaire."

She smiled, but he could feel her pulse fluttering against his fingers, her breath skittering across his face, and knew she felt the electricity strumming the air between them, too.

He lowered his mouth to hers, sipping the Chianti from her lush lower lip before delving deeper, feeling the hot connection zing between them that happened every time their mouths met. Kept kissing her as she slid her arms around his neck and pulled him close. Felt her melting into him, and he lowered her slowly to the blanket before both of them ended up just toppling over.

His hand found its way to the soft skin of her thigh, tracking up inside her skirt, and her gasp into his mouth inflamed him. The only thought in his head was getting her naked and kissing and touching her everywhere and he was making progress on that mission until the sound of voices and laughter somehow made it through the sexual fog in his brain.

He barely managed to break the kiss, lifting his head toward the sounds. Sure enough, not too far down the grassy area, a group of people, likely tourists who'd decided to go off the beaten path, had unloaded off a hired boat.

"Well, damn." He dropped another quick kiss to her mouth before he made himself sit up, taking her hand to help her do the same.

"I thought you said this island is practically deserted." Somehow her eyes were laughing a little at the same time they looked as dazed as he felt. Her tongue slipped out to lick her lips, and he nearly groaned, thinking about what they'd been doing just seconds ago and how good it had felt and where it might have been headed next.

"It is. Usually. Just our luck, hmm?"

"Maybe the gods of professional relationships are looking out for us."

That got a laugh out of him. "I hope not. Roman gods can be pretty ruthless. And I don't know about you, but I'm seriously thinking about crossing them."

Golden fingers of light spilled across her shining hair as she let out a low laugh, which had him pulling her close for another soft kiss. Behind her, the sun sank to just above the grasses and murky water, and Enzo let go of her to pick up his wineglass and tip the last of it into his mouth. But the taste of Aubrey still lingered.

"We better get going before it's so dark you can't see a bit of the lagoon life."

"Okay." Her last sip of her own wine was followed by what sounded like a very happy sigh, and she sent him a smile almost as brilliant as the setting sun. "I bet I'll more than like it. This has been wonderful. Thank you for bringing me."

"Thank you for joining me." He helped her back into the boat and couldn't remember a time he'd felt quite this deeply connected with a woman. "I love it out here. Haven't found a good reason to come lately. You're my reason."

"I like being your reason."

Their gazes met and held. Something about the words made them seem more important than they should have. He didn't know exactly why, but the feeling hung between them, sweet and intimate and suspended in the thick lagoon air. Enzo found himself just looking at her as they sat close on the small seat, her hip and arm warm against his, and it felt about as right as anything he'd ever felt before.

"I have to ask you something," she said, her gaze steady on his. "Why didn't you ever call me when I was in Rome?"

An easy question with a hard answer. "I thought about it more times than I could count. Had the phone in my hand ready to dial, but stopped myself. I wasn't sure about Shay and my brother, and if she had planned what happened. And you were her friend, which seemed like it could be a problem. Plus I had the issues with the house going on, and I just… I guess I felt like being with you was a complication I didn't need."

"And then it just got more complicated."

"Yeah. But somehow that complication seems more than worth it now." He drew her close for another long, sweet kiss, until he managed to pull back to get the boat on its way. The movement put an inch or two between them, and he instantly missed the feel of her body touching his.

"Soon I'll be turning off the motor and using the oars so we can slip quietly through the channel. Parts of it are only two feet deep." Maybe talking about the place would get his mind back on track. Away from her soft skin and lush mouth. "Depending on the flow of the rivers and wash of tides from the Adriatic, if you lean over you'll see fish, crab, squid—all of the many things you can find on restaurant menus in the city."

"It almost reminds me of the fish farming on the coast near my house."

"Venetians like to scoff at talk about the 'new' art of fish farming, since we've been doing it for hundreds of years."

"You Venetians seem to like to scoff a lot at anyone who doesn't have the history you do."

"Which is most everyone, Ms. New World."

They exchanged grins as he cut the motor and let the boat slide into the marshy channel. Aubrey leaned over just a couple inches to peer over the side of the boat, then, as the boat slightly rocked, grabbed his arm so tightly it hurt.

"Ouch," he said, extricating her fingernails from his skin, holding her arm up against his body instead. "I'm wishing this boat had a mast for you to hold on to instead of my flesh." He dropped a kiss onto her cheek and smiled at her, hoping she'd relax.

"I'm sorry."

"No need to be sorry. But remember what I said? Only two or three feet deep here. If you did fall out, you'd get a mud bath as much as you'd get wet. But you won't fall—the boat is steady, promise. I'm here to steady you, too. Making you feel safe is, right now, my priority in life."

"That's a…a very sweet thing to say. And being scared is so silly, I know." She sat up straighter and looked embarrassed, which made him wish he hadn't teased her. "I'm trying."

"I know. And that impresses me more than you know." He stroked her soft inner arm as he tucked her closer. "Do you have any idea how many people just accept their fears and don't try to do a thing about it? You're already way ahead of every one of them."

"Thank you." Her eyes were wide and troubled as they clung to his. "I'll get there. I— Oh!" She pointed behind him. "Look at that huge bird! What is it? Is it stuck in the lagoon?"

CHAPTER EIGHT

ENZO TURNED TO see the bird, which had doubtless just dived into the water. "It's a cormorant. They're everywhere out here. The lagoon's bounty of fish and shellfish are a daily buffet."

"It looks trapped or something."

He looked again, then even closer. Was the bird really floundering? "Let's go take a look." With the oar shoved into the mud, he pushed the boat through the marshland.

"You look like a gondolier when you do that. Is that another of your many skills?"

"Is that a real question of a man who grew up here? I look exceptionally good in the striped shirt and be-ribboned hat."

Her laughter faded as they drifted up close to the bird and it became clear that it truly was in distress. "Is that…? What is that on it? Oil?"

"Don't know. Something like that." He tried to maneuver the boat close enough to see if there was something they could do without making the bird panic, jamming the oar deep into the mud to bring the boat to a stop. "With the industrial plants at Marghera and near the causeway, chemicals from agriculture, and all the tankers and cruise ships that come by, our pollution problems have gotten worse. We've put in buffer strips of trees and shrubs along the edges of the lagoon to try to catch it, but it's not a perfect solution."

"Poor bird!" Aubrey leaned over the edge of the boat toward the bird, obviously forgetting about being afraid of the water. "What can we do?"

"It's not completely covered in the oil, so that's good. Probably just dived into a single gob that had fallen off a ship. It still looks fairly healthy, I think." He glanced at her. Normally, when things like this happened, he'd get the bird on the boat and take it to one of his veterinary friends, but he knew from experience that sometimes the birds didn't like that too well. He didn't want to see Aubrey get splattered with the oil or, worse, pecked and injured, especially when they were on the water, which worried her.

"It won't be healthy for long. You know as well as I do that it won't be able to clean itself enough, or if it does the oil it eats off its feathers will make it sick."

"And how do you know this?"

"Just because you're a doctor and a prince and a native Venetian doesn't mean nobody else knows as much as you, Dr. Affini," she said with great dignity. "I volunteered off the coast of California when there was an oil slick once."

"A woman of many talents." He had to laugh as he said it, even as one or two of those talents that came to mind weren't funny, they were amazing, and he shouldn't be thinking about them. "So you won't freak out if I bring it on board and it flaps around? We'll have to try to secure it with something."

"The blanket will work." While she rummaged through the picnic bag, he got the medical bag he always kept with him in case there was an emergency, and snapped on the gloves.

"If we do this, I can't promise that you won't get covered with oil, or even bitten."

"I can handle both of those things. And I know a certain quack doctor who is very knowledgeable about bird bites and pecks." Her eyes laughed into his. "But we just need to hold him tight, right?"

"Hopefully right. But sometimes things don't always go as planned, you know?" He grinned back. "All right, then. After I put him in it, I'll keep his beak closed while you wrap him and hold him as tight as you can. Tell me when you're ready."

"Ready."

He draped the blanket over her shoulders, then smoothed it down over her legs as much as possible, and was it his fault he had to linger on each of those spots as he did?

"What kind of man uses rescuing a bird as an excuse to fondle a woman?"

"A man who keeps trying not to touch you, but can't help himself."

The seductive look she sent back to him jabbed him right in the solar plexus, along with a few other notable places, and that thing that kept shimmering between them lit the air. This time it was Aubrey who leaned in for the kiss, and he was only too happy to meet her halfway. Her mouth was sweet and soft and pliant, and if he hadn't had the damn gloves on he would have held her face in his hands, tipped it back, and kissed her until neither of them could think anymore, but that would have to wait.

He pulled back, loving the way her lips stayed parted

as she stared at him. "Hold that thought, okay? We have a good deed to do."

Maybe she was having as much trouble talking as he was, because she just nodded. He turned to slowly, carefully reach for the bird, bracing himself in case it tried to fly up into him. When he grasped its body, holding its wings down as firmly as he could, he was glad the bird only wrestled weakly to get away.

"Coming to you on the count of three. One, two, three." He pulled the bird from the water, pressed it into the cloth over Aubrey's waiting arms, then lifted one hand to slide his fingers around the bird's beak as she wrapped it and held it close to her breasts.

Lucky bird.

"I…I think I'm good," she said. Enzo used his free hand to help wrap it, while holding the beak tightly as the bird jerked its head up and down, trying to get loose. He took from his wrist the rubber band that he'd grabbed from his bag earlier and wrapped it around the beak. For having fairly small arms, it looked as if Aubrey had the huge bird held good and tight.

"I'm going to let go now, okay?" He watched carefully, ready to contain it if he had to, but the bird seemed to have given up the argument, and Aubrey's elated eyes met his.

"We did it!"

"Haven't gotten him back yet. So don't count your cormorants before they're hatched. Or something like that." She laughed as he snapped off the oily gloves to get the motor going. "I'm not going to go too fast, so it doesn't get scared."

"And so *I* don't get scared, wimp that I am." She said it without one bit of fear on her excited face, and Enzo's chest filled with something absurd, like maybe pride in her toughness, as he reached to stroke her soft cheek.

"You? A wimp? Wonderful nurse, fear-facer, and bird-rescuer? You, Aubrey Henderson, are a warrior."

All the way back, she talked to the bird in a soothing voice, and Enzo had to smile at how cute she was. His vet friend, Bartolomeo, met them at the dock, and the handoff proved to be a little awkward. Getting Aubrey out of the boat at the same time she held the bird tight wasn't easy, but finally she was standing on the walkway, able to carefully pass the bird to Bart.

"Is it going to be all right, do you think?" Aubrey asked, her happy expression dimmed with concern now.

"Do not worry, *signorina*," Bart said. "You have brought him in good shape. I have all I need to get it cleaned up and hydrated, and an assistant who enjoys helping with birds in trouble. Come to our office to see it in a few days—with a little luck, I think you'll be pleased."

"I'd like that. Seeing how you do things there would be interesting, too."

"Aubrey has told me about some of her many interests, Bart." Enzo smiled at the excitement on her face, despite the splotches of oil on various parts of her skin and dress. "She's participated in bird rescue in the past."

"Maybe you could come work at my veterinary clinic. We can always use extra hands."

"No way," Enzo said, stepping in fast before she had a chance to think about that. "I need her nursing skills at the clinic more than you need her giving shots to dogs and cats."

"No promises that I won't try to woo her over to my clinic instead, Enzo."

His friend's face might be grinning, but it showed

loud and clear that he was attracted to Aubrey, too, and what man in his right mind wouldn't be? The feeling of possessiveness that suddenly filled Enzo's chest was unfamiliar, but there was no denying that emotion was what drove him to reach for her hand. To place a kiss to her forehead in a clear message to Bart as to whom she belonged to.

For the moment, at least.

"I appreciate the offer, but I think nursing humans is my calling at this point. Thank you, though," Aubrey said, and Enzo felt relieved that she didn't scowl at him for answering before she could say a word, but squeezed his hand instead.

"Let me know if you change your mind. And now I'd best get this bird taken care of before he decides to dive back into the lagoon. *Arrivederci.*"

Glad the man and the bird were gone, Enzo was able to focus on just Aubrey again. He ran his fingers across the black smudges on her forehead and jaw, only managing to smear them even more. "You're a bit of a mess. And I am, too. The clinic is close by, so I suggest we go there to shower. Unless you gave away my change of clothes again?"

"Funny." She playfully swatted his arm. "I don't have extra clothes there, though. Maybe you should just take me home so I can clean up there."

"No. Because that would be the end of our evening together, and I'm not ready for that." The truth of his statement had him tugging her against him, not caring that the bits of oil on her skin would find their way to his shirt and pants. "Are you?"

"No," she said softly, and the way she smiled into his eyes and snaked her hands around his neck stole his breath. "I'm not."

He touched his lips to her nose and the places on her face that weren't smeared with oil before kissing her for real, and the heat of her mouth felt so arousing, so right, he had to break the kiss and suck in a deep breath before he stripped her naked right there in public.

"Come on. Let's get that oil off you." He grasped her hand and nearly ran the few blocks it took to get to the clinic. He quickly pushed the code into the keypad outside the back door and practically hauled her inside, not able to stop until they were in the locker room next to the shower.

"I'll go in first," she said in a prim voice totally at odds with the twinkle and heat in her eyes. "I'll let you know when it's your turn, Dr. Affini."

"Uh-uh. This job requires two people." He grabbed towels from the stack on the shelf, then washcloths, too, before reaching for her hem. He had the dress off and over her head in one quick movement, then reached around her to get the bra off, too.

"What kind of job are you referring to?" Her fingers were already working his belt, then the button and zipper, too, shoving his pants down his legs. One second later, she had her hands around the waistband of his boxer shorts, inflaming his obvious desire even further until he nearly groaned. "I think I'm handling this okay solo, don't you?"

"You're doing a fine job, yes," he said, his voice a little hoarse. "But once we've taken care of this part, the next jobs will take both of us."

"Jobs, plural? I might need more instruction on this job you're referring to. You might do it differently in this clinic than we do at home." Those beautiful, mysteriously colored eyes met his, and the heat and humor in them weakened his knees almost as much as the way she was touching him.

He opened the shower door, turned the water on, and finished getting both of them naked as fast as he could. "Pretty universal techniques around the world, I'd think. Except there's not one single thing that's just 'usual' when it comes to you, Aubrey Henderson."

The water spraying his back was still a little cold, so he pulled her in front of him to shield her from it until it warmed. Once he'd gotten a washcloth wet, he slathered it with soap. "Here's the two-person job. You can't see the black stuff smeared on your face, and this oil is tough stuff, so I'll have to wash it for you."

The frustration on her face made him chuckle as he gently washed the spot on her forehead. "If this is strictly medical, with you cleaning me like your friend is cleaning the bird, I might have to kill you."

"You had something else in mind, *bellezza*?" He scrubbed off the spot on her jaw, then slowly moved the washcloth down her throat, across her collarbone, and down to her nipple, following with his lips and tongue.

"Um…no. I can see this is…an excellent way to address the problem." She tipped her head back, and as he licked the water from the hollow of her throat and slid the cloth slowly back and forth across her breasts and down between her thighs, her little gasping breaths and the way she touched and stroked him back nearly sent him to his knees.

Which might not be a bad place to be.

So go there, he did. Kneeling before her, he held her sexy, round bottom in his hands and drew her to his mouth. Kissed and touched the slick sweetness of her center as she tangled her hands in his wet hair and made little sounds and it was so good he didn't notice how much her legs were shaking until she dropped to her knees, too, pushing him back onto his rear as she did.

"That was… I couldn't…" She stopped talking. With her lips parted, she stopped talking. Just stared at him with eyes that were filled with the same intense want that rushed uncontrollably through his veins and his mind and his heart.

"I know."

It was good that words weren't necessary any longer, since neither of them seemed able to say more than two of them in a row. She reached to touch him, her hands caressing his cheeks down to his shoulders as he lifted her to him, pressing her warm, wet breasts against his chest. He was barely aware of the water pouring over their heads and bodies. All he could think about was how she felt against him as she positioned herself and eased onto him. All he could see was how incredible she looked as she moved on him, needing to touch every part of her he could reach as she did. Her breasts, her hips. Her thighs and waist and where they were intimately joined. Her soft cheeks as he brought her mouth to his for a deep kiss that seemed to shake his very soul even as their orgasms shook their bodies. And when she pressed her torso to his, resting her face against his throat as their chests rose and fell in unison, he knew with certainty that he'd never before experienced anything like the physical pleasure and emotional closeness and mental connection all layered together that he felt at that moment with Aubrey in his arms.

Which was incredible and confusing and scary as hell.

CHAPTER NINE

AUBREY BLINKED AT the orange-yellow early-morning sunlight that spilled through the huge windows of Enzo's childhood home and across the thick cotton comforter. She turned her head and focused her bleary eyes on the oh-so-close chiseled features of Enzo, his head propped up on one hand and his sculpted lips curved in a smile.

"Buongiorno, mia bellezza," he murmured.

He pressed a soft kiss to her forehead, then lazily began twining a strand of her hair through his fingers. His slumberous dark brown eyes were looking at her in a way that told her he was ready to take up where they'd left off last night, and how that could be she had no clue, since three times in one night had been more incredible sex than she'd ever enjoyed in her life.

Than she ever expected to enjoy as much again.

"How can you be so wide-awake? We were up half the night." She rolled slightly toward him because she wanted to feel the warmth of his skin again. Wanted to feel the thud of his heart against her hands as she pressed them to that wide, well-defined chest. Wanted to slip her arms around his strong body and stay held close in his arms for the rest of the day.

For the rest of the time she'd be in Venice, and suddenly a few months didn't feel nearly long enough.

"Sleeping seems like a waste of time when I'm with you."

Oh. Well. When he put it that way, she'd have to agree. "Except sleep is kind of a necessity when we have to be at work in an hour. Or at least I do. Are you working today, too?" It suddenly struck her that Enzo might have scheduled her to work with the other clinic doctor—the one she hadn't even met yet—since their plans to keep that professional distance had gone up in smoke, then seriously hot flames, last night.

"You think I'd have you work with Antonio instead of me? No way. Women fall all over him, and he takes advantage of that. You're stuck working with me instead, Nurse Aubrey, for better or for worse."

She sat up. Did he mean that the way it had sounded? "So what you're saying is you think I'd sleep with any handsome man? Just because I slept with you that first night we met, I want you to know—"

"No, feisty one." He effectively stopped her by pressing his mouth to hers before propping his head on his hand again. He tugged at the strand of hair in his fingers, and the way he grinned in response seemed to show he was enjoying her annoyance. "I'm saying that I don't trust him to not come on to you, then I'd have to beat him up, and the clinic would be down to one doctor. Not the best thing for our many patients, do you think?"

She sank back into the mattress and snuggled up against him, liking his words more than she should. Since when had she ever been attracted to a possessive man?

Apparently, when that man was fun, smart, delectable Enzo Affini. And since they'd now moved way beyond a simple hookup, she wanted to learn more about him.

"That first night we met," she started to say, "you—"

"Couldn't resist kissing you."

"And prying for information about Shay. Which I told you I know is why you went out with me at all."

"Ah, you're wrong about that. I did want to find out more about the woman my brother was going to marry, but that was most definitely not the only reason I went out with you." Heat emanated from his body as he tugged her closer, and as he nuzzled her neck it was very apparent that he was ready for round four. "The second I spied you from across the room, I was extremely attracted, which alarmed me greatly."

"Alarmed you?"

"Because I thought you were Shay. Remember I told you I'm slightly color blind? Dante had told me she was wearing a green dress, and I thought yours was green." She could tell that the lips traveling across her throat and down to her collarbone were smiling. "Very bad form to lust after your future sister-in-law."

She started to laugh, then squeaked when his mouth found her breast. "I'm trying to have a conversation with you here." He didn't seem to listen, as he moved his attention lower to start nipping at her ribs, but maybe that had something to do with the fact that she was clutching the back of his head and holding him close.

"Converse away." His tongue slipped back up across her nipple and she gasped with the goodness of it before she managed to speak again.

"Tell me why you say you and your brother are bad bets."

She hadn't necessarily wanted to stop his very exciting ministrations, but her question had him lifting his head to look at her, all playfulness gone from his face.

"Because we are."

"People aren't just born bad bets, Enzo."

"And you would be wrong about that." His heavy sigh slid across her skin as he rolled to his back, bringing her with him. He just looked at her, seeming to think awhile before he finally spoke. "The Affini men are afflicted with a bad personality trait. My father's father was notorious for the number of women he kept, with my grandmother pretending to look the other way. My father was even worse, but my mother didn't pretend it wasn't happening. She spent their whole married life trying to change him."

"Did they fight?"

"I'm not sure you could call it that." He turned his head to look at her, and his dark eyes were filled with a peculiar mix of pain and anger and disgust. "My mother would cry and beg for him to stop and love only her, and he would respond that he knew she loved him enough for both of them. I never understood why, but that appeared to be the truth."

"That's…that's terrible! Why did she stay with him? Because of you and Dante?" Aubrey just couldn't imagine having the man she loved constantly cheating. She looked at Enzo as he held her naked body close to his, and realized that if she found out he'd been with another woman while they were sleeping together, it would tear her up inside. That they'd been together only once over two months ago, and a matter of days since then, wouldn't change that. Being together for years? Having children together? Impossible to imagine.

"No." He stroked his finger down her cheek. "We wanted her to leave him. My mother was a happy, loving, joy-filled woman except for this one, terribly painful thing in her life. We knew our home would be a more cheerful place, a better place, if he was out of the house. But even on the day she died, as he stood by her bedside, she told him how much she loved him."

"He must have felt terrible then. Must have told her how much he loved her, too."

A bitter laugh left Enzo's throat. "No. The only person my father loves is himself."

Her throat clogged for the poor woman who had loved a man who hadn't loved her back the same way. For the sons who'd grown up with a cold, selfish man for a father, doubtless feeling confused and hurt about all of it. Thought about her own mother. She'd never spoken of Aubrey's father, which had left Aubrey's imagination to create a larger-than-life dad.

Had her mother loved him? Had he left her? Was that why she'd done what she'd done?"

"And so you see why we are bad bets." He brought her mouth to his for a kiss so sweet, it was hard to imagine that he truly believed that about himself.

"Just because your dad isn't a good person doesn't mean you're not. You know that."

His answer was to kiss her again. "Your turn," he said, tucking her close and playing with her hair some more. "Tell me about your family."

She didn't really want to talk about it. But he'd answered her questions, hadn't he? Fair was fair.

"My mother was a very special person. So smart, and a wonderful, loving mom. We did everything together, until she got sick with cancer." She closed her eyes against the tears that threatened, but he turned her face to make her look into his warm and sympathetic eyes.

"Aubrey. It's okay to cry. I cried when I lost my mother, too. Sometimes I still do, when I think about losing the house she loved. So tell me about the wonderful woman who created such a special daughter."

She swallowed and forced herself to go on. "I told you she was afraid of crowds, of being around more than a few people. But in small groups, she was such an amazing leader. Her passion for the history of our city in Massachusetts, for our home and the other historic homes there, led her to start a number of architectural boards, and to get laws passed that would keep that history, that heritage, from being torn down or irreparably changed."

"We would have gotten along well, your mother and I."

"Yes." That thought managed to make her smile. "You would have."

"And your father?"

That, she definitely didn't want to talk about. "Let's just say he and your father have a lot in common."

"He cheated on her?" His voice had gone low and hard.

"No. Or at least, I have no idea about that. I never knew him until after she died. Other than telling me she got pregnant accidentally when she was only nineteen, she never talked about him. So, growing up, I created who he might be in my mind. Strong and handsome and fun. Someone everybody adored. My imaginary dad loved to fish with me, to travel places my mom didn't like to go. He loved to ride our horses, and he loved me."

Hearing herself say her childhood fantasies out loud made her feel ridiculous and embarrassed, and she turned her head away from the serious dark eyes listening so intently. "What time is it? I need to get showered. Get ready to go to the clinic."

"In a moment." A large, gentle hand nudged her gaze

back to his. "So you met him after your mother died. And he wasn't anything like your imaginary dad."

"At first, I thought he was. I was so thrilled to meet him, and he seemed like everything I'd ever dreamed he'd be. So handsome for a man in his fifties, well-groomed, with an easy, charming smile. He told me he hadn't known about me until my mother died, when her lawyer contacted him about some money in her will. Said he felt terrible he hadn't been part of my life growing up, but that he couldn't wait to make up for all the time we'd lost together." She shut her eyes, hating to think about how gullible she'd been. In some ways, still the little girl who'd long dreamed of her superhero dad. When she opened them, she could see Enzo's were still warm and sympathetic, but getting a little hard again, too. Smart man knew this story wasn't going anywhere good.

She was silent a long moment, but Enzo didn't speak. Just ran his hand slowly up and down her side, over her hip and back, not in a sensual way, but in a caring, soothing way. Giving her time. And that comforting touch made her want to talk about it after all.

She sucked in a breath and forged on. "He started coming around all the time, four or five times a week. We rode the horses together. Went on quite a few excursions. He seemed so interested in my nursing career, even sometimes came to a few of the architectural review meetings that I'd taken over for my mom, saying he wanted to support her passion, too. He was fun and exciting and I just felt so blessed to have finally met him. I'd lost my mom, but, after all these years, God had helped me find my dad."

"And then what happened?"

"He told me about a project he needed money for.

Just a loan, to help him refurbish a few old homes he'd bought in another state. It was a lot of money, but I knew my mom would have wanted that, too. So I gave it to him."

"Oh, *tesoro*." The hand cupping her face was full of tenderness. "I'm guessing that was the last you saw of the money."

"The money, and my father." It angered her that it still hurt. She didn't even know the man, really. They shared only genes. So how could she let his dishonesty, his manipulation, his lack of moral character, hurt her at all? "Once he had the money, he disappeared. No more visits, no more telling me how happy he was to have me in his life. I soon found out through my mom's lawyer that she'd been paying him money for years to stay away, and when it stopped coming, that's when he found out she'd died. I have no idea if she paid him because she didn't want to see him, or if she knew her teen crush had turned out to be a gambler and a con man, or what. All I know is that she didn't want him to be part of my life. And I feel so stupid that I fell for the charade and for his lies."

"What a terrible thing for you to have to go through." The way he tucked her face against his neck and hugged her close felt so good, she found herself clinging to him. Hungrily soaking in the warmth and comfort he offered. "But you must tell yourself what Dante and I eventually learned. Our father's cold, selfish heart isn't the way it is because of anything we did, and no amount of love from our mother could've changed him. That's true for you, too. You wanted and deserved a good father who loved you, and it's his loss that he will never have the kind of relationship with you that you could have offered him. I'd feel sorry for him if I didn't want to beat the hell out of him."

"Thank you." Trust him to make her smile, even as she thought about how much she hated being used by the man. "If he shows up again wanting more money, can I give him your address as the place to pick it up, so you can punch his lights out?"

"It would be my pleasure. As is this, *mia belleza*." He ran his hand down her hip again, before pulling her thigh over his. It was very apparent that their serious conversation hadn't affected his libido, and even as she was thinking they were going to be late for work, she wrapped her leg farther around him, tangled her fingers in his hair, and kissed him.

Bing-bong. The jarring sound was so loud, she jumped and nearly knocked her skull into the huge, carved wood headboard as she clutched her hand to her chest. "What was that?"

He frowned and sat up. "The doorbell. Is there another UWWHA nurse coming to stay here?"

"Not until next month, as far as I know." She hated to leave the sizzling warmth that had been zinging between them, but maybe it was for the best. "Saved by the bell, maybe? Otherwise we might have had an annoyed line of patients at the clinic before we even got there."

He responded with a heated grin as the bell gonged again, and she slid out of the bed to shove on her robe and see who the heck could be ringing.

"I'll get it." Enzo was putting his pants on with some difficulty, since his body apparently hadn't figured out they weren't doing *that* after all.

"I have my robe on already. Besides, I don't want to get a bad reputation around here with a sexy, half-naked man answering my door. Be right back."

She ran her hands through the current mess on her head as she trotted down the stone stairs, not wanting to look as if she'd just gotten lucky, even though she sure had last night. Very, very lucky. The giant door was heavy, and she slowly pulled it open to see a man standing there, formally dressed in a suit and tie and carrying a briefcase.

"May I help you?"

"Are you Aubrey Henderson?"

"Yes."

"The owner of this house has informed the UWWHA about this but wants to let you, as the current tenant, know personally, as well."

"Know what?"

"This property is almost in contract with a new buyer. The funding will be finalized within the next few days. When the purchase is complete, I'm afraid this home will no longer be available to rent, as it will go under construction immediately. The UWWHA tells me they will be contacting you about new housing. My client is giving you a three-day notice to be moved out. You will be refunded your rent accordingly."

He pulled several papers from his briefcase to hand to her, but Aubrey could barely see them as she reached for them with icy hands. All she was seeing was Enzo's determined face when he said he'd do anything he could to save the house he'd grown up in. All she was hearing was his voice telling her how much he loved this home.

Her voice shook with the big question she needed answered. "May I ask who the new buyer is?"

"Proviso Hotels. They will do a magnificent job re-modeling this run-down place. You will have to come stay here again when it's finished. I am sure you will marvel at its transformation to the kind of new and modern hotel tourists will love."

CHAPTER TEN

"I TOLD YOU to sell those a week ago! Why aren't I seeing the funds as available in the account yet?"

Enzo paced his small office in the clinic, worry and frustration gnawing at his gut. Was Leonardo inept? Hadn't he made it clear to the man that he needed to immediately liquidate the assets that he'd outlined in detail?

"I did sell them. I don't know why it's not showing up as cash yet, but I'll find out right now."

"Find out sooner than right now. I need to know exactly how much more I need to outbid Proviso so I can figure out a way to get the rest by tomorrow."

He flicked through the reams of papers he'd pulled from his briefcase and laid on his desk at the clinic. He leaned his palms on his desk as he did, fighting a sickening feeling of impending defeat. Never before had he brought this kind of work to the clinic. Had always tried to keep his medical work separate from the vineyards and wineries he and Dante helped operate, and from his other business investments.

But today wasn't the day to care about that kind of separation. Desperate times called for desperate measures, as the saying went, and if he had to stare at the numbers and what else could be quickly sold to get fast cash in between seeing patients, that was what he'd have to do. Maybe there was some solution he wasn't seeing yet. Or maybe there was no solution, and his fight would end in failure, which he'd refused, until this moment, to believe could really happen.

In the midst of his intense concentration, he heard a soft knock on his office door. *"Entra."*

"Enzo."

He looked up to see Aubrey staring at him, her fingers twining anxiously together as if she had some bad news.

"What is it? Someone I need to see?"

"No. The last couple of patients have all had simple problems I could take care of without bothering you."

"Then…?"

"I want to talk to you about your house."

"Aubrey." For some inexplicable reason, just looking at her sweetly earnest face helped his lungs breathe a little easier. Which made no sense. Her caring and warmth and beauty weren't going to save his mother's house. The house she'd loved so much, that he had, too, and that he'd so wanted to keep forever. The house he'd never dreamed would be lost to him in yet another selfish sweep by his father.

Her worried eyes stayed glued to his for a long moment before she spoke again. "Your house. We need to talk."

"I appreciate that you care. I do, more than you know." And the truth of that loosened the tense knots bunching in every muscle. "But talking isn't going to fix this problem, *bellezza*. Money is going to fix this problem, and I'm doing all I can to get it together in time to save it."

"Well, that's what I want to talk about." She licked

her lips, and just as he was going to tell her not to worry, that it wasn't her problem to stress about, Nora swept into the room.

"Franca Onofrio just called. She said Carlo looks very ill, but he is refusing to go to the hospital to see what the problem is. Are you able to go see him today?"

"You want me to go by myself while you work on this?" Aubrey asked. "It might be something I can handle on my own, and if not I can call you."

"A very nice offer that I appreciate. But my first responsibility is to my job and the patients in this city, and Carlo's English is hard to follow. He's diabetic and had to have one leg removed below the knee a couple years ago. I should come to see what's going on."

"All right. I'll get both our bags together and meet you out back in, what, five minutes?"

"Yes. *Grazie.*"

He watched her rush out, wondering how he could ever have been suspicious of her motives for coming to Venice, and for working in his clinic. The woman was not only beautiful and exuberant, she was all about what she could do for others, not for what others could do for her. Something not at all true about many of the women he'd dated over the years.

After gathering the items he always took on house calls, they walked through narrow passageways and over cobbled bridges on their way to Carlo's house. "Are you glad he lives close enough that we didn't need to ride on the *vaporetto*?" he asked.

"I'm slowly getting used to the water. The risk of hyperventilating the next time I'm on a boat is getting less and less, I think."

"*Bene.*" He liked the cute way she poked fun at herself, and, since he seemed to always be looking for a reason to touch her, he put his arm around her and tugged her against him, dropping a kiss on her forehead. "You may end up buying a boat of your own when you go back home."

He'd said the words without thinking, but when they came out of his mouth it struck him how much he would miss her. The months would go by too quickly, of that he was sure. But he also knew, deep in his soul, how lucky he was to have met her for this brief time. And since he'd been given that unexpected gift, maybe that meant he'd find a way to save his mother's house, too.

"Maybe." She looked away from him and after a pause began exclaiming brightly about the various doorways she liked to admire. Too brightly, really, and he looked closer at her, wondering if she was bothered by walking so close to the canal, or if her chatter was hiding something else.

Then she abruptly stopped talking, turning to him with an odd look of determination on her face. "About your house."

"So that's what's bothering you." He pressed a lingering kiss to her soft cheek, wanting to show her how much it meant to him that she cared. "Please stop worrying about it. I hope to have some numbers in hand later today, and I need to talk to Dante about a few of our joint liquid assets, as well."

She opened her mouth to say something else, but he dropped a quick kiss to her lips before she could speak. "Here we are at the Onofrios'. It's time to get to work."

They rang the bell and within seconds Franca had opened the door for them, ushering them inside. Enzo nudged Aubrey in ahead of him, following her through the arched stone doorway that was so low, he had to duck his head beneath it.

They followed Franca to another room, listening to her talk the whole time about how stubborn Carlo was, and how he wouldn't do a thing she asked him to. Enzo smiled to himself, thinking Aubrey would have appreciated the diatribe if she understood fast Italian, but when her amused eyes met his he could tell she got the gist of it anyway. Because it was in the center of a row of houses, the interior was fairly dark, and it took a moment for his eyes to adjust before he spotted Carlo sitting in a chair in the corner.

"I hear you're not feeling too well. What's the problem?" He felt a little rude speaking in Italian when he knew Aubrey couldn't follow, but their patient's comfort was the most important thing and he'd fill her in as he could.

"I'm okay. Franca just likes to worry and nag me."

"Which makes you a lucky man."

Carlo huffed an annoyed breath, and Enzo noted how dry his lips looked. Eyes looked a little sunken, too, so he'd guess the man was very dehydrated. He switched to English. "Aubrey, please take his vital signs. Also check his blood sugars."

She nodded and went about getting his blood pressure and sugar levels while Enzo listened to his chest. "Have you been taking your insulin the way you're supposed to?"

"Yes. Well, not this week, because I ran out."

"You ran out?" Enzo looked at him in surprise. "You know how important it is to keep your insulin levels on target. Did you—"

Franca interrupted him to loudly scold her husband, even smacking him on the shoulder as he shook his head and apparently tuned her out. Enzo glanced over to see Aubrey's eyebrows raised at the argument, and he gave her a quick grin. He'd been taking care of both of them for quite a while and couldn't remember a single time when they hadn't gotten into it over something.

"Aubrey, what's his sugar reading?"

She peered at the monitor, then her mouth dropped open as she stared up at him. "Top reading is five hundred, and it's over that."

Enzo cursed under his breath and turned to the fighting couple, needing to get this thing moving before Carlo got any worse. "You two do know I'm charging you by the minute, don't you?" He said it with a grin and this time it was his arm that Franca whacked. "In all seriousness, Carlo, your sugars are way high. Your potassium is high, and your sodium is low. Since you don't have any insulin in the house, and since you're obviously dehydrated, too, I want you to go to the hospital to get insulin right away, and some fluids."

"I don't want to go to the hospital. Franca will go get my insulin, and I'll be fine."

"I'm not arguing with you about this. I'm calling the ambulance boat, and you're going."

The man looked mulish, as if he was going to argue some more, but apparently could tell Enzo meant business and just scowled. Enzo quickly called the ambulance with the information, then turned to Franca, telling her about how soon they'd arrive. "I'll come back in a couple days to check on him. And please get his insulin prescription filled right away."

Thanking him, and nicely including Aubrey in her nods, she told them to wait a moment, returning with a bag of cookies she insisted they take. "You'll love Franca's biscotti," he said to Aubrey as they headed out the door. "Maybe we should take a coffee break to enjoy them with." Taking a short break with Aubrey, away from the clinic and the financial statements hanging over his head in his office, sounded better than good.

"I thought you had more paperwork you had to deal with."

"An hour isn't going to make a difference." He looked at her and realized how badly he needed and wanted a break that included spending real time with her. "There's no doubt in my mind that an hour with you would boost my spirits."

"Sounds like a lot of responsibility, Dr. Affini, but you know what? I just might have an idea on what would cheer you up."

Bright sunshine poured down on them as they walked down the canal toward one of Enzo's favorite coffee shops. He wrapped his arm around Aubrey's waist, and just tugging her close was enough to boost his spirits already.

"Isn't it a beautiful day? Not a cloud in the sky." The smile she turned to him was wide and full of the joy he'd seen in her so often, but at the same time he could tell it was shadowed with concern. "Though I know it's hard to enjoy when you have such a tough situation going on right now. I can't tell you how sorry I am about that."

"I'll figure it out." He had no idea if that was true, but what was the point of her worrying, too?

They moved from the narrow passage to a walkway by one of the small canals. Children were kicking a ball back and forth across it, laughing and good-naturedly arguing when the ball plopped into the water.

"Is this a game you played as a kid?" she asked, holding her hand above her eyes to shield them from the high, midday sun.

"Dante and our friends were always cooking up new

games to play when older games got boring, but I'm not sure about this one. Looks like they're trying to either catch the ball, or kick it into one of the boats."

"I can just see you as a boy playing here."

"Because I seem childlike to you?"

"Um…that would be a definite no." There was a teasing smile on her lips as she looked up at him, but her gaze didn't seem smiling at all. It seemed hot and filled with sexy thoughts, and he was so mesmerized by it, he didn't see the ball heading straight toward his head until it smacked right into him, practically knocking him sideways.

"Oh, my gosh!" Aubrey rested her soft palm against his temple. It throbbed and hurt like crazy, but he wasn't going to let her know that. "Are you all right?"

"Good thing it hit my head. Dante would say it's the hardest part of me."

"That's because he doesn't know what's *really* the hardest part of you."

That made a laugh burst out of his chest, which made his head ache even worse. He leaned toward her, loving the coy look on her face that was making that sometimes hard part of him start to do exactly what she was talking about. "Ah, *bellezza*. I'm more than happy to—"

The boys interrupted him with a spate of shouts, and he turned to see the ball floating down the canal, out of their reach.

"They want you to fetch the ball, I'm guessing?"

"Your Italian is getting good, Ms. Henderson."

"Don't have to speak Italian to figure that out." She grinned. "Need help?"

"No. I'll use a fishing net from one of these boats. Be right back."

It took just a few minutes, and as he was shaking

water from the ball before he carried it back he heard the children screaming, then Aubrey shrieking.

What the…? He looked up just in time to see Aubrey's white skirt flying into the air in front of her fluttering legs and shoed feet before she did a belly flop straight into the canal.

CHAPTER ELEVEN

Mio Dio. With his heart pounding straight up into his throat, Enzo sprinted to the spot she'd gone in, about to jump in himself when Aubrey's head came back up. Her soaking hair was streaming into her eyes and he could tell she was catching her breath, but was obviously treading water as she held a crying, very small little girl in her arms. She was talking in a breathless but soothing voice to the child, pushing the girl's black hair out of her eyes as she did. Since Aubrey wasn't using her hands to swim, she must have been doing some kind of scissor kick, as she was making her way over to the wall of the canal. Several children were standing there ready to grab the little one, but Enzo stepped in front of them, pulled her from Aubrey's arms, handed her to one of the older kids, then reached for Aubrey.

Hardly able to breathe, as if he'd been the one underwater, he shoved his hands deep down to grasp her waist. Lifting her out of the canal and high into his arms, he smashed her tightly against his chest as he pressed his cheek to hers. After barely starting up again from the scare of seeing her go into that water, his heart now slammed hard against hers, and he wasn't sure if it was her shaking from the chill of the water, or him shaking, or both of them.

"What were you thinking? Why in the world did you do that? Can you even swim?"

"I told you, I can swim. I swim in pools all the time. It's dark lake and river water that scares me."

"Which the canal is. *Dio!*" He lifted his head just enough to look in her eyes, and that they were shining and happy made him want to shake her. "Seeing you go in that water took ten years off my life."

"I'm sorry." From the gleam in her eyes, it didn't seem like she was sorry at all. "But we need to check on the little one. Hold on."

She pulled herself from his arms, smoothed the rest of her wet hair from her face, and crouched down to the child, who Enzo could now see was probably only three years old, or so. She was still crying, but just a little, sniffling and nodding and looking a little shy as Aubrey spoke to her. Enzo had a feeling the child had no idea what Aubrey was saying, but the way she smiled at her was a universal language, wasn't it?

Aubrey gave her a quick hug as the older children thanked her, picked up the ball Enzo had dropped when he'd fished them both out of the canal, and went off to play again.

"Are you done playing hero for today?" He folded his arms across his chest, wanting her to know that, even though it had turned out well, he still couldn't believe she'd put herself at risk like that, scaring him to death in the process, when it should have been him going in after the child.

"For today, yes." She grinned at him. "Oh, come on. If you'd been standing there, you would have gone in, too."

"In case you hadn't noticed, I was plenty close enough to have done the jumping in. Not to mention that I'm not afraid of water, which might have sent you into a panic, which you know as well as I do is often the reason people drown."

"You're being dramatic. I knew you were close by." She waved her hand before she used it to pull his wet, clinging shirt away from his skin. "But I am sorry I got you all wet. And that you were worried."

Exactly how worried still shocked him. He couldn't deny that the instant terror he'd felt had been a little unnecessary. Extreme, even. And what exactly that said, he didn't want to analyze too much.

"We should get back to the clinic." His voice was gruff, and he knew the arm he wrapped around her waist was a little too tight, but that was too bad. He needed to feel it there. Needed to hold her close.

That closeness had him finally thinking less about how upset he'd been and what had just happened and more about her and her discomfort when he felt her shivering against him. He stopped to rub his hands briskly over the goose bumps on her arms. "You're cold. How about I get you a water taxi back to the house? You can take a hot shower, change into dry clothes, and relax without worrying about coming back to work."

"I'm fine." She ran her hands up his damp shirt to wrap them around his neck as she pressed her smiling mouth against his as he folded her close, feeling the tension of the past five minutes slip away as he held her. "I'll take a shower at the clinic. Get into a dry uniform there. But you're sweet to want to take care of me."

Surprising was the word he'd use, since wanting to take care of her seemed extremely important. Remembering all they'd done in that shower got his heart rate cranking all over again, and he kissed her again, a little deeper this time. When he came up for air, he heard some giggling and realized a few of the kids were watching.

"The Italian version of the peanut gallery," he said drily as he took her hand. "Let's get you into that shower, and, Aubrey?"

"Yes?"

"Warning you that I just might use having my clothes wet, too, as a great excuse to join you there."

With the last patient of the day gone and the clinic closed, Aubrey paced in front of Enzo's office door. After they'd returned yesterday to dry off after her canal plunge, he'd spent most of the afternoon in there. Today, he'd been closeted inside the entire time he wasn't seeing patients, studying spreadsheets, making long private phone calls, and disappearing periodically. Clearly, he hadn't found a solution yet.

She wasn't sure she should disturb him, and even less sure what exactly she should say, even though she'd been pondering it for two solid days. Thinking about her forced move date from his house—former house—tomorrow. He'd been so busy with it, the other doctor had come to the clinic for a few hours to take over some of the patient load. And while Dr. Lambre was nice enough, and a good doctor, work hadn't been the same without Enzo patiently working along with her. Exuding his potent charm and sending that impish grin to some patients, while getting gently tough—a seeming oxymoron he amazingly managed—with the most difficult patients.

Despite their rocky start when she'd first returned to Venice, she'd come to see that he was a good man. A very special man. And because he was, and because she wanted to help him and *could* help him, she stiffened her spine and forced herself to knock on the door.

"Entra."

Holding her breath, she pushed open the door, expecting him to be looking up at her. Instead, his head was lowered to the papers in front of him, a deep frown creased his brow, and, even worse, his fingertips were pressed against his closed eyes.

That utter picture of stress and despair made her heart squeeze hard in her chest. Made her wish she were a huge, burly man who could go find his father and beat the heck out of him for doing this to his son, the way Enzo had said he would do to her own father if he could. But it also made what she had to say easier.

"I'm sorry to bother you. But can we talk for a minute?"

His hands dropped to the desk as he looked up and gave her a smile. If you could call it a smile, because it was a forced, gray shadow of his usual, adorable grin. "Of course. I'm sorry that I've been busy and…absent. I hope working with Antonio has been okay?"

"It's been fine." She sucked in another fortifying breath and forged on. "I know you have a lot going on, but can we maybe get a drink somewhere in the fresh air? It's a beautiful evening, and I know you probably need a break."

The eyes that looked back at her were dark and scarily lacking all their usual warmth and vivacity, but she could see him trying hard to push past the darkness obviously consuming him right now.

"A break and a drink sounds good. Better than good, if it's with you."

Relief weakened her knees, and she walked to his desk to reach out her hand. "You promised to be my

Venetian tour guide, His Excellency Dr. Prince Affini. Where's the best place close to here for a perfect Italian Bellini?"

"Bellinis are a bit fruity for my taste, but, if that's what you want, I know of a good place a bit past all the tourist spots, but not too far."

That it had taken a long moment for him to grasp her hand worried her, and the half smile he gave her worried her, too, but she'd get him out of the clinic any way she could. Because they had important things to talk about, and maybe those things would bring the smile she'd come to love back to his handsome face.

The sun was hiding behind thick clouds on the horizon as they walked along the Riva Degli Schiavoni toward the restaurant and bar Enzo had suggested with obvious reluctance. Aubrey pondered when and how to broach the subject they needed to talk about. The evening was alive with tourists walking the promenade, and vendors of all kinds were working to sell their wares, but one in particular caught her eye.

"Those watercolors are beautiful, don't you think? Do you mind if we look? I'm going to need a few souvenirs to take home."

She didn't really want to think about souvenirs, and about going home, but hoped maybe a benign distraction and conversation would be a good thing before she tackled what she really wanted to talk about over that Bellini.

"You do realize there are dozens of artists selling paintings of Venice everywhere you go here." The smile Enzo sent her was better, a little more real, than the one they'd started this excursion with, and her heart lifted a little that it was a start.

"I know. But I might find the perfect one when I

least expect it, right? Why wait until the day before I'm leaving for the States?"

He seemed to look at her a long time before he answered. "Yes. Why wait?"

Her stomach jittered with nerves, and she made some lighthearted conversation about all the touristy stuff for sale, trying to bring them back to their former relaxed banter. As they walked along there were artists who were painting at the same time they chatted to tourists. Others sat on folding chairs, looking a little bored as people walked by to admire their work.

"I can guess which artists are selling more, can't you?" Just as she said it in a grinning undertone her heart jolted in her chest at one of the watercolors on display.

"Look!" So surprised, she felt a little breathless as she tugged him toward the various canvases propped on easels next to stacks of other artwork. "It's your house. Your beautiful house. Right there, in the painting!"

"Sì." His arm wrapped around her waist and held her close to his hard body as he looked down at her, and not the painting. "It's a very famous house. One often photographed as being quintessential Venetian, standing tall and proud in the middle of two canals. You've already noticed its unique design. One of the many important buildings that are part of our history. Part of the fortunes and extravagance of nobles and aristocracy from bygone days."

She stared up at him as his dark gaze met hers. For those who might not know him, his expression seemed impassive. Matter of fact. But she knew differently. Knew that beyond the calm facade he tried to portray to others lay a world of emotion. A deep love for this city and his ancestral home and, yes, for his mother. A love that went far beyond the connection Aubrey felt to her house in Massachusetts that her mother had held dear to her heart. The home in this painting, this amazing place built more than seven hundred years ago, the house he'd grown up in, could never be replaced. Because it was irreplaceable.

That certain conviction gave her the strength she needed. "Are we getting close to that Bellini? Because I'm dying of thirst."

"That's surprising, since you decided to drink some canal water yesterday." He dropped a smiling kiss to her forehead. "Don't worry, it's not much farther."

Aubrey was glad that an outside table set slightly apart from the others was available for them. Sitting there looking out over the darkening water, she clutched her cold glass and glanced at Enzo as she breathed in the lagoon air for strength. Nerves jittered in every muscle, and, while it seemed ridiculous, she knew it wasn't because what she was about to say was important to only her. She knew it was important to him, too, and also knew it was going to be very hard to convince him to accept her help. And learning exactly where everything stood and what weighed in the balance had to come first.

"So, tell me what progress you've made on buying the house back."

His eyes met hers, dark and brooding and so somber, she wanted to reach for him before they said another word. She tightened her fingers on her drink and bit her tongue to keep from touching him or saying anything else, because, as hard as it was to be patient, she knew she had to give him a chance to talk.

"If you're wanting me to say that all is fixed and I've

bought the house back and you can keep living there, I'm afraid I can't."

"The house sale is due to close day after tomorrow."

"This I know. Your point?"

"I want to help."

His chest heaved in a deep sigh as he reached for her hand. "And I thank you for that. But this is a battle I must finish on my own."

"Why? Are you too proud to accept help?"

"Aubrey. There is no way for you to help." He said her name on a long breath, a quiet defeat in his voice as he brought her hand to his mouth, holding his lips there until she loosened it to hold his cheek in her palm instead.

"Maybe that's because you haven't yet listened to what I have to say."

A sad smile that was so unlike any Enzo smile she'd seen before touched his lips. "Then of course I'm more than willing to hear it. You have much wisdom in that amazing brain of yours."

"Thank you. But this isn't about wisdom." She licked her lips and stared into the brown eyes she'd come to care about so much, praying he'd accept her proposal. "This is about practicality and business, pure and simple."

"You have a business proposition for me?" This time, his smile looked a little more real. "Talented nurse, architectural historian, child rescuer, and a businesswoman, too? I'm all ears."

"I'm glad to hear that. How much money do you still need to outbid Proviso?"

"About one hundred thirty-five thousand euro. Which today is approximately one hundred fifty thousand dollars."

"I'm guessing you're having a hard time getting it by tomorrow."

"You already know that most of the land we own is held in trust, and I don't have access to it to sell it. I've liquidated a number of my assets, but many others aren't liquid. And I can't take out more loans, because that would be irresponsible. I have to think about the people who work for me on my various properties. Dipping into the accounts that pay them would be wrong. So I'm coming up short but am still working on it."

"But it's not looking good."

"No." The dark eyes that met hers communicated much more than that simple word. "It's not looking good."

"I have a solution." She drew breath, afraid to say it because she had a bad feeling he'd flatly say no. "I'd like to give one hundred fifty thousand dollars to the fund you have set up to buy it back."

His stunned expression would have been comical if there had been anything funny about the situation he faced. "What? No."

"Yes." She reached for his hand. "I love that house, too, and I've lived there barely two weeks. I can't imagine you losing it when you and your mother grew up there. You know that saving historical homes is important to me and was important to *my* mother. Seeing her money, which is now mine, go to keeping a historic landmark from being gutted would make her happy. And it would make me happy, too."

"Aubrey." He shook his head as he stared at her. "I can't accept that. It might take me a long time to pay you back."

"You wouldn't have to pay it back. It would come out of the same fund I accessed to adopt the fresco. That my mother set up years ago for preserving homes like yours. Well, not exactly, because there's nothing like yours in the US." She smiled, wanting to make him smile, too. To see that it really was all right for him to accept her offer.

He lifted her hand and brought it to his lips as he had before, then leaned across the table to kiss her mouth. Soft and sweet and so full of emotion, it felt as if the kiss sneaked all the way into her heart. She clutched at his shoulders to draw him closer, and when their lips finally parted, their eyes met in the silent connection she'd felt since the first moment they met.

"Say yes," she breathed.

His lips brushed hers as he shook his head. "No, *tesoro*. I can't. I'm moved more than I can say by your generous offer, but this is my battle to fight."

"So you won't let anyone else on the battlefield to fight with you?"

"Not you, not anyone except my brother and my bankers. But there is one thing you can do for me."

"What?"

He held her face in his hands, and the eyes meeting hers held something like awe along with the heat that made her quiver. "Let me spend one more night in the house with you. One more sweet night with a special woman to join the many important memories I already have there. Please?"

As if he had to ask. And maybe, just maybe, after another night of lovemaking she could change his mind. She pressed her lips to his and whispered, "Your wish is my command, Your Excellency."

CHAPTER TWELVE

ENZO WAS GLAD that the clinic had been filled with patients all morning, and that Aubrey hadn't been there with him. Focusing on work was probably the only way to take his mind off the reality of what was happening today. That it was moving day for Aubrey, with the sale of the house going through soon. His stomach had churned about it for days now, but today he felt more resigned to the harsh reality that it would soon no longer be the house it had been for so many centuries, but transformed into some monstrosity instead.

He knew that making love with Aubrey again last night was part of the reason he felt calmer about it. Something about being with her had filled the empty hollow in his chest when he'd finally seen there was almost no chance that he could buy the house in time. Took some of the sadness away, too. Even some of the exhaustion he'd felt when it became painfully clear that defeat was imminent.

That she'd offered him so much money to help him blew his mind. Free and clear and with no strings attached just because she knew it was important to him. Yes, he knew she liked the house, and was fascinated by its history, but that could be said of any number of houses in Venice ready to go on the chopping block, and probably a few of the older homes in the States that her mother had cared about.

No, he knew she'd offered it because she cared about him. Which humbled him. Overwhelmed him. And when he'd made love with her last night, his heart had felt strangely light and heavy at the same time. Had felt a reverence for her when he'd kissed her and touched her that was completely foreign to his existence. Emotions he'd never felt or experienced before, and he knew he was teetering dangerously close to loving her.

And that would be bad. Very bad for her. He knew it but selfishly couldn't bring himself to end things just yet. They both knew there was an end date for their relationship, didn't they? She had a life and home to go back to in the States after she was done with her tenure here. Just thinking about how much he would miss her when she left stabbed his heart before it had even happened. But he knew that a few more months with her would be more than worth the pain and emptiness he'd feel after she was gone.

The ring of his cell phone startled him and he fished it out of his pocket to see it was Leonardo. A few days ago he might have gotten hyped up about a phone call, wondering if there was good news, but today he knew the conversation would be more about closure. About what to do with the funds they'd liquidated into cash now that they couldn't buy the house.

"Have you seen this, Enzo?" Leonardo's voice was loud and excited and Enzo strode into his office, wondering what the man could possibly be so excited about.

"What?"

"There's enough money in the fund!"

"What do you mean?"

"There's been a big cash transfer. We've done it!

I've sent it all over to the Realtor and lawyer to get the transaction expedited and completed, hopefully today. If all goes well, that house will be yours again by tomorrow, Enzo. Congratulations."

He dropped down into his chair, and a sudden, sickening feeling joined the cautious optimism that swirled around his gut. "Where did this cash transfer come from?"

"It's from a trust in the States. Henderson LLC. Do you know who that is?"

Dio.

He scrubbed his hand down his face. What should he do? Should he accept Aubrey's incredibly generous gift? Let the sale go through? Getting to keep that house and eventually renovating it would all be due to Aubrey if he did.

A deep sigh left his aching chest. He wanted to. *Dio,* he wanted to more than he could say. But what kind of person would that make him? Taking that kind of money from a woman so incredibly special, so amazing, so loving and giving, while offering her absolutely nothing in return would be all kinds of wrong.

He wasn't a fool. He knew women. He knew Aubrey was coming to care for him the way he was her, even though he didn't deserve it. That she was on the verge of loving him, which last night had proven to both of them.

He couldn't let himself be the kind of rat his father was, using her to his own ends without being able to commit to her. Loving her while she was here, yes, but he couldn't love her forever because that would just end up in pain and sorrow for Aubrey, and she deserved so much more than that.

She deserved the world from a man who wasn't a bad bet, and he knew at that moment with absolute certainty that he had to save her from him. He already wanted to keep her close. The way he felt about her filled his chest and heart in a way he'd never experienced before. Big and overwhelming, and because of that he could see himself making promises he couldn't keep.

He absolutely could not selfishly hurt her that way.

No. He'd send her money back to her and keep his distance. Work opposite shifts, and have Antonio work with her instead of him. Maybe he'd even take some vacation time away from the clinic, go see how the vineyards and wineries were doing. Spend time with his brother and get to know Shay.

Losing both Aubrey and the house at the same time made his heart feel as if it had turned into a heavy stone weight, but it was the only choice he could make.

He refused to be the man his father was. He would not be the man who broke Aubrey Henderson's beautiful heart.

"We can't accept the money, Leonardo. Don't argue with me, please. I'm telling you we can't. Transfer it back to the trust with our thanks and regrets."

"*Buongiorno*, Aubrey." Antonio Lambre gave her a smile as she walked into the clinic. "No patients here yet, so take your time changing."

"Thanks, Dr. Lambre. I'll be ready shortly." She moved to the locker room, and her stomach lurched the way it had the past seven days. A rising anger had joined her confusion and the sick feeling in her belly every day that she'd come to the clinic and Enzo hadn't been there.

She knew he'd been in Venice the entire past week, because of course she'd had to look at the work schedule. Which he'd carefully written to have them work on days opposite one another. She'd called him a couple times, too, to see how he was feeling now that the house sale had gone through and ask if he was happy and if he was going to move there, since the UWWHA nurses weren't renting it anymore. To ask if he wanted to come see the awful little modern apartment they'd stuck her in and laugh about it.

And how unbearably humiliating was all that? Calling him like a moonstruck teen, even though it was now beyond clear he was avoiding her big-time. Embarrassing beyond belief that she'd secretly hoped he'd ask her if she wanted to move back to his house, now that he owned it free and clear. The paperwork from her financial advisor and lawyers had come through showing he'd happily accepted the money he'd claimed he didn't want. And she'd seen in the newspaper just that morning that the house was officially back in the royal family again.

Was it possible that he was just super busy with finalizing everything? But how could he be so busy that he wouldn't even call her? Wouldn't want to celebrate with her?

She moved toward the new week's schedule, hating to have to see how he'd written it this time, at the same time stupidly hoping she was wrong, that he wasn't avoiding her, that there was some other explanation. That they'd be working together again. Sharing picnics again. Making love again. Then stared when she saw he wasn't on the schedule at all.

"Just step right in here, Madame Durand. The nurse will be with you in a moment."

Aubrey ran her suddenly icy hands down her skirt and stepped to the hallway as Nora closed the exam-room door.

"I have a patient for you, Aubrey. Room two."

She nodded and licked her lips to moisten her dry mouth. Her heart was thumping so hard she could hear it in her ears, and she was having so much trouble breathing she had to suck in air twice before she spoke. "Nora. I see that Dr. Affini isn't on the schedule for this next week. Do you know why?"

"He took some time off to go to his home in Tuscany. Left a couple days ago. He has property there, you know, and needs to check on it now and then, I think. He hasn't been there for quite some time. I'm not sure how long he'll be gone."

"Thank you." She needed to get out of there for a minute before she saw her patient. She stumbled out the back door and breathed in the lagoon air she'd come to love almost as much as she loved Enzo.

Lying, deceiving rat that he was. Because the only explanation for his suddenly steering clear of her, even leaving for another part of the country, which he apparently hadn't done for a long while, was loud and painfully clear.

Funny how he'd been so unpleasant to her until the meeting where he'd learned she'd donated money to restore the fresco. Suddenly he was apologizing, then all nice and charming the following day. He'd accused her of having an agenda? What a joke.

He'd gotten what he wanted, then he'd taken off, just like her father.

Barely able to swallow the bitter taste of that reality, she forced herself to go back to do her job. But as she walked inside the clinic she thought about all he'd said about his mother. How she'd loved his father even though she knew he didn't love her back, and here Aubrey was, doing the exact same thing.

Pining for a man who didn't truly care about her.

She stood there a long moment, facing that horrifying realization. Pictured herself working in this clinic day after day, checking the schedule over and over again. Knowing she'd dread seeing him at the same time she craved it, might even forgive him the way she had after he'd been so nasty just a few weeks ago. Thinking about how easily she'd done that forced her to see what had to happen.

She couldn't stay in Venice any longer.

She had to go home. As soon as possible. And yes, that made her weak and pathetic, but being those things was better than staying in this city she loved without the man she'd pitifully come to love, too. Thinking of him as she walked along the canals and looked at all the fascinating buildings, hearing the sexy rumble of his voice as he talked about it all. Wishing he were beside her as she rode the *vaporetto*, telling her how brave she was. Missing his touch, his kisses, the way he'd looked at her and held her with such an incredible intimacy, she'd fallen headlong in love with a lie.

Except there was one thing he'd said that hadn't been a lie. He'd been absolutely truthful when he'd told her he was a bad bet for any woman. She could only hope her battered, deluded heart would eventually truly believe it.

Enzo tipped his forehead against the airplane window and looked down at the city he loved, waiting for the smile that always came as he did. Instead, a peculiar mix of anxiety and nervous anticipation roiled in his belly. There was a sense of grief, too, over losing his mother's house, but he'd worked hard to put that behind him. To roam the beautiful hillsides of the Affini estates, to walk the vineyards and enjoy time in the villa he still owned that had always been an enjoyable respite for him and Dante and his mother when they'd needed a short break from the close quarters and summer heat of Venice.

He tried to conjure the bit of happiness he felt that his brother, at least, had saved his own properties from their father's selfishness. Dante hadn't planned it, but clearly it had been meant to be for him to have a child with Shay. And Enzo had to admit he was looking forward to playing with his niece or nephew in the same rolling hills he and Dante had played in as kids.

How to handle being back at the clinic and having to see Aubrey was something he hadn't figured out yet. Scheduling Antonio to work the same shifts she did had worked in the short-term, but he knew there would come a time when that wasn't feasible. So then what?

Working with her again would be sweet torture. He wanted to look into her beautiful eyes, see her dazzling smile, listen to her laugh. But he knew not reaching to touch her and hold her, not kissing her or wanting to enjoy more time with her on the lagoon or anywhere else would be nearly impossible. He honestly didn't know if he could do it, so where did that leave him?

In serious trouble, that was where.

He leaned his head back against the seat and closed his eyes. Aubrey. How had she become so deeply nestled inside him in such a short period of time? She was on his mind as he rode the water taxi from the airport, looking out over the island where they'd picnicked and laughed and kissed. He thought of her as he watched the cormorants fly and dive for fish, remembering the oil smudged on her beautiful face, her happy smile as they'd rescued the bird. The way she'd clung to him on both his small boat and the *vaporetto*, forcing herself to face her fear, then actually leaping into the canal to save that little girl.

Whenever he'd been gone from Venice for a while, the lagoon air filling his lungs on the taxi ride from the airport was another thing that usually made him smile. This time, the air felt thick and heavy instead of invigorating.

He slowly walked from the *vaporetto* stop to his house, feeling as if he had lead weights in his feet. Aubrey was still on his mind as he passed the old doors that fascinated her, and he wondered where the UWWHA had put her up after she'd had to move from his old home. Was she happy there? Finding new places in Venice to explore without him? He hoped she was. Hoped she didn't miss him the way he was missing her. Which brought back to mind the huge problem of working with her again.

How was he going to handle it?

Piles of mail that his housekeeper had stacked on the old wooden table in his foyer needed attention and he started sifting through them to see which seemed the most urgent. A larger envelope delivered by certified mail was tucked in between bills and letters and catalogs, and he tore it open. Then stared.

It was the deed to his mother's house.

What the...? His breath backed up in his lungs, and it felt as if his heart stopped for a long moment before lurching back into rhythm. He stared at it again, but there it was in black and white. His name on the deed. He owned the house.

How had this happened?

A letter was enclosed in the envelope, too, and he slowly slipped it out to read it. Then read it again. His lawyer outlined the details of the transaction and the final price, ending the letter with a hearty congratulations on his success getting the funding together in time.

Except he hadn't. Which left only one explanation. Somehow Aubrey's money hadn't been sent back to her, after all.

Head spinning, he hoped he was wrong. That something else had come through in time. He practically staggered to a chair and dropped into it, pulling out his phone to dial Leonardo.

"Can you explain why the deed to the house is now in my name and in my possession? Can you also tell me why all this went through, and nobody bothered to tell me? Would maybe a phone call have been in order?"

"I assumed you knew. I got a copy of the letter the lawyer sent you weeks ago."

"I was out of town and didn't get my mail." Hiding away from Aubrey, and look what had happened because of his cowardice.

"Well, there was a little mix-up." Now Leonardo sounded sheepish and contrite and a little worried. "I did what you asked with the Henderson money, except I'd already transferred the fund over to the Realtor and your lawyer before I'd talked to you. Then neither of them answered my call at first, and by the time they called me back, it was a done deal. Because we—you— bought it with cash at a slightly higher price than Proviso had offered, the seller was happy to take it and run. So, um, a belated congratulations!"

Dio mio. "Leo. This is a huge problem." He rubbed his hand across his forehead as emotions ping-ponged all over the place. The house was his. For real. The house he loved more than anything. Except maybe not. The way he felt at that moment told him that maybe he loved Aubrey even more, and if he did how could he possibly accept her gift? Giving her nothing back but probably a deep disappointment in him that he wasn't the man she'd doubtless believed he was? That he wished he could be?

"Why is this such a big deal?" Leonardo asked. "If it's the money from Henderson LLC, we can always pay it back, you know. Consider that it just bought you more time to raise the money you needed. So we keep working to raise more cash over the next few months, then you can pay it back. With interest, if that's important to you. This isn't the problem you're making it out to be, Enzo. Consider it heaven-sent, instead."

Heaven-sent. That was Aubrey, not the money, and he had to go see her right away. Talk to her about all this.

"Plan to pay the money back, Leo. I'll be working on raising it."

He hung up and called Aubrey, shocked that his hand was actually shaking as he dialed. Then everything inside was shaking, too, when it went to voice mail. He strode out the door again and headed straight to the clinic. It wouldn't close for another hour. He had no idea if she'd be there, since he'd been gone for almost three weeks, and Antonio had been doing the scheduling. But if she wasn't, at least Nora would surely know where Aubrey was living now.

He went in the back door, his stomach in knots. The exam doors were both closed, so presumably patients were inside, and he headed to the front desk to find Nora. More patients waiting to be seen sat in the few chairs, and he came up behind Nora, leaning down close to her ear.

"Can we talk for a minute?"

She looked up and her mouth dropped open in surprise. "Dr. Affini! When did you get back?"

"Just now." He lowered his voice even more. "Is Aubrey working today?"

She looked perplexed, tipping her head sideways to look up at him. "No. She apparently told the UWWHA she wanted to be reassigned somewhere else later in the year. I believe she went back to the States."

Enzo stared at her, wondering if he'd heard right. "She's not in Venice?"

"No. She left about two weeks ago. Do you want to meet the new nurse? She's—"

"I'll meet her another time." Since the world seemed to tilt on its axis, making Enzo feel a little dizzy, he'd barely been able to answer. "Do you by chance know where Aubrey lives in the States?"

"I have no idea. You could probably find out from the UWWHA." Nora was looking at him with great interest, which made him wonder what his face looked like.

"Good suggestion." He drew in a deep, shaky breath. "Thanks." His legs felt a little numb as he walked out the door, having no idea where he was even going.

Aubrey had left Venice? Gone home, or maybe even somewhere else in the States? How in the world was he going to find her? He had to clear up this mistake. Let her know how much he appreciated her help and that he'd pay her back.

He walked through the city he loved, and every step he took made him think of her. All the things she loved about it, all the things he'd loved showing her. His feet took him past the artists selling paintings of the buildings and his house and that made him think of her, too.

How had every part of this city become filled with memories of her in a matter of weeks? *Dio*, he wanted to have her there with him. Kiss her and hold her and make love with her again, but as he stood there he forced himself to realize that her being gone was for the best, taking all temptation with her. He wouldn't have to go through trying to work with her while keeping his distance, which had been torture before he'd gone to Tuscany.

She was the most special woman he'd ever been privileged to be with, and nothing had changed about that. Which also meant nothing had changed about needing to stay away from her so there was no chance he could hurt her. She deserved a man who could give her his heart and soul and a forever after, and as he stood there picturing her beautiful face and shining eyes, hearing her inquisitive questions and infectious laughter, the thought of her with someone else made him feel as if he were bleeding inside.

None of that mattered. Her feelings were what mattered. And as he stared out over the water, the deep ache in his chest he wasn't sure would ever completely go away told him that calling her would be a bad idea. Hearing her sweet voice might make him do something stupid, like beg her to come back to Venice, or let him visit her in Massachusetts or wherever she was so he could see her one more time. Touch her once more. And how selfish would that be?

No, as soon as he was able to find out from the UWWHA where she was living, he'd have his lawyer send her a letter about the transaction. Tell her that he would be returning the money with interest as soon as he had it. He'd write her a letter, too, thanking her for her generosity and telling her he wished her all the best for her life.

Somehow, he'd keep it cool and professional as he'd

tried to do before, until he'd completely caved to the allure of Aubrey Henderson. Then he'd go back to his old life. Except that life now, at the clinic and this city, would hold memories of her everywhere, and he had no idea how he was going to deal with the pain of her being gone.

CHAPTER THIRTEEN

AUBREY STOOD IN the old bedroom she'd grown up in and changed out of her uniform, thinking about how mundane her life felt now. Hoped that feeling would change once some time had passed, bringing back her interest in all the places nearby she'd always loved to go. Assumed that working at the nearby hospital again would start to feel challenging and interesting instead of days she just needed to get through.

As she wandered across the grass to the stable she scolded herself for that thought. She'd had some lovely patients she'd enjoyed taking care of, and had managed to have some fun with friends, too, right? And with her old nanny, Maggie, who lived in one of the guest houses. Anyone would feel a little let down coming back to the life they'd lived for years after the adventure of living and working in a place as incredible as Venice.

Maybe it was because she'd been feeling tired. Kind of sick, really. Queasy and a little dizzy, and she hoped she wasn't coming down with some kind of stomach bug.

That must be it. Her malaise had nothing to do with Enzo Affini. Okay, maybe it did, but that just made her mad because he didn't deserve for her to be moping around about him. Wasn't worth her heart still hurting and her stomach feeling all twisted around at the way he'd used her.

How had she let herself fall in love with a mirage? A prince doctor used to having people fall all over him, and using that to his advantage, deceiving them with his charm and easy smile and a sexiness that would wow anyone?

No, it wasn't her fault. If she kept reminding herself she disliked him now, one of these days her heart would finally catch on and life would get back to normal.

Except right now, normal felt very, very dull compared to being with a handsome, charming, manipulative man in beautiful Italy.

She made her way into the barn, waving when she saw that Maggie was at the far end, feeding one of the horses a treat. "Hey, Maggie! Going riding tonight?"

"Planning to." The nurse and nanny who had been part of the family for years beamed her sweet smile. "Want to join me?"

"Thanks, but not today. I'm not feeling too good." She put her hand to her stomach because the queasiness seemed worse. Maybe after she went back inside, she'd make herself some chicken soup or something to see if that would help.

But first, she'd say hi to one of her favorite horses. She headed to his stall to rub his nose. "Do you think I'm an idiot, Applejax? You know how my dad turned out to be a jerk. But you had no idea he was like that, did you? Should I have known? Am I just a really bad judge of character, being taken in by both of them?"

The horse bobbed his nose up and down in agreement, and she grimaced. Yeah, maybe she was just bad at reading people, and she wondered if there were lessons on how to get better at it.

Her stomach lurched a little more, and the realization that she might actually get sick had her deciding to get back to the house sooner rather than later. But as she turned, her head strangely swam, the light seemed to glitter, then fade, and her legs felt as if they just crumpled beneath her.

Blinking open her eyes, she looked up into Maggie's anxious face just above her. It took her a second to realize she was lying flat on her back, and when she lifted her hand to her head she felt some straw stuck in her hair.

"What...what happened?"

"You fainted dead away, sweetie. About gave me a heart attack."

"Fainted? What?"

She could see Maggie looking at her closely as she helped her sit up. "Feel like you can stand now?"

"Yes. I feel okay. I can't imagine how that happened."

"Well, there could be lots of reasons. Take your time walking, and lean on me, okay?"

They slowly walked back to the house, with Maggie's arm wrapped around her waist as she'd often done when Aubrey was little. "How are you feeling now?"

"I'm fine. Really. I think I have a bug. Been feeling light-headed and queasy on and off the past couple of days."

Maggie didn't speak for a long moment, then asked, "Any chance you could be pregnant?"

"What?" She stared in disbelief that Maggie had even asked her that. "Of course not! I'm on the Pill. I mean, I did miss a couple of periods, but that happens sometimes with the one I'm taking, and, well..." Her voice faded off as a cold chill came over her that didn't have anything to do with her bug.

Surely there was no way she could be pregnant. Was there?

"You know I have all kinds of nursing supplies at my house, including a pregnancy test." She tucked Aubrey into her favorite chair and briskly plumped pillows behind her head, then got her a cold drink. "You get comfy and I'll be right back."

With her figurative nursing hat firmly in place, Maggie was speaking in a no-nonsense voice, and while Aubrey wanted to say she didn't need the test, the suddenly really scared part of her had to know.

Getting comfy wasn't possible, despite sitting in the plush chair with her feet up while she waited for Maggie. Aubrey sipped her water and thought about Enzo.

What if she really was pregnant? As Shay had gotten pregnant by Dante? What in the world would she do? And would Enzo think she'd done it on purpose, since he'd been suspicious of why she'd shown up to work at the clinic that first day?

The thought sent another cold chill sliding down her spine and made her feel even sicker than she had before.

It seemed like an eternity before Maggie got back with the test. All too soon, the answer was terrifyingly clear in the form of an intense pink dot. She stared at it for long minutes, feeling as if she might faint all over again. She sucked in deep breaths and looked into the mirror to see her shocked eyes staring back at her.

How in the world had this happened?

Somehow getting her wobbly legs to work, she finally made it back to the living room to see Maggie. The result must have been more than obvious on her face, because Maggie stood up and came to hug her.

"Ah, sweetie. Come sit down and let's talk."

"Oh, my God. What am I going to do?"

"Who is the father? Someone you like?" She gently pushed Aubrey back into the chair and patted her knee. "Is he here or in Italy?"

She stared up into Maggie's wrinkled face, and the calm, nonjudgmental way she asked the question helped Aubrey start breathing again. "He lives in Venice. He's a doctor. And a prince." *And a jerk.*

Maggie grinned. "Trust you to do it right, little one."

"Do it right? This is awful!"

"Is he a good man?"

"I thought he was. But then he did something that showed me he isn't." And was that an understatement, or what? Took the money, then ran hard and fast the other way.

"Well, I'm sorry to hear that." She patted Aubrey's knee again. "But you'll have to tell him soon, and, after you talk, you both can figure out how you want to handle this."

The thought of telling Enzo made her feel faint all over again. He'd be horrified to be having a child at all, let alone with her, since he obviously didn't feel any of the things for her that she'd believed he did. Not to mention he'd all but accused her of trying to trap him when she came to work at the clinic. He'd probably think this was proof of that, since she must have gotten pregnant that very first time they were together. "I don't think I'll tell him, Maggie. I'll just raise it myself. He lives halfway across the world, anyway."

"Italy isn't exactly halfway across the world from the east coast of the US, now, is it?" Maggie said with a chiding smile. "And do you really want to raise a child alone? Have it grow up like you did, always wondering who your dad was?"

Everything inside her stilled at Maggie's words. All

the memories came tumbling back, all the fantasies, all the melancholy she'd felt her whole life knowing that her father must not love her, because if he did he'd come around sometimes. Memories of drawing pictures, imagining who he might be. A pilot or a football player or a dragon slayer. Memories of asking her mother questions that were never answered. Memories of that sad, empty feeling inside that other kids had a dad, knew who he was, and spent happy times with him.

They never had to imagine who he might be, because they knew.

She lifted her gaze to Maggie's face and reached for her gnarled hand. "Thank you. You're right. No matter how hard it will be to tell him, I have to. I can't let my baby grow up like I did, not knowing. Because that was the only thing about my life that wasn't good."

"That's my girl." Maggie's hand squeezed hers. "And do it soon, or otherwise you'll be stewing about it instead of planning your future, and the future of your baby."

"Thanks so much for your good advice." She leaned forward to hug the woman who'd always been there for her since she was eight years old. "I feel so lucky to have had both you and Mom in my life. Two people who loved me and who I knew always had my back."

It was true. And as she pictured Enzo's impish smile, remembering how wonderful he'd been with little Benedetto, reassuring him and fixing his bike, and with all the other children they'd taken care of, she knew, in her heart, that he'd be there for his own child. Not what he'd planned maybe, but he would be. Yes, he'd used her in a way that hurt even more than her father's betrayal. One thing she knew for sure, though?

Family was important to him.

"You know, I think I'm going to call him right now, before I lose my nerve. Get it over with."

"Way to go," Maggie said, and the high-five hand-slap the older woman gave her, as she'd done since Aubrey was a kid, actually managed to make her smile as she faced the toughest thing she'd ever done.

"I don't understand why you can't give me her address," he said to yet another UWWHA employee. "She worked for me!"

Enzo felt as if all he'd done since he'd gotten back to Venice was pace the floor somewhere. His other house, the clinic, the walkway streaming with people as he'd spoken with his lawyer and the UWWHA and the guy he'd bought his house back from, since he'd been renting it to Aubrey before she'd had to move out.

Pacing this house, too. The one he now owned only because of Aubrey. He'd made so many of the calls from here, now that he'd moved back, because this house somehow felt as if Aubrey were a part of it. But every person he'd reached had claimed they either didn't have her address, or couldn't legally give it to him.

He was close to pointing out he was Italian royalty to see if that loosened their tight lips, which was something he never did. But if he had to, he would, and just as he opened his mouth to see if that would work he heard another call coming in. When he looked at his phone to see who it was, he almost fell over.

"I have to take this call." He abruptly hung up on the person and punched the answer button with a shaking hand. "Aubrey."

"Hi, Enzo." The sound of her voice poured into him like the finest wine, and his fingers tightened on the phone, holding it like a lifeline. "I…I have to talk to you about something. Something important."

"I have to talk to you about something important, too." *Dio*, his heart felt as if it were pounding in his throat, making it hard to breathe. "I've been trying to get your address to send you a letter about it. You need to know that the money transfer from your trust wasn't supposed to go through. It was supposed to go back to you because I couldn't accept it, but there was a mistake and it went through anyway."

The silence from the other end rang in his ears. It struck him that he hadn't thanked her for her incredible generosity, even though he couldn't take the money, and stumbled to get it out coherently. "And I want to thank you for…for caring about the house and I do own it now, so thank you, it's amazing to have it when I thought there was no way it could happen, but I'm in the process of raising the money to pay you back. With interest. So you don't need to worry about that."

He cursed under his breath, knowing he sounded like a raging idiot. But he might never have the chance to talk to her again, and the stress of that knowledge made it difficult to know, exactly, what to say. Difficult to remember how to talk at all.

More silence. "Hello? Are you there?"

"You were going to send me a letter."

She said it in a flat voice as a statement, not a question, and Enzo hurried to answer. "Yes, I wanted to tell you all that I just said, about the mistake, and that I was going to make it right."

"Make it right." Another flat statement. "Picking up the phone was out of the question because you didn't want to talk to me, apparently."

It was true, he hadn't wanted to talk to her. Hadn't

wanted to risk letting her know how much he'd come to care for her, had needed to keep her safe and far away from a man who couldn't be the kind of lover she deserved. "It wasn't that I didn't want to talk to you, it was—"

"Save it. I don't need any explanation. It was all crystal clear. You got the money, then suddenly we were working different shifts, you weren't answering *my* phone calls, then you disappear to Tuscany without a word to me. I may not be very smart, but I figured out pretty fast that our…relationship wasn't as it had seemed to me."

"Aubrey." Horror left him frozen to the floor. Did she really think he was that kind of monster? Hearing her voice so hard and cold showed that the awful truth was that she did. "That's not how it happened. I enjoyed our time together. I—"

"Again, save it, please. That's not what I called about. I'm calling about the time we enjoyed together, unfortunately."

Surely, after lambasting him for the past few minutes, she wasn't about to tell him she wanted to see him again, was she? And if she did, what should he say? He'd already told her he was a bad bet, which she apparently fully believed.

This time, he was the one who stayed silent, deciding he'd blabbered and upset her too much already and needed to listen instead.

"I hope you're sitting down, because—" he heard her draw a deep breath "—I'm pregnant. And you're the father."

"What?" The floor beneath his feet felt as if it were moving, and he had to try twice before he could say more. "How do you know?"

"How do I know that I'm pregnant, or that you're the father? Thanks for the insult."

That hard voice had gotten even harder, which kept him from saying, *both*. He stumbled to a chair to sit and try to process the grenade that she'd dropped in his lap.

Thoughts of his brother slowly came to mind, about Shay showing up pregnant and his wondering if that had been her plan all along. Wondering about Aubrey, too, and now he couldn't help but wonder again how much Shay had told her about the Affini family trust that said his properties would all come to him if he married and produced an heir by age thirty-five.

"I know this is a shock. It was for me, too."

Her voice had softened into the Aubrey he knew. He absorbed the sound of it, and as he did his blood seemed to finally start pumping again, reducing the numbness he'd felt creep through every muscle at her stunning announcement.

He thought of all the wonderful things he knew about her. The way she stepped up to take care of everyone around her. Her bravery facing her fear of the water. Her adventurous spirit, and her sweetness with patients and with him. Her genuine love for the architecture and history of the city he loved, too.

The truth came as clear as the glass windows in his library that she'd admired.

She hadn't done this on purpose. She hadn't planned to manipulate him or force him into marriage. She hadn't wanted anything from him, other than the very special time they'd spent together. Instead, she'd given him so much, expecting nothing but his friendship and caring in return.

"We need to talk." He wasn't sure about what, other than their baby. Confusion and fear blurred his vision, and he needed time to think. But he had to see her. Look into her eyes and see her beautiful face as they worked through how to handle this. "Come back to Venice. Or I'll come see you. Which would you rather?"

"Neither. There's no reason for us to see one another right now. I knew I had a responsibility to you and to our baby to tell you, and I've done that." He heard the sudden tears in her voice, heard her breathe in a long, shuddery breath, and the sound of her distress made him want to reach through the phone and hold her close. Let her know that he was here for her. Tell her it would somehow be okay.

"I should be available to you if—"

"There's no 'should' in this. I don't want you to do anything you don't want to do. I'm not like your mother, Enzo, who kept a man in her life who didn't love her. I'm perfectly fine on my own. I'll let you know when it's getting near the time it will be born. We can talk then about when you can come see it, and how we're going to handle things after that."

"Aubrey, no. We need to—"

"*Arrivederci*, Enzo."

The way she said goodbye, low and gentle, pulled hard at his heart. Because goodbye sounded so final, and he realized he'd avoided saying that to her before by leaving Venice altogether. Her soft tone reminded him of the times they'd made love, and that she'd spoken to him that way after being so angry, and then telling him she didn't want to see him, brought a lump to his throat, too.

He sat with the silent phone held limply in his hand for a long time after she'd hung up, finally getting up to move in a slow stride that was far different than the agitated pacing he'd been doing before she called.

Dio mio. A baby. A child created through lovemaking as he'd never experienced in his life, with a woman so beautiful and special in every possible way. Missing her filled him with a hollow ache. Of not getting to see her joyous smile, or feel her silky skin, or tease her inquisitive mind. Of never again sharing coffee with her, or holding her close on a boat ride, or listening to her many knowledgeable ideas.

He moved through his mother's house—his house—and thought of Aubrey as he had nearly every moment since he'd been back. Had slept in a different bedroom than the one she'd used because he couldn't bear to be in it without seeing her beautiful hair spilling across the pillow, her eyes smiling at him as she awakened, feeling her warm, soft body tucked closely against his.

Thought about her as he wandered through each room, picking up the artwork and little things she'd admired. Touched the books in the library she'd loved, and thought about her comments about the windows, and the light in the room. Looked up at the painting on the ceiling, and realized one of the angels depicted there looked a little like her.

Slowly, he made his way into the office he'd just recently brought all his things to, and picked up the deed to the house. Stared at it for a long time, and as he did the confusion he felt lifted, cleared, and he knew with absolute certainty what he wanted to do. Because there was nothing confusing about how he felt about Aubrey.

He loved her.

Loved her in a way he'd never loved anyone before. A woman who deserved a man who would care for her and be loyal and faithful to her forever. He wanted to be that man, so much that for a long moment he tried to convince himself he could be. But he was his father's son, and he couldn't bear to ever hurt her the way his father had hurt his mother.

He couldn't give himself to her, because that wouldn't be the kind of gift she deserved. There was one thing, though, that he could give her. The perfect and right thing. He would give this house to the woman he loved, and to the unborn child they'd made together. She loved Venice, had said she loved this house, and he knew she would bring their child here to learn its history, and discover his or her own deep heritage. An Affini growing up right here where he and Dante had grown up. A new child following a long line of generations of his mother's family, and he actually smiled when he pictured his mother smiling, too, because he knew she would be.

Of course he'd be a part of his baby's life and help it grow up as best he could. Seeing Aubrey and not being able to hold her and love her would unbearably hurt, he knew, but he'd keep away from her as much as possible to protect them both.

CHAPTER FOURTEEN

AUBREY STILLED WHEN she saw the certified letter post-marked from Venice, Italy. There were two possibilities what it could be. One: that it was from the UWWHA about the brief time she'd worked there. Or two: it was from Enzo.

With her heart skipping around and her stomach tight, she opened the envelope and slid out a folded letter, along with an official-looking document and a piece of stiff manila paper. Then stared at the document, her heart now in her throat, barely able to process what she was looking at.

The deed to Enzo's house. With her name on it.

What in the world…?

With shaking hands, she slowly unfolded the letter, handwritten in the familiar bold scrawl she'd seen Enzo use on clinic paperwork and prescriptions.

Dear Aubrey,
It is my privilege to be able to give you and our baby this house beloved by my mother's family, by her, and by me. I believe it was beloved by you, too, in the short time you were here.

Thinking of our child spending time there with his or her very special mother makes me smile

*more than anything has made me smile in a long
time. Except for my time with you, because that
brought me many smiles, as well.*

*I hope you'll decide to live there at least part
of the year, which also will give me a chance to
spend time with our child while you're in Venice.
Also know, of course, that if you choose to stay
in the States, I'll visit regularly to be a part of
our baby's life.*

*I look forward to hearing from you when the
time comes for our bimba to be born, because I
want so much to be there with you for what will
be an incredible moment in both of our lives.*
All my love,
Enzo

Aubrey stared at the letter, then the deed, then read
the letter three more times, not quite believing what
she was seeing.

He'd given her the house he grew up in? The house
he loved so much; that he'd worked so hard to try to
buy back? The house that had been so important to
him, he'd made her think he liked her so she'd help
with the purchase?

Except, that obviously couldn't be true. If it was, she
wouldn't be holding this deed in her hand.

She laid the deed and letter on the kitchen counter
and picked up the third paper that had been enclosed
with them in the envelope, turning it over to see what
it was. Then what little breath she had left swooshed
from her lungs.

It was the watercolor painting of Enzo's home they'd
seen when they walked along the waterside. The place
considered to be a particularly special example of an

amazing house in a city full of incredible houses. The rich colors leaped from the page, bringing memories of the short time she'd been able to live there, of making love there with Enzo, of his plans to restore it to its original glory.

It is my privilege to be able to give you and our baby this house beloved by my mother's family, by her, and by me.

She stared at those words on Enzo's letter, then looked back at the beautiful painting he'd obviously made a special effort to get for her.

Did her being wrong about him using her to buy the house for himself mean she could also be wrong about how Enzo felt about her? Was there any way it was possible that he loved her the way she loved him?

*All my love,
Enzo*

Slowly, she shook her head. Who knew, maybe a deceitfully charming man like him signed letters like that all the time. But as she thought about him, this crazy man she stupidly still loved, the man who'd given her this incredible gift and, unexpectedly, a baby as well, she knew that, no matter how hard it might be, she had to find out.

The thought of baring her soul and telling him how much she loved him felt beyond terrifying. But hadn't he said she was brave? Amazing to face her fears?

Dealing with her fear of water was a good thing, but not essential to happiness and living her life to the fullest. Risking telling Enzo she loved him? Shoving that fear aside to find out if maybe he loved her, too? That was worth everything. She had nothing to lose but her pride, right? And if he didn't, she'd simply be standing in the same place she stood right now.

A place that didn't feel nearly full enough without Enzo by her side.

How the tiny premature infants in the neonatal intensive care unit at the Hospital San Pietro could stand the glare of harsh white light above them was beyond Enzo. Not to mention the annoyance of the steadily beeping screens above the bassinets, and the way they were hooked up to IVs and external monitors of all kinds. He'd never been bothered by it before, when he'd taken care of patients in the hospital, and knowing all that was helping them get well. But thankfully the babies seemed utterly oblivious to it, sleeping peacefully.

Especially his new little niece, Sophia Maria Affini.

Looking at her tiny face, he couldn't help but think about how much his mother, with only two mischievous sons growing up in her house, would have loved having a granddaughter. Hoped that maybe his niece might look a little like her someday. Dante was convinced that the baby looked just like him, except for the heart shape of her face like Shay's.

Enzo personally thought that, at the moment, the skinny baby looked more like a tiny monkey than his mother or brother or sister-in-law, but he'd kept that to himself. Had a feeling Dante wouldn't appreciate that opinion.

What would his own child look like? Would it be a girl with gray-blue eyes and golden-brown hair? A boy with his beautiful mother's coloring, or would it, girl or boy, be darkly Italian?

Never had he imagined his brother or himself having a new little life they were responsible for. And yet staring at Sophia Maria's tiny pink face, he knew both he and Dante had been given an amazing gift. Gifts they hadn't planned on, and maybe didn't deserve, but perhaps that was the best kind of gift. The kind you didn't even know you wanted until you held it in your hands.

His gift wasn't here yet, wouldn't be for too many months, and it took nearly all his strength to not hop on a plane, find Aubrey, and bring her back to Venice until their baby was born. Take care of her, and be there for her in any way she wanted him to be.

Except she'd made it very clear she didn't want that. Respecting her wishes was more important than his need to see her. More important than pandering to his own desires, which was something he'd spent his lifetime doing. But that was about to change. Soon he'd have a new life to think about, and he'd already realized that having a child was going to make him a better man.

"Goodbye, little one." He patted the glass surrounding the sleeping infant. "Sweet dreams, and your uncle Enzo will come see you again very soon."

He pushed to his feet and headed to a local restaurant, leaving with his dinner in a bag to head back to his house. The worry that had been nagging at him for the past few days came back as soon as he was in his boat.

Why hadn't Aubrey ever called him about the deed? What if she hadn't gotten it?

Then told himself—again—that his worry about that was stupid. He'd received notice that it had been delivered to her house and signed for, hadn't he? So the reason he hadn't heard from her was obvious.

Clearly, she still didn't want to talk to him, and he could hardly blame her. Hadn't he avoided calling her from the day he'd left for Tuscany while she was still in Venice? He probably wouldn't have talked to her ever again if she weren't pregnant with his baby, and thinking about that reality squeezed his heart so hard he wondered how it could continue beating.

He pulled the boat up to his dock and secured it, leaning down to grab the dinner he'd be eating alone, and a heavy feeling hung on his shoulders. He couldn't remember ever feeling lonely before, but loving Aubrey and missing her were all new things he would just have to get used to.

He fished his house key from his pocket as he rounded the corner to the front door, stopping abruptly when he saw two sandaled feet with pink toenails... shapely legs stretched across his doorstep. He let his gaze travel up those beautiful legs to the yellow skirt skimming her thighs, and his stomach dived and pitched and smashed right into his heart at the sight.

"Aubrey?"

"*Buonasera*, Enzo."

He stared down into the eyes he'd missed so much, at the curve of her sweet lips, and practically fell to his knees as he crouched down in front of her, dropping the bag to reach for her hands. "Are you all right? Is something wrong?"

"I'm fine. The baby is fine, too."

His heart started up again in slow, lurching thuds as he sucked in a steadying breath. "Then why are you here, sitting on a hard stone step? You need to take better care of yourself! How did you even know I would be here? You might have sat there for hours, getting a chill." He lifted her to her feet and it was all he could do to not pull her into his arms and beg her to stay with him forever.

"I got Shay to ask Dante which house you were living in, and if you were in Venice. Then I talked to Nora, and she told me you'd worked today. Then I came here, though I admit I was a little worried you might not come home, or would have some woman with you."

He could tell the joking tone and half smile on her face were forced, and her gaze was searching his for something, but he had no idea what.

"I haven't wanted to be with another woman since you left Venice that first time." Had wondered if he'd want to be with anyone other than Aubrey ever again. "For heaven's sake, please get up off the hard pavement and tell me why you're here."

He knew why he wanted her to be here, which was to take up where they'd left off, but he couldn't let that happen, could he? His important reason and conviction about staying away from her faded from memory as he absorbed the feel of her hands in his, that she was here in this house again—her house now—where every room he went into she was on his mind and in his heart.

"Why I'm here? Are you accusing me of stalking you again?"

"You're ridiculous," he managed to mutter. "I want you to be here, but I'm confused because you said you didn't want to see me."

"I didn't. But now I'm here because I have something to say that couldn't be said on the phone."

She licked her lips and he could almost see her shoring up the inner strength she had that made her fight her fear of water and go for what she wanted.

"What?"

"I'm here to tell you that I love you. Not because I'm pregnant with your baby, because I loved you before I left Venice. I think I fell a little in love with you that very first night we were together, and every time I was with you, I fell a little harder. When you fixed Benedetto's bike, and when you were so sweet with the lady who had heart failure. When you held me to make me feel safe on the water, and when you rescued that bird. And I decided that I had to tell you. Even if you don't love me back, I wanted you to know."

His heart pounded hard in his chest as he looked into the beautiful eyes he loved, reflecting that love right back at him. To see it there humbled him more than he'd ever been humbled in his life, because he knew he'd never done a thing to deserve the love of a woman like her.

She took a step forward, looking up at him with hope and fear and uncertainty swimming in the blue-gray depths of her eyes. His hands closed around her arms, but he didn't let himself pull her close. Didn't speak. Didn't know what to say or how to say it.

"Enzo, I flew across the ocean to tell you I love you, and to see if you might love me, too. I need for you to give me an honest answer back. Please. That's all I'm asking for."

All she was asking for. So easy to give her the honest answer she wanted, but so incredibly hard to know if he should. "You know I'm a bad bet, Aubrey. Remember?"

"I don't believe that. You might not love me back, but, no matter what, I would bet on you any day." She brought one of her hands to his cheek. "You're a good man. A special man. A man who would give the house he loves to a woman he may not love, and to an unborn child he didn't plan on and hasn't even met yet. That tells me you have the kind of deep moral character that should tell *you* that you're not at all like your father."

Admiration had joined the other emotions in the

eyes gazing into his, and his hands tightened to tug her closer. Whether or not she was right, he owed her the truth. "I do love you, Aubrey. I love you more than I knew it was possible to love a woman. And because I love you so much, I'm afraid to ask you to be with me forever. I'm afraid I might hurt you, and I couldn't bear for that to happen."

"You helped me with my fear of the water. What do you say I help you with your fear of hurting me? We spend the next six months making love and fixing up this house and working and adventuring together. After little Prince or Princess Affini shows up, if you feel like being with another woman, feel those bad genes taking over, I won't try to keep you. You can decide then to let me go. What do you say?"

Another emotion in those eyes. Trust. So clear and real, it brought a thick lump to his throat. Listening to her words, looking into her eyes as he held her close, made him finally know.

He'd never be like his father.

Aubrey was the only woman he would always want to be with. To love her and cherish her and do whatever he could for her. He wanted to marry her and spend the rest of his life with her and be the best bet she'd ever made in her life.

"What do I say?" His answer was to kiss her. Softly and slowly the way he'd thought about kissing her every hour of every day for the past six weeks, breathing in her sweet scent, tasting the lips he'd never thought he'd get to taste again.

When she eventually broke the kiss and leaned back, she gave him the smile that had dazzled him from that very first day they'd met. He held both their hands to the slightly rounded belly that, incredibly, held the baby they'd created together, and pressed his forehead to hers, swallowing down the emotion overwhelming him. "I say that I don't need six months. I only need as much time as you want to put a wedding together. Can't have little one born out of wedlock, can we?"

"I guess Prince or Princess Affini won't need that kind of attention from the tabloids." She wrapped her arms around his neck. "What do you think about getting married on a boat out on the lagoon?"

He laughed against her mouth. "A celebration of both of us moving past our fears? I can't think of anything better than that."

EPILOGUE

AUBREY KNEW THAT no one expected peace and quiet at a one-year-old's birthday party, but she had to wonder if the insistent banging on the ancient *terrazzo* floor just might be getting on the nerves of at least one of the thirty or so guests by now.

She crouched down next to her baby son, Gabriel Dante Affini, and waved a new toy in front of him. His instantly fascinated eyes were so like his daddy's, it filled her heart with overwhelming emotion the way it did every time she looked at him. Gabriel's focus switched to the dangling, colorful rings from the plastic hammer he had been pounding.

"How are we ever going to get the renovation on this house finished if you won't let him work on it?" Enzo said in her ear as he leaned over both of them, his warm lips sliding down her cheek while his big hand rested on their son's soft black hair.

"With or without his help, we have a long way to go, and I think he's examined the floor enough for today. But we'll get there, don't you worry." She lifted her lips to meet his, still amazed that this man was hers. That he loved her as much as she loved him. That the touch of his mouth always made her feel breathless. "Even though it's not close to livable yet, I'm so happy we decided to have Sophia Maria's one-year birthday party here. In the house where her *nonna* and daddy and uncle grew up. Do you think the smell of paint and sawdust will make everyone extra hungry for the cake?"

Enzo chuckled and glanced over at his niece, who seemed deeply focused on taking off her pink birthday hat, then trying to put it back on again, much to her parents' amusement. "I find the construction scent very pleasing and appetizing. But not nearly as pleasing and appetizing as you."

His mouth met hers again for a long kiss that had her clutching his shirt as he sat on the floor to pull her close, until something fluttered into their faces to separate them.

Aubrey and Enzo both turned to see the birthday hat lying between them, and Sophia laughing as she lurched in her adorable, learning-to-walk way to retrieve it.

"Hey, you two, enough of that. This is a birthday party, not a date night," Dante jokingly chided as he pulled Shay close against him.

"Every night is date night with my wife," Enzo responded with a grin. "And the sooner your daughter opens her presents, the sooner we can get on with our date."

"Enzo!" Aubrey swatted his arm as Dante and Shay laughed.

"My brother and I have always had an understanding. And today that means he knows I'd just as soon finish celebrating, too, then get home with my wife and daughter to celebrate some more. After Sophia Maria is in bed." Dante kissed Shay's forehead as she rested against his shoulder, turning to Aubrey with a wide smile.

"We had no idea what we were getting ourselves into when we came to Italy, did we?"

"No, we sure didn't." Aubrey watched her handsome

husband lift their baby into his arms, who gently bonked him on the head with the plastic hammer as Gabriel laughed. "I thought I was coming here to work. To cure my fear of water and have an adventure. And what did I get?"

She stood to lean over Enzo and Gabriel, wrapping her arms around them. Holding them close to the wonder that filled her heart.

"I don't know, *bellezza*," Enzo murmured against her temple. "What did you get?"

The answer was so enormous, a mere sentence couldn't cover it. "I got our beautiful son. A new life and new dreams. This wonderful and special house. And you." She kissed him again, not caring if Dante complained. "My perfect and amazing husband, who I'm betting will keep making me happy every day for the rest of my life."

* * * * *

If you missed the first story in the
ROYAL SPRING BABIES *duet, check out*

HIS PREGNANT ROYAL BRIDE by Amy Ruttan

And if you enjoyed this story, check out these other great reads from Robin Gianna

REUNITED WITH HIS RUNAWAY BRIDE
THE PRINCE AND THE MIDWIFE
HER CHRISTMAS BABY BUMP
HER GREEK DOCTOR'S PROPOSAL

All available now!

MILLS & BOON®

MEDICAL ROMANCE™

THE ULTIMATE IN ROMANTIC MEDICAL DRAMA

A sneak peek at next month's titles...

In stores from 23rd March 2017:

- **Their One Night Baby** – Carol Marinelli *and*
  Forbidden to the Playboy Surgeon – Fiona Lowe

- **A Mother to Make a Family** – Emily Forbes *and*
  The Nurse's Baby Secret – Janice Lynn

- **The Boss Who Stole Her Heart** – Jennifer Taylor *and*
  Reunited by Their Pregnancy Surprise – Louisa Heaton

Just can't wait?
Buy our books online before they hit the shops!
www.millsandboon.co.uk

Also available as eBooks.

MILLS & BOON®

EXCLUSIVE EXTRACT

Dr. Dominic MacBride had no intention of falling in love—yet now he's fighting for paramedic Victoria Christie…and their surprise baby!

Read on for a sneak preview of
THEIR ONE NIGHT BABY

'You got your earring back.'

'They were a gift from my father.'

'That's nice,' Dominic said.

'Not really, it was just a duty gift when I turned eighteen. Had he bothered to get to know me, then he'd have known that I don't like diamonds.'

'Why not?'

'I don't believe in fairytales and I don't believe in for ever.'

There was, to Victoria's mind, no such thing.

She held her breath as his fingers came to her cheek and lightly brushed the lobe as he examined the stone.

If it were anyone else she would have pushed his hand away.

Anyone else.

Yet she provoked.

'It was the other earring that I lost.'

And he turned her face and his hands went to the other.

This was foolish, both knew.

Neither wanted to get close to someone they had to

work alongside but the attraction between them was intense.

Both knew the reason for their rows and terse exchanges; it was physical attraction at its most raw.

'Victoria, I'm in no position to get involved with anyone.'

They were standing looking at each other and his hands were on her cheeks and his fingers were warm on her ears. There was a thrum between them and she knew he was telling her they would go nowhere.

'That's okay.'

And that *was* okay.

'If you don't like diamonds, then what do you like?' he asked. His mouth was so close to hers and though it was cold she could feel the heat in the space between them.

'This.'

Their mouths met and she felt the warm, light pressure and it felt blissful.

Don't miss
THEIR ONE NIGHT BABY
By Carol Marinelli

Available April 2017
www.millsandboon.co.uk